WHITE TIGER

JENNIFER ASHLEY

BERKLEY SENSATION, NEW YORK

BERKLEY
SENSATION

An imprint of Penguin Random House LLC
375 Hudson Street, New York, New York 10014

WHITE TIGER

A Berkley Sensation Book / published by arrangement with the author

BERKLEY SENSATION® and the "B" design are registered trademarks of
Penguin Random House LLC.
For more information, visit penguin.com.

ISBN: 978-0-425-28135-2

PUBLISHING HISTORY
Berkley Sensation mass-market edition / April 2016

PRINTED IN THE UNITED STATES OF AMERICA

10 9 8 7 6 5 4 3 2 1

Cover art by Tony Mauro.
Cover design by George Long.

Penguin
Random
House

CHAPTER ONE

It was almost time. Addison Price slid the coffeepot back on the heater, unable to keep her eye from the clock.

The diner closed at midnight. Every night at eleven fifty-five on the dot, he came in.

Tonight, though, eleven fifty-five came and went. And eleven fifty-six, eleven fifty-seven.

She'd have to close up. Bo, the owner, liked everything shut down right at midnight. He'd come in about fifteen minutes later and start going through the accounts for the day.

Eleven fifty-eight. The last customer, a farmer in a John Deere cap he must have picked up forty years ago, grinned at her and said, "Night, Addie. Time to go home to the wife."

He said that every night. Addie only nodded and gave him a warm good-bye.

Eleven fifty-nine. In one minute, she'd have to lock the door, turn the "Open" sign around to "Closed," help with the cleanup, and then go home. Her sister and two kids would be asleep, school day tomorrow. Addie would creep in as usual, take a soothing shower, play on the Internet a little to unwind, and then fall asleep. Her unwavering routine.

Tonight, though, she wouldn't be able to analyze every

single thing the white-and-black-haired man said to her and decide whether he liked her or was just making conversation.

The second hand on the analog clock above the pass to the kitchen swept down from the twelve toward the six. Eleven-fifty nine and thirty seconds. Forty. Forty-five.

Addie sighed and moved to the glass front door.

Which opened as she approached it, bringing in the warmth of a Texas night, and the man.

Addie quickly changed reaching for the door's lock to yanking the door open wide and giving him her sunniest smile. "Hello, there. Y'all come on in. You made it just in time."

The big man gave her his polite nod and walked past her with an even stride, his black denim coat brushing jeans that hugged the most gorgeous ass Addie had seen in all her days. Because this diner's clientele had plenty of men from all walks of life, she'd seen her fair share of not-so-good backsides in jeans or showing inappropriately over waistbands.

Her man was different. His behind was worth a second, third, and fourth look. He was tall but not lanky, his build that of a linebacker in fine training, his shoulders and chest stretching his black T-shirt. The footwear under the blue jeans was always either gray cowboy boots or black motorcycle boots. Tonight, it was the motorcycle boots, supple leather hugging his ankles.

And, as always, Addie's man carried the sword. He kept it wrapped in dark cloth, a long bundle he held in his hand and tucked beside his seat when he sat down and ordered. At first Addie had thought the bundle held a gun—a rifle or shotgun—and she'd had to tell him that Bo didn't allow firearms of any kind in his diner. She'd lock it up for him while he ate. They had a special locker for the hunters who were regulars.

The man had shot her a quizzical look from his incredibly sexy eyes, pulled back the cloth, and revealed the hilt of a sword.

A sword, for crap's sake. A big one, with a silver hilt. Addie had swallowed hard and said that maybe it was okay if he kept it down beside his chair. He'd given her a curt nod and covered the hilt back up.

But that was just him. He was like no man Addie had ever met in her life. His eyes were an amazing shade of green she couldn't look away from. The eyes went with his hard face, which had been knocked around in his life, but he still managed to be handsome enough to turn the head of whatever woman happened to be in this late. Which, most nights, was only Addie.

His hair, though, was the weirdest thing. It was white, like a Scandinavian white blond, but striped with black. As though he'd gone in for a dye job one day and left it half finished. Or maybe he simply liked the look.

Except, Addie would swear it was natural. Dyes left an unusual sheen or looked brittle after a while. His hair glistened under the lights, each strand soft, in a short cut that suited his face. Addie often studied his head as he bent over his pie, and she'd clutch her apron to keep from reaching out and running her fingers through his interesting hair.

In sum—this man was hotter than a Texas wind on a dry summer day. Addie could feel the sultry heat when she was around him. At least, she sure started to sweat whenever she looked at him.

For the last month or so, he'd come in every night near to closing time, order the last pieces of banana cream pie and the apple pie with streusel, and eat while Addie locked the door and went through her rituals for the night. When Bo arrived through the back door, the man would go out the front, taking his sword . . . and the other things he always brought.

They came in now, walking behind him—three little boys, the oldest one following the two younger ones. The oldest's name was Robbie, and he brought up the rear, looking around as though guarding his two little brothers.

"Hello, Robbie," Addie said. "Brett, Zane. How are you tonight?"

As usual, the two littlest chorused *Fine*, but Robbie only gave her a polite nod, mimicking his father. Although Addie thought the man wasn't actually Robbie's father.

The youngest ones had the man's green eyes and white-and-black hair, but Robbie didn't look like any of them. He

had dark brown hair and eyes that were gray—a striking-
looking kid, but Addie figured he wasn't related to the others.
Adopted maybe, or maybe a very distant relative. Whatever,
the man looked after all three with protective fierceness, not
letting anyone near them.

They took the four stools at the very end of the counter
away from the windows, almost in the hall to the bathrooms.
Robbie sat on the seat farthest from the door, Zane and Brett
perched in the next two seats with their dad next to them, his
bulk between them and whoever might enter the diner.

Addie took up the coffeepot and poured a cup of fully
caffeinated brew for black-and-white guy and three ice
waters for the boys. She'd offered them cokes the first time
they came into the diner but their dad didn't like them having sugared drinks.

Considering how much pie they put away, Addie didn't
blame him. Sweet sodas on top of that would have them
wired to the gills all night.

"You almost missed the pie," Addie said to the boys as
she set dripping glasses of water in front of them. "We had
a run on it today. But I saved you back a few pieces in the
fridge." She winked. "I'll just run and get them. That's three
banana creams and an apple streusel, right?"

She looked into the father's green eyes, and stopped.

She'd never seen him look at her like that. There was a
hunger in his gaze—powerful, intense hunger. He skewered
her with it. Addie looked back at him, her lips parting, her
heart constricting.

Men had looked at her suggestively before but they'd
always accompanied the look with a half-amused smile as
though laughing at themselves, or telling Addie she'd have
a great time if she conceded.

This was different. Black-and-white man studied her with
a wanting that was palpable, as though any second he'd
climb over the counter and come at her.

After a second, he blinked and the look was gone. He
hadn't intended her to catch him.

The blink showed Addie something else. Behind the
interest, his eyes held great distraction and deep worry.

Something had happened tonight, some reason he'd come here going on five minutes late.

Addie knew better than to ask if everything was all right. He wouldn't tell her. The man was not one for casual conversation. The boys talked but kept their answers general. They had never betrayed with one word where they were from, where they went to school, what they liked to do for fun, or why their dad kept them up this late every night.

Addie simply said, "I'll be right back," and ducked into the kitchen to fetch the pie.

She took out the pieces, already sliced on their plates, and sprinkled a little extra cocoa powder on the banana cream ones from the dented shaker on the shelf.

Jimmy, the guy who washed dishes, wasn't there. He liked to duck out for a smoke right at closing time, coming back in when Bo got there to finish the cleanup. Addie hummed, alone in the kitchen, her pulse still high from that look black-and-white man had given her.

If Addie marched out there and said to him, sure, she was interested—in a discreet way in front of his kids—would he break down and tell her his name?

Or would he take her somewhere and make love to her with silent strength, the same way he walked or ate his piece of pie, as though he savored every bite? Would Addie mind that?

She pictured him above her in the dark, his green eyes on her while she ran her hands all over his tight, beautiful body.

Nope, she wouldn't mind that at all.

She picked up two pieces of pie, still humming. At the same time, she heard a scratching at the back door.

Bo? Addie set down the pie and walked over. Bo always used his key to get in—they kept the back door locked. Even though the small town of Loneview was pretty safe, robbers passing through might seize an opportunity.

Bo often couldn't get his key into the lock—his h shook with a palsy that ran in his family. Jimm to help him, or Addie would open the do a bit early, but he was sometimes

Addie reached for the door just as something banged into it.

"Bo? You okay?" Addie unlocked the deadbolt and carefully turned the doorknob.

The door fell inward, a heavy weight on it. Addie looked down.

A curious detachment came over her as she saw Jimmy the dishwasher, a guy of about thirty with greasy brown hair and beard stubble. He was dead, his brown eyes staring sightlessly. She knew he was dead because he had a gaping red hole where his heart used to be.

If this had been a movie, Addie would be screaming, fainting, sobbing, saying, *Oh my God,* or running outside crying, *Somebody, help!*

Instead, she stood there, as though caught in treacle, unable to move, think, talk, or even breathe.

A faint noise sounded outside, and Addie raised her head. She saw the round muzzle of a gun, one of the automatic ones that shot however many rounds a minute. Her breath poured back into her lungs, burning, and she knew she was looking at her own death.

A rush of air passed her, and the door slammed shut. At the same time a pair of strong arms closed around her, propelling her to the floor, the man with black-and-white hair landing on top of her.

In the front of the diner, every window shattered as bullets flew through them. Glass exploded through the open pass between the kitchen and dining area, as did bullets, shards of cups and plates, tatters of napkins.

The kids, Addie thought in panic. *Where were the boys?*

There they were, huddled against the door to the freezer. How the man had gotten them in here so fast and out of sight Addie didn't know, but her body went limp with relief to see them.

"Who's doing this?" Addie squeaked. "What—"

The man clamped his hand over her mouth. "Shh." His voice was a low rumble. "I need to you to be very quiet, all right?"

CHAPTER TWO

Addie, mouth dry, nodded. The man took his hand away after a few seconds but he didn't rise or move from her, the weight of him warm.

The boys, Addie noticed, were utterly still. No panicking, no crying—they lay silently on the floor, heads down, as though they did things like this all the time. Sad thought.

The deadly barrage of bullets ceased after a few heart-stopping moments but the man still didn't lift himself from Addie. He lay full-length on her on the grease-spattered floor, too strong for her to slide out from under him. His face was turned away from hers, bringing his hair and the curve of his neck in front of her eyes.

Addie smelled leather and musk, the scent of wind and rain. The color of his hair was indeed natural, she saw now, the black and white strands starting at the roots and mixing together in wide streaks across his head.

Tiger-striped.

Why the thought popped into Addison's mind, she didn't know. The man said nothing, did nothing, only waited. As though *he'd* done this before.

"Kendrick!" The shout came from beyond the broken front windows. The voice was harsh, a mean edge to it. "Get your sorry ass out here!"

Kendrick. Addison wouldn't have pegged that name on the solidly built guy on top of her, but, then, it kind of went with his odd hair and green eyes.

To her alarm, Kendrick started to rise.

"No, don't!" Addie whispered frantically.

The kids remained in place, eyes wide, frightened but waiting. The man called Kendrick got his feet under him but remained in a crouch next to Addie. His motorcycle boots were dusty, creased with wear. Denim stretched over heavily muscled thighs directly in her line of sight.

"If you go into the freezer and shut the door, can you get out again?" he was asking her. "You won't be locked in?"

Addie stared at him, barely registering the question, then she nodded. Bo wasn't stupid enough to have a freezer without a handle on the inside. He'd be the most likely person to get caught in there, and he knew it.

Bo—dear God, he'd be coming in soon, and these guys would shoot him like they shot poor Jimmy. She had to warn him . . . with her cell phone all the way across the room in her locker.

Kendrick's voice rumbled next to her. "When I give you the signal, I want you to take the cubs and go into the freezer with them. Shut the door and stay low. Can you do that?"

Cubs? Oh, he meant the little boys. Addie cast an eye over them where they lay close together, bodies touching. *Cubs—why the hell did he call them that?*

"If I don't come for you in fifteen minutes, take them out the back way and drive them toward Rock Springs. There's a shut-down gas station just before you get to town. If I don't meet you there . . ." Kendrick stopped, the ache in his eyes real as he cast his gaze over the boys. "Take them somewhere safe. Take care of them. Promise me."

Addie put her hand on his arm, sinking fingers into the warm denim of his coat. "You can't go out there. Let's run out the back together. My car's not far from the door." If it didn't go into one of its hissy fits and refuse to start, if it had enough gas to make it thirty miles down the highway.

Kendrick's green gaze fixed on her, and he put a broad finger over her shaking lips. "Promise me, Addison."

He'd never spoken her name before. The kids called her Addie, since Robbie had read her name tag and asked her what kind of name Addison was. She'd told them to use the shortened version. Kendrick had listened but never called her by name. Never said much to her at all, actually.

Now his deep voice around the syllables tingled through her blood, and Addie's heart squeezed to one hot point.

She gulped a breath. "I promise. But what the hell do you think you're going to do against a bunch of guys with automatics?"

Guys who were getting impatient. "Kendrick!" the man outside shouted. "You don't want us coming in there. Come out and face us."

Kendrick turned from Addie and grabbed the long bundle that held his sword. He'd even managed to bring that back here with him.

He quickly unrolled the folds of the cloth and drew from a sheath a long broadsword with a wide blade and a thick hilt. The sword looked very, very old, the blade a soft silver color, not shiny like modern steel. The hilt and blade were covered with symbols that looked like writing but no writing Addie had ever seen.

"You can't fight guns with a sword," Addie protested. "Are you nuts?"

Kendrick's eyes sparkled with sudden heat. "If you mean crazy, yes I am. I'm one crazy bastard, which is what's going to save my sons. Be ready."

"But what are you going to *do*?" Addie asked in a worried whisper.

"What I have to." Kendrick reached out and traced one scarred finger down Addie's cheek.

Addie lost all her breath again. His touch traced fire, his eyes softening as the rest of his square face remained grim. Dark whiskers brushed his skin, the bristles also black mixed with white. Addie had a sudden, insane curiosity about whether his hair was like that all the way down . . .

The look in Kendrick's eyes changed to one of consternation, and Addie realized she'd become fixed in place, staring at him.

"Right." Addie broke away and quickly scrambled the short distance on hands and knees to the freezer door, sitting down next to the three boys.

"Robbie." Kendrick transferred his hard gaze to the oldest boy and took a firm grip on the sword. "Take care of them."

"Yes, Dad," Robbie whispered, his gray eyes round, his look old for his age.

"*I'll* take care of them," Addie said, putting her hand on Robbie's thin back. "You just take care of yourself."

Kendrick sent her another long look that held a hint of a smile, a feral one. Then he . . . leapt.

It was weird—he sprang from a crouch up to the pass— the shelf where the cook put the completed dishes—then was through it and down the other side. It happened in only a second, from the time Addie drew a breath to releasing it again. Kendrick was gone, making no noise at all.

Signal—Addie was supposed to wait for a signal. Kendrick hadn't said *what* signal. She should have had him make that clear, but then, she'd never been in a situation like this before. She didn't have a checklist of what she needed to know.

Shouting sounded outside, but she heard nothing from Kendrick. If he'd hidden himself somewhere in the diner, he wasn't making a sound.

Robbie sat up next to Addie, huddling with his arms around his knees. The two littler boys remained on their stomachs, silent and waiting. Addie's body was cold, the floor hard under her butt, fear making her chest ache. She put her arm around Robbie but he didn't lean into her. He was trying to be brave but she felt him shiver.

The kids shouldn't be here. She had to get them to safety, call the police or the sheriff or at least 911. But, as Addie had realized, her cell phone was across the room in her locker, along with her purse. She kept the keys to her car in her pocket, but the rest of her life was in the small locker on the other side of the kitchen.

More shouting came from outside, men's voices raised in anger, then gunshots, violence boiling around her world.

All at once a man screamed, the sound high, harsh, and full of terror.

Had that been Kendrick? *Please, no.* Addie's heart thudded until it sickened her.

Another male scream came, and then a long, low growling filled the spaces between the noise, like a wild beast on the loose.

At the animal sound, the boys perked up. Brett and Zane sat up, eyes sparkling. Robbie even grinned.

The growling escalated and became snarls of vicious rage. There was more shouting, screaming, gunshots. A man, yelling, charged straight into the diner, glass crunching under his feet. Addie saw him through the pass, a big man, who turned around and fired behind him. The sound of the gunshot was right on top of them, deafening.

Addie clapped her hands over her ears. The man swung back to the pass and tried to jump up through it. He saw Addie and their eyes met for a brief moment, his wide and frantic.

And then what looked like two giant white paws caught him around the waist. His mouth opened, and his face screwed up in terror.

Addie couldn't hear his screams—the pistol banging at close range had robbed her of that sense. She was grateful because the man's open mouth must be emitting horrible sounds.

He grabbed at the pass, his fingers finding no purchase in the stainless steel. Then he was gone, dragged down, a bloody streak left in his wake.

A moment later, Kendrick's sword clattered through the pass, the blade falling hilt downward into the kitchen. Robbie scampered forward and grabbed it.

"Freezer," he said, his small mouth exaggerating the word. Addie suspected he couldn't hear either.

She and the little ones got the gist. Addie reached up and pulled open the freezer door, shoving the boys inside. Robbie ran in, dragging the sword that was longer than he was.

Addie flicked on the light inside the freezer, then closed

the door and dragged a few crates of frozen meat in front of it. The door opened outward, but anyone coming in would have to fight their way past the heavy crates after that.

It was cold in here but would be bearable for a short amount of time. The single light bulb illuminated shelves filled with boxes and boxes of frozen beef, veggies, premade pies, anything the customer wanted. Bo wasn't a great believer in organic, or even fresh, food.

Fifteen minutes. That was about how long they could stay in here without getting hypothermia, or so Bo had told her. Addie checked her watch, her heart pounding, her blood hot. Her body temperature had to be so high that hypothermia wouldn't stand a chance.

She worried about the youngest boys, though. They were small and wouldn't be able to survive this cold as well as she or even Robbie could. Especially when they were . . . taking off their clothes?

"Stop!" Addie said. She could hear again finally but it was as though someone had stuffed cotton into her ears. "I don't have any blankets in here. What are you . . . ?"

Zane and Brett calmly finished stripping off their jeans, shirts, and underwear, even socks and shoes, folding them into neat piles. Robbie stepped in front of Addie as she tried to go to them.

"Let them," Robbie said in a loud voice. "It's the only way they'll survive."

"What are you talking about . . . ?"

Addie choked to a halt as the two little boys' bodies began to jerk. She started for them again but Robbie grabbed her hand and held her back with a surprisingly strong grip.

The outlines of Zane and Brett blurred, and then, before Addie could register what happened, she was staring down at two very small white tiger cubs, both of them blinking green eyes like Kendrick's up at her.

Addie opened her mouth, barely able to hear the surprised sound that came out of it.

"It's okay!" Robbie called up to her. "They'll stay warmer with fur."

Addie gaped down at him. "What about you? Are you a tiger too?"

Robbie shook his head. "Lupine. But I'll be all right. What time is it?"

Addie for a moment couldn't remember how to find out. Her watch burned cold on her wrist, and she jerked it up in front of her eyes. When she figured out how to read it again, she deduced they'd been in there maybe three minutes.

What the hell was happening to her life?

Those men shooting up the place were after Kendrick specifically—they'd called him by name. This hadn't been a random act. They'd been chasing him, and Kendrick had known someone was after him.

They must have been after him for a while. Why else would he always take such care not to sit in front of the windows, to keep himself between his sons and the door?

And why hadn't he mentioned that his sons were *white tigers*?

The cubs' black-and-white stripes matched the stripes in Kendrick's hair, and their eyes were the same shade of green as his. That must mean that Kendrick was a . . .

No, that was insane. People didn't become wild animals, unless they were . . .

Shifters.

Addie never seen a Shifter before in her life. She'd watched documentaries about them on television, seen news reports, had heeded warnings to stay away from them.

Not that she'd even needed to worry about it before. Shifters didn't run around in middle-of-nowhere towns like Loneview, didn't mix much with people at all. What were called Shiftertowns had been formed in Austin and around San Antonio, but Shifters didn't leave them to come visit this out-of-the-way place. Addie never paid much attention to Shifters—they weren't part of her world.

And now one had come to her diner to eat pie.

Four Shifters, actually. The two little tigers huddled together and against Robbie. They blinked for a while, then Brett and Zane closed their eyes, and danged if they didn't drift off to sleep. Addie pulled a crate full of frozen pies over to them and sank down on it.

Addie's hands were growing numb, from fear or cold, she wasn't sure. She checked her watch every two minutes—the minute hand had never moved so slowly. Finally she simply started counting seconds to give her agitated mind something to do.

On the dot of fifteen minutes, Addison rose, signaled the cubs to stay behind her, and softly clicked open the freezer door.

The waft of warm air felt good. She'd never complain about Texas heat again.

Her foot crunched on glass, but other than that, all was silence.

That silence was broken when a man stumbled in through the open back door. He was big and hard-muscled, like Kendrick, but his clothes were in shreds, and blood coated his face and body.

The man saw Addie. He stared at her in great surprise, eyes of a very light blue widening. Then his knees bent, and he sort of folded up and collapsed to the floor, landing on his back. His head made an audible crack on the tile.

Addie started for him. He'd been one of the shooters, she was certain, but he wasn't armed now. He looked beaten down and pathetic.

Another sound made her look up. Kendrick came through the door, likewise bloody, and he was stark naked.

Kendrick gazed at Addie, and she looked back at him. His green eyes stood out in his dirt-and-blood-streaked face, holding both insane fury and great unhappiness.

Addie heard the tiger cubs and Robbie come out behind her, but the three remained together, huddled against the door of the freezer.

Kendrick and Addie studied each other over the body of the injured man, Addie barely able to breathe.

"Guardian," the man whispered.

Kendrick dragged his gaze from Addie and moved it down to him. The man looked back up at Kendrick, fear and shame in his eyes. The one word had been a plea.

Kendrick growled in his throat, his fist closing as though he held his sword, though Robbie still had the blade, guarding it across the room.

"You endangered my cubs," Kendrick said, the rage in his voice making the man on the floor flinch.

"I'm sorry," he said. "I'm sorry. I didn't know they would be here with you. Forgive me, Guardian. Take them far away, because more will be coming."

"How many more?" Kendrick asked him, voice hard. "And why? Why have you turned on me? I put my ass on the line for twenty years making sure you stayed free, no Collars, no Shiftertowns."

The man shrugged wearily against the floor. "There are at least fifty of us, maybe more. They're tired of hiding, tired of running."

"Dying is better?" Kendrick demanded. "Or living imprisoned?"

"We made *ourselves* prisoners. You know we did. We want out."

Kendrick said nothing. When he looked up at Addie again, she saw stark grief in his eyes, not outrage, that this man, whoever he was, had turned against him. As though the betrayal had been Kendrick's fault. He flicked his gaze away once more, back to the man at his feet.

"It's over, my friend," Kendrick said.

"I know." The man could barely speak. "I've lost. I accept my defeat."

"Your defeat is your death."

"I know. Please, Guardian, don't let me linger here."

Addie knew she should call the police, an ambulance. She should haul ass to her locker, grab the phone, and call. No way could she or Kendrick save this guy on their own. The man was going into shock, his eyes unfocused, body shivering, breath ragged.

But Addie couldn't move. She remained fixed in place, staring at the tableau—the bloody man on the floor, Kendrick above him, gazing down at him in anguish.

"Robbie," Kendrick said, without looking up. He held out his hand.

Robbie immediately lifted the big sword, laying the blade gingerly across his other palm so he wouldn't drag it on the floor as he carried it to his father. Kendrick gave his son a look of thanks as he closed his hand around the hilt. Robbie backed away as though he knew what Kendrick was about to do.

No! the thought shrieked in Addie's head. *No, he can't just kill this guy . . .*

Kendrick dropped to one knee. He put his hand on the man's forehead, his arm shaking but his bloodstained fingers rock steady. The man's body relaxed, his eyes softening as he sighed with relief.

"Thank you," the man said. "Forgive . . ."

Kendrick gave him a nod, then stroked the man's hair, as he might do with one of his sons, to comfort him.

"Goddess go with you," Kendrick said softly.

Then he rose, raised the sword overhead, and plunged the blade into the dying man's heart.

CHAPTER THREE

Addie cried out and leapt at Kendrick, but too late. The sword went straight through the man's chest.

The man grunted in pain, then his eyes cleared, and he looked suddenly happy. "Thank you," he whispered.

Those were the last words he spoke. His body shimmered with a silvery light and then, before Addie's eyes, the man dissolved into dust. The dust fell to the floor, swirled into a fine mist, and was gone, out the open door.

"Holy shit, you killed him!"

The words sprang from Addie's mouth before she could stop them. Kendrick, who'd bowed his head, the sword's point resting on the floor, looked up at her, his green eyes luminous with tears.

"He gave me no choice," he said.

"What about the others out there?" Addie's voice went up a notch. "Did you kill them too?"

Kendrick took one stride to her where she stood frozen and terrified. "You need to go, Addison. Take the cubs to safety for me, as you promised."

"But—"

"Your police will come. I can't let them find my sons. *Please.*"

Addison had never heard anything as heartfelt as the plea. Kendrick was afraid, scared for the kids, angry, dangerous.

And naked—had she mentioned that about seven times already? His body was hard and tight, strong, formidable. She kept her eyes averted so she wouldn't see anything too personal, but *not* looking was one of the hardest things she'd ever done.

He was right, though. This was a small town. News traveled fast; any trouble was instantly reported. If Robbie, Zane, and Brett had been normal kids, she wouldn't worry about the police so much, but they were Shifter, and their dad had just killed a man—possibly all the shooters. She knew enough to realize that cops would take the kids—the cubs—and keep them who knew where. Maybe never let them go again.

Addie looked at them, two little tigers huddled against the older Robbie, the three of them alone and vulnerable.

"Yes," she found herself babbling. "Yes, I'll take them."

"Now," Kendrick said, cutting through her stammering. "Robbie."

"I'm on it, Dad."

Robbie, small himself, picked up the tiger cubs by the scruffs of their necks. He cradled them against his chest and looked up at Addie in total trust.

Addie felt a brush of air, and when she looked back for Kendrick, he was gone, vanishing out the door into the hot night.

Four Shifters had attacked the diner, two of them with guns, *the fucking cowards*. What Shifters used guns?

Kendrick had taken down the one he'd just sent to dust— a Lupine called Ivan—who'd never been the most obedient to Kendrick but had never outright opposed him before. Kendrick had caught and fought a second Shifter, a Feline, and also sent him to dust with the sword before he'd gone after Ivan.

Kendrick's heart ached from the deaths, each one a gaping loss for every Shifter.

He changed to his tiger again and found the trails of the two remaining Shifters, who'd fled when he'd attacked. They'd taken to vehicles about a mile away and driven off down a dirt road heading straight west.

Returning to where he'd hidden his clothes and sword on his motorcycle, Kendrick saw Addison come out of the diner's back door, a big floppy purse at her side. She herded Robbie and the cubs into her car, a well-used Camry that had seen better days.

Kendrick had a momentary flash of anger. This woman should have a bright, beautiful car and be dressed in the finest clothes, not the ill-fitting waitress uniform and the flat, dull-black shoes on her shapely feet.

He'd recognized in Addison, the moment he'd first walked into her diner, a beauty that he'd never before encountered. He'd gone in with the cubs to find them something to eat late one night, choosing an out-of-the-way town where Shifters didn't go.

One look at her had floored Kendrick, made him want a second look. She'd cheerfully served them pie, the last pieces of the day, confiding to Kendrick that apple with streusel was her favorite as well. She'd spoken without worry to the cubs, gaining smiles from even Robbie, who was slow to trust anyone. She'd won over Brett and Zane by squirting extra whipped cream onto their pies, making a game of swirling it around.

Addison had hair the color of darkest coffee—the way he liked it—and eyes the blue of sudden violets in the snow. She wore her hair in a ponytail, which swung against her back as she ushered the cubs into the backseat.

Kendrick had looked at her and seen a diamond among pebbles, a vivid and striking brightness in a world of grays. Something had awakened in him when he'd heard her voice, seen her smile. He didn't know what that something was—his mate had been gone since Zane had come into the world, too soon for grief to be over.

But for a brief moment, his life had not been so dark or

uncertain. There was Addison, beaming her smile, winking at the cubs, always with a welcome.

That was her job—Kendrick understood that—but in that space of time in her diner, Addison had seen Kendrick as *himself*. Not a Guardian, a Shifter leader, an errand boy for Dylan Morrissey, or a Shifter trying to draw his clan together again. He'd been Kendrick, father to three cubs, man who ate pie.

When Robbie had asked the next night, "Can we go see Addie again?" Kendrick hadn't been able to say no.

Addison secured the cubs in the back then slid into the front seat and started the car. She scanned the parking lot, searching the shadows, not seeing Kendrick where he'd parked his bike well back from the lights. Kendrick watched her square her shoulders and drive away.

The place Kendrick had told her to take the cubs was straight south, a few miles outside San Antonio, where Dylan patrolled regularly. No one would dare harm Kendrick's cubs in Dylan's territory.

Now to make sure no other Shifters lingered here, waiting to corner him.

Kendrick had always had unrest in the Shifters he led. How could he not, with different species living together, hiding from humans, keeping their true natures a secret?

Unlike most Shifters these days, Kendrick and his band didn't wear Collars. They'd hidden away when humans came to round up Shifters years ago, and had lived free of Shiftertowns, covertly, for the last twenty years. But they'd had to follow Kendrick's stringent rules to remain hidden, and Shifters hated confinement. Restlessness turned to resentment and anger. Kendrick had been challenged for leadership more than once, though he'd always prevailed.

At the moment, Kendrick's Shifters were in limbo. They'd been living in secret in an underground bunker in South Texas that they'd made into a functioning if inelegant hideaway. But then a human man working for Shifter Bureau and his Collared Shifter mate—a Kodiak bear—had found the compound, broken in, and destroyed it. Kendrick's Shifters had gone to ground as per their standing contingency plan, hiding out the best they could.

When Kendrick found a new place for them to be safe, he'd contact them. But his Shifters, never the tamest, must have decided to break away and even to try to take over in the meantime. Kendrick had failed them, they must have reasoned; therefore, Kendrick had to die.

At least, he assumed that was what these attacks had been all about. He'd have to find one of these assholes and shake answers out of him.

Shifters who wanted new leadership were supposed to challenge the leader directly. They didn't fire guns—*what the hell were they thinking?*—and try to simply kill that leader and his cubs.

Kendrick dressed in the darkness next to his motorcycle with its sidecars, made specially for the cubs. He mounted it, started it up.

Sirens blared into the night, law enforcement responding to whoever had called in the violence at the diner. Kendrick rolled out of town in the opposite direction from the flashing lights, the Sword of the Guardian once more strapped to his back.

Addie had one of the tiger cubs—she wasn't sure which one —on her lap by the time she pulled into the parking lot of the closed gas station just off the 377. The other tiger was curled up in the front passenger seat. Robbie sat in the back, his lap full of the cubs' clothes, his face too serious.

Addie had called her sister as she'd driven, knowing Ivy would have heard about the shooting already—nothing stayed quiet long in Loneview. Ivy had been frantic, but Addie reassured her she hadn't been hurt. "I'm really fine. I'll be home in a little bit," she'd said. Ivy assumed it was because she had to talk to the police, and Addie didn't correct her. "Tell Tori and Josh I'm all right. Give them a kiss for me."

She'd clicked off the phone before Ivy could ask any more questions.

Addie parked and turned off the car's lights but kept the engine running. She turned to look at Robbie, who watched her with grave eyes. "You okay back there?" she asked him. "You haven't said much."

Robbie shrugged. "Nothing much to say."

"I know, sweetie." Addie reached back and patted his jeans-clad knee. "I just want to make sure you're all right. You want to come up here and sit with us?"

Robbie shook his head, though Addie saw in his eyes he did want to. He thought he had to be brave.

"You're good to take care of the little ones," Addie said. "Are they your, what—cousins?"

"We're not related," Robbie said without changing expression. "They're Feline. I'm Lupine."

"I'm not sure what that means, honey."

Robbie pointed at the sleeping tiger cub in the passenger seat. "Feline—big cats. Lupine means wolf." •

"Oh." Addie studied him. "That's why you have such nice gray eyes, I bet. You take care of them well."

"Kendrick takes care of me," Robbie said. "It's the least I can do."

He was far too young to speak in phrases like that. Addie had grown up fast, but not *that* fast. She'd still had a childhood, thanks to her sister.

"Why don't you stretch out there while we wait," Addie said. "I have a blanket—we can pull that over you, make you all cozy."

Robbie obeyed and lay down, but Addie suspected it was to please her, not because he wanted to. He was tense, waiting, much like Kendrick had been when he'd crouched in the kitchen, just before he'd launched himself through the pass to fight to the death. Cats jumped like that, she realized.

Addie pulled an old wool afghan from behind the driver's seat and tucked it around Robbie's small body. He didn't say anything and didn't close his eyes, only stared into the darkness.

Poor kid. Addie smoothed his hair, which he didn't fight, and left him alone.

Fifteen minutes later, a motorcycle headed out of the darkness at her. Addie clutched the steering wheel, ready to gun the car and race away if she had to. As the bike slowed and turned into the empty parking lot, she saw the flash of Kendrick's white and black hair in the moonlight, the sword on his back.

The cubs woke as soon as they heard the motorcycle. Both tigers bounced to Addie's lap, put paws on the open window ledge, and started yowling.

Kendrick swung off the bike with easy grace, balancing the sword without trouble. The cubs scrambled onto the window ledge as he reached the car, then hurled themselves at him. Kendrick caught them in his arms, cradling them with his big, gloved hands.

It was an interesting sight, the large, tall biker, holding two little white tiger cubs.

Robbie had sat up and now climbed out of the car without a word. He went straight to Kendrick and wrapped his arms around the man's waist. Kendrick smoothed Robbie's hair the best he could with an armful of cub.

"Addison, thank you." Kendrick's eyes held true gratitude.

He gazed at her for a moment longer, as though wanting to say more but not finding the words. Then he abruptly turned away, still carrying the cubs.

Addie scrambled out of the car. She knew that when he rode out of here, she'd never see him again. No way was she about to let him race off into darkness without answering a few questions.

"What happened?" she demanded. "Who were those guys? Why did they want to kill you? You stuck the sword into him and he disappeared. Where did he go?"

"To the Summerland," Kendrick said, cutting through her jumble.

"Oh?" Addie planted her hands on her hips. "What the hell does that mean? If you stuck that sword into *me*, would I become a puff of dust too?"

"He was Shifter," Kendrick said. "So, no."

One thing Addie had learned about Shifters in the documentaries was that they wore Collars, with a capital C. The

Collars were designed to shock them and shut them down if they grew violent. *Control them—humanely*, the documentary had claimed.

Addie had seen nothing around Kendrick's throat when he'd stood up, unclothed, in the diner. The Shifter who'd run into the diner hadn't had a Collar either.

"Who were they?" she repeated. "Who are *you*?"

He gave her a hint of a smile. "Who do you want me to be?"

"Come on," Addie said in exasperation. "I just went through hell. Tell me *something*."

Kendrick's mouth hardened. "They were Shifters who used to work for me. I thought they still did work for me. I thought . . ." He shook his head. "Someone has been stirring up trouble, and I need to find out who."

Robbie had let go of Kendrick. While Addie blurted questions, he brought the cubs' clothes from the car and tucked them into one of the two wide saddlebags on the bike. The saddlebags had been modified to have small seats inside them, and the two cubs scampered down Kendrick's arms and fixed themselves onto these seats.

"Where are you going to go?" Addie asked.

Kendrick kept his eyes on her, the green visible in the dark. "Someplace safe for them. I want *you* to go somewhere safe, Addison. Take a vacation; go far away. You'll have my scent on you—leave Texas for a while. And burn this." He reached out and took a fold of her sleeve between two fingers. He didn't touch her, but she felt the heat of him brush her arm.

"Your *scent?* What the hell does that mean?"

"They can track you through it. Any Shifter can. I can't risk that they won't use you to get to me."

"I can't just leave. I have a job . . ." In a shot-up diner that would need a hell of a lot of work before Bo could open it again. She probably wouldn't have a job at all for a while.

"Safer for you to be nowhere near here." Kendrick reached into his coat and took out a thick wad of rolled-up bills. "I don't know how much this is but it will help you travel."

Addie stared at the roll, which was very fat, her eyes widening. The top denomination, as far as she could see, was *100*. "I don't want your money. Besides if I showed up at an airline counter looking like this and tried to pay for a ticket with *that*, they'd call security."

His lowered brows told her he had no idea why. He took her hand and pressed the roll of money into it. "However you go, take it. Buy a new car." Kendrick's glance at the vehicle behind her was full of skepticism that she'd reach anywhere in it. "Go far, Addison. Don't go home."

Addie's heart burned. Ivy would be up waiting, worried about what had happened at the diner. Tomorrow it was Addie's turn to drive Tori and Josh to school after Ivy made breakfast, and Addie had planned to look some more into signing up for college classes before heading in to work. A normal day in Loneview.

Kendrick closed Addie's hand around the cash, the warmth of his fingers coming through the cool leather of the glove. "I thank you, Addison. Truly."

The words told her more certainly than anything that she'd never see him again. He'd ride off down the road and disappear, his cubs with him. Addie would have to find a new job—she needed the money too much to wait for Bo to put the diner to rights, if he ever did. There would be police reports and insurance . . . insurance could take forever.

Kendrick would become a memory, his strange hair, his intense green gaze, the powerful way he moved, his voice deep and resonating, the way he was so careful with the little boys. He'd fade into her past and become a strange, confusing, heart-pounding memory.

"Oh, what the hell," Addie said softly.

She closed the space between them, flung her arms around Kendrick's neck, and pulled him down to kiss him fully on the lips.

CHAPTER FOUR

Addie felt Kendrick's body move in surprise under her kiss, then he went very still. She expected him to not respond, to freeze until she stepped back, embarrassed and apologetic.

Then Kendrick growled low in his throat. He wrapped his arms all the way around her, and Addie went breathless at his strength, his warmth. He cradled her in the darkness, shutting out everything terrible, all the fear and horror of the last hour.

He eased away from her first kiss, only to bring his mouth back down on hers. His body was a place of heat as he kissed Addie slowly, his lips parting, his tongue tangling hers with a bite of spice.

Kendrick's arms were hard on her back, crushing her against the solid power of him. Addie felt every inch of his body through her thin polyester dress that ended at her knees, the heat of him against her bare legs.

She held on to him as the kiss strengthened, the two of them seared together in the cool of the Texas night. His breath was hot on her cheek as he pulled her closer still, his strength astonishing. He kissed with aching intensity, the hunger she'd seen his eyes in the diner manifesting in this savage, amazing kiss.

Another growl, and Kendrick abruptly released her. Addie staggered back, fighting for breath. She put out her hand, but found nothing to steady herself on. She had to back away until she bumped into her car.

Kendrick said nothing. He didn't reach for her again, didn't apologize, didn't do anything. He simply looked at Addie for a long moment as she struggled to stay upright.

Another sound came from him, like a snarl in the darkness. "Go," he said, his voice fierce. "*Now*. Stay away from me."

Addie's throat didn't work, nothing emerging in answer. Kendrick watched her a moment longer, his chest rising in a sharp breath, then he turned away and mounted his motorcycle.

Moonlight flashed on his sword as he kicked the bike to life. He didn't look around at her, didn't say a word. Addie supported herself on the ledge of the driver's open window while Kendrick eased the bike forward, then out of the abandoned parking lot.

Robbie was the only one who looked back, his small head covered in a helmet, as Kendrick turned onto the road. Robbie raised his hand in a wave, which Addie shakily returned.

The motorcycle picked up speed, the bike's taillight flashing as Kendrick slowed for a turn, then they were gone.

Addie was left alone in dark, silent warmth, amidst the smell of exhaust and dried grasses, her mouth raw from Kendrick's hard kiss.

Addie took the 377 and kept heading south. The money Kendrick had left with her burned in the pocket she'd shoved it in. She'd run her thumb over the wad and realized it was about five thousand dollars. She could consider it a tip, she supposed. She'd served some really good pie.

Addie started laughing, the laughter turning hysterical. She took a deep breath, trying to stifle it. Losing her mind right now wasn't going to help her.

Kendrick had told her to leave Texas, to go anywhere. Addie's heart pounded as she contemplated what to do. Ivy would be scared for her. Her big sister didn't handle life as well as Addie did—Ivy had a comfort zone she'd rarely left since her divorce.

But then, if Kendrick was afraid the guys who'd attacked the diner would look for her . . . Addie couldn't lead them back to her sister's house, where her innocent nephew and niece lived.

Kendrick was right—she should leave the state and just keep driving. The only trouble with that was, Texas was such a damn big state, and Loneview was more or less in the center of it. It would take a long time to cross a border. But she had a change of clothes in her trunk—she often changed into and out of her uniform at the diner—and now the money Kendrick had pressed upon her.

She could go to New Orleans, lie low there in a motel somewhere—however low a person could lie in New Orleans. She could blend in with the tourists, at least.

Addie's fingers firmed on the steering wheel. She'd drive on through the night, call Ivy and assure her she was all right, that she needed to get away after the trauma. She'd even mail Ivy some of the money.

She knew these back roads pretty well and started looking for the turnoff that would let her head east. A little maneuvering would get her into San Antonio, and the 10, which would take her straight to Houston and then to Louisiana and New Orleans.

A flash of light caught her attention, and Addie glanced into her rearview. Her heart sank as she saw the unmistakable lights of a police car coming up behind her. Had they followed her from the diner? Did they know about Kendrick? The dead Shifters?

She soon heard the wail of a siren as the car came closer. This might not be about her. *Might* not. But there was no one on this back road but herself.

The lights grew closer until they were right on her bumper. She knew better than to try to floor it—they'd chase her, and life could get bad after that.

Their headlights flashed, and they sounded the horn that meant, *Yes, we're following you, lady, and you need to pull over.*

Swallowing, Addie put on the brakes and halted on the highway's shoulder.

A glance into the mirror showed that much of her hair had escaped its ponytail and hung in long hanks down her face. She hoped by all that was holy she hadn't looked this bad when she'd thrown her arms around Kendrick and kissed the hell out of him.

The heat of that kiss still lingered on her lips, the sensation of his hands on her body imprinted there for life.

Two men approached the car. One leisurely strolled toward her window while the other remained at her taillight, almost in her blind spot.

The one who approached her open window wore an immaculate khaki-colored uniform, his short hair combed and perfectly straight. He wasn't Loneview police, she realized; he wore a county sheriff's department badge on his chest and his name tag read *Alvarez*.

He stood at her window, leaning slightly to look inside. "Ms. Price? Can you step out of the car for me?"

Addie tried to hide her agitation as she opened the door and got out. Cool wind wrapped her bare legs. She saw that the other deputy remained at the rear of her car, and he had his gun in his hand.

"Mind telling me where you were going?" Alvarez asked her.

"I don't know, really," Addie said, her voice shaking. "Anywhere."

"Your car was seen heading out of town after the trouble at your diner," he went on. "You were a witness."

Not a question. A statement. He knew she'd been there. But then, if he'd talked to Bo, Bo would have told him she'd been working her shift tonight.

"Yes," she said, her mouth dry.

Alvarez was watching her with a calm, steady look, but she read the suspicion behind his eyes.

"Wait," she said. "You think I had something to do with it? I didn't. I was scared out of my mind."

"I can imagine," Alvarez said, continuing with the calm tone. "I'm going to ask you now why you were driving down this highway instead of going home. You're not obligated to tell me, but I'm going to ask. Seems a kind of strange thing to do."

He wanted her to confirm his suspicions, that she was involved somehow, that she knew all about who had done the shooting and why. His eyes and tone of voice encouraged her to.

Addie thought of Robbie's too-serious gray eyes as he looked after the smaller cubs. She also remembered the way Robbie had momentarily let down his guard when he'd seen Kendrick, to run to him and cling to his legs.

No way was she giving up those kids to the cops. Not their fault their father had been hunted, not their fault he'd killed a guy with a sword. Kendrick had been defending them against men who'd tried to shoot them all dead.

If she gave up Kendrick, the cubs would be taken. To where and what would happen to them, she didn't know. She was equally certain that Kendrick could take care of them now, wherever they'd gone.

"I was just so scared," Addie said. Her voice quavered— not a lie. "I don't know where I was going. Driving around to clear my head."

Alvarez pinned her with his dark stare then grudgingly gave her a nod. "Understandable. But I need to ask you to—"

He broke off sharply. Addie went ice-cold as she realized he was staring at her pocket, which was bulging with the money roll Kendrick had handed her.

"Ms. Price," Alvarez said, voice sharp. "I'm going to ask you now to empty your pockets. Again, you don't have to comply, but I'm going to ask."

Addie heaved a sigh. If she didn't do what he wanted, he could arrest her or at least take her in for questioning, advising she call a lawyer. Not that Addie had one.

She drew a breath, reached into her pocket, and took out the bills. "It's mine. A friend gave it to me."

There was no law against carrying around a lot of money. But an underpaid waitress racing down an empty highway with thousands of dollars in her pocket after the diner where she worked had just been shot up didn't look good.

Alvarez stared hard at the money. Then he looked back at Addie, anger in his eyes.

"Ms. Price, I'd like you to come to the sheriff's department with me. There are few questions you need to answer."

No telling her she had a choice this time. Sighing, Addie nodded. At least they didn't cuff her before they put her into the back of the sheriff's car and drove away.

"Dad," Zane asked Kendrick in their motel room well south of the I-10. "Is Addie going to be our new mom?"

Kendrick glanced down at his youngest son, barely four years old now. Kendrick's heart constricted. Zane had the look of Eileen, Kendrick's mate, who'd passed bringing this lad in. The eyes that looked up at him, thought they held the green of the white tiger, were hers.

Kendrick shook his head but kept his voice gentle. "I don't think we'll be seeing Addison anymore, son."

Zane's eyes filled with distress. "But I like Addie. She gives me pie."

"I know." Kendrick's voice was harder than he meant it to be. "But it's too dangerous for her to be around us right now. We don't want Addison getting hurt."

It had been a hell of a hard thing to unwrap his arms from around her and tell her to go. The sudden joy of her kiss, the taste of her sweetness, the feeling of her body the length of his had awakened a hope he'd not felt in a long, long time.

Grief and pain had consumed him for years, and then Addison had smiled at him, her blue eyes warm. The hot promise of her body had made aching need, long-suppressed, spring to life.

He had to send her to safety, away from the Shifters who'd turned on him, from humans who might find out she'd helped him. From himself.

Zane nodded at Kendrick's words, but Kendrick knew he didn't really understand.

Robbie, flipping through channels on the television, the sound muted, did understand. He said nothing though, only his hunched back betraying his unhappiness.

Damn it. Kendrick hadn't meant for his cubs to be out in the wide world any longer than they had to be. He was supposed to find a new safe place for them, for all his Shifters.

He was working on it, but slowly. Kendrick had hoped he'd find a new site for his Shifters quickly, far from here, possibly in Alaska.

That plan had fallen apart as soon as Kendrick, trying to take his cubs to safety from the collapsing compound last November, had been found by Dylan Morrissey. Dylan was an alpha stronger than any other Kendrick had met, didn't matter that Dylan had a Collar firmly around his neck.

Dylan had decided that Kendrick, an un-Collared Shifter that Shifter Bureau didn't know about, could help him with covert operations he was running. They were so covert, even the Shifters in the local Shiftertowns didn't know about them.

Dylan promised protection for Kendrick and his sons and for any un-Collared Shifter that Kendrick had led, as long as Kendrick stayed around and helped him. Kendrick saw no reason not to—he could keep looking for a new place while he assisted—but he knew deep down inside that Dylan wouldn't let Kendrick go until he was ready.

Dylan had not been happy that Kendrick had set up his "Shiftertown" in Dylan's area of control, though Kendrick hadn't realized until too late he'd violated Dylan's territory, an unforgivable act. He hadn't understood how far Dylan's power reached.

Kendrick sat down heavily on the bed. He should never have gone to Addison's diner, never endangered her, or his cubs. But they'd clamored to go, happy to get out of the boring motel room and eat some real food.

Addison, her name tag read. Kendrick hadn't been able to stop looking at the name, the label hung on her so all would know who she was. Humans so readily gave each other their most intimate names.

The cubs called her Addie. Not the same thing. *Addie* was cute and bouncy. *Addison* was more remote, lovely, like coming upon a sudden beautiful vista after climbing through a dreary, desolate landscape.

Addison had smiled at Kendrick and the cubs, her eyes warm. No distance. Addison was open, friendly, kind.

Tonight, he'd found her in his arms, her mouth crushing his in that burning kiss . . .

"Dad," Robbie called in agitation. "Look!" He was standing up, staring at the television, his small fists balled. The younger boys, who'd been dozing at the end of one bed, sat up to see what had caught Robbie's attention.

Kendrick fixed his gaze on the screen, the picture playing with no sound. He saw Addison being led up the steps into a building in the middle of a dark town, two men in law enforcement uniforms on either side of her. Words and numbers poured across the bottom of the screen, stock quotes, game scores, and the highlights of the story unfolding.

Shootout in Loneview. Suspected accomplice taken in for questioning.

"Turn that up," Kendrick said.

Robbie, who'd figured out how to work every remote in the room five minutes after they'd checked in, clicked a button.

". . . The county sheriff's department suspects this woman of having a hand in the shooting, though it's unclear whether she let in the shooters or covered their escape, or whether she was coerced or working with them. Police haven't discovered the motive for the shooting—a robbery gone wrong, or an act of terrorism."

Addie glanced once over her shoulder, her face fixed with fear she was trying not to show.

"Son of a fucking . . ." Kendrick's words faded into snarls. "Robbie."

Robbie gave him a solemn nod. "I'll take care of them, Dad. Are you going to go save Addie?"

Kendrick didn't know if he could. She was in custody of the human police, and Kendrick was an un-Collared Shifter who was breaking the law simply by existing. What the hell he could do, he didn't know.

He'd think of something. He'd spent his whole life making things up as he went along—why stop now?

"Be ready," he said to Robbie.

The lad knew what he meant. Robbie had learned how to lie low and then move at the drop of a hat—he'd have their collective belongings together and the littler boys prepared to go.

Robbie nodded. "Goddess go with you," he said.

Zane and Brett sat quietly, their large eyes on Kendrick. He went to them, bending down to give them tight hugs, kissing the tops of their heads, before he made himself turn and leave them.

He heard, before he mounted his motorcycle he'd parked next to the door, Robbie clicking all the locks home and dragging a piece of furniture in front of the door.

Kendrick slung his sword on his back, started the Harley, and rode away north.

A ddie sat with her hands folded in front of her in the interrogation room. Alvarez still hadn't handcuffed her, but he'd made it clear she'd be restrained if she tried to leave before they were finished.

Alvarez faced her, his partner, whose name was Hickson, beside him. Hickson started a recorder.

"For the record, Ms. Price," he said. "Let's go over events one more time. I want to emphasize that you're simply here so I can ask questions. You haven't been charged. Now . . . who was in the restaurant?"

Addie swallowed. "No one. The last customers had gone." She cleared her throat, trying to sound helpful, not worried. "I was locking up, and Jimmy stepped outside for a smoke." She didn't like to think about Jimmy, falling in the door, surprised and dead. He hadn't deserved that. "The shooting started and I hid until they were gone."

"Hmm." Alvarez shifted in his seat as though growing comfortable for a long chat. "When we went over the diner, there were four place settings and four glasses at the counter. One set of dishes at a booth. Who were those for?"

Addie wet her lips. "Oh—just regulars. They'd gone. I was locking up, like I said. I hadn't had time to clear the tables."

She thought hard about when the guy in the John Deere cap had left—she was positive it had been before Kendrick had arrived. Kendrick had been late. But if John Deere Cap had seen Kendrick on his way . . .

"No one was there," she repeated.

Alvarez didn't believe her. Addie read that in his eyes. Hickson didn't either, but he was remaining deferentially silent, letting Alvarez lead.

Alvarez leaned forward and asked, "What about the pie?"

CHAPTER FIVE

Addie started. "Pie?"

"There were four plates behind the pass, pie boxes open, and a spatula thing for scooping pieces out."

Addie had forgotten about that. She'd set up plates in the back just before the shooting started. "Oh. That. I was going to serve some customers out front, but they left before I could bring the order."

"Yeah?" Alvarez looked interested. "Why do you think they did that?"

Addie wet her lips. "How should I know? Maybe they were tired and didn't want to wait. Maybe they had to go to the bathroom. They didn't say."

"Did they pay you?"

"For what?" Addie asked, bewildered. "The pie?"

"For the drinks you'd already served. And for the pie, since they'd obviously ordered it."

"I don't remember." Addie pressed her hands to her face. "I really don't remember."

"And what did you do to get that very large tip? You were carrying around five thousand dollars. You know that, right?"

Addie jumped again. Yes, she'd guessed at the amount Kendrick had simply handed her. Which the police now had as well as her purse.

"Who were these last customers?" Alvarez prodded. "What did they look like? You said they were regulars. Do you know any of their names?"

"I . . ." Addie couldn't think. Which was exactly what Alvarez intended. He'd ask her the same questions over and over until she couldn't remember what she'd told him and blurt out the truth when she couldn't hold it in any longer.

Addie tried a faint laugh. "If you think the farmer who comes in every night had anything to do with the shooting, you're wrong. I don't know his name, but he's a nice guy. He doesn't get along with his wife, so he eats in the diner a lot. Mostly for the company. Couldn't be the food."

Alvarez listened with seeming patience. "He might have had nothing to do with the shooting, but he might have seen something. Maybe he saw these other customers when they suddenly decided to leave. Tell me about them."

"About who?"

"The four customers at the counter." Alvarez spoke slowly, as though Addie had trouble understanding English. "Did you know their names?"

Kendrick, Robbie, Brett, Zane. Good thing telepathy wasn't real or Addie would have just given them up. *I hope they're all right.*

"Or at least what they looked like," Alvarez prompted. Hickson simply sat and listened, and the recorder made a faint, electronic hum.

Someone knocked on the door of the stuffy room. Hickson calmly rose and answered it.

Kendrick walked in. His hair was slicked down on his head, the strands arranged so the white wasn't as obvious through the black. He carried a leather folder in one hand, and he was wearing a suit. Coat, slacks, ivory-colored shirt, tie and all.

Where the hell did he get a suit? was Addie's first dazed thought. *And doesn't he look good in it?*

No, he looked *damn* good in it. The coat hugged broad

shoulders, the collar and tie framed his square face, the slacks skimmed athletic legs. He looked like a corporate pinup guy, like the billionaires on the covers of romances her sister devoured.

Addie imagined him coming home after a hard day's work, loosening his tie, slinging down his coat, unbuttoning his shirt, giving her a promising look from his green eyes . . .

She nearly swallowed her tongue. Once she regained control of it, she realized he was speaking.

"I'm Ms. Price's attorney." Kendrick produced a business card from his pocket and set it on the table in front of Alvarez. "I'm advising her to answer no more questions and requesting that you release her if you have not brought formal charges. She is an unfortunate victim here, not a perpetrator."

Well, that at least was true. Addie pressed her mouth closed and tried to look like an unfortunate victim.

Alvarez studied Addie for a time. He didn't want to let her go, she saw. He wanted to charge her for maybe being an accessory to the shootout, maybe for robbery. But Bo could not have reported five thousand dollars missing, because he never kept that kind of money in the diner. Five hundred possibly, but never five grand.

Alvarez had no evidence. Hickson had searched Addie's car, finding nothing but her change of clothes and her purse. No weapons, ammunition, a phone with calls to a boyfriend to come and open fire on the diner. Addie's call log showed her sister, a few girlfriends, and that was it. Addie, since her bad breakup a while back, didn't have much of a social life.

Alvarez scowled at Kendrick, then he hid his disappointment and nodded at Hickson. "Stay close to home, Ms. Price, in case I need to speak to you again."

Kendrick closed his hands around his folder and waited. Addie, after a heartbeat or two, sprang to her feet. "Right. Thank you." She nodded at Alvarez and Hickson with as much dignity as she could and followed Kendrick out.

Addie managed to keep her mouth shut all the way down the white-tiled halls of the courthouse and sheriff's department. At the door, her purse and clothes were returned, but not, she noticed, the money. She could protest about that, but then they might come up with a charge to keep her there.

She took up her stuff and jogged along beside Kendrick, out into the cool darkness of the Texas night.

The courthouse in Loneview, the county seat, was typical old-style, sitting in a square, surrounded by quiet streets of an aging Texas town. Kendrick headed around the corner in a long stride, and Addie trotted to keep up with him, her purse flopping against her hip.

Kendrick reached a motorcycle parked around the corner of the next block, hidden behind a convenience store. He dropped the leather folder into one of the saddlebags and loosened and pulled off his tie.

"Can you ride?" he asked her.

Addie dragged her gaze from the open buttons at his throat and fixed it on the large Harley. "A motorcycle? I don't know. I never have."

"Time to learn." Kendrick mounted the bike and handed her a helmet. He pried the purse from Addie's shoulder as she stood there, tucked it into the saddlebag, and patted the seat behind him.

Addie settled the helmet with shaking fingers and tried to swing her leg over the bike's seat. She kicked the seat with her clunky shoe, her toe bouncing off, and ended up hopping on her other foot, trying to regain her balance.

Kendrick, for the first time since she'd met him, twitched his lips into the ghost of a smile. He grabbed her leg, pushed it over the bike, and helped get her butt on the seat. Addie settled herself, the imprint of his hand warm on her skin.

"Where are the boys?" she said to him as he started the bike. "Are they all right?"

"Yes." Kendrick's body moved as he balanced the throbbing motorcycle. "Put your feet on the footholds and hang on to me."

Addie's feet slipped off twice before she figured out how to plant them onto the metal bars. She grabbed Kendrick around the waist as he lifted his feet and guided them out of the small parking lot, holding on tighter as he glided around a corner.

Kendrick headed away from the courthouse, using streets that would take them out of town the fastest. Addie expected him to turn around and head for the 10, but Kendrick took the road south, out to open country.

Wind, speed, and the roar of the motor prevented Addie from asking him questions, like *Why did you come back for me?*

There wasn't much traffic out here, and Kendrick sped up, leaning into the wind. This part of Texas was flat, dry, spreading out under endless sky. Stars unfurled in a multitude above them, glittering against the black of nothingness.

Addie wrapped her arms more firmly around Kendrick, the power of him vibrating against her. She moved with him, the two of them one as cool air flowed around them and the land rolled on forever.

I love this, Addie realized. *No wonder bikers are so obsessed with the road.*

The freedom of riding, being part of the land instead of shut away from it, was exhilarating. Riding at this speed, holding on to a hard-bodied man who'd just rescued her, the wide world spinning under her, made Addie laugh out loud. The danger of it simply made it more exciting.

They rode ever southward, until Addie started to wonder if they were heading into Mexico. Alvarez had asked her not to go far—Mexico could be considered far.

But for the moment, Addie didn't care. She was now without a job, and she had no ties except to her sister, no obligations. No money either, but that didn't seem to matter right now.

She was almost disappointed when Kendrick slowed in another small town and made for a motel a little way from the highway.

Seeing Robbie and the little guys inside the room after Robbie unlocked the door and peered out cautiously, made up for the disappointment, however. Brett and Zane cried out in delight and rushed Addie, throwing their arms around her legs. Robbie gave her a calmer but no less exuberant hug.

"Addie!" Brett yelled. "Did you bring pie?"

"No, sweetie, sorry," Addie said.

Kendrick closed the door and locked it, then dropped the folder onto the bed and sent the suit coat and tie after it.

Addie disentangled herself from the cubs, watching as Kendrick unbuttoned the shirt's collar, just as she'd imagined him doing. His eyes took her in, his hair mussed from the ride. His hand went to another of the shirt buttons, and another.

Just when Addie thought, breathlessly, that he'd pull open the shirt and let her gaze at his firm, well-muscled chest she'd seen in naked glory at the diner, he turned from her and headed for the bathroom.

To hide her regret, she picked up the leather-bound folder he'd dropped, and opened it. Inside she found a yellow legal pad, brand new and unused, and the pockets of the folder empty. The folder too was new, probably purchased at an office supply store on Kendrick's way to Loneview.

Glancing at the closed bathroom door, Addie dipped her hand into his coat pocket. She found three cards, also new, possibly printed off at the same office store. *Miles Standing, Attorney at Law, Standing, Standing, and Davis.*

She was staring at the card, mystified, when Kendrick came out. He'd changed back to jeans and a black T-shirt, looking like he always did when he came into the diner. Addie wasn't sure which she preferred—bad-boy biker or well-dressed attorney.

Addie held up the card. "Who is—?"

"No one," Kendrick said. "It's a name I use sometimes when I have to deal with humans."

His clear eyes scrutinized her, taking in her waitress dress, which was limp and tired now, the ugly shoes she wore to keep her feet from getting too sore. She flushed, knowing she looked like crap but not sure what to do about it.

Addie studied Kendrick in return. The white streaks in his hair were more prominent now that it was messy from the wind. The T-shirt hugged every muscle, which he hadn't hidden at all when he'd fought at the diner. His neck remained bare, no Collar in sight.

"All right, next question," Addie said, her tongue finally loosening. "Why did you come rescue me?"

Kendrick's stare didn't waver. "Because you were innocent. And because you didn't betray me."

"Yes, I am, and no, I didn't. Wait—how do you know I didn't tell anyone about you? Can you read minds? *That* would be embarrassing."

"I'm Shifter."

Addie waited but Kendrick seemed to think the two words were an explanation.

"What does that have to do with anything?" she finally asked.

Kendrick's voice was a low and pleasing rumble. "If you'd told them I was Shifter, Shifter Bureau and every law enforcement agency from Austin to the border would be hunting me right now. There'd be news reports telling people to call in any sight of me or any unusual Shifter activity at all. *That's* how I know."

His gaze was unnerving but Addie continued to meet it. "Well, *you* didn't do the shooting. You were shot *at*. You killed that guy in self-defense. But there's no body, no evidence that you hurt anyone or he hurt you. I don't think anyone would have believed me when I said you stuck a sword into a man and he disintegrated." She ran out of breath, rubbing her hands over her arms. "They took your money—the deputies did. I'm so sorry."

Kendrick shook his head. "It doesn't matter."

Addie's eyes widened. "Seriously? Five thousand dollars is gone like a puff of dust and it doesn't matter?"

"Getting you away from them matters." Warmth entered Kendrick's gaze. "You're a very strong woman to resist speaking of me and my cubs under interrogation. Most humans would have given me up."

Addie went on rubbing her arms. "I didn't feel strong. I just didn't want the kids pulled in by the cops or you arrested. I bet if you were imprisoned, the kids wouldn't go into foster care, unless there's some Shifter equivalent—not that I'd want them in foster care at all. I didn't want to see Robbie and Zane and Brett hurt, so I kept quiet."

Kendrick gave her a nod that was almost a bow. "And for that, I thank you."

Addie looked him over again. "Are you always so formal?"

Kendrick gave her another nod, a sparkle lighting his eyes. "Yes."

Addie became aware that other eyes were on them, two pairs of bright green ones and one steadfast gray.

"Dad," Zane said in his small but surprisingly strong voice. "Addie *is* going to be our new mom, isn't she?"

Addie turned to him in surprise. Zane was looking up at her, so much eagerness in his expression that it broke her heart.

"Zane," Kendrick said, admonishing.

Addie held up her hand, her heart beating faster. "No, wait. This is interesting. Has there been discussion on the topic?"

"No." Kendrick's brows came down, and the word was abrupt. "The cubs, they're . . . missing their mother."

Who wasn't around anymore, Addie took it. "What happened to her?"

"Dead." Again Kendrick's word was abrupt, devoid of emotion.

"I'm sorry." Addie felt bad for prying but she was coming to understand that with Kendrick, information had to be dragged out of him a piece at a time. "What about Robbie?"

"His parents were killed. They left him to me."

"I'm sorry, Robbie," Addie said, turning to him. "I lost my mom and dad too. My sister took care of me from the time I was fourteen."

Robbie only looked at her. She read sorrow in him, sorrow he tried to hide while he dealt with it. It was wrong for kids to lose their parents, their anchors in the world, too soon.

All of them, Zane, Brett, Robbie, and Kendrick, had sadness in their eyes. Too much of it. Addie wanted to do something to see the kids laughing and happy, if only for a few moments.

"So, now what?" Addie lifted the purse she'd dropped to a chair and rummaged through it. "I should call my sister and let her know I'm all right—"

A large hand clamped over her cell phone and firmly took it from her. "No."

Addie reached for it. "She'll be worried about me. I was arrested—well, almost arrested."

"Addison." Kendrick held the phone away from her. "I can't let them track a call here."

"I understand that. But I'm going to have to call someone, somehow. You've kind of stranded me out here."

"I know." Kendrick remained in place, the phone in his hand. He stood rigidly, his eyes holding a darkness but also the tiniest hope. "Addison, I don't have anywhere to take you where you'll be safe. Not right now."

A lump lodged in Addie's throat. She hadn't really thought he'd brought her here so he could sweep her into his arms, shower her with more wads of cash, do a striptease for her . . . The tingle in her heart swelled to scorching.

"I was thinking about heading to New Orleans," she said. "You could always buy me a bus ticket."

Kendrick's brows slammed together again. "Bus. Alone and vulnerable, prey to any human who looks at you and wants you."

"Paranoid, much," Addie said, folding her arms. She felt suddenly cold, though the small room was warm, the AC faulty. "What do you suggest? I'm in a tiny town in the middle of nowhere with no transportation. Sure, I'll just walk out onto a lonely back Texas highway and hitch a ride. Nothing can possibly go wrong with *that*."

CHAPTER SIX

Kendrick couldn't move. Addison stood like a sharp blade of grass, or maybe a strong young tree, ready to face the world and not be broken by it. Fragile and not knowing she was.

Human women couldn't defend themselves like Shifter women could. A female Shifter could kick a male Shifter's ass, and everyone knew it. Human males over the centuries had subjugated their females until their women believed themselves weak.

Addison was human, and vulnerable. The thought of her wandering in the dark, open to every person driving by, made him furious. "You won't have to walk away alone," Kendrick said, his voice edged. "I'll take you somewhere safe."

"And then where will you go?" Addison looked pointedly at the boys' bags Robbie had readied and lined up, waiting to be loaded onto the motorcycle in case they had to go. Which they did now.

"Far from here."

Addison met his eyes without fear. Humans weren't supposed to be able to do that. Kendrick was an alpha, a

Guardian, and few were his equal. Most Shifters dropped their gazes or looked away to avoid his stare.

Addison simply looked at him, unimpressed. Her blue eyes caught him, and he saw in them a spark of lightness that his life had forgotten.

He'd known her only a brief time, and they'd barely spoken, but Kendrick knew that if he said good-bye to her tonight, he'd grieve. He should send her away from him, safe and free, but the very selfish part of him, the one he'd never been able to indulge, wanted her close. Wanted her where he could put out his hand and touch her.

"You mean you'll never tell me," Addison was saying in her cheerful voice. "You won't get in touch or let me know how the kids are doing or come into whatever diner I work in next for a slice of pie."

Kendrick cleared his throat. "It has to be so."

Addison took a step forward. "Why does it?" She drew a breath then blurted out the next words. "Take me with you, Kendrick. Wherever it is you're going. You need someone to look after your kids . . . I mean, your cubs. Right? If you're going to be fighting people, you need someone to take care of them. And I need a job. So . . . how about it?"

Kendrick stopped. "So you want to, what? Be my cubs' nanny?"

"Sure, why not? You can pay me a little salary, I'll look after them, and you keep the cops from putting me in jail. You owe me, since they suspected me of robbing the place because of your overzealous generosity."

She was serious. Addison stood there, quivering with optimism, and with worry that he'd walk away from her, like he should.

"You have no idea what you're offering," he said, voice hard. "No idea of the danger."

"Probably not. But people shot at you, Kendrick. I won't sleep easy thinking that your kids—cubs—are in that kind of situation again. I want to *know* they're safe."

She didn't mention it, but it was also Kendrick's fault she was now jobless. If Kendrick had kept himself away from the diner and not given in to the temptation of seeing her, she'd be happy and well, at home with her sister, anticipating another day waiting tables.

Again, his anger stirred. Addison was watching him, eyes wide, still wearing the ugly salmon pink one-piece dress that hung shapelessly on her body. The dress was supposed to hide her—though nothing could ever truly hide her beauty.

She should be in lovely clothes that complemented her curving body, with jewels on her wrists and at her throat. A man should be taking her out in a luxurious car, showing her off to the world. But no, she was in a dingy motel room, with a man who had the money to give her everything, and didn't dare.

Kendrick hardened his voice. "Addison, if you came with us, it would be the end of your life as you know it."

"Oh, yes?" Addison put one hand on her hip. "The end of my low-paying waitress jobs? Hoping I don't get stiffed on tips too many times, working late into the night, with maybe one day off a week if it's not too busy? The end of that life? Yeah, 'cause that would suck."

"I meant being with your sister, her children, your friends."

Addison's gaze flickered but her lips firmed. "My friends all grew up, got married, and had kids. They remember to invite poor Addie over once in a while and they try to fix me up with friends who either turn out to be total losers or interested in someone else. My sister is divorced, devoted to her kids, and making ends meet. She lets me live with her because she feels sorry for me. I almost got married once but it didn't work out."

He heard anger, sadness, and frustration. Kendrick wanted to know what dickhead had let her go but he had no time to ask for details.

He tried to sound stern. "If you come with me and it gets too dangerous, I'd have to ditch you somewhere. For your own good."

Addison's blue eyes sparkled. "Who decides if it's too dangerous?"

"Me. If I say go to ground, you go to ground."

"With the cubs?"

"If necessary."

Addison bounced on her toes, like Robbie did when he

grew excited. "Well, we can argue about that later. Where exactly are you going?"

"I don't know yet." Kendrick hated that. "I need to find a place that's safe, round up my trackers, start over."

"I see. While we're on the subject, why aren't you with other Shifters in the places called Shiftertowns? And why don't you have a Collar-thingee?" Addison waved her hand at his bare neck. "Not that I think you should wear one—I'm just curious why you're not."

"Now that is a very long story." Kendrick broke from her, swept up the bags Robbie had gathered, and dumped them on the bed. "I can't promise you safety," he said. "I'll do my best but the Goddess only knows what I will find when I start looking. Or I can send you somewhere safe, far from me. Make your choice now."

Kendrick snapped his mouth closed, waiting for her answer with more anticipation than he'd have liked.

He wasn't sure why he was giving her the choice at all. He didn't have time to look after a human woman, even if she'd offered to play babysitter for the cubs. She was excess baggage, and he needed to keep everything simple right now.

And yet, he knew if Addison didn't come with him, Kendrick would forever be looking for her—around every corner, waiting to hear her voice, see her face. He'd been forced to sever many ties over the years—this one wasn't even a knot yet—but he didn't want to cut it loose.

They were both on the brink of something, Kendrick and Addison, and he wasn't quite sure what.

Robbie broke the silence between them. "Please, Addie. Come with us?"

Zane and Brett took up the chorus. "Yes, Addie, *please!*"

Addison turned her cocky smile on all three. "Of course I'm coming with you. Your dad is just making things complicated, like guys do. Let's go. Oh, yeah, I'll need a toothbrush."

Addie asked Kendrick to at least let her change her clothes. With relief, she shed her uniform in the bathroom and pulled on the jeans and loose, flowered shirt she'd kept in her car. She was tempted to dump the now smelly uniform in the trash but someone might find it, and who knew what suspicions that would lead to?

Addie unhooked her name tag from the uniform and dropped it into her purse. She wadded up the ugly dress and tucked it under her arm before she left the bathroom. When she emerged, Kendrick was studying her phone, which he still had, turning it over in his hands.

As she opened her mouth to ask him to return it to her, Kendrick ripped the back from the phone, took out the sim card, and broke the phone into two pieces.

Addie gaped. "Hey, those aren't cheap!"

"I'll give you the cost of it." Kendrick cracked the case and card into smaller pieces, stepped into the bathroom, and flushed them down the toilet. "They can be used to track us," he said when he emerged.

Addie had known that, but her heart beat faster. "I still need a toothbrush," she pointed out.

"I have one you can use."

Addie put her fists on her hips, hands shaking. "Now, hey, I like you, but that's going a little too far . . ."

Kendrick flicked her a surprised glance. "It's in a package."

Addie had figured that's what he'd meant, but Kendrick obviously took things literally. She was going to have to work on that. Addie winked at the boys. They drew closer to her, their eyes shining with delight.

Kendrick picked up the bags and slung them over his shoulder, heading for the door.

"You still haven't told me where we're going," Addie said.

"Somewhere not here." Kendrick opened the door and led the way out.

Kendrick paid for the room at the office, then returned to the bike where Addison had already gotten the boys settled in. He helped her on, started up the motorcycle, rode from the parking lot, and flowed out of town, heading south into the night.

No one followed. This late there were no vehicles at all on the highway, only Kendrick's motorcycle in the darkness, with his cubs, Addison clinging to his back. The warmth of her cut the growing chill of the wind, and her arms around him were more comforting than anything had been in a while.

Her impulsive kiss earlier tonight had tapped at the mate frenzy inside him, the needs he'd suppressed for years. Something had snapped in him and Kendrick had fallen into the kiss, crushing her up to him, imbibing her, feeling her wrapped around him.

He felt as though he'd been sleepwalking for years, and Addison's kiss had jolted him awake.

Too dangerous to be awake and aware of Addison. Kendrick had to concentrate on rounding up his trackers, finding a new home for his Shifters, taking care of his cubs. No time for indulgences like mate frenzy or even burying himself in a woman and breathing her scent. His body throbbed with her nearness, berating him for his denial.

The moon had set and the night was dark. Typical for nights in the open desert in spring, it started to get cold. No lights shone anywhere, the darkness complete.

South Texas was vast, miles upon miles of flat country, towns few and far between. The land was filled with ranches, some working, some abandoned, and oil wells, pump jacks cranking, their heads going up and down like strange, rusting, hungry beasts.

Kendrick and his cubs knew how to spend the night outdoors, huddled together for warmth in sleeping bags, the little ones curled up in their animal forms. Addison wouldn't be used to sleeping rough, though, and he doubted she'd ever had a wolf and two tigers trying to share space with her.

Kendrick would need to find a house, even an empty one, to get them out of the cold. Storms could brew up quickly out here as well, the weather going from calm to tumultuous in a matter of minutes.

His fuel would run out soon, so he'd need to find a town somewhere. He'd gassed up once he'd reached the motel last night but then he'd driven north to fetch Addison and back, and now they moved down this highway at a fast pace.

A length of split-rail fence loomed up out of the darkness, marking the edge of a property along the road. Barbed wire was more commonly used out here, effective for keeping cattle within a range, but ranchers sometimes lined the drives to their houses with split rail, a decorative choice.

Kendrick saw no lights, no closed gates, nothing to tell him the place was inhabited. The house at the end of the drive might be half fallen down or abandoned and full of vermin. Most mice, rats, and snakes would vanish when a wolf walked in, however, even if he looked like an innocent little boy. They knew. A full-grown white tiger was nothing they wanted to encounter either.

Kendrick slowed and turned onto the rutted track that met the road at the end of the fence. Addison's hands tightened on his middle but she said nothing, asked no questions. Kendrick sensed her exhaustion, her need for rest.

The dirt drive led up over a rise filled with mesquite and scrub, effectively curtaining whatever was back here from the little-trafficked road. About half a mile later, Kendrick pulled the bike to a halt in front of a long, low house whose windows and roof were still intact. A front porch ran the length of the house, and rocking chairs had been placed at intervals so inhabitants could sit and watch the night.

Kendrick turned off the motor, carefully swung his leg over the front of the bike, and stood up.

The silence was immense, which Kendrick liked. Cities made him itch. He couldn't properly use his Shifter senses in a town—he was assaulted by too many scents, sights, and sounds, which ran together to form a jumbled mass.

Out here, the night was vast, the sky thick with stars, the constellations that humans called the Big and Little Dippers hanging sharp against the fainter stars around them.

Addison swung down from the bike, yanked the helmet from her head, and rubbed her backside. "Where the heck—"

Kendrick motioned her to silence. The cubs hadn't said a word. They knew to let Kendrick surveil a possible campsite, waiting quietly while he sussed out any dangers.

He approached the front door of the house from an oblique angle, staying in the blackest shadows. The place didn't smell deserted but he detected the scent of only one human.

That human yanked open the door and shone a lantern flashlight full in Kendrick's face. "Can I help you with something?" A voice belonging to an elderly man came at him, and Kendrick heard the click of a cocking shotgun.

If Kendrick hadn't heard that sound earlier tonight, hadn't thrown his sons over the counter and rolled after them, he wouldn't be standing here, and neither would the cubs or Addison. But his reactions were those of a cat, and Kendrick could move fast.

He had the shotgun out of the man's hands in a heartbeat, pointing the barrels well away from his cubs and Addison.

The lantern dipped, and the gray-haired man raised one hand in surrender. "Now, no need for violence," he said in a slow Texas drawl. "I just need to be careful about who walks up to my door in the middle of the night. What y'all want?"

Addison, who truly needed to learn about caution, approached. "We hate to bother you, sir," she said in her pleasant waitress voice, "but we saw your house, and there isn't much else out here, is there? Is there a town close by where we can spend the night?"

The man glanced at Kendrick, who still held the gun by its barrel, and Addison, who was smiling, a Texas-born girl who knew how to be polite.

"Ain't no towns around here," the man said. "There's Marfa, but it's about a hundred miles that way and the hippies have taken it over. No, this is the best place to stay in these parts. Welcome to Charlie's Dude Ranch. Can I book you a room?"

CHAPTER SEVEN

"What's a dude ranch?" Brett wanted to know.

The man called Charlie showed them the way in with a big flashlight—after Kendrick had gone in first to check the place out. Not until after he'd decided the house was safe did he allow Robbie, Brett, and Zane off the motorcycle. Charlie handed Addie flashlights to pass around—electricity hadn't worked since his generator went out, he said.

"This is where city slickers come to pretend to be cowboys," Charlie said in answer to Brett. "They help round up the cattle and such. Not that there's any of those around anymore."

"We're not city slickers," Zane said. "Addie, what's a city slicker?"

Addie handed Zane a flashlight and showed him how to work it. "It's someone who's lived their whole life in a city and doesn't know anything about the country. I'm not one, either. My grandparents had a little ranch when I was about your age. I learned how to ride and use a lariat. That's a rope you throw around a cow to catch it."

Kendrick said nothing at all. He looked around the house

thoroughly, flashing his borrowed light on walls, beamed ceiling, and the large stone fireplace in the main room. He'd already locked the shotgun into a cabinet in a closet—he hadn't wanted to hand it back to Charlie.

"Well, the slickers all used to come out here," Charlie said as he took them through a door that led to a long hallway. "Celebrities too, to get away from it all. Guest bedrooms are back here."

"You don't have any guests now?" Addie flashed her light into the first room he opened, seeing a comfortable double bed in an old-fashioned bedstead. "It looks nice."

"Not for a good many years, young lady," Charlie said. "Bathroom's in there." He fixed his light on a door on the other side of the room. "Plumbing still works. It's just the lights that go haywire. No, we haven't had guests in—oh, ten years now. Not since Mrs. Charlie passed away. That's what everyone called her. Mrs. Charlie. I called her Edna. Sweetest woman you ever want to meet."

"I'm sorry," Addie said. Ten years, and deep sorrow still filled his voice.

"She wouldn't like it if I weren't hospitable, so as long as you can put up with the busted generator, you can stay. You and your husband can sleep in here and the boys can have the big bedroom across the hall."

"Oh," Addie said, her face growing hot. "We aren't—"

"That's fine," Kendrick broke in. "Thank you."

Charlie turned away without noticing any hiccup. "No mice or snakes—I have a bunch of cats out there who keep down the critters. Coyotes come right up to the porch, though. They'll eat cats, so the cats run and hide when they come. Here you go, boys."

He opened the door to a large bedroom that had been lined with wood to look like the inside of a log cabin. A bunk bed filled one wall and a small trundle bed lay against the other. A soft braided rug stretched across the wooden floor, and shelves were filled with books and old-fashioned wooden toys.

"I know kids are lost without their Xboxes," Charlie said, "or whatever they're called nowadays, but you'd be surprised how many abandon them to play with the wooden horse and toy soldiers."

Robbie and the two younger cubs walked into the room and looked it over as though they'd never seen anything like it.

Zane and Brett lost no time in swarming up the short ladder to the top bunk and perching there. Addie watched them in alarm for a heartbeat or two before she remembered they were cats, in truth. *Would they land on their feet if they fell?*

"You can sleep up there only if your dad says it's all right," she admonished them.

The two boys stopped and stared down at Addison in puzzlement. She turned away quickly and focused on Robbie, who was still looking around then sat tentatively on the lower bunk.

Kendrick slung a small duffel bag to a chair. "Settle yourselves in." He looked pointedly at Robbie.

Charlie said, "Well, I'll leave you to it. I have some cold sandwiches if you want supper. Can't cook anything."

He gave them a genial smile and clumped down the hall to the front. Kendrick gave Robbie another look before he shut the boys in the bedroom. He put his hand on the small of Addie's back and guided her inside the room Charlie had designated as theirs.

"Why didn't you ask for separate bedrooms?" Addie said as soon as the door closed. "You could have said I was the nanny."

Kendrick studied her with eyes that told her he didn't understand her objection. "He thinks we're husband and wife or at least a couple," he rumbled. "He thinks we're a normal human family. As it should be."

Addie wanted to laugh. The bubble of hysteria rose. "The fact that you can say *normal* and *family* in the same sentence shows you don't know a lot about human families."

"Doesn't matter. I only care what *he* thinks." Kendrick set the larger duffel bag and the long bundle with his sword on an empty table. "I have some shirts in there you can wear for something to sleep in."

"Sleep." Addie turned her gaze to the bed. It was a high

wooden bedstead, the kind with steps. It looked comfy, but . . .

When she turned around, she saw that Kendrick was no longer watching her. He was pacing the room, examining the walls, ceiling, windows, flashing his light everywhere. A fireplace took up the far wall, which backed onto the fireplace in the big living room. The same stone lined it, the whole wall part of the chimney.

Kendrick ran a hand over the fireplace wall, then slapped the stones, which gave off a solid sound. He glided his light over the ceiling, examining the beams.

He reminded her of a guy on one of the house remodeling shows. Any second now he'd say something like, "Good bones."

"You planning to buy it?" Addie leaned against the bed, the mattress soft against her back.

"Maybe," Kendrick said absently.

"An old house in the middle of nowhere with a busted generator." Addie nodded gravely. "The ideal home. I bet you could get a good deal on it. The question is—why?"

Kendrick switched his light from the ceiling to her, snapping off the beam just before it would blind her. "We have to live somewhere. A den in the ground might have done for my ancestors but I like indoor plumbing."

He was trying to be funny. Addie's big, silent warrior had tried to make a joke.

The only light came from her lantern flashlight now, which she'd set on a nightstand. By it she saw his eyes on her, glittering like a cat's.

"Very amusing," she said. "But you're avoiding the question of our sleeping arrangements."

Did he expect her to curl up in bed with him? Did he expect she'd throw off her clothes and demand to have sex with him? She imagined his welcoming look as he drew her against his big, strong, unclothed body . . .

Addie sucked in a sharp breath that nearly drowned out Kendrick's next words.

"You take the bed," he said, sounding indifferent. "I rarely use a bed, and I need to have a look around."

"Ah. Right." Addie kept the disappointment from her voice. Not that she'd been ready to throw off her clothes and slide into bed with him . . . All right, maybe she had been.

"Settle yourself in and get some sleep," Kendrick said. "I'll go see if I can help Charlie with his generator."

"Are you an electrician?" Perhaps that's how he made a living and was able to buy pie every night.

"I know something about it."

"What about the cubs?" Addie asked. "Are they going to be all right?"

Kendrick hesitated. "They're off the road, safe for now, under my protection. They'll be fine. Robbie knows how to look after the little ones."

"Yes, but who looks after Robbie?" Addie thought about the look Kendrick had given him, the one that told Robbie he needed to make sure the smaller cubs were okay. Robbie sometimes looked crushed under the weight of responsibility.

"*I* look after him," Kendrick answered. "Go to bed. Long day tomorrow."

"Why? What's tomorrow?"

Kendrick gave her an unreadable look. "I don't know. We'll find out tomorrow."

"Kendrick." Addie took a step forward.

Kendrick turned back to her, looking impatient to be gone. "Something you need?"

"A lot of things. Like who is after you, why you don't live in a Shiftertown, why you don't wear a Collar, and why you want to buy this house in the middle of nowhere. The documentaries say Shifters aren't allowed to buy houses. Which is a stupid rule, but I don't want you getting into trouble."

Kendrick came back from the door to halt a foot or so away from her, right in her personal space. He could change from quiet, enigmatic man to dangerous predator in a heartbeat.

He leaned down and spoke quickly and softly, his eyes glittering in the shadows. "I want Charlie to think us a human family so he won't catch on I'm Shifter. Humans would be together like this. I'll buy this place, like a normal human, and he never has to know. I need you to help me with that, Addison."

His warmth came to her, his eyes holding vehemence but also fear. Kendrick demanded, but Addie realized his demand was actually a plea. Kendrick wasn't a man who had to ask for help very often.

"So did you escape from a Shiftertown?" Addie asked in a whisper.

"No. I was never in one." Kendrick took a step closer her. "That's the point. I've kept myself, my family, and an entire group of Shifters from being forced into Shiftertowns. For twenty years."

Addie's lips parted. From what little she'd gleaned, Shifters could not be without Collars and were not allowed to live anywhere but a Shiftertown. Those were the rules, enforced pretty hard. Shifters caught not following those rules were called "rogues" and could be arrested and killed.

Kendrick and his sons, walking around in the world un-Collared, were in a dangerous position.

"How can you?" she asked, her voice hushed. "Isn't it safer for you in the Shiftertowns?"

Kendrick's look of rage nearly made her step back, but Addie held her ground.

"Not safer," Kendrick said, the words containing a snarl. "More convenient for humans. They're terrified of us, but they never gave us a chance." He'd begun to curve over her, a beast enraged, and now eased back down. "You didn't give us up to the police. I'm trusting you to not give us up now."

"Like I would." Addie pinned him with an annoyed look. "I really don't care whether you live in a Shiftertown or not. Just . . . promise me you won't let your kids be hurt for what you believe in."

His scowl deepened. "I am doing this to make sure my cubs are free and far from harm. Do you think they'd let me keep Robbie? He's without clan, without pack. Humans would shove him in with a different wolf family who might not accept him. Pack affiliation is taken seriously."

"But you're not even a wolf," Addie pointed out.

"He's with me because I'm leader. All my Shifters are my pack, as it were. Though Felines say *pride*."

"What about me?" Addie asked. "Will I be part of your pride?"

Kendrick stopped. He stared at her as though she'd stunned him. His face went very still, his jaw firming then easing.

He skimmed his gaze down her body, taking in her shirt that was about four years old, her generic blue jeans, her sneakers. Then, very slowly, Kendrick lifted his hand and smoothed back a lock of her hair.

He'd stripped off his gloves, and the touch of his bare fingers tingled heat through her blood. Kendrick's jaw tightened again, his lips compressing until little creases formed in the corners of his mouth.

Addie resisted leaning into his hand, much as she wanted to. His palm was large, which would nicely cup her cheek, warm her cool skin. She closed her eyes and let out a small sigh.

Kendrick abruptly dropped his hand, and Addie opened her eyes in time to see him turning away. The draft of his swift withdrawal chilled her.

"Get some rest," he rumbled, then yanked open the door and took himself out.

Addie blew out her breath as the door clicked closed behind him. She needed to flop somewhere, as she liked to when the world got too much for her. In this room, she had to climb the ladder to the bed before she could throw herself down on her back.

The bed was as comfortable as it looked. Addie's bones began to soften, her sore muscles and her shakes relaxing.

She was far, far from anyone and anything she knew, with a taciturn Shifter biker with a sword and his three kids, in a run-down dude ranch with no electricity, its proprietor a sad old man taking care of it in memory of his late wife.

Addie should be terrified. Kendrick could do anything to her—he was a Shifter without a Collar, uncontrolled, unregulated. She should fear him.

But she'd seen the sadness in his eyes when he'd run the sword through the other Shifter, even though that Shifter had been doing his best to kill Kendrick and his sons. Addie had witnessed Kendrick's protectiveness with the cubs, and now with Addie.

He wasn't a rampaging, killing beast . . . All right, at least not all the time. He cared about his kids, he'd not let Addie take the blame for the shooting, he'd handed Addie five thousand dollars to help her out, and then shrugged when the police took it away from her. He'd spoken casually about buying this house, which was large, and probably on a lot of land. Not cheap. So somewhere, Kendrick had enough stashed that he didn't have to be concerned about money.

Addie spread out her arms and breathed in the silence. She'd regain her equilibrium then check on the boys and get them to bed. No worries about springing up tomorrow morning, with nothing to look forward to but putting on her waitress uniform and heading to the diner for another grueling day on her feet.

Addie was here by her own choice, lying on a very comfortable bed, while a hot man who didn't look at her with boredom was running around somewhere, insisting she take it easy while he did all the work.

Dreams really did come true.

Kendrick fixed the generator, which was located in a room under the house entered by the outside. A storm cellar, he reflected, built to withstand the tornadoes that sometimes marched across this land.

Charlie helped him by training the flashlight on the gears and wires while keeping up a stream of talk.

This had been a pretty famous ranch at one time, Charlie was saying. All the greats came out here in the early days of Hollywood—John Wayne, Clark Gable, Gary Cooper, Audie Murphy, Gene Autry . . . Charlie and his wife hadn't taken over until the seventies but they'd seen their share of movie stars of that day. Kendrick let him natter on, suspecting the man hadn't had anyone to talk to in a very long time.

The generator's problem was age and lack of lubricant.

Kendrick cut out old corroded wires and spliced in good ones, then greased up the contacts. That would help out for a while. The entire generator would have to be overhauled or replaced, but Kendrick's trackers could do that once the house was his.

Kendrick nodded at Charlie to start up the machine again, and Charlie flipped a switch then pressed a dirt-encrusted button. The generator coughed once, then clattered to life.

"Hot damn," Charlie said. He slapped Kendrick on the back, which felt like a brush from dry twigs. "You did it, son. Will make a huge difference when it gets hot tomorrow. And a better breakfast."

Kendrick and Charlie cleaned up, then Kendrick told Charlie he'd go for a walk. He agreed to Charlie's warning to watch out for the snakes and coyotes—he'd lived in Texas for a while and knew what it was like.

The challenge of repairing the generator had kept Kendrick's mind off things for a while but now he needed to explore, to find out where they were and what was out here.

At least, that's what he told himself as he walked away into the dark, quietly setting down his flashlight once he was far enough from the house.

Kendrick did need to roam the bounds and make sure they were truly alone out here, but another reason he needed to leave was Addison.

She'd gazed wistfully at him as she'd leaned against the bed, her top with its floaty material outlining every soft curve of her. She'd looked worried when she mentioned their sleeping arrangements, but then when he'd touched her hair, she'd closed her eyes, her body relaxing, wanting to move against his.

Kendrick's dormant mating frenzy had taken another breath. He'd had to get out of there before he did or said anything stupid—and irreversible.

I wouldn't want just sex with you, Addison. Not like your "normal" human couple.

I'd want it hard and fast, basic and raw. I want you on the ground, against the wall, you riding me, me on you, locked together, inseparable. I want you groaning my name while I shout yours, and I want you begging me never to stop . . .

Kendrick started to run. Faster and faster, until his breath came in gasps, and his mouth was parched.

He paused long enough to slide out of his human clothes, then he hit the ground on all fours as tiger.

CHAPTER EIGHT

Kendrick ran until he could run no more. Even tigers got tired, especially after they'd battled, rescued a woman in distress, and then ridden the rest of the night.

He slowed to a walk and ambled along, breathing hard, paws barely making an indent on packed Texas earth. The run had calmed him enough that every beat of his heart didn't make him want Addison, only every other beat. Still, he was too agitated, too charged with adrenaline. He needed to climb down from frenzy and *think*.

He'd liked the ranch as soon as he saw it, and now, slowing to stroll its perimeters, he liked it even more. Kendrick didn't know the exact boundaries of the property, although a barbed wire fence along the east side likely marked it from its neighbor. He scented no other Shifters out here, and not even any humans. Few would come this far from a road. A determined hiker might strike out across country but Kendrick could deal with that as it came up.

He only cared that the ranch was hard to find and the house was out of the line of sight from the roads due to a slight rippling of the land around it. Defending such a large area wouldn't be easy, but Kendrick's top trackers—Seamus, Francesca, Dimitri, Jaycee—could do it.

He wondered momentarily whether they, his closest friends, had also turned on him, like the Shifters who'd cornered him in the diner. He hadn't been in touch with any of them for a long time, though he knew that Seamus and Francesca were well. He hadn't heard anything from Dimitri or Jaycee.

Kendrick pushed those thoughts aside for now. More immediately, he'd have to deal with Addison threatening to tear his mating frenzy out of the cocoon he'd stuffed it into. He'd vowed to protect her, so she needed to stay here for now. He'd simply have to suppress his need for her until this was over.

Right, like that was so simple.

Maybe he could pound his head against the ground until all thoughts of her smile, the sly look she'd given him when she'd confessed she liked the same pie he did, the feeling of her against his body on the motorcycle went away. Sure, there was a good solution.

Kendrick huffed a breath and turned his steps for the house. He couldn't put off facing Addison, so he had to find a way to suck it up, as Brett liked to say. He had his cubs to take care of.

Didn't help that the phrase *suck it up* made him think of covering Addison with whipped cream and licking it off her.

Halfway back to the house, Kendrick halted. Addison filling his thoughts had distracted him from a faint scent on the edge of his senses. Not human, not Shifter. Not Fae either—he'd encountered a few of those in his day, and their smell was nose-curlingly distinctive.

The scent faded. Whatever, whoever, it had been, was gone. Kendrick let out the breath he'd been holding and moved silently through the dark to where he'd left his clothes.

Addie woke shortly before six in the morning—according to the luminous digital clock next to the bed. She took a moment to realize where she was, and another to realize the electricity must have been restored if the clock worked.

The room was cold, no air flowing. Charlie had probably turned off any fans, heat, or AC once the generator was down. All the lights were off too—nothing shone under the door.

Addison groped for the lamp she'd seen on the table by the bed, groped some more for a switch, and flicked it on.

She blinked at the glare, then swallowed a strangled yelp when she found the reclining form of a giant white tiger on the floor beside the bed.

"Holy . . ." She cut off her exclamation and lowered her voice to a whisper. ". . . shit."

The tiger released a breath and slowly raised his head. Addie found herself meeting Kendrick's green eyes in a broad white face. Black stripes formed a series of upside-down Vs on his forehead, and black spots dotted the base of his white whiskers. His ears, round, furry, and sticking straight up, moved in her direction, then one swiveled, listening behind him.

"Please tell me that's you, Kendrick," Addie said in a hushed tone. "Not a white tiger that's escaped from a zoo, walked a hundred miles, and broke into the house to find a snack."

The tiger huffed again, eyes glinting in amusement. Kendrick heaved himself to his feet, which put his back level with the high bed. He butted Addie's hand, like a cat might do, and her palm landed on the top of his head.

"Well, aren't you warm and soft?" Addie stroked him a couple of times then daringly scratched behind one ear. The tiger's eyes half closed, and he let out a quiet growl.

The growl would have been a purr on a cat but the tiger was so large the vibration shook the bed. He rubbed against her hand, pressing so hard he threatened to dislodge her from the mattress.

"I don't think there's much room for a tiger up here," Addie said as she continued to bask in the silken feel of his coat. "Though you'd be soft to sleep against."

She had a sudden flash of curling up against him, gathering this wild beast into her arms as she slept without fear.

The tiger ducked away and Addie's fingers slid from him.

She bit back disappointment then uttered a soft cry as the tiger's fur rippled. Its limbs shrank, and the tiger's head flattened until it became Kendrick's face. Only his eyes didn't change, the green pinning Addie with a piercing stare.

Addie was left looking at a black-and-white haired man standing fully illuminated by the bedside light, not wearing a stitch of clothing.

The last time Addie had seen Kendrick unclothed, he'd been covered with blood and grime at the close of a deadly battle. At the moment, he was clean and unscathed, the quiet bedroom a very different scenario.

His hard chest was dusted with dark hair and another arrow of hair pointed from a firm abdomen to a place that wasn't in shadow. No modesty for Kendrick as he remained standing two feet from her, every inch of him showing. The hair there was purely black, Addie saw. Not mixed as she'd wondered.

"Well," Addie said shakily. "Good to see you're not a real tiger."

"I *am* a real tiger," Kendrick answered in his low rumble. "The beast is the real part of me. *This* is what I show to humans to live in their world." He splayed fingers across his chest.

"I see." Addie realized she was having a philosophical discussion about whether he was tiger-man or man-tiger, while he stood naked in front of her. "Clears that up. Don't you want to . . . um . . . put anything on?"

Kendrick shrugged and turned his back. "I will if it bothers you."

"It doesn't *bother* me," Addie said quickly. His back was as enticing as his front, his well-muscled torso narrowing to tight buttocks and strong thighs. "I'm as happy as the next girl to have a good-looking man like you on full display." She let her gaze rest on his backside as he reached for clothes draped over a chair. "But Charlie might be embarrassed if he came in."

"Why should he come in?" Kendrick pulled underwear on over his delectable ass, to Addie's regret. Although . . . he still looked pretty good in only the underwear.

"I don't know," Addie babbled. "To check on us? Bring us a midnight snack?"

Kendrick turned around, underwear in place. The briefs were dark blue and very small. "Charlie is asleep. I heard him snoring in a room at the other end of the house."

Addie's need to gaze at him hungrily kept her nervous questions coming. "What were you doing out until o'dark thirty in the morning?"

His quizzical expression told her he didn't know what her idiom meant, but he answered. "Walking the bounds, making sure all was safe. The one horse in the barn wasn't happy with a visit from a tiger, but otherwise, we're alone here."

"Good. I like that." Addie folded her arms, cold. She'd put on one of the shirts he'd offered, a big T-shirt, faded from washing, with an INXS logo on it. She wondered how long he'd had it—Shifters, it was rumored, lived for several hundred years.

Kendrick's gaze was steady. "You like being alone?"

Addie hugged herself tighter. His shirt was roomy on her, which was a nice change. Usually clothes hugged her too much, revealing more of her plumpness than she was comfortable with.

"I'm by myself a lot," she said. "When I'm not at work. Sometimes it's refreshing."

"I hate it." The words were vehement, Kendrick's eyes burning.

"I thought tigers were solitary," Addie ventured.

"I'm Shifter. It's different. We're not meant to be alone. I surrounded myself with Shifters to take care of them. Their bodies, their souls. I'm not only Shifter, I'm Guardian."

Kendrick's muscles were tight in the dim lamplight, his fists curled.

"You're the protector," Addie said, trying to understand. "Of other Shifters."

Kendrick shook his head, his look still savage. "I stand between them and terrifying darkness. I don't let their souls be enslaved. Ever. But they are scattered from me, gone. If they die . . . I can't help them."

And that was hurting him. Addie didn't really understand

what he was talking about, but she threw back the covers and slid from the bed. She managed to remember at the last minute to use the steps and made it to the braided carpet without mishap.

"We'll find them." Addie went to him, stopping a foot or so away. If she got too close, she might not be able to talk. "Tomorrow, we'll go out and start looking for them."

Addie had no idea who *they* were or how to find them, but Kendrick's expression was so bleak she felt the need to comfort him.

Kendrick didn't soften. "No, I will stay here. This is a good place. But I will look for them all the same."

Addie stared—he made no sense. "You know, you are seriously confusing."

"I know that. I confuse myself. What the hell? I've learned to live with it."

The spark of humor in his eyes was self-deprecating. Addie drew a breath and jammed her arms over her chest again, mostly to keep from reaching for him.

"Who are these Shifters you need to find? Maybe I can help."

"They are very good at hiding. I doubt you'd know where to start looking." Kendrick let out a breath, a sound much like his tiger had made. "Twenty years ago, when humans began rounding up Shifters, I escaped them." He pitched his voice very low, so that anyone listening at the door or through the fireplace would hear only sound not words. "I found others like me, and we came together for protection. We stayed hidden, surviving, and I became their leader. We moved to Texas several years ago. Last year, we were found by other Shifters, who destroyed our place of hiding. We ran, breaking into small groups, to hide until I find a new place to gather again. But it has been some time—six months or so—since we scattered. I might never find some of them again."

He finished and closed his mouth with a sudden snap, as though he'd not meant to say so much.

Well, that explained a bit—why he didn't wear a Collar, why he wasn't in a Shiftertown. She was still unclear on a few things, but she realized this close-mouthed man telling her even that much was a victory.

Her urge to comfort him rose strongly once more, and she took the last step between them and touched his arm.

"You'll find them," Addie said. "I know you will."

Kendrick's gaze swept down to her, landing on her fingers on his forearm. The muscles twitched there. She'd seen, before he'd flicked his eyes past hers, the hunger he'd shown last night in the diner.

Beneath her fingers, Kendrick's skin was smooth and tight, warm. The wiry hair on his arm was nothing like his tiger's fur but Addie wanted to stroke him all the same.

His entire body was warm, the heat radiating from it embracing her. Addie had pictured wrapping herself around the tiger—even stronger came the vision of her twining herself around his human body.

He wasn't comfortable with her touch, Addie sensed. When she'd stroked him as tiger, he'd purred. Now he stood rigid, as though not wanting her near.

She tried to smile as she slid her fingers away. "Well, if we're going to start looking for a bunch of Shifters tomorrow, we'll need to sleep tonight."

Kendrick caught her hand. His gaze fixed on her again, predator's eyes, before he pulled Addie to him with sudden strength.

One arm went around her, holding her tightly against his body. His hand went to her hair and gently tipped her head back, Kendrick's look still haunted as he came down to her and covered her mouth in a kiss.

CHAPTER NINE

Kendrick kissed Addison with fierce need. The craving sprang up inside him, making him drag her closer, press her body the full length of his. Her softness called out to him; her breasts crushed against him and heightened his longing.

She tasted of sweetness and bitter coffee, loneliness and joy. Her body moved under his, the thin T-shirt catching in his hands. Kendrick hid a growl as he swept his tongue into her mouth, opening her farther to him.

She filled him. He'd wanted her from the moment she'd smiled at him when he'd slid onto the stool at her counter. Her open friendliness had caught at him, her entire being seeming to embrace him. Even her name tag had invited him in—*Hello, My Name is Addison.*

Kendrick knew he'd returned night after night only for the flash of her blue eyes, the curve of her smile.

He kissed the mouth that smiled so readily, locked his hand behind her neck to pull her harder into him. Addison's fingers sank into his arms, her body curving under his. She made a small noise in her throat, which turned up the flame inside him.

Want this woman. Want all of her.

Pouring out his story had seemed natural. She'd put so much on the line helping him—she deserved to know what she was getting into.

Kendrick's hand found the curve of her waist, the warm flesh under the shirt. The loose fabric let him slide up under it to the smoothness of her back, which was bare, she having removed her bra for sleeping.

He could have this shirt off her, catch the weight of her breasts, taste them. *Basic and raw,* he'd thought before. Yes, it would be, and it would be the most pleasure he'd ever known.

Kendrick deepened the kiss, liking the little start she gave, tasting her surprise in his mouth. She flowed against him, not fighting, not shoving him away. His hand went to her stomach, up to the firm round of her breast, the nipple tightening against his palm. Kendrick stroked the hardening tip, loving the little sound Addie made in her throat. He scented her rising need, the dampness that would be beginning between her thighs.

What he wanted wasn't tame and tender. He wanted to take Addison to the bed and climb into her arms, thrusting into her welcoming body. Harder and faster he'd go, until his burning need for her was sated. If it ever could be.

Addison . . .

A yowling cry shattered the silence. The sound was like a fall of ice on Kendrick's heated skin.

He fought his way back from drowning in Addison and took a sharp breath. The only thing that could cut through mating frenzy was his cub's cry of distress.

Kendrick released Addison, but she was already back-pedaling from him, then ducking around him, hurrying from the room. Kendrick dragged in another breath, the absence of her warmth like a slap, and followed her.

Addison was across the hall and running into the boys' room before Kendrick could leave their bedroom. He stifled a growl of admonishment—she didn't understand that she should wait for him to assess the danger.

He scented no danger, however, nothing in the room but

his cubs. Zane and Brett had become their tigers and were on
the upper bunk. Brett was sitting on his haunches blinking at
Zane, who was howling a small tiger roar, the sound filled
with anguish. Brett, watching his brother, whimpered.

Robbie was clinging on to the ladder, trying to pet Zane.
He looked as though he wanted to cry as well but he was
holding it in to comfort the younger ones.

Addison went straight to Robbie, lifted him from the
ladder, and gave him a big hug before setting him down.
"What's wrong?" she asked him.

Robbie shrugged his slim shoulders. "They're scared."

Kendrick reached to the top bunk and scooped up his
cubs, one in each arm. "Hey now," he said softly. He rumbled low in his throat, a wordless sound that made the cubs
snuggle into his bare chest.

Brett recovered first, nuzzling his father and then licking
his cheek. Zane shivered, still mewling.

Addison gave Robbie another hug. Robbie usually dis-
liked anyone but Kendrick touching him, but he didn't shrug
off Addison's touch. He clasped her in return, his small body
trembling.

When Addison finally released Robbie, he looked calmer,
less likely to give in to tears. Addison, her hair mussed from
Kendrick furrowing it, her lips wet with his kiss, reached
for Zane. "Let me hold him."

Zane continued to cry. Kendrick quietly relinquished him
to her, and Addison lifted the cub into her arms.

She staggered a little as she discovered that a baby tiger
was heavier than he looked, and very squirmy. Addison got
Zane firmly into the crook of her arm then stroked the top
of his head.

Zane opened his eyes, realized Addison held him, and
quieted down. Brett remained with his father but watched
Addison with watery green eyes.

"There you go," Addison crooned at Zane. "Feeling better? Want to sleep now?"

Zane squeezed his eyes shut again and let out a little
yowl. Kendrick knew exactly what he was saying—he didn't
want to be left without Kendrick or Addison.

"How about if I sleep in here with them?" Addison asked, turning her violet blue eyes to Kendrick. "You're beat—you take the bed and get some rest, and I'll bunk down in the trundle bed."

Kendrick tamped down his need and disappointment. He'd assumed the night would end with him inside Addison, but his sons came first. Not trusting himself to speak, he gave Addison a nod.

Zane clung to Addison, but Brett climbed down from his father's body, leaving a few light scratches on Kendrick's bare flesh. Brett scampered across the room to the trundle bed that rested against the wall and leapt onto it. Robbie, more quietly, moved after him and sat down on the bed's edge.

Addison jounced Zane as she went to join them. Kendrick watched in silence, feeling cold.

Addison looked up at Kendrick as she sat down with Robbie. "Go away now. You sleep, and I'll tell stories."

Kendrick felt no incentive to turn and leave the room. He wanted to linger, to curl up in the tiny bed next to Addison while his sons draped around them, and Addison's clear voice told bedtime stories.

"If you start, they won't let you stop," he warned.

"Yes, we will," Robbie said. "Good night, Dad."

Kendrick didn't move. Addison waved a hand at him, as though reassuring him that all would be well.

It would be, he knew. Addison had no treachery in her. Kendrick would have sensed it, scented it. The cubs liked her, and they were in a strange place, alone and cold. Addison, right now, was their beacon of warmth.

Kendrick made himself turn away. Stiffening his resolve, he walked to the door.

His resolve hadn't been the only thing stiff as he'd kissed her. Even now, his cock was ready to resume its hardness, wanting to ease itself inside her.

"Good night, then," he said without turning.

He took the last steps out into the cool hall, and closed the door firmly behind him. On the other side of the wood panels, he heard Addison say. "All right, then. I'll start. Once upon a time . . ."

There was a beautiful waitress and a fugitive white tiger Shifter . . .

Kendrick had no idea how that story would turn out.

Kendrick stood a long time in the middle of the empty bedroom he was supposed to share with Addison, his body throbbing, before he climbed up into the bed.

Addie's warmth lingered in the nest she'd made, and her scent. Kendrick knew he should leap up, walk out of the house, shift to tiger, and sleep under the stars somewhere over the rise.

Instead, he pulled the covers over him and lay with his eyes open, letting her surround him.

He needed her with terrible fire. Kendrick had lived so long suppressing his libido, that its awakening had him in impossible pain.

Kendrick's mate, Eileen, had passed bringing in Zane. Females dying in childbirth was much rarer these days but it still happened.

The problem with being Guardian was that Kendrick had been the one to send her to the Summerland. He'd kissed Eileen's cold lips, smoothed her hair, and closed his eyes as he'd driven the sword into her chest.

He'd risen and walked away, not opening his eyes until he'd been far from the pile of dust that had been his mate. He'd walked for days, trying to shake off the pain that clung to him like fog.

He never wanted to be in the position to do that again.

Kendrick drifted into a half slumber, his exhausted body forcing him into shutting down.

Addison stood six feet from him on a sunny, flat stretch of ground. She was so real that Kendrick reached for her, but he couldn't quite touch her. There seemed to be a barrier between then, like a soapy film in the air.

"What are you doing out here?" he asked. "Are you all right?"

"Of course," Addison said. "The boys are fine too, Kendrick. What about you?"

"They like you." Kendrick reached again, his fingers sinking into the spongy barrier. "*I* like you."

"I'm glad." Addison gave him that sunny smile again. "What is it you want?"

Kendrick narrowed his eyes, confused at the question. Who was he speaking to? Addison in a dream? Coming to him because he knew he needed her? Or someone in her guise?

Kendrick said nothing. He was standing in his underwear, wanting to go to her, enfold her in his arms again, but he couldn't move.

The barrier broke. Kendrick had been leaning on it, and he stumbled through. Addison turned and ran from him. Kendrick easily overtook her, sun warm on his back, and he caught her in his arms. She was laughing when he kissed her.

Down to the warm grass, her clothes and his underwear melting away until they were body to body. Addison tilted her head back, her face softening as he slid straight into her.

The sensation shot his heartbeat high, his body squeezing in triumph. But it wasn't enough. Something kept him from feeling it all the way, kept him pumping into her in a desperate quest for it.

This was a dream. It would never, ever be as satisfying as being with the real Addison, and everything within him knew it.

Addison touched his face. "Kendrick, I lo—"

She broke off, and her mouth opened in a sudden scream. The scream was muffled, as though the barrier had descended over both of them again.

Kendrick looked up to see the Shifter, Ivan, whom he'd sent to dust in the diner. The man had an automatic pistol in his hand, great sorrow in his eyes.

"I'm sorry, Guardian," Ivan said. "I failed you."

Addison was still under him. Kendrick looked down and saw blood on her chest, her eyes vacant, her face gray. She was in her waitress uniform again, scarlet blood on the salmon pink material.

Feral rage rose up inside Kendrick, blotting out every other thought, ever other sensation. He leapt to his feet as Addison shimmered and fell away to dust.

He grabbed Ivan, yanking the pistol from him and breaking it into many pieces. Then he threw Ivan to the ground and spun around to find Addison standing behind him, alive, in the jeans and pretty shirt she'd put on in his hotel room.

"Live your life, Kendrick," Addison said. "You have so much. Live with every ounce of strength you have. Live it for your sons—for *you*."

Kendrick gave her a look of anguish. "*This* . . . isn't . . . life."

Addison cocked her head. "Yes, it is. You'll figure it out. Look around you, white tiger. *Live*."

The dream was ending. Kendrick felt himself swimming toward awareness, reality kicking in.

The light that surrounded Addison grew brighter and brighter until it stabbed into Kendrick's eyes. Kendrick screwed up his face and turned away . . . and found himself waking in the guest bedroom, sunlight streaming in through the uncovered window into his face.

The digital clock said it was nine, he heard the voices of his cubs on the other side of the fireplace wall, and smelled frying eggs and bacon.

Kendrick rubbed his face, finding it wet. He groaned a little as he came off the bed. He was sore—he must have lain in one position, muscles rigid in his dreams.

He was straightening up when he heard Addison's voice, muffled but sharp with fear. "Whoa. Who is *that*?"

CHAPTER TEN

Kendrick was in his jeans and pulling on his shirt, racing barefoot through the giant living room and into the kitchen on the other side before Addison said another word.

He found her at the sink, staring out the uncurtained window. Charlie was at the stove and the cubs were at the table, human and clothed, each drinking a glass of milk.

Kendrick stopped close behind Addison and peered over her shoulder. "Who is who?"

Addison shook her head, her newly shampooed hair brushing his nose. She still wore his T-shirt, tucked into her jeans. In spite of his worry, Kendrick wanted to slide his hands around her waist and find the warm woman underneath. The memory of being with her in the dream stabbed into him.

Addie continued to stare outside. "I thought I saw someone. But he's gone now."

Kendrick didn't relax. Shifters could fade into shadows quicker than anyone, were masters at hiding. He didn't scent any Shifters from here, not that it would be easy with the sharp bacon smell in the room and Addison filling all his senses.

"I'll check it out," he said for the benefit of his cubs, who were watching with worry.

"You'll wear shoes, I hope," Addison said, glancing at his bare feet. "That's Texas out there."

Charlie gave a chuckle. "She has a point."

Kendrick conceded, though he knew he'd only take them off again if he had to shift.

As he ducked back to the bedroom for socks and boots, he heard Addison say, "If you didn't have any electricity, Charlie, how did you keep the food so fresh? The milk was good and cold and so were the eggs."

"I have an icebox," was Charlie's good-natured response. "A real one, with ice. A big old tin-lined wooden thing in the cellar—it was my granddad's. I just drive into town, buy a mess of ice, and keep it going. It's as good as a real refrigerator and doesn't use any power."

Addison turned as Kendrick came back into the kitchen.

"Be careful, now," she said, concern in her eyes.

The admonition, spoken in her fine Texas accent, warmed him all the way through. He gave her an acknowledging nod, opened the door, and slipped outside into the growing heat.

K endrick knew it wasn't a Shifter. Shifter scent was distinctive to another Shifter, no matter what form he or she was in.

That left human, Fae, animal, and other.

Humans were harder for Kendrick to distinguish but he was familiar enough with them to know it wasn't human. Fae could be tricky, so he'd hold that idea in reserve. Animal—no.

That left *other*.

The host of supernatural creatures that populated fiction mostly weren't real. Vampires existed, but they weren't the Boris Karloff type or the modern take of Anne Rice, *Buffy*, *True Blood*, or the host of popular novels that had poured out to be eagerly devoured by Jaycee, one of his trackers. Real vampires were creations from an ancient time, who'd survived by being extremely elusive. They didn't form communities, like Shifters, and kept their lineage a deep secret. In fact, Kendrick wouldn't be surprised if they'd died out over the centuries.

The other supernatural creatures that were real kept to realms like Faerie, a place where they were considered more or less normal. Everything else—ghosts, demons, and other hellish types— didn't exist.

So what was it?

One thing Shifters were good at, Felines in particular, was waiting. Kendrick slid into the shadows and did so.

He could hear Addison inside the house chatting to their host, making him laugh. The cubs cheered when breakfast landed on their plates, Addison's voice joining them.

Like a real family. A real life.

That was all Kendrick wanted, why he'd fled the humans who were passing out Collars twenty-odd years ago. The dream he'd had—was it a warning that he'd never have a real life? Or had it been a simple manifestation of his needs and fears? Just his brain blowing off steam?

Kendrick didn't deny to himself that making love to Addison would be deeply satisfying. Dream Addison had also been right that he had been resisting living his life. Taking care of his Shifters had always been his first priority, having a life of his own second. His mate, Eileen, had known this and Kendrick had always considered that he'd failed her because of it. Would he fail Addison too? And his cubs?

These thoughts poured through his head as Kendrick waited but they didn't interfere with his watching. He'd had a hundred years of experience at seeing without being noticed.

Then a man walked out of nowhere, up to the back porch, and knocked on the door.

Kendrick swarmed up the porch steps, grabbed the man by the neck, and pulled him back down.

With surprising strength, the man wrenched himself out of Kendrick's grasp and swung to face him. He had buzzed short black hair and dark brown eyes, looked Native American, and had a broad, hard-muscled body, like a Shifter, but lacked Shifter height. He was tattooed on his neck, arms, and hands but not all over as Dylan's tracker Spike was.

"Before you go all Shifter on my ass," the man said. "Dylan sent me. And before you panic, he doesn't know exactly where I am."

"Good," Kendrick growled, "then when I break your neck, only the coyotes will find your bones."

The man raised his hands. "It might be *your* bones, so don't mess with me. I'm trying to say that Dylan might ask me to do something for him but that doesn't mean I work for him."

"What does it mean then?" Kendrick asked in a hard voice.

"It means I like to find things out for myself. What are you doing out here?"

"What are you?" Kendrick countered. "*Who* are you?"

"You can call me Gil if you want. Dylan's looking high and low for you, but I like to assess a sitch for myself before I decide what to do."

Addie watched out the window while Kendrick faced the unknown man. She remained poised, ready to grab the kids and hide them—maybe in Charlie's cellar with the icebox—until Kendrick finished with the intruder.

The man wasn't very tall, only reaching Kendrick's shoulders, but he was bulky with muscle. The tatts on his neck and the ones cupping his elbows were the kind men gave each other in prison, at least as far as Addie knew. One of Bo's dishwashers had been in prison a while and he'd explained what his tatts meant to Addie one slow night.

The tension between the two men crackled. Addie held on to the lip of the sink and watched.

Kendrick's hand flashed out and gripped the man by the neck again. The man did nothing this time, didn't fight. Kendrick marched him up the steps and into the house.

"Another for breakfast?" Charlie asked without surprise.

"Yeah," the man Kendrick had captured said. "Eggs over

easy if it's not too much trouble. Lay off, Kendrick, I'm only being hospitable."

"Do you know him?" Addie asked Kendrick, her eyes widening.

"No," Kendrick said sharply.

The man turned to Addie and looked her up and down with appreciation. "He*llo*, pretty lady. I'm Ben."

Kendrick didn't release him but steered him to a chair he pulled well away from the table and his cubs. "You said your name was Gil."

"It's Gilbenarteoighiamh, but I'm not sadistic enough to make people say that. Pick a syllable, I'm fine with it." He sat down before Kendrick could push him down and winked at the cubs.

The three boys stared at him, openmouthed. Addie noticed that they kept quiet, cautious, unlike other children who might relax under Ben's friendly wink and smile. The cubs had been almost gregarious with Charlie, but in Charlie they recognized harmlessness, while this man could mean danger.

"Coffee?" Addie offered. She picked up the pot, which she could also use a weapon. Scalding liquid could be distracting.

"Don't mind if I do," Ben answered. "Dylan is not happy with you, my friend," he said to Kendrick.

Kendrick remained in place behind Ben's chair. Addie plucked a coffee mug from the cupboard and carried it and the pot to the table.

She poured a cup for the stranger then stepped back, clutching the pot. "You have it tattooed on your fingers." She gestured to Ben's hands he'd wrapped around the cup. Letters on the first three fingers on the right hand spelled out *Ben*; on the left, *Gil*. "So you won't forget?"

Ben rumbled with laughter. "Exactly. I like her, Kendrick. She's funny. Where did you find her?"

Kendrick only scowled. "If you work for Dylan, why don't I know you? He's had me running errands for him for six months."

Ben shrugged. "Dylan has fingers in many pies. You'd be surprised at the number of people he controls. He compartmentalizes. We don't always know about each other. He says he's worried about you and asked me to find you."

"He's worried he'll lose control of me," Kendrick said.

Ben gave another shrug. "You aren't wrong. He doesn't control *me*, and he knows it, but he thought I had the best shot at running you down. I wouldn't have found you at all if you hadn't gone back for *her*, but hey, I don't blame you." He pointed at Addie then raised his cup to his lips.

Addie set the heavy pot back on the coffeemaker. "All right, let's be clear about everything. Who is Dylan, who are *you*, and Kendrick, why is he trying to find you? Does this Dylan have anything to do with the shootout at my diner?"

Charlie broke in, surprised. "Were y'all involved in that? I heard on the radio about a shooting up in Loneview. One reason I don't live in a big city. They were shooting at *you*? I'm glad you're all okay."

Ben fixed Kendrick with a hard stare. "This is news to me. Who shot at you?"

"Some of my own. Long story."

"Story I'm going to need to hear." Ben gripped his coffee cup as though prepared to settle in for a tale on a long winter's night.

"Not until I know whose side you're on."

"My own side." Ben glanced at Addie. "Hers, actually. She's prettier than you. And the cubs. I'm as protective of kids as Shifters are. More, probably."

Addie widened her eyes at Ben. "We weren't going to use the *S* word," she said in a frantic half whisper. She'd told the cubs not to mention Shifters in front of Charlie.

"Oh," Ben said. Charlie was cooking at the stove, back moving as he flipped eggs. "I thought you'd found refuge with a friend or would have won over his loyalty by now."

"Stealth," Addie said, leaning to him. "That's what we were going for."

"Stealth is an *S* word," Ben pointed out. "I can make it so he doesn't remember, or has a compulsion not to talk about you, or something."

Charlie turned around and marched over to the table with

the frying pan and spatula, an irritated look in place. "I don't know who you people are, but you can trust me to keep your secrets. I respect the privacy of my guests—that's why all those celebrities were happy to stay here. So say what you like. It's not like I'm not burning with curiosity."

So speaking, he slapped eggs, perfectly cooked, to the plate in front of Ben. He slammed a couple pieces of bacon beside the eggs and stalked back to the stove.

"There you go." Ben made an expansive gesture with his coffee cup. "Tell us everything, Kendrick."

"How about this instead?" Kendrick said tightly. "If you're working for Dylan, go back and tell him I'll stay out of his territory if he stays out of mine. I'm done working for him, and he can keep up his end of the bargain. And tell him to send my trackers to me. The ones he has—Seamus and Francesca. The others if he's caught them too."

Ben's brows climbed. "Seriously? Me give orders to Dylan, the biggest badass in South Texas? In the world maybe?"

"I've done what he asked. He knows that."

"I haven't hung out in the Austin and San Antonio Shiftertowns very long," Ben said. "But I know that Seamus has shacked up with a human woman. Lives in her house somewhere south of Austin. Francesca, the Lupine, is living in the Austin Shiftertown with a bunch of bears, taking care of a cub. I haven't heard about any others that were yours."

Kendrick had already known about Francesca, a bear Shifter, and Seamus McGuire, a lion, even if he hadn't been in contact with them. Dylan had told him their story. Kendrick worried, though, about Dimitri and Jaycee—he hadn't heard a thing from them since the compound was destroyed.

"Find out about the others," Kendrick said. "And send word to me."

"So, what, now I'm *your* errand boy?" Ben thumped down his coffee. "What makes you think I'll do all that?"

Kendrick leaned to the table, resting his fists on it and looking into Ben's face. His black T-shirt stretched over his large biceps as his muscles tightened.

"Because you tried to come into this house where my

cubs were," Kendrick said carefully. "I'm being polite not killing you."

Ben looked hurt. "I told you, I'd never hurt the cubs."

Addie broke in. "You have prison tatts."

"You mean these?" He rubbed his hand over the Celtic-looking symbols on his inner arm and the spiderweb on his elbow. "I got these so I'd blend in where I lived. You'd be surprised how much people leave me alone when they see them."

"Goodness," Addie blinked. "Where on earth do you live?"

"Around. But trust me, I'm a big sweetie. Your cubs are safe with me."

Kendrick didn't look convinced. "Finish your breakfast and go." He rose from the table and moved to stand a little behind Ben, like a sentry.

"Or what?" Ben asked, picking up his fork.

"I'll stop being polite." Kendrick folded his arms and waited.

"Right, right." Ben tore apart his eggs, the yolks spreading bright gold across the plate. "Errand boy."

Kendrick didn't move. He could do that—go absolutely still, his green eyes fixed, watching. When he was like that, Addie could see the cat in him, the tiger that could kill with one swipe of his huge paw.

Kendrick the man, on the other hand, was delectable. His arms bulged against the shirt, the fabric clinging to his chest. His hair was messy from sleep, the white and black tangled together, and bristles covered his jaw, but he didn't look bedraggled. He looked like he'd just risen from bed, warm and tousled, and lucky was the woman who got to see him first thing in the morning.

Addie hoped no one else noticed her devouring him with her gaze, but Ben concentrated on his breakfast, the man effusive in his praise to Charlie. He took his time, enjoying it, then rose, held out his fists to bump with the cubs', who'd softened to him a bit. Ben gave Addie another once-over, winked at her, and walked out, Kendrick close behind him.

Addie followed them, standing on the back porch as

Kendrick ushered Ben down the steps. Ben had left a motor-cycle parked close to Kendrick's at the back of the house, and Kendrick walked him every step to it.

Ben and Kendrick had more conversation as Ben checked his bike, but they were too far away for Addie to hear it, and they leaned in, voices low. Kendrick regarded Ben with a hard stare, while Ben gestured with his hands as he argued.

It was clear who lost the debate. Kendrick's body was tilted forward over Ben's, an aggressive stance, while Ben was trying not to back down.

Finally, Ben climbed aboard his bike, started it up, and drove it around the house to the dirt drive, a wake of dust climbing into the clear, blue sky.

Kendrick turned around, regarding Addie on the porch without surprise, as though he'd known she'd followed to watch.

"Kendrick," Addie said. "We need to talk." She stepped off the porch and marched toward the barn on the little rise behind the house, without waiting to see whether he'd follow.

CHAPTER ELEVEN

Watching Addison walk up to the barn, her backside swaying in tight jeans, woke Kendrick's hunger with a vengeance. Too long burning, too long alone. The non-satisfaction of the dream rose up and bit him.

Addison was angry. Kendrick noted that with the same awareness that followed the noise of Ben's motorcycle far into the distance.

Addison slowed her pace as she entered the barn. Kendrick caught up to her, finding himself in a shadowy interior with a lofty roof, smelling of dust, hay, and horse.

Only one horse stood in this vastness, in a stall that was one of a dozen. The horse hung its head over the partition when Addison approached and gave a heartfelt little whinny. It was lonely, just like the rest of them.

"How are you, girl?" Addison halted in front of the stall and rubbed the horse's nose. "It's too hot for you to run in the corral right now. Later, I'll ask Charlie to turn you out."

"How do you know it's a she?" Kendrick asked, using the words to deflect his roiling desire. "Because your grandparents taught you about horses?"

"Because Charlie told me." Addison turned from the

mare but kept her hand on its neck. "I'm not expert enough to tell the difference by one glance—well, I mean except for the obvious way." She patted the horse again. "Not what I came here to talk to you about."

Kendrick didn't think she had.

"You need to be straight with me." Addison stepped away from the horse. She kept her voice low, trying not to startle the beast, but she stared straight into Kendrick's eyes. Brooking no nonsense, her look said. "I know you didn't want to say much in front of Charlie or your cubs, but we're alone now. That Ben guy obviously found you here pretty easily. Who is this Dylan, and why was he looking for you?"

"There's a lot of Shifter business going on," Kendrick said. "Dangerous business."

"I figured that. You're a Shifter Guardian, whatever that means, who kept your friends from being put into Shiftertowns. I know you told me this—I'm trying to get it all straight. How does this guy Dylan figure into it?"

Kendrick regarded her for a moment while putting in order what he'd tell her. He longed to protect her from all the shit in his life, but he also knew that ignorance might get Addison killed. Maybe that's what the dream had meant.

"Dylan Morrissey is father to the leader of the Austin Shiftertown," Kendrick began. "Last year, he helped organize a raid on my compound—he thought we'd kidnapped a woman. When my Shifters scattered, Dylan found me. I thought he wanted to Collar me and force me into his Shiftertown, but instead, he recruited me to help him track down a band of Shifters who used to follow a feral Shifter in Mexico. Those Shifters are dangerous, most of them gone totally feral, and many are roaming free. He knew I could help him track them under the radar—humans don't know about me. Dylan promised that if I helped him, he'd keep humans away from *my* Shifters forever. I couldn't say no to that. But I soon realized I was under his thumb, and time was going by. I just told Ben to tell Dylan that I'm finished, I'm out. Time for Dylan to keep up his end of the deal."

Addison listened—what she thought, Kendrick couldn't tell. He'd left out the days and nights of hunting along the border, standing by while Dylan meted out his brand of rough justice. Dylan had either dragged the Shifter back to a Shiftertown, fitting him with a Collar to calm him down, or killed the Shifter outright if they'd been too far feral. Kendrick was a Guardian—he was there to send the Shifter to dust.

Kendrick no longer wanted to be the Guardian in Dylan's pocket.

Addison listened, her blue eyes wide. "Do these rogue Shifters have anything to do with the ones who shot up the diner?"

Kendrick's fears lashed at him. "I'm not sure. There have always been elements among my Shifters that were factious, but none rebelled openly. But since my Shifters dispersed last fall, it seems that some of them have decided to break from me and join a contingency of Collared Shifters who want out of Shiftertowns. Shifters are dangerous, Addison. I don't care what the human-made documentaries say or how harmless you think my cubs are. Shifters are volatile and unpredictable. I tell you all this so you understand that. Sending you to New Orleans—by private plane, not bus—is looking better and better to me."

"Is it?" Addison cocked her head, as she had in the dream. "Who is going to watch out for your cubs while you face all these dangerous Shifters? From what I heard, you asked Ben to find some of your Shifters and send them to you. Sounds risky. I think I'd better stay right where I am."

Kendrick went to her swiftly. The horse threw up her head and backed up in her stall, her eyes white. She knew the creature who moved toward her was predatory, a beast in the guise of a man.

Addison, on the other hand, stood her ground. She also knew Kendrick was a predator, and she didn't care.

Time to teach her a few things.

Kendrick gripped Addison by the shoulders. "I didn't want you to come with me in the first place. Dragging you into danger wasn't what I needed."

"Yes you did," Addison said quietly. Her sure gaze met his agitated one. "You wanted me to come or else you'd have put me on that plane or left me in the motel or even at the side of the road."

She was right that he'd wanted her with him. Even in Kendrick's anger, he had to acknowledge that. He hadn't wanted her to go, not yet. Even now, as he told her he wanted her gone, he knew he didn't mean it. He needed her here, next to him. That's also what the dream had told him.

"If you stay too long, Addison, then I can't ever let you leave. If Shifter Bureau catches you, they won't let up on you. They'll keep at you until you tell them everything about me."

"Fine then," Addison said. "I won't leave."

Kendrick's grip tightened. "If you stay with me, your greatest danger is *from* me. You need to understand that."

"Because you can change into a big tiger and take me out with one paw?" Her smile came. "I'll risk it."

Kendrick's blood fired. "It's more than that, Addison. It's so much more than that."

"Oh?" Addison's tone sharpened with curiosity and behind that, excitement. "What exactly do you mean, then?"

"Damn it."

Kendrick's words turned to a growl. His hands began to change, claws extending from fingers that turned furry. The claws snagged the material of the T-shirt on her shoulders and tore through it.

Kendrick never broke her skin. He knew exactly how much pressure to use, and when to stop.

He was hot, his blood beginning to sear. He felt as though he'd run too long, oxygen squeezing out of him and leaving him breathless.

He brought his claws down the front of the shirt, ripping it away. No thought about how she'd get back to the house with her clothes in shreds crossed his mind. At the moment, Kendrick didn't care.

Addison drew a quick breath, her curiosity changing to surprise but not fear. Her lips parted, became moist, as Kendrick's claws receded, his hands became fully a man's, and he dragged his fingers down the shirt, pulling it away.

Her bra beneath was a neutral-colored satin with a white bow, cupping her full breasts like loving hands. The bra was too dull for her, too thick and masking. Kendrick would buy her beautiful lingerie—he had vague visions of floating white, red, or black fabric that enhanced rather than hid her.

Addison made a small noise when he tore open the bra, pulling it away to free the fullness of her.

This is what Kendrick wanted to see—Addison the woman, no cloaking herself in awkward clothes, no effacing herself so she could make a living. She had round, full breasts, as he'd felt last night, the tips dusky pink, rising with her intake of breath.

Kendrick changed his touch to a tender one, cupping her with his palms where the bra had. Addison leaned into him, her eyes half closing.

Hell. Kendrick brought his thumbs up to touch her nipples, a shudder going through him at the hot softness of her skin. *I need this.*

He found himself dropping to his knees before he consciously decided to, the last remnants of the shirt she'd borrowed from him falling at his touch.

Kendrick pressed a long kiss to her belly, and her hands came around him to cradle his head, fingers stroking his hair.

"Your beauty blasts from you," he whispered into her skin. "It cuts me."

"I'm a waitress who needs to eat less pie," Addison answered. Her supple abdomen moved with her laughter.

"It hurt me." Kendrick pressed another kiss to her stomach, licking where his lips touched. "I told myself never to go back after I first saw you, but I couldn't stop. I had to see you every night, just to look at you."

"And here I thought you really liked the apple streusel. I can make some for you, if Charlie has the ingredients."

"Stop." Kendrick nipped her skin, then licked her again. He couldn't cease tasting her. "Stop making this a joke. I brought you into danger, because I couldn't deny myself. You call to me."

Addison stroked his hair once more, fingers languid. "I can't help making jokes. It's how I deal with stress."

Stress. Something humans went on and on about. Shifters

had stress too, but usually it manifested in fights to the death or something as terrible as a Shifter giving in to anguish and ending his own life. Kendrick had felt that anguish but he'd grabbed on to all his strength and fought to stay alive. His cubs needed him.

"This is how *I* deal with stress," Kendrick said. He popped open the button of her jeans and pulled down the zipper. He was kind and didn't tear the fabric this time—he merely yanked the jeans and underwear beneath down to her ankles.

"Kendrick . . ."

Kendrick waited for what she wanted to say, but Addison fell silent. She was beautiful standing there, fully bare except for the fabric bunched around her sneakers. He looked up to her round breasts, the dark ponytail flowing over her shoulders, her blue eyes filled with need. Her stomach was soft, hips wide, and curls as dark as those on her head waited between her legs.

Kendrick brushed his hand to the join of her thighs, finding her moist. He leaned forward and kissed her there, liking the way she gave a startled jump.

Kendrick stilled her with one hand. "You taste like . . ." He groped for what he wanted to say. "Desire."

She tasted exactly like he wanted her to, exactly as he needed her to. Her scent, honey with a slight tang of salt, entered him and became a part of him.

"You taste ready for me," Kendrick finished.

Addison pushed at him with feeble hands. "I'm not sure what I'm ready for."

"Greedy," Kendrick said. "Me for you, you for me."

"You're confident." Addison gave a shaky laugh. "Though it's me standing in a barn with my clothes off."

"You are hungry for me, Addison. I can taste it." Kendrick kissed her again, then slid his tongue straight into her heat.

"Oh, my . . ." Addison broke off in a cross between a gasp and a moan. "Shit, Kendrick, you can't . . ."

She trailed off, not finishing what he couldn't do. Kendrick drew her closer to him, his hands on her hips, and drank her in.

The tang of her rolled over his tongue, her wanting, her dismay at wanting it, every need she had. Kendrick knew all.

At the same time, he tasted only *her*, the bite of her sending his lusts soaring. His cock tightened, wanting him to take her *now*. On the dusty straw, on the hard floor, to drive into her until every ache was gone. That would take a long, long time.

Addison groaned, her fingers twining in his hair. Kendrick sped his tongue's strokes, drinking her. He wouldn't take her fully here, in the dirt—not now. Later, though . . . He compensated for his kindness in not simply ravishing her by pleasuring her with his rapid tongue, making her hips rock with joy.

"Oh . . ." Addison pushed forward, reaching with all of herself for the sensation of his mouth. *"Oh . . . Holy f—"*

Her word trailed off into a long cry of joy that became a wail. One hand left his hair to be pressed over her mouth, choking off the sound.

Kendrick kept on her as she twisted and writhed but never tried to dislodge him. She was breathing hard, perspiration shining on her skin.

"Kendrick. You have to *stop*." Her voice was raw, hoarse.

No, he didn't. Kendrick renewed his attack, his fingers pressing into her buttocks, kneading them as he lifted her against his mouth.

Addison gave up trying to stem her cries, which came out of her in loud *Ohs*. Her body arched to him, her hands pulled him closer, the heat of her flowing into his mouth. She wanted him inside her—his tongue was only the warm-up.

But not yet. Kendrick shook deep inside, holding back and hating it. She was human, fragile, in spite of her claims to the contrary. He'd die if he hurt her.

Kendrick gradually slowed his licks, nips, thrusts. Addison dragged him closer, wanting more, but Kendrick forced himself to back away, pressing a final kiss to her sweetness.

He climbed to his feet, not in the least stiff from kneeling on the hard floor. In fact, he wanted to race away, to run, until he dropped in exhaustion. Only then would his frenzy abate, only then could he leave her alone.

Addison was flushed, her hair in tangles, her shaking hands balling at her sides. Her eyes shone, though, and when Kendrick took a step back from her, her smile blossomed.

She gave him a shy but happy look and started to reach for her sagging jeans, but Kendrick caught her around the waist. Addison started, but he pulled her to him, tight against his body, loving the feeling of her bare flesh against his clothes. He didn't try to kiss or caress her, he simply hugged her.

For a Shifter, holding was the next best thing to sex. Hugging meant touch, soothing, warmth, protection, happiness, safety, complete trust. Kendrick held on, burying his face in the curve of Addison's neck.

She hugged Kendrick in return, laughing softly as he squeezed her. They swayed back and forth as heat sifted around them and dust hung in the air.

Addison suppressed a small sneeze. Kendrick raised his head but he didn't want to let her go.

He had to, though, or he'd say to hell with it and take her. Kendrick would mate-claim her, go into mate frenzy, and forget about Dylan, his Shifters, those hunting him.

A snarl worked its way up through his throat. Kendrick's skin was hot, itching, but there was no relief because the wild heat was *inside* him.

The snarl came out. Kendrick pushed away from a startled Addison and stripped out of his clothes. He tossed his own T-shirt at her feet right before he shifted to tiger.

He heard the horse whinny in terror, Addison cry out. But Kendrick was gone, the white tiger sprinting out into the sunlight and rising heat of the desert morning.

Addie managed to pull up and fasten her jeans before her strength left her. Then she fell back against a stall door and pressed her hands to her face.

She'd just had the most brilliant orgasm of her life, with a man who could change into a *tiger*. Her body was still shuddering with it, hot all over, a tightness within her easing.

She realized she'd just changed somehow. The Addie

who'd walked into the barn, ready to pry out of Kendrick a clear explanation of events, was gone. A new Addie stood in her place, and she wasn't sure what she'd learn about her.

One thing—she loved what Kendrick had done with his tongue. He'd done it to pleasure her and also to frighten her, to show he could do anything to her.

Well, if he'd been going for terror, his plan had backfired. Addie felt cleansed, as though some darkness she'd been holding on to without knowing it had been ripped free.

Kendrick had only made her want him more, hope he'd continue what this first pleasuring had meant to lead to.

The sound of voices cut into her afterglow. Addie jumped then swooped down and snatched up the shirt Kendrick had dropped. She stepped back into deeper shadow and slid the shirt on, kicking Kendrick's empty jeans into a corner just before Charlie and the three cubs walked up to the barn.

The barn had no doors, and she could see the four clearly in the sunshine—Charlie with his slightly stooped shoulders, the littler cubs dancing around, Robbie walking more sedately. Addie scooped up the tattered remains of the other shirt and her bra and crumpled them into a ball in her hand.

The horse had ventured forward again after Kendrick departed and now watched in curiosity as the boys and Charlie came in. She whickered a greeting to Charlie but gave the cubs a wary eye. She knew that they, like Kendrick, weren't human.

Addie patted the horse, calming her. Charlie's glance took her in, noting at once that she wore the shirt Kendrick had left the house in. The man was no fool.

"Do you still ride her?" Addie asked to cover her awkwardness.

Charlie laughed, going along with it. He wouldn't embarrass her. "Me? No. But you're welcome to, and the boys might want to."

"Nah," Robbie said at once. "She won't let me. Wolves eat horses."

"*I* wouldn't eat her," Brett said. "What do tigers eat?"

"Well, now, let's see," Charlie said. "Tigers mostly live in India, so they'd eat elephants, wouldn't they?"

Brett and Zane went round-eyed. "A whole elephant?" Zane bleated. "I don't think I could eat a whole elephant. What else do they eat?"

Charlie shrugged. "Well, sometimes, people."

"Ewwww," the cubs said at the same time. Brett finished, "I'd never eat people. People are nice, like Addie. She gives us pie. Can we have some pie, Addie?"

Addie shook her head in wonder. "You just had breakfast."

"I know, but we're hungry again," Brett said, and Zane agreed.

"They're always hungry." Robbie shared a look with Addie, one that adults might as they contemplated the antics of the kids.

"'Course they are," Charlie said. "They're growing. Like you, Robbie. Tell you what, I'll have Addie come and look at what all I have, and see what we can do. I might have to go to town for supplies," Charlie said to Addie. "Wasn't expecting company."

"The ranch has been closed ten years, you said?" Addie asked him.

Charlie shrugged. "I didn't close it down, not really. Edna wouldn't have wanted that. But guests just stopped coming."

"We're guests," Brett announced at the top of his voice. "We'll be the best guests, ever."

The horse danced back nervously at his loudness, and Robbie rolled his eyes. He didn't admonish the little ones though.

"All right, then, let's go make a shopping list," Addie said.

Charlie was as eager as the cubs. "Come on, then—" He stopped and cocked his head, frowning suddenly. "Do I hear a cell phone?"

Addie looked down. Something was ringing under a hunk of straw in the corner, the sound incongruous with the peaceful barn.

Robbie and the cubs ran forward, Robbie reaching the source of the noise first. He pulled out an old-style flip phone from the layers of straw. The little window in front showed a number and a name in tiny letters.

"Seamus," Robbie read.

Brett and Zane shouted with excitement and started jumping up and down. They grabbed hands and kept jumping. "It's Seamus. It's Seamus. It's Seamus. Answer it, Robbie!"

Addie had heard Kendrick and Ben mention Seamus. "Who is he exactly?" Addie asked them.

"One of Dad's trackers," Robbie answered, more subdued. He opened the phone and said cautiously, "Hello?"

CHAPTER TWELVE

"**D**ad's not here," Robbie said into the phone, his brow puckering. "I mean, he's here, but not *right* here. What do you want me to do?"

Addie didn't like this. While Kendrick had spoken about contacting Seamus, she wasn't certain this was a Shifter who could be trusted. Plus, just because the caller ID read "Seamus," anyone could have stolen the phone and called in an attempt to locate Kendrick.

She took the phone from Robbie so quickly he didn't have time to fight for it.

"Hello," she said into it, voice firm. "I can't let you talk to the cubs. If you want, I'll take a message and have their father call you back."

"Who—" The word cut off, and there was a long silence at the other end of the line.

Addie suspected that the *Who?* had been the first word of *Who the hell is this?* But Seamus—if it were Seamus— obviously didn't want to speak to Addie.

"I'll tell him you called," she said. "Good-bye."

Another startled exclamation came through before Addie clicked off the phone and closed it.

This wasn't Kendrick's phone, she was certain. Kendrick had broken and flushed *her* phone, and she was pretty sure he'd done the same to his, not wanting it to give away their position. If he'd had a phone, he wouldn't have had to ask Ben to deliver messages for him.

Should she take it into the mare's stall and let her stomp on it? A thousand pounds of horse would probably smash it pretty well.

Addie brushed off the last of the hay from the device, slid it into her pocket, and pasted on a smile for the waiting cubs. "Come on. Let's go see about those groceries."

Kendrick walked the bounds a good long time before he trusted himself back in the house with Addison. The small taste of her hadn't eased his need; it had only flared it to life.

He didn't sense anyone else out in the wide vista behind Charlie's house, not another creature like Ben, no other Shifters. They were alone, for now.

When Kendrick believed himself calm enough—or at least convinced himself to go make sure Addison and the cubs were all right—he shifted back to his human form, recovered his jeans from the barn, and entered the house through the front door. He was ready to slip down the hall and find another shirt to cover his sunbaked torso, but Robbie saw him through the open kitchen door.

"Dad! We're making a list. What do you want?"

Brett and Zane added their chorus. Kendrick made his way across the giant living room to the kitchen, pausing in the doorway.

Addison was talking with Charlie, the two getting along famously, as they debated how many eggs they'd need for breakfasts to come. Kendrick had anticipated Addison being awkward with him, or even fully afraid of him, but she broke from Charlie and came close to him without worry.

"Found this," she said in a low voice, pressing something cool and hard into his hand. "Seamus called."

Addison gave him a significant look, then turned around and went back to drawing up her shopping list.

"We'll pay for all this, of course," Addison said in a loud voice. "Kendrick?"

"Yes," he said, distracted. He always made sure he had a stash of money where he could easily get to it. The five thousand the police had taken from Addison was a drop in the bucket.

The advantage of not wearing a Collar was that he could walk into a human bank, open an account, and pull money from it whenever he wanted. Unless he decided to shape-shift in the lobby, the humans would never know the difference.

More pressing was this unfamiliar cell phone in his hand and Addison's words, *Seamus called.*

His heart beating faster, Kendrick moved down the hall to the bedroom, opened the phone, and pressed the keys to call back the last number.

The phone rang twice before a familiar voice with a Scots accent answered with a cautious, "Who is this?"

"Me," Kendrick said.

"Kendrick?" Seamus's voice went soft and at the same time filled with relief. "Where the hell are you, man?"

"Safe. Tell me how I got this phone. It's not mine."

"I don't have the faintest fecking idea. I got a text from Ben—weird guy who's doing some work for Dylan—that said I should call this number, and I'd find you. Except I found Robbie—and a woman."

"That's Addison. She's human."

Seamus's tone turned amused. "What, you had time to go to a groupie bar?"

"No," Kendrick said, his voice going harsh. "She's not a groupie."

"Hey, don't knock Shifter groupies—I found me a real sweetheart of one. We want to be mated, Kendrick. Except I want you to do it, not these Collared shites. Where are you?"

Kendrick paused. Seamus, one of his closest friends, sounded happier than Kendrick had ever known him. He looked forward to presiding over the joining under sun and moon *after* he'd solved the problems raining on him now.

"We need to meet," Kendrick said.

"I agree. I want to see you." Seamus waited a beat. "Don't let this go to your head, tiger-man, but we miss you."

Kendrick warmed. "I'm your leader." It was natural for Shifters with less dominance to want to be with those of higher dominance.

"No, shithead. Not you, Oh Great Leader. You, yourself, and your boys. They all right? Robbie sounded scared."

"They're fine. Keep your phone on you. I'll pick a place and let you know. Do I have to tell you to keep it quiet?"

"Don't get all emotional on me now." Seamus's voice was full of laughter, so good to hear. "I'm not Dylan's man, if that's what you're worried about."

"Thank you for that. I'll be in touch."

Kendrick punched the hang-up button and closed the phone, sliding it into his pocket.

Ben had left it, he suspected. While the man had been wandering the grounds before Addison spotted him at breakfast, he could have dropped a cell phone for Kendrick to find, then told Seamus to call it. Kendrick wondered how the hell he'd missed it.

Addison walked into the bedroom even as he had the thought, and shut the door, and Kendrick realized exactly how he'd missed it. He'd been focused on Addison alone. He'd been trying to tell himself that his sudden need for her was simply hormonal, after being celibate for so long.

Right. His urge for her sprang to life as soon as he saw her. He wanted to pull her to him, kiss her, climb with her to the absurdly high bed, finish what he'd started in the barn. His whole body sang for her.

"What do you want from the store?" Addison was asking. She stood against the closed door, a position which pushed her ample breasts at him. She'd grabbed the T-shirt he'd flung at her, this one black with a Harley logo on it.

Kendrick turned away to take another shirt from his duffel bag . . . and found the bag empty. Everything that had been inside it was gone.

"Dresser," Addison said before he could ask. "Second drawer. I took the top one. That is, I'll take it after I buy myself some more clothes."

Kendrick opened the drawer to find his shirts, underwear, and socks in careful rows inside. She'd even folded his underwear, by the Goddess.

"I don't want you going with Charlie," Kendrick said, pulling out a shirt. "Tell me what you need, and I'll get it for you."

Addison's eyes widened. "I'm going to let a *man* buy my clothes? Are you kidding me?" She studied him, her eyes dark blue and beautiful. "Besides, if people are looking for you, you showing up in a town will only alert someone to your presence. I bet there are Shifter spies all over South Texas. None of your enemies—or friends for that matter— know me. I'll pretend I'm Charlie's niece or granddaughter going with him to help him shop."

Kendrick knew she was right, but the thought of her out of his sight, unprotected, made his fur itch. "Charlie can go on his own."

Addison let out a sigh. "*Kendrick.* No one knows me. I can't trust Charlie to pick out clothes for me either. I like him, but he's still a guy."

Kendrick grunted. "Tell Charlie to go to a town where he's not known—not his regular places. I don't need anyone commenting on how much food he's buying. He'll need a ton for the cubs. They eat a *lot.*"

Addison gave him her little smile, which made her eyes dance. "Most boys do."

"These are Shifter boys. You have no idea." Kendrick took his wallet from his pocket and pulled out about out a thousand dollars. "Give this to Charlie. I hope that's enough."

Addison's eyes widened as she stared at the wad of bills. "Damn, Kendrick, do you always carry around this much money?"

Kendrick shrugged. "I never know when I'll need it.

Addison's fingers brushed his as she took the money. Kendrick quickly withdrew before he could grab her and not let go.

"Where'd you find the phone?" he asked.

"Barn." Addison folded the bills and tucked them away. "I think Ben left it up there, don't you? We didn't hear the horse fuss, so Ben must not be a Shifter. Y'all make her nervous."

"Ben's not a Shifter," Kendrick said. "I'm not quite sure what he is." He didn't like that.

"About this Seamus," Addison said. Her smile was gone. "You trust him?"

"I've trusted him with my life. I'm going to meet with him— in a place I choose—and find out if I still *can* trust him."

"Okaaayy. And when will you tell me all about that?"

Kendrick let his grin come. "When you get back from your shopping trip."

"Oh, so now you're going to let me go?"

"Yes, if you do what I say and go someplace Charlie doesn't know anyone."

"Are you having fun being arbitrary?"

Kendrick considered. "Yes." He was, he realized. Fencing with Addison was more enjoyment than he'd had in a long time. Tasting her had been even better.

Addison pointed one finger at him. "I'll hold you to it."

She swung around, jerked open the door, and stalked out, her unfettered torso under his shirt a wonderful sight.

Charlie decided he and Addie had better go into San Antonio, even though it was about a hundred miles away. Everyone in every small town in South Texas pretty much knew Charlie or had known Edna or her family—or his parents or his kids. His kids now lived in Houston doing highfalutin jobs he didn't really understand, he said.

Kendrick told Charlie to watch over Addison, and Addison to watch over Charlie. Charlie promised to check in via his own cell phone, calling the phone Ben had left—a burner, Kendrick discovered. No name associated with the number.

Brett and Zane wanted to go with Addison.

"It's a big trip, sweeties," Addison said as she opened the door of Charlie's pickup. Unlike the house, the pickup was nearly new, with four-wheel drive, good for the middle of nowhere.

Zane threw himself on Addison's legs and hung on. Brett stood next to his brother, looking as though he was trying not to cry.

"They're afraid you won't come back," Robbie said behind them. "You'll come back, won't you, Addie?"

Kendrick had the same fear but he would never admit it out loud. Addison could drive out of his life right now—he wouldn't blame her if she did. The thought tore at him, making him want to join Zane in hanging on to her.

"Of course, I'm coming back," Addison said. "Just try and stop me. And I'll have all kinds of fun presents for you."

Zane wouldn't let go. Kendrick stepped forward and unhooked him from around Addison's legs. Zane struggled but his strength was no match for his father's.

Zane threw his arms around Kendrick and clung to him, refusing to look as Addison climbed into the truck and slammed the door. Brett and Robbie watched forlornly as the pickup rolled away, though they returned Addison's cheerful wave. Kendrick wanted to join Zane in yowling, feeling empty as the truck turned the corner, and was gone.

The trip to San Antonio was uneventful, to Addie's relief, except for two incidents.

The first happened after Addie had enjoyed herself buying new tops, shorts, jeans, underwear, and a cute skirt she couldn't resist. She felt a little guilty that Kendrick was paying for all this, but Addie had become an expert at finding the very best clothes for the least amount of money possible. Her sister, Ivy, said she should be called Shopping Master and give classes.

Addie would pay back Kendrick every penny when she could, she vowed. She made it her policy not to be in debt to anyone.

As they emerged from the discount store, Charlie insisting on carrying the bags, Charlie stopped her and gestured into the crowd. "Are those Shifters?"

He whispered it, and Addie came alert, her heart beating faster.

She glanced to where Charlie indicated. There were two of them, a couple lanes of parked cars away from Addie and Charlie. The two men strolled easily through the lot, making their way to the hardware store in the strip mall, but they attracted attention just by being there. Addie wasn't the only one who'd turned to stare.

The Shifters resembled Kendrick, but then they didn't. Both were large and solid in body, strength obvious. They didn't display themselves—they wore modest T-shirts and jeans—but sunlight glinted on their Collars.

They shared with Kendrick the extreme confidence that ran to arrogance, the graceful way of doing something as simple as walking, and a way of being aware of every detail around them.

A third Shifter, younger than the other two, jogged through the parking lot toward them. The first two stopped and waited for him.

One of the older Shifters was tattooed on his neck, down his arms, and on his chest—the tatts obviously ran under the T-shirt. He had more swiftness of movement than the other two, his brown eyes quick. He wore his hair buzzed almost completely, with only a black shadow on his head.

The younger was restless, but no less large than the tattooed guy. He had dark hair, a thick shock of it, and unlike the other two, had a ready smile and laughter.

The third made Addie halt for a stride. He was larger than the others, and he looked uncomfortable to be in this parking lot, surrounded by people, cars, and even his fellow Shifters. His hair, though, caught her attention most of all. It was black streaked with a distinctive red-orange.

Except for the color, it looked very much like Kendrick's hair.

A tiger.

At that moment, the tiger Shifter's gaze moved to fix directly on Addie.

His eyes were yellow-gold, distinct even at this distance. His face was still, as was his body, no movement at all, though his friends were speaking to each other, their voices rumbling with the same deep timbre of Kendrick.

Addie made herself continue walking but the golden gaze trained on her, and she couldn't look away.

The younger Shifter noticed the tiger's motionlessness. "What's up, big guy?" The sentence floated across the shimmers of heat off the parked cars.

The tiger dragged his gaze away from Addie and answered in a low growl. Addie, released, jogged a few steps to catch up with Charlie.

Her breath came fast, her need to rush to the safety of the pickup overwhelming. From the vantage point of the passenger seat in Charlie's truck, Addie watched the three Shifters move on together toward the hardware store.

The tiger one turned around, and Addie was sure she felt his stare go right to the truck, and to her inside it.

CHAPTER THIRTEEN

The second incident wasn't so much an incident as it was Charlie. In spite of Addie's nervousness at seeing the Shifters, Charlie followed the plan of stopping at the big grocery store a few exits down the freeway and loading up with food and other supplies.

No Shifters appeared, and Addie told herself to relax. Those Shifters couldn't possibly have known who she was or that she even knew Kendrick. She was just another Texas girl shopping in town with her elderly relative.

She made herself enjoy picking out the foodstuffs she'd use to create meals and buying kitschy toys for the cubs, but she remained nervous until they had the truck loaded up and were heading back out of the city.

Once they were on the road, Charlie decided to grill her. "You and Kendrick aren't husband and wife, are you?" He gave her a stare as perceptive as any Shifter's.

Addie's face went hot. "No. We're not."

Charlie shrugged, hands on the wheel. "Well, now, I'm not a stickler for getting a piece of paper saying a couple is together. I grew up in the sixties and was a wild boy for a time. Edna and me lived together for a couple years before we finally tied the knot—to the relief of our parents." He chuckled in memory. "But that's not what I meant. You two aren't together at all. It's like you're strangers."

"Sort of," Addie said. "Kendrick was a customer in the diner. I came here with him to help him look after his cubs." She paused as Charlie watched her, the man knowing there was more to it than that. Addie groped for explanations, uncertain of her own motives. "I wanted to make sure the cubs were all right. And Kendrick. I just wanted to."

"Uh huh. But he doesn't wear a Collar like those Shifters we saw did."

"I know." Addie closed her mouth after that. What Kendrick had told her could get him killed.

"Hmm." Charlie pulled out around a slow car on the two-lane highway then concentrated on getting back before an oncoming eighteen-wheeler reached them. "You need to be careful, honey," he said as soon as he was back in the right lane. "Shifters aren't like us. I don't mean he's evil or anything, but they have different ways of looking at things. I mean, I wouldn't be a bit surprised if we got back and found him and his cubs gone. Nowhere to be found."

"I know," Addie said, glumly this time. She feared that too. Kendrick had no obligation to her. He'd sprung into her life and could disappear back out of it without much effort.

"So don't pin your hopes on him," Charlie said. "You're a nice young woman. I'd hate to watch you get your heart broken."

"It might be too late." Addie let out a sigh. "I've been burned in relationships before. You'd think I'd learn to be cautious."

"The heart does what the heart does," Charlie said. "We can't pick and choose who we fall for. Nothing's that nice and neat. You might find yourself madly in love with someone who doesn't have any feelings whatsoever for you back. It's the chance we take."

"You and Edna worked out," Addie said. She'd seen plenty of pictures of the woman around the house, from very young woman to an older woman still flushed with the beauty of her youth.

"Don't try to change the subject." Charlie's mouth twitched. "It wasn't all sunshine and roses for us either. Her father couldn't abide me, a ranch hand who was always dirty. He wanted Edna to marry someone rich and powerful, who worked in an office. That was never going to be me. I was drafted into 'Nam, and when I came back—thanking God every day that I'd made it—I grabbed Edna and said we were going to be together. I wasn't risking losing her. Her parents kicked up a fuss, and we ran off together, joined a commune, and shacked up." He laughed. "We thought we were rebels. We were just poor as dirt and madly in love. We finally decided we wanted a real house with a bathroom we didn't share with ten other people, and left. I went back to ranching, and Edna and me married. We still didn't have much money, but we didn't care. We were together forty years."

Addie listened, her eyes moist. "That's a sweet story."

"It ain't sweet, young lady. It was real life."

"Yeah, but I like your real life."

Charlie softened. "My point is, me and Edna both wanted the same thing. That's important. You need to find out what Kendrick wants, what he can give you. If you both need something too different, you should brace yourself for having to say good-bye. Sorry to have to tell you that."

Addie nodded, not trusting herself to answer. The green fields around Hill Country gave way to hot, dusty flatlands as they went south and west, back into the nothingness from whence they'd come.

Charlie was right, and she knew it. Kendrick's life was vastly different from Addie's. He was running from people who wanted to shoot him, hiding out from other Shifters. She understood why he'd needed to hide from humans, who wanted to sequester Shifters for the good of humanity, which Addie had never agreed with. Not that she'd ever given it much thought, she realized uncomfortably.

The three Shifters in the parking lot had seemed like friends to each other, companions. The younger one had stood close to the others, talking and laughing in perfect trust. In that respect, they didn't seem much different from humans.

But they were different, the news media was always quick to emphasize. Shifters looked human and could take human traits, but they were different, *other*. And always would be.

Charlie pulled into to his drive past the split-rail fence and headed up for the house. Addie held her breath as she looked about for signs of Kendrick, then released it in relief when she saw the motorcycle still parked behind a clump of mesquite. Kendrick hadn't gone.

No one was in the house, however. Addie checked all the rooms but found no Kendrick, no Robbie, no Zane and Brett.

She was about to rush back out to voice her worries to Charlie when she spotted them outside the back door, in the shade of a clump of live oak Charlie said he'd planted once upon a time.

A huge white tiger lay stretched out on the ground, his large paws in front of him. As Addie watched, one very tiny white tiger jumped onto the tiger's back and slid off; another was busily chewing on one of the big tiger's ears. A wolf pup, tail waving, darted in and out, avoiding the smaller cubs' claws and teeth, while he teased both them and the large tiger.

Kendrick kept a careful eye on where the cubs were, Addie saw, while he let them tug on his ears, his paws, his tail. He rumbled deep in his chest, and the tiger cubs answered in mewls and yowls. Robbie gave the occasional yip.

"Oh, I wish I had a camera," Addie said.

Kendrick raised his head. His green eyes focused on her, and the rumble grew to a soft snarl.

The cubs leapt away from Kendrick and swarmed to Addie. They ran around her feet, bodies wriggling in excitement, the tiger cubs trying to climb her blue-jeaned legs.

Kendrick rose to his feet and ambled over in a stride that showed the rippling strength of his shoulders, the power of his tiger body. He caught the cub trying to climb Addie by the scruff, lifting him high.

Growling admonition, he carried the tiger cub, dangling from his mouth, into the house. Charlie held the door wide for him. The other two cubs abandoned Addie and rushed after their father.

By the time Addie entered the house, the four had

disappeared, but soon the little boys, shifted and dressed, ran back to the kitchen.

"What did you bring us?" Brett demanded at the top of his voice.

"Lots of stuff," Addie said, as excited as he was.

She rummaged in the bags and brought out little cars and other toys her nephew had liked when he'd been their age, coloring books and crayons, colored pencils for Robbie. She'd also brought comic books and magazines, not knowing what little Shifter boys would like to read, or even if they could. They lost no time in grabbing everything in sight and racing back to their room to go through it.

Addie helped Charlie put away the groceries. By the time they'd finished Kendrick emerged, the sheathed sword in his hand. He'd dressed fully, but the eyes regarding her were pure Shifter.

"I need to talk to you," Addie said to him, jerking her head at the back door.

Kendrick's brows went up, but he walked past her without a word and outside. Charlie watched them go, giving Addie a warning look.

"You like to talk," Kendrick said as they stopped in the middle of the backyard. He laid the sword beside him. Charlie had once had a lawn here, it was obvious, but weeds had taken it over and now it was a field of brown, dried wisps. "Maybe we should go to the barn."

"I don't think so." Addie shivered then gave him a severe look. "I want to actually *talk* this time."

The amusement in Kendrick's eyes was warm. "I can't for long. I've set up the meeting with Seamus. He'll be there soon."

Addie's worries returned. "Do you still think you should meet him alone? Can you trust him?"

Kendrick shrugged. "I have to find out one way or another."

Addie looked up at him. "Kendrick, when I was in San Antonio, I saw some Shifters."

He stopped, any merriment he'd found in the conversation gone. "Where?"

Addie quickly sketched the scene and described the Shifters. "I think one of them was a tiger."

Kendrick's face had gone grim, his eyes lightening almost to gray. "Did he see you?"

"Yes."

"Shit," Kendrick said softly.

He turned away from Addie, put his hands on his hips, and stared up at the cloudless sky. His fingers quivered against his jeans.

"I don't think they could have known I had a connection to you," Addie said. "I was just another customer coming out of the store, for all he knew."

Kendrick turned around. "How close were you to them?"

Addie thought about it. "A couple car lengths plus the width of the lane, I think. How much is that? Twenty feet? Thirty? Hell if I know how long cars are or how much space is in parking lot aisles."

Kendrick's jaw tightened. "It might have been far enough. Especially with all the cars, exhaust, people . . ."

He was speaking to himself, Addie realized, trying to sound reassuring. "Far enough for what?"

"Shifters can scent. Sometimes that sense is stronger than sight or hearing. If they were close enough, they could have scented me on you."

Addie wrinkled her nose. "Seriously? That's unsettling."

"It's normal. But those Shifters have never met you, and I met them only once. They might not remember my scent from so brief a meeting six months ago. Since then, no Shifter from their group has seen me except Dylan." Again, he sounded as though trying to reassure himself.

"Would they smell your scent on Dylan?" Addie asked, thinking it through. "If he spends time with you, then goes back home . . ."

"Dylan's careful about what scents he carries. He's the most cautious Shifter I've ever known. If Dylan didn't want his son's trackers to know my scent, he'd keep it from them."

How, Addie wondered? Long showers? Special soap? Her thoughts kept turning. "How do you know they were Dylan's son's trackers? They could have been Shifters from anywhere, right?"

"If they're in South Texas, Dylan knows them. Besides, you described them to perfection. There might be other Shifters who look like Spike and Connor, but there aren't any other tigers. Except me."

The note of sadness in his voice tugged at Addie. Of course, his parents would have been tigers, and he'd never spoken of them. Because they'd passed away? "No? I thought there'd be all kinds of big cat Shifters, tigers most of all."

Kendrick shook his head. "Felines tend to be mostly lions and leopards, with a few jaguars and smaller cats. There might be more tigers in the world but I don't know about them. I didn't know about that particular tiger until I met Dylan."

"He watched me pretty closely," Addie said. "Scared me a little."

"Good. You should be scared of him." Kendrick stepped to her, his hands on her arms cutting the chill. "Be a little scared, Addison. It will keep you safe."

"Maybe, but what will keep *you* safe? I want to go to this meeting with you."

Kendrick's gentling look hardened again. "No."

"Come on, Kendrick, think about it. What if Seamus turns on you? Who's going to run for help? Plus I could keep him covered with Charlie's shotgun. I know how to use one."

Kendrick growled, fingers pressing down. "The last thing I need is you waving around a firearm. Humans with guns are even more dangerous than Shifters. If I think Seamus is about to betray me, I'll . . . take care of it."

Addie stopped. "You mean you'd kill him." She let her voice go quiet. "Like you did those Shifters at the diner."

Kendrick gave her a brief nod. "If I have to."

The pain in his eyes told Addie much. He wanted this Seamus to be trustworthy, his friend, but he feared betrayal. The look of grief she'd seen when he'd thrust the sword through the other Shifter hadn't been feigned.

"You need someone you can trust to watch your back," Addie said.

"I need someone I can trust to watch my cubs," Kendrick

returned. "Looking around at all the candidates, that would be, hmm, *you*."

Addie gave him a stubborn look. "They'll be much safer inside the locked house than you will be waiting alone for a Shifter who might or might not try to hurt you."

Kendrick's brows drew down, completing his scowl. "I know that. But right now, there's no one in this world I trust to leave with my cubs. Only you, Addison Price. Not even Charlie—I don't know enough about him. I need you to keep an eye on *him* too."

"But do you know enough about me?" Addie met his gaze. "I served you pie, then I climbed onto the back of a motorcycle with you and rode away. That's it. That's all you know."

Kendrick's grip eased, and so did the harsh note in his voice. "What I know is that you're loyal and you care about the cubs, and you'll break rules if you have to in order to protect them." His look softened, and he cupped her cheek with one big hand. "I know that you love without restraint, and that you put others' needs before yours all the time, as much as you pretend you don't. I'll have to teach you how to sometimes put yourself first. I also know that, right now, I trust only you."

Addie warmed, his touch bringing a wash of fire. "You're good at flattery, I'll give you that."

"It's the truth. All of it. Please help me, Addison."

If Addison heated anymore, she'd dissolve into a puddle of goo. "You're good at looking at me with your hot green eyes and making me melt too."

Kendrick caressed her face. "Please."

"Charlie's wrong—you *are* evil."

Kendrick looked briefly puzzled, but he only pulled her closer.

His mouth was warm as it came down on hers, his eyes a flash of green before he closed them to enjoy the kiss. His hand on her cheek held her steadily, his thumb at the corner of her mouth opening her to him.

Addie's knees started to fold. She wrapped one arm around Kendrick to keep herself upright and let herself succumb.

His hand moved up her shirt—the Harley T-shirt that belonged to him. Addie loved wearing it, feeling close to him inside it. Kendrick's large palm cupped her breast, reminding her how good it had felt against her bare flesh.

His hand was hot through the fabric, the rest of his body hotter still. His hardness pressed against her abdomen, the line of it rigid and so very long. Documentaries never said Shifters were bigger than their human counterparts, but that's what rumor implied. Addie, feeling the evidence first-hand, believed it.

She slid her fingers between them and pressed the ridge inside his jeans.

A strong hand clamped around her wrist and pulled her away. Kendrick glared down at her, fire in his eyes.

"Addison. No."

Addie sent him a coy look. "No? You're the only one who can dole it out?"

His grip didn't loosen. "Touching me is very, very dangerous."

"For you or for me?"

Kendrick growled. "For both of us. Now go." He shoved her from him.

Addie took a few steps back, rubbing her wrist. "All right, all right. No need to get touchy."

Kendrick's look turned concerned. "Did I hurt you?"

"No." Addie showed him her wrist, which wasn't bruised, not even with a red mark on it. He knew how to mitigate his strength. If he ever lost it, he'd be powerfully strong. Addie shivered, but knew it was more with excitement than fear.

"I'll go look after the cubs," she said when he said nothing further. "You're right—we don't want anyone sneaking in to grab them. But the second you're done with Seamus, you *find me* and tell me you're all right. Don't make me come looking for you now, you hear?"

Kendrick spent a long time trying to get his mating frenzy under control before he picked up the sword and moved off toward the meeting place he'd designated for Seamus.

Part of his mind was rejoicing. Her deliberate stroke along his cock told him that she was willing, that she wanted it as much as he did. The other part of his mind that lived in caution stopped him. *She doesn't understand what it means to be with a Shifter.*

Sex with a Shifter could be straightforward and loving, or it could get . . . creative. Shifter women knew how to take the strength of a Shifter male. Some Shifter women only wanted to do it if both were in animal form, though Kendrick had found too much joy in human form to agree with that.

Addison in his shirt, her thick dark hair in her sloppy ponytail, made him crazy. Kendrick yearned for her, and he kept getting interrupted by Shifters stalking him, Dylan sending weird messengers, and worry that Tiger, a very perceptive Shifter, had made Addison and was even now searching for Kendrick.

One day, when his Shifters were rounded up again and safe in a new place, he would take Addie to a private room, post a guard, and not come out for days. Weeks, if necessary. He'd teach her all about Shifters and what they liked, and all about pleasure. He'd let her dark hair fall over his bare body, lick every inch of her, then hold her while she rode *him.*

He'd never want to come out, and his Shifters would tease him like hell, but it would be worth it.

Weeks wouldn't be long enough. A month or two *might* suffice.

Kendrick had debated long and hard before choosing the place to meet Seamus. He wanted to be close enough to the ranch house to get back if anyone attacked while he was away, but far enough that he could keep the house a secret if necessary.

In the end, Kendrick had chosen a place about a mile from the ranch, down a slope where the house could not be seen. This field could be reached by roads that didn't run past the ranch's entrance.

Kendrick had actually told Seamus a *different* meeting place at first, but when Seamus called now and said he was nearby, Kendrick told him the real spot. Seamus declared good-naturedly that he'd see Kendrick soon, not at all surprised or offended by Kendrick's precautions.

Open desert was one place where low ground could be good. The high ground offered no cover unless a person hunkered flat against the earth and hoped the weeds were tall enough to block him. Down in a dry wash, on the other hand, Kendrick could stand motionless in the shadows of well-clumped mesquite and keep watch.

Snakes liked it down here too. A thick-bodied diamondback came slithering through the wash, poking out its tongue to test Kendrick's scent.

Kendrick growled, letting the rumble vibrate the wash's floor. The snake snapped its tongue back in and flowed rapidly away under a cluster of rocks.

A man appeared on the horizon, striding without hurry toward the place Kendrick had told him to go. He was tall and lithe, with dark hair cut short and the sure stride of a Feline Shifter. A Collar glinted on his neck.

Kendrick's heart gladdened. He hadn't realized until this moment just how much he'd missed his trackers—Seamus's good-sense opinions, Jaycee's wicked humor, Dimitri rhapsodizing over every woman he met. Nothing could take away the comradeship that had been built over years . . . at least, Kendrick hoped not.

Seamus reached the gathering of brush Kendrick had chosen, checked his phone, and waited.

Kendrick let him stand there for a few minutes, making sure Seamus hadn't been followed or wasn't signaling anyone. Seamus only stood still, patient, unworried, knowing Kendrick would come when he was ready.

Finally, Kendrick moved from his cover and approached Seamus obliquely, staying out of sight until he was behind the other Shifter.

Seamus never turned around. He knew damn well Kendrick was there, but he only said, "Kendrick, my friend. I've missed you, ye shite."

Kendrick reached Seamus's side, and only then did Seamus turn. Kendrick's relief when he studied Seamus's steady golden eyes and saw no duplicity in them made him forget caution.

He opened his arms and enfolded Seamus into a warm embrace. Seamus's strong arms came around Kendrick's back, the welcome returned. The two men held each other close as a hot wind whipped by them, and Kendrick nuzzled Seamus's cheek.

"My friend," Kendrick said. "Damn, I've missed you."

CHAPTER FOURTEEN

Kendrick breathed Seamus's scent, letting the familiarity of it soothe his troubled soul. He'd been so afraid, so bloody afraid that Seamus would turn against him.

Kendrick drew back, hands still on the man's shoulders. "So you want to take a mate, do you?" he asked, giving Seamus a wry look. "Did I hear you say she was a Shifter groupie?"

Seamus nodded, and his cheekbones stained red. "Bree is something special, Kendrick. You'd like her."

Kendrick grinned. "Seamus, the loner; Seamus who lived to be tracker to his leader." He shook his head in mock sorrow. "I turn my back, and you pick up the closest woman and shack up with her."

"About right." The relaxed look in Seamus's eyes told Kendrick that this woman, Bree, had a calming effect on him. He'd never seen Seamus so at ease. "She saved my ass from getting caught and executed. Least I could do was mate-claim her."

"Yeah, I'm sure you had to thank her somehow." Kendrick looked Seamus over a moment, then jerked the man back into a hug.

Seamus closed his arms around Kendrick, and for a time the two men held each other, soaking in warmth and touch.

Kendrick at last made himself release Seamus and return to business. If they'd had time, they'd have shifted to their big cat forms and spent an hour or so lazing under the sun, heads together, paws resting on each other, taking comfort in each other's presence.

Kendrick flicked his fingers over the black and silver Collar around Seamus's neck. "Why are you wearing *this*?"

"It's fake," Seamus said. "Dylan asked me to put it on— okay, he pretty much demanded me to. At the time, I needed to pretend to be a Collared Shifter, or I would have been arrested."

Kendrick let out a breath. "At least it isn't real. But you look strangled in it."

"I don't like it." Seamus fingered the Collar, which didn't move. It must have been fused into his skin, like the real ones. "But it's better than being rounded up and caged. I go back and forth from Shiftertown to my girlfriend's house— this makes it easier."

"I understand. Dylan gave me a fake but leaves it up to me when to wear it. He probably knows I'd make him eat it if he didn't give me the choice."

"Dylan is . . ." Seamus trailed off, searching for the right words. Seamus had never been an eloquent man, preferring a simple and straightforward fight to conversation. Take it down first, ask questions later. ". . . complicated," Seamus finished. "You see him with his granddaughter and grandsons and think he's the most loving man ever. Then he turns around and becomes the most terrifyingly ruthless shite I've ever laid eyes on. Hot and cold."

"I noticed," Kendrick said. "I told him I was done working for him. Do you know if he got my message?"

Seamus nodded. "He's not happy with you, but understands—so he said. He'll not pursue you, if that's what you're worried about."

The knots in Kendrick's stomach loosened one strand. "Good."

"But I wouldn't write him off just yet. If he decides he

needs you, he'll come after you. I'm willing to bet he knows exactly where you are even now."

"Probably." Addison describing how she'd seen Spike and Tiger in the parking lot in San Antonio had unnerved him. Regardless of whether they'd ever seen Addison, Tiger was uncanny at putting things together and finding out who people were. Spike would follow right along with Tiger and stop at nothing to track Kendrick down.

Or so Kendrick understood. He'd met Spike and Tiger only once, as he'd told Addison—Dylan had kept Kendrick separate from the Austin Shifters. Compartmentalizing, as Ben had said.

Which reminded Kendrick . . . "So who is this Ben?" Kendrick asked.

Seamus shook his head. "I don't know much about him, but I understand the wolf leader in Las Vegas sent him. Graham—that's the wolf alpha's name—says Ben is good at what he does—too good, which is why Graham wanted him out of there."

"*What* is he?" Kendrick went on. "I've never scented anything like him. And what is it he's good at?"

"No idea. Want me to find out?"

"Discreetly. It's not top priority." He firmed his tone. "What is top priority is finding out which of my Shifters have turned on me. Are you one of them?"

Kendrick didn't change expression while he waited for the answer, and he remained standing easily, not tensing.

But he knew that in the next moment or two, he would either be embracing Seamus again or killing him. Didn't matter that Seamus now had made a mate-claim, had a new life—Kendrick's tiger wouldn't care. The Sword of the Guardian waited in case Kendrick had to send his best friend to the Summerland.

Seamus's gaze didn't waver. "No," he said quietly. "I'm loyal to you."

Shifters had difficulty lying, because scent, body language, and an indefinable sense of wrongness would alert those who were lied to. Things humans might miss screamed *false* to a Shifter. So, most Shifters didn't bother with lies.

Seamus was usually polite enough not to pin Kendrick with his gaze, making sure he in no way challenged his alpha's dominance. At this moment, though, Seamus was meeting Kendrick's eyes not so much to challenge, but to bare himself. He wanted Kendrick to see everything.

Kendrick exhaled in more relief than he had in a long time. Only tasting Addison today had given him more joy.

He dragged Seamus into another embrace, squeezing the man hard. Seamus hugged him back as robustly, and Kendrick's eyes moistened.

Kendrick eased off the hug and held Seamus at arm's length. Seamus's lion eyes were full of warmth, happiness to see Kendrick, and a spark that had been missing before.

"It is good to see you, my friend," Kendrick said, heartfelt. "Let's go home."

Addie burned with worry the whole time Kendrick was gone. She helped Charlie plan and start dinner, but she chafed at Kendrick's absence.

What if this Seamus *did* turn on him? Kendrick seemed confident he could fight the man, but the other Shifters had carried guns. What if Seamus came packing heat? Or brought others to ambush him?

Addie could only watch for Kendrick's return and try to stay calm—not easy. Robbie was just as worried, though he kept saying that of course Seamus wouldn't hurt Dad. Seamus was loyal. He spoke as though if he said the words often enough, he'd believe them.

When Addie saw Kendrick and another man come walking over the rise, she nearly wilted in relief. The second Shifter was as tall as Kendrick though not as broad of shoulder. They strode comfortably side by side, the still-bright sun glistening on Kendrick's black-and-white hair and his sword's hilt above his back.

Addie abandoned chopping carrots and raced out the door.

She was supposed to wait until Kendrick let her know for certain that all was well, but screw it. Addie couldn't be the meek little woman waiting at home for word of her man. She'd never been able to do that, which was why her idiot fiancé had dumped her. He'd even said, *You should do what I say, Addie, until I tell you otherwise. You're not respectful.*

Unfortunately most guys she'd met after that had been cast in the same mold. True, Kendrick also told her what to do, but his attitude said that he'd rely on Addie's good sense rather than unquestioning obedience.

Good sense deserted Addie now as she raced up the low hill to meet them.

Seamus—if this was Seamus—was more loose-limbed than Kendrick, and a Collar hugged his neck, a Celtic knot resting on his throat. He had black hair and eyes a shade of gold Addie had never seen on a human being before.

"Well?" Addie asked as she stopped before them. "I see you didn't kill each other. I assume he's all right?"

If Kendrick had been Addie's ex-fiancé, he'd have grown angry that Addie had left the safety of the house, would growl at her to get back to the kitchen where she belonged. Kendrick only met her gaze with one that held reassurance.

"Addison, this is Seamus McGuire, my tracker and my second. Seamus, this is Addison Price. I trust her."

The last words were said emphatically, as though imparting that if Seamus didn't also trust her, there would be a problem.

Seamus roved a thorough gaze over Addie. Not as a man might check out a woman, but as a stranger assessing another stranger. Finally Seamus gave her a formal nod.

"Nice to meet you, Addison." Seamus's accent was Scottish, Addie thought. "Kendrick has told me absolutely nothing about you."

"He's told me nothing about *you*, so we're even," Addie returned. She looked Seamus over as fully as he'd studied her. "Can we trust him?" she asked Kendrick.

She already knew the answer. Seamus wouldn't be standing next to them if Kendrick couldn't.

"Yes." Kendrick said simply. "What's for dinner?"

Addie rolled her eyes in feigned annoyance. "Men—

always thinking with your stomachs. It's going to take a little while, but I think you'll like it."

She turned her back on them and started down to the house.

Seamus and Kendrick didn't follow right away. Addie felt the weight of their stares on her, and she turned back. They were watching her, both of them with odd looks on their faces.

She had no idea what puzzled them so much, but she was sure it was a Shifter thing. She continued down into the house, where Robbie was watching out the window.

Brett and Zane tumbled out of the back door toward Kendrick and Seamus as the two approached.

"Uncle Seamus!" They chorused. Brett grabbed Seamus's leg and jumped up and down. Zane climbed Seamus as easily as he would in tiger form.

Seamus, laughing, caught them both and hoisted them into his arms. "How are you, lads?" He bounced them and gave them each a noisy kiss on the tops of their heads. "How are you holding up, Robbie? I bet it's tough having to look after this lot, including your dad."

Robbie shrugged, trying to hide how happy he was. "They mostly behave. Brett and Zane do anyway."

Brett and Zane were busy hugging Seamus, tugging at his hair, each vying for his undivided attention as they all ducked into the house.

"Where have you been, Uncle Seamus?" Brett asked on one side.

"We've been hiding," Zane said on the other.

"Isn't Addie pretty?" Brett continued. "She likes us. She's going to be our new mom!"

Addie swallowed a breath, which came out a cough. Kendrick reached out and firmly took his sons from Seamus. Seamus gave Addie an interested glance with tawny eyes that twinkled with good humor.

"Out of the mouths of babes," Seamus said.

Addie flushed. "Well, not out of the mouth of me. We need to finish helping Charlie with supper."

The younger boys wriggled out of Kendrick's grasp.

"We're having lots of meat," Brett declared, and Zane finished, "And yucky vegetables. I'm not eating *them*."

"You don't have to," Kendrick said. "Shifters are different," he said to Addie. "Different metabolism."

Seamus skipped the discussion and lifted Robbie into his arms. "How are you, little lad?"

Though Robbie tried to be more dignified than his adoptive brothers, he was still very young. He hugged Seamus with enthusiasm and laughed out loud when Seamus tossed him up in the high-ceilinged kitchen and caught him.

"So," Charlie said, looking up from the stove. "That's another for supper, is it?"

Addie was amazed how open and relaxed Kendrick was with Seamus. She watched them with a little envy while the Shifters, including the cubs, devoured the entire shank of beef in five minutes, leaving the large portion of roasted potatoes and other veggies for Charlie and Addie.

Kendrick joked and laughed with Seamus, unbending in a way he'd not yet done with Addie.

Then again, Kendrick had known Seamus for years. The man was a trusted friend. Seamus apparently was *still* a friend, and Kendrick was busy enjoying that fact.

After dinner, Kendrick suggested that Seamus walk out with him to look at the stars. Can't see the constellations stuck in a city, Kendrick said, and Seamus agreed.

They weren't going to stargaze, they were going to talk, Addie knew. She was determined to listen but she hated leaving Charlie to clean up the mess. And the cubs could sure make a mess.

Robbie pitched in and helped. Addie carried plates from the dining table in the big room to the sink but she had her eyes on the back door where the two Shifters had departed into the darkness.

After she dropped a dish, watching it shatter on the slate floor, Charlie growled to her, "Go on. You know you want to."

Addie apologized profusely, wiped her hands, and charged outside.

CHAPTER FIFTEEN

She found the two men in the dark at the top of the hill. She almost missed them—they blended so well into the night. Kendrick's ability to do so was uncanny. He could suddenly become unnoticeable, standing in perfect stillness while shadows seemed to swallow him.

Both of them were doing that now. They were also standing very close together; in fact, they were embracing. Not just a manly clasp with a few back pats, but a long, bodies-pressed-together hug.

Addie stopped, her mouth going dry. Seamus lifted his head from Kendrick's shoulder, nuzzled the bigger man's neck, then leaned into him again.

Addie couldn't look away. She'd never thought about it before, but watching two very hot men hold each other was . . . hot.

The two men must know she stood there. She hadn't tried to approach softly, and she understood by now that they'd catch her scent.

Even so, they took their time unwinding from the hug, giving each other one last nuzzle.

"I know you didn't come to eavesdrop," Kendrick said

easily, turning to her. "Join us, Addison. We have much to discuss."

Addison looked surprised to be included, but Kendrick figured it would save time. Addison would need to know what was going on, and this way he could have one conversation instead of two similar ones.

That's why I'm leader, he told himself dryly. *I'm so damned efficient.*

"I told you I'd brought my Shifters to Texas and set up in a bunker off that way." Kendrick pointed an arm to the northwest. "We fixed it up until it was a nice place to live."

"For a bunker," Seamus put in. "No windows."

"Then, as I mentioned, it was destroyed," Kendrick went on. "The Austin Shifters thought we'd abducted a young woman, when all she'd done was move into our compound with her boyfriend. And, as you know, I've been working with Dylan since then, while looking for a new place for my Shifters."

Seamus frowned at him, clearly uncomfortable with all Kendrick was revealing. But Kendrick wanted Addison to know, to understand.

Kendrick continued. "As I said, I was helping him round up feral Shifters who'd followed a leader he took down in Mexico. But lately, there's been other strange shit happening in the Shiftertowns around here. Shifters are disappearing for days, not saying where they're going or where they've been. They haven't exactly challenged their hierarchy, but they don't obey when they should. Dylan asked me to help him find out what these Shifters were doing, and to catch and interrogate them when we can."

"And what," Seamus asked slowly, "have you found out?"

"They're trying to form their own Shifter communities," Kendrick said. "Out from under the hierarchy imposed on them by the human government. Like we did." His voice took an ironic note. "Only a little less civilized. They're choosing their clan leaders based on dominance and want to run things by a council of clans."

"That doesn't sound too unreasonable," Seamus said. "Optimistic, but not unreasonable. Shifter clan leaders don't always get along."

He shot Kendrick a look. A long time ago, Kendrick had been forced to challenge another Shifter, a Lupine clan leader, for control of their group, and Kendrick had won. Kendrick had killed the other Shifter and taken over, which had been one of the hardest things he'd done in his life.

The other Shifter had been, up until his betrayal, Kendrick's closest friend. The pain of the man turning on him and forcing Kendrick to kill him had lingered for years. Still lingered.

Kendrick shook his head, pulling himself back to the present. "If it stopped at them wanting to form their own enclave, Dylan would simply keep an eye on them, maybe figure out how he could use them. But they've moved one step beyond. These Shifters want to remove their Collars, and then destroy the Collared Shifters. Shifters happy to stay under the yoke of human rule are endangering all Shifters, they say, and so must either be recruited or killed. They're trying to recruit the cubs first, because many of them now don't have Collars and never will."

"Shite," Seamus said, his slow anger rising. "Are they out of their minds?"

"Seems that way. I was able to infiltrate one of the groups, wearing a fake Collar and keeping a low profile. Unfortunately, at one meeting I saw Ivan Cranford. And he saw me."

Seamus stared at him for a few heartbeats. *"What?"*

"I evaded Ivan when I left and told Dylan I couldn't go back. I thought I'd given Ivan the slip, but next thing I knew, he was looking for me. A couple nights ago, he found me. He and his backup had guns and they opened fire. I'm guessing he meant it to look like a gang shooting—a tragedy, but nothing to do with Shifters."

"Oh, holy . . ." Seamus put his hands on top of his head and walked a few paces away.

Kendrick was aware of Addison, listening hard, her arms tightly folded as though she were cold in the hot late-May night. Her eyes were filled with horror as she realized they were talking about the Shifter she'd watched Kendrick send to dust.

Kendrick drew a long breath. "He's dead, Seamus. I killed him."

Seamus kept his back to them for a long time. He let his hands drop and looked up at the stars, which swam thick and white across the black backdrop. The night was clear, no clouds between them and the heavens.

Seamus turned around again. He didn't approach, keeping a distance between himself and Kendrick.

"Did ye give him a chance?" Seamus asked.

"Yes." Kendrick's body tightened with anger as he remembered. Ivan had aimed at Kendrick as he'd flowed out of the diner, a tiger, then cursed as Kendrick flattened himself to the ground just in time for the bullet to soar over Kendrick's head.

Then Ivan had thrown the gun aside and shifted, meeting Kendrick as his wildcat. They'd fought savagely. Kendrick, filled with the rage of a Shifter protecting his cubs, hadn't held back.

Ivan, lower in dominance than Kendrick, hadn't stood a chance. Kendrick had tried to make himself ease off, give Ivan the opportunity to surrender, but Ivan was determined to fight on. Conquer or die. Kendrick, enraged and fearing for his cubs, couldn't stop himself. He'd torn Ivan apart.

Then Ivan had *apologized* but warned Kendrick at the same time that he could expect more Shifters to fight him. Kendrick had wanted to lie down and weep after he'd sent Ivan to dust but he'd had to get his cubs to safety.

Seamus's breath came faster, sharing Kendrick's grief. Seamus flinched, as though a cramp had clenched his body, then he let out a soft sound of distress.

Kendrick went to him, his instinct as leader and Guardian to comfort him. "I gave him what chance I could."

Seamus twisted away. "No, don't touch me."

"I never meant it to go down like that," Kendrick said. "I was protecting my cubs."

He placed a hand on Seamus's arm, and Seamus jerked from him, eyes wide. "Ye don't understand. I can feel it—all ye did. Your anger, fear, grief—I *feel* it." He thumped both hands to his gut. "Ye have to back off, leave me be."

Seamus didn't explain his bewildering statements, simply pivoted and strode away. He didn't go far, stopping to throw his head back and study the stars.

Kendrick's chest tightened, his hands clenching. He didn't know what Seamus meant or how the death of Ivan would affect Seamus's loyalties to him. He couldn't lose Seamus, not after all they'd been through.

Kendrick felt a hand touch his. Addison had come to stand beside him, her fingertips on his hot fist.

"You didn't have a choice," she said quietly.

Kendrick didn't move, letting her touch ease him. "A leader pledges to protect his Shifters. That means *all* of them, regardless."

"You *were* protecting them," Addison pointed out. "Why was defending your cubs wrong?"

"If I had an easy answer, my life would be so much better," Kendrick said with grim humor. "I hurt him. That hurts me." He gestured at Seamus, who'd drawn into himself.

Addison's fingers caressed his. "You can't think that what everyone in the world does is your fault."

"Not everyone in the world," Kendrick said. "I'm not that crazy. Just people I pledged to take care of."

Another caress. "You'll figure it out," Addison said softly.

Kendrick stopped. In his dream last night, Addison had stood with him under the sky and said the same thing. *You'll figure it out. Look around you, white tiger. Live.*

Had the dream been premonition? Or his brain trying to get him to understand?

Voices floated up the hill from the house, small ones with determination only tigers could have. "They want to stargaze too," Robbie called as he walked with the younger boys toward them.

Zane stared up at Robbie in outrage. "No, *you* wanted to," he said when they reached Kendrick and Addison. "And told us we had to come with you."

Robbie flushed, but Kendrick didn't admonish him. Robbie had to give in to Zane's and Brett's needs all the time—once in a while they should give in to his. "Is Uncle Seamus all right?" Robbie asked.

Seamus straightened up and came back to them. He had a welcoming look on his face but Kendrick saw the strain.

Robbie seemed to notice the tension as well. He was perceptive, for a cub. He pointed upward. "Look, there's the Great Bear."

Addison glanced skyward, following his finger. "Ursa Major," she agreed. "I never knew it was a bear when I was little. I only knew it as the Big Dipper. And the Little Dipper over there." She pointed to the north sky.

"That's not a dipper," Robbie said, with the incredulous tone of a boy who knows something an adult doesn't. "The Great Bear is a mother bear Shifter searching for her son. When bear Shifters were first created by the Fae, a mother and her cub escaped out of Faerie into what would become America. One day, the cub went missing and the mother bear searched for him frantically. The native people of the place where she found refuge told her to look in the sky. That night, she looked up, and saw the little bear."

Robbie pointed at Ursa Minor—the little bear, Addie realized—and continued. "The mother bear leapt high, swung up on the stars, and started chasing her errant son. The Fae came boiling out of Faerie, ready to shoot them both down. The shamans of the native tribe used their magic to change the mother and son into stars. The Fae couldn't reach them and went back home. So now the mother chases the son around and around the North Star."

Robbie moved his arm to illustrate as he talked, and Addison listened, enchanted.

"It's not the story I learned," she said when he finished.

"There's all kinds of stories about the stars," Robbie said. "Dad knows them all. He told us."

Addison sent Kendrick a look. "Did he?"

Kendrick rounded up his sons. "Inside, you three. It's getting late and colder. Seamus?"

Seamus, without saying a word, started for the house. He leaned down and picked up the smaller boys on his way, and Robbie, with a hopeful look at Addison, went after them.

"I'll be in to put you to bed," Addison promised, then she turned to Kendrick. "Is he going to be all right? Seamus, I mean."

Kendrick looked after his tracker, who had reverted to his good-natured ways with the boys. "I don't know. There's something going on with him."

"Will you tell me?" Addison gazed up at him as wistfully as Robbie had. "The Shifter stories of the constellations?"

There were many—the Lovers, which humans thought of as the twins of the Gemini, the Tiger, and the Wolf Cubs. Kendrick had a tale for each of them.

"Yes," he said in a low voice. "When this is done, I'll tell you the legends of the stars."

Addison didn't answer for a time. She studied him with her clear-eyed watchfulness, then gave him a nod. "Good. I'll hold you to that."

C harlie made no comment about having to accommodate yet another Shifter in his house and had a bedroom ready for Seamus by the time Addie walked back in with Kendrick.

"Does me good to see the place so alive again," Charlie said to Addie as he bustled around with pillows and blankets.

Seamus disappeared into his room, and Addie heard him on the phone as she lingered in the hallway. Seamus was speaking in a gentle tone, obviously to someone he cared about.

"I'll be all right, sweetheart," he said. "Home as soon as I can."

His voice was so full of love that Addie's heart ached. How wonderful to have someone care that much for you that every word was a caress. She thought of her conversation with Charlie when he said that not everybody was lucky to love someone who loved them back.

Addie sighed, hid her longing, and went to put the boys to bed.

The little ones seemed happier tonight, less afraid. Uncle Seamus was here, they were safe in Charlie's house, and Addie could tell them more stories.

Addie repeated stories from the *Oz* books, which she knew by heart—the originals, not the 1939 musical. All three boys were fascinated, listening, mouths open, until they finally drooped and slept.

Addie had to wonder whether she'd be sleeping in the bed in this room or in the big bed across the hall, and whether it would be with or without Kendrick.

When she checked their bedroom, it was lit but empty, as was the living room. Charlie must have gone to bed, because he was nowhere in sight.

Addie poured herself a glass of water in the kitchen and carried it back down the hall with her. She heard voices from Seamus's room but it didn't sound like he was on the phone anymore. Kendrick's rumble answered Seamus and Addie tiptoed along the hall until she stood outside Seamus's door.

"I don't know when it started," Seamus said. "I had it all my life, maybe, and it finally was noticeable when terrible things happened."

"But terrible things have happened to us before," Kendrick said. "We've had death, outright slaughter, had to flee for our lives. Why didn't you know about it then?"

"I have no idea," Seamus said. "All I want to know is, what the hell is a Shifter empath, and how did I get this way? Dealing with it, Kendrick, has been a bitch."

CHAPTER SIXTEEN

Addie had no idea what a Shifter empath was, and her curiosity stirred. She leaned closer, listening without shame.

"Dylan didn't tell you about what happened to me?" Seamus asked.

"Dylan didn't tell me a lot of things," Kendrick said. "Not that I've actually had many conversations with him. He gave orders; I gave him information. I don't really blame him. It's tough for leaders to know who to trust."

"Yeah, I get that." Seamus's growls softened. "Thank you for trusting *me*. Now, what are we going to do?"

"Can you find Jaycee? Or Dimitri?"

"I don't know." Seamus sounded troubled. "Haven't heard from either of them since we went to ground. Of course, I've been inside a Shiftertown and both of them must think I went over to the dark side. But I'll try to find them. Francesca can help."

"Only if Francesca can get away from the Shifters. I don't want her or Katie to be hurt by this."

Amusement entered Seamus's tone. "You're not going to believe this, but the two that broke our compound—Rebecca and Walker Danielson—are pretty good people. They take care of foster cubs and help a lot of Shifters. We've become good friends."

"I might choke on the sentimentality," Kendrick rumbled. "But I'm going to trust you to know which Shifters *you* can trust. Try to get hold of this Ben guy too. Seems like he's resourceful." Kendrick paused. "Addie saw Tiger and Spike yesterday when she went into San Antonio. She said they saw her but they have no reason to connect her to me. Do they?"

Seamus whistled. "If Tiger saw her . . . He's something different, is Tiger. That might be a problem."

"Do you trust him?"

"With my life. But . . ." Seamus trailed off. "Then again, it depends. Tiger obeys only Tiger. Even Dylan can't control him. No one can, except his mate, who is half his size—it's adorable. Tiger doesn't wear a real Collar either. I mean, who would be fool enough to put one on him?"

"Hmm." Kendrick's concern touched Addie through the door. "Well, I'll worry about him when I need to. Sleep on it." He gave a laugh. "That is, if you aren't busy calling your mate again to coo at her."

"I don't coo." Seamus didn't sound the least bit embarrassed. "And Bree's a wonderful woman. You'll see."

Kendrick made another growling noise, then there was a rustle, both men going silent. Addie pictured them hugging again—they liked to do that.

Before she knew it, the doorknob was turning. Addie fled down the hall, trying to move swiftly and silently, the water in her glass sloshing over.

She made it to the bedroom but a second later, Kendrick was there, pushing her inside, rescuing the water before she dropped it.

He closed the door and leaned against it. "Never think a Shifter can't hear the softest footfall, Addison."

In the dim light cast by the lamp on the nightstand, Kendrick's face faded into shadows, but his green eyes were sharp.

Addie shrugged, trying to be nonchalant. "I was curious."

"If you want to know anything, all you have to do is ask."

Addie snorted a laugh. "Yeah, right. When you first met me, you wouldn't even tell me your name."

"I told you plenty tonight."

Addie could not decide whether Kendrick was angry or not. He remained against the door, blocking her way out but not advancing on her.

"Not everything," she countered. "What's a Shifter empath?"

Kendrick finally left the door. He went to the dresser and drew off his shirt. His firm back came into view, criss-crossed with fine white scars.

"I don't really know," Kendrick said. "Seamus says he can sense strong emotions in others, feel what they're feeling. That's why he was so upset on the hill—he caught my grief at having to kill Ivan. So he says, anyway."

"I'm sorry about that," Addie said. She remembered the deep pain in his eyes when he'd used the sword on the dying Shifter. She came to him, putting her hand on his bare arm. "You okay?"

Kendrick looked swiftly down at her. "Addison, it's best not to touch me."

Addie blinked and withdrew. "No? I was getting the idea that Shifters liked the touchy-feely stuff. Or maybe it's only Shifter guys with Shifter guys?" She sent him a sly smile.

She only meant to tease him, but Kendrick stared at her as though he had no idea what she was talking about.

"Every time you touch me, I want you more." Kendrick turned around and stepped to her. Addison had to crank her head back to keep her eyes on his face. "I want you so much it's killing me."

Addison let her hand drift to his. "Kendrick, I've probably made it obvious I don't mind." She softened her voice. "I really don't."

The snarl that worked its way from Kendrick's throat was harsh. His big hands closed over her arms, and he lifted her from her feet and carried her backward to the bed. Addie stifled a yelp, his strength powerful.

She'd thought the height of the bed would stymie him,

but Addison found herself on her back on the mattress, Kendrick on hands and knees over her.

"You tempt your fate," he said, his words soft as a whisper. "I'm not gentle, Addison. Never have been."

Addie disagreed, having seen how tenderly he held his cubs and Robbie. She recalled how careful he'd been with them when they'd played on the grass in their animal forms. He'd made sure he never hurt them.

"Tell you what," Addie said, trying to keep her voice steady. "How about we just sleep? We both need it." She stroked his arm, finding his skin hot and tight.

Kendrick leaned close, his eyes hard. "You want me to lie here with you, holding you for comfort? You think we can do something that tame? Every time I'm with you, I want you, and not in a nice way. What happened in the barn is only the barest beginning. I want you every way I can have you, and I don't want it gentle. I've only ever been with Shifter females, and they can take what I need to do. You can't. And so I'll be sleeping on the porch tonight."

Addie's eyes widened but her heart beat faster in excitement. "You have no idea the harassment I took at the diner. Most was in fun, but some of the guys were mean, and rough." She thought of a few pats on her ass that had stung, some that had been accompanied by a grip of hard fingers. "You're not like that. No matter how badass you think you are."

"Addison." Kendrick leaned closer, his body heat covering her. "You play with fire."

"Fire can be good." Addie dared put one finger to the hollow at his collarbone, touching where a Shifter Collar would be. "It warms you and cooks things."

"It can also be the most destructive thing on earth."

Kendrick's growl came again. He leaned even closer, fists tightening on either side of her head, and licked her from chin to the bridge of her nose.

His tongue was hot, his breath scalding. Kendrick came down again, this time licking across her mouth. The third time, he dipped between her parted lips, stroking inside, nudging her tongue to respond.

Addie took the weight of him, wrapping him in her arms.

She slanted her mouth across his, opening for his kiss, which was deeper than any he'd given her yet. Kendrick moved his tongue inside her mouth the same as when he'd gone down on her in the barn. The sexiest moment of her life.

This one was rivaling it. While she was clothed this time, the heat of Kendrick's bare chest through her thin shirt was intoxicating. She skimmed her hands down his smooth back, his muscles working as he strengthened the kiss. She felt his cock through his jeans as she had earlier today, his wanting clear.

Kendrick moved one hand to her shoulder, pressing down with powerful fingers. She was pinned to the mattress, Kendrick's hold not letting her move. His kiss turned hard, almost savage, Addie sinking into softness with him on top of her.

Instead of terrifying her—which was what he was trying to do—Addie felt exhilarated. She wrapped her foot around his firm calf and pulled him closer still.

Kendrick snarled and ripped his mouth from hers. His eyes had lightened, the green so pale it was almost white. He lifted his hand from her shoulder, the other off the bed. Bedding tore, the fist that had braced him having become a paw with claws.

Another snarl and he sprang away from her, landing on his feet beside the bed. "No!"

Addie grabbed the edge of the mattress and peered over it. "What's the matter?" Her breath came swiftly, the chill of his leaving sharp.

"If you have to ask . . ." Kendrick's eyes held more anger than she'd ever seen in him. His fists balled and she realized he was barely containing his shift.

Addie swallowed her impulse to reach for him again, come what may. "Are you all right?"

"No!" Kendrick swung abruptly away, grabbed a shirt out of the dresser drawer, leaving it open and askew, and headed for the door. "Stay away from me, Addison."

He opened the door and paused a moment, his head turned deliberately away from her. Then he squared his shoulders, dragged in a breath, and went out.

The *bang* of the door resounded through the house.

Addie flopped back down on the bed, hugging her arms over her chest. Her heart was pounding, her blood hot, her body still feeling his weight, the imprint of his hand, the sensation of his mouth.

I want you every way I can have you, and I don't want it gentle.

Addie let out a sound between a sigh and a growl. *I don't want it gentle, either*, she longed to call after him. *I just want it to be with you.*

Addie was up early the next morning, after a night of fitful sleep. She got out of bed at dawn, showered, dressed, and walked out the front door, nearly tripping on a large white tiger who was stretched across the front porch, sound asleep.

The tiger blinked open his eyes when she stopped short, then he gave her a baleful green stare.

Addie pressed her hands to her chest. "So sorry to disturb his majesty. Oh, no, wait, it's the *lion* that's king of the beasts."

She enjoyed Kendrick's irritated growl for a few seconds, before her words shot back down her throat. A full-grown male lion with a thick black mane emerged from around the corner of the house and started up the porch steps.

Addie's mouth went dry, and then she saw his eyes—golden-tawny and full of good humor. "Seamus?"

The lion gave her a little huffing bark, walked well around Kendrick, and butted his head into Addie's side.

A thrill went through her as the huge, ferocious lion bumped her with affection, and again when her hand stroked his wiry, warm mane. At least not all Shifters were afraid to let her touch them.

Kendrick heaved himself to his feet and faced Seamus, his eyes narrowing. Seamus continued to lean against Addie, rumbling in enjoyment as Addie scratched under his mane.

From Kendrick's throat came the grating sound of a tiger's long growl, a noise that would send terror through the jungle. Seamus met Kendrick's gaze, unimpressed.

Leisurely, he stepped away from Addie, shook himself out, yawned, then strolled off the porch again, sauntering away.

Addie found herself smiling in delight, her face aching with it. She wanted to laugh, and when Kendrick turned a look of fury on her, Addie couldn't help herself. She let the laugh come out.

"The look on your face," she said, pointing at Kendrick's great, beautiful tiger visage, with his black stripes on snow white, his eyes luminous green. "It's priceless."

The tiger began to distort, and in a few seconds, Addie's laugh choked off. Before her stood not a man or a tiger, but a half man, half tiger. White tiger's fur spread over the steel-muscled armature of a man, the face Kendrick's but with fur, tiger ears, and the teeth of a beast. His hands ended in claws, dark and sharp.

"He defies me." Kendrick's voice was guttural.

"He's giving you a hard time," Addie said, trying to hide her nervousness. "I heard him on the phone with his girl-friend. It's painfully obvious how much he loves her."

The tiger-beast-man rippled, the fur flowing away, Kendrick shrinking down to be Kendrick-sized again. He was completely naked, the morning sun kissing his skin.

"He's never defied me," Kendrick said, now sounding confused. "Not even as a joke."

"People change. Seamus is madly in love with this woman, and he lives with her now, right? Wouldn't that make him different?"

Addie saw him turn these thoughts over in his head, uncertain. "Yes," he conceded.

Addie resisted the urge to reach a comforting hand to him. She liked that Kendrick stood here before her, bare and unashamed. If last night were anything to go by, touching him would make him retreat and run.

"Breakfast?" she suggested instead. "I'll cook this morning and give Charlie a break. I make a mean pancake."

"Pancakes!" Small voices chorused inside the house.

The three cubs pressed against the front window, not in the least surprised to see their father standing naked on the porch, facing Addie.

Addie gave them a shaky wave. "Probably you should get dressed," she said to Kendrick, as though every inch of his body didn't make her hot all over. She gave him an encouraging smile then made herself stroll, as leisurely as Seamus had, into the house.

Kendrick ate breakfast at the far end of the table, trying not to watch Addison's warm eyes as she conversed easily with Seamus, Charlie, and the boys.

He burned for her, and nothing was going to be simple. Addison was right that Seamus had been teasing the hell out of him by nuzzling her this morning. Seamus would have sensed Kendrick's need for Addison and decided to play with him a little—Kendrick hadn't exactly hidden his interest.

If Kendrick kept Addison at arm's length and focused on the problems at hand, he'd be fine, he told himself. *Yeah, and snakes will sprout wings and fly.*

His resolve went out the window as soon as Addison laughed out loud at something Charlie said. She was like sparks from a firework, filling the space with beauty and heat.

Kendrick could easily solve the problem by sending her away. He didn't believe she'd instantly send the police and Shifter Bureau out here to arrest them all, though his trackers like Jaycee and Francesca would tell him he was thinking with his hormones.

The thought of Addison being out there in the bad world, though, where he couldn't reach her and protect her, was anathema. She was staying. Kendrick would just have to deal with his mating frenzy.

Like he'd dealt with it so well last night. The only reason Kendrick had come to his senses and gotten away from her was because he'd started to shift while he kissed her. Terrified he'd hurt her, he'd forced himself off the bed and gotten the hell out of there.

He'd spent the night on the porch, as a tiger, too hot and needy. And crabby as hell when he woke up. Seeing Seamus nuzzling her had been too much.

Seamus left after breakfast, though. Kendrick held himself in check to take Seamus aside and talk with him a moment, leader to tracker, laying plans.

Seamus then said good-bye to the cubs and Charlie, and approached Addison, enfolding her in a hug right in front of Kendrick. When Kendrick growled, Seamus released her and shot him a grin.

"Keep it together," Seamus said to him. "Or go for it. I guarantee, it's better to give in."

Kendrick only growled again. Seamus, laughing, walked out to the dusty little pickup he'd driven here. The truck didn't look like much but its motor hummed with smooth efficiency when Seamus started it up. He raised his hand in farewell, the cubs excitedly waving back to him.

He was gone. Now all Kendrick could do was wait and keep himself away from Addison.

Addison made it easy for him by plunging seriously into her nanny duties. She had the boys washed, helped them clean up their room, then helped Charlie in the rest of the house.

Kendrick followed her example and went around fixing numerous things that needed repair in the basement, barn, and sheds around the property. When he returned, Addison was baking pies.

The smell of warm baking filled the kitchen, fruit pies from the fresh berries Addison had found in town—blueberry, blackberry, strawberry. Odors wafted from the oven and lingered in the house.

They ate the pie after dinner that night, the only time Kendrick allowed himself to sit down with Addie near. The blackberry pie melted on his tongue, the crust crisp and tangy.

"These are better than the pies at the diner," Brett said. He looked perplexed. "How can that be?"

"Homemade is always better," Addison said, her fork loaded with blueberry pie. "That is, when you have a big kitchen and lots of good ingredients."

And a fine cook, Kendrick thought but didn't say.

"My mom could cook," Robbie said.

Kendrick's gaze shot to him. Robbie rarely mentioned

his family, not at all if he could help it. The fact that he volunteered the information meant . . . something, though Kendrick wasn't sure what. He was a Shifter leader, not a psychologist.

Robbie said nothing more, only went back to eviscerating his pieces of pie.

"More of my friends might be here soon," Kendrick said to Addison abruptly. *If I'm lucky.* "Jaycee can be . . . forthright. Go easy on Dimitri—he has a speech impediment and is shy around people he doesn't know."

"He stammers a little," Zane said. "But when you get to know him, you don't notice. Is Dimitri really coming, Dad? When?"

"I don't know, son." Kendrick's blackberry pie suddenly tasted like dust. "I told Seamus to put the word out. We just have to wait."

"I hate waiting," Zane said.

So did Kendrick, but he didn't have much choice. Waiting was always the price when un-Collared Shifters did anything in the human world. They had to not hurry and keep silence.

Kendrick spent another night walking the bounds and sleeping on the porch to keep himself from Addison. She again busied herself with the cubs, as though doing her best to keep from *him*. He wasn't sure he liked that.

He did, however, enjoy being able to sleep out of doors in his tiger form, something he couldn't do when they lived in the compound. He was starting to truly like this place.

At dawn he was dragged out of sleep by the scent of another Shifter screaming into his brain. Kendrick was on his feet, snarling, even as he recognized the scent.

Jaycee Bordeaux, in human form, sprang from the shadows of shrubs below the porch and landed on the railing with the grace of her leopard.

"Psych!" she said. "Never thought I'd catch you napping, Kendrick."

Kendrick remained where he was, waiting, as he had done with Seamus, to see whether she had turned against him.

Jaycee, who had plumpness and strength at the same

time, leapt down from the railing and threw her arms around his neck without inhibition. "Damn, it's good to see you, Kendrick. If I didn't want to just hang on to you and cry, I'd ask you for a shag."

"Figures," said another voice. A tall man with short red hair and the dark gray eyes of a wolf, who'd climbed leisurely off a motorcycle, walked up to the porch. He spread his arms. "Dimitri's here. Time to s-start the . . . party."

CHAPTER SEVENTEEN

Addie heard the rumble of the motorcycle that stopped in front of the house. She grabbed a robe and hurried to the big living room.

On the porch was Kendrick, as a tiger, with a red-haired man and a woman with golden hair and brown eyes hugging him and crooning over him. Kendrick rolled onto his side, not objecting to them holding and petting him. The woman was busy covering his face with kisses.

"Uncle Dimitri!" The shriek came from Zane, who shot out past Addie before she could stop him. Hard on his heels was Brett, and then Robbie.

"There's my b-boys." Dimitri rolled to his feet and caught the little tigers in his arms.

For Robbie, Dimitri leaned down and growled at him. Robbie put his hands on his hips and growled right back. Then Robbie broke off and started laughing. Addie hadn't heard such merriment from him before. He sounded like a normal, delighted little boy.

"I missed you!" Robbie yelled up at him. "Addie, come and meet Uncle Dimitri! And Aunt Jaycee!"

Addie stepped out onto the porch, very aware she was in a robe with her uncombed hair hanging every which way. She smoothed the hair out of her face and found herself pinned by the stares of the new Shifters.

Dimitri gazed at her in open appreciation. "Who's this b-beautiful thing? Don't worry, baby, my stutter goes away when I'm wolf, and *howlin'*." His words were softened by the warm wink he gave her.

"Goddess, do you have a hose?" Jaycee gave Dimitri a disgusted glance and turned her gaze back to Addie. Jaycee sniffed delicately, then a sharp, jealous light entered her eyes.

Oh, great. She's in love with Kendrick, Addie realized. Addie might not be Shifter, but she recognized when another woman coveted a man. *That makes me her new enemy.*

Well, Addie would have to show Jaycee that she had nothing to worry about. Kendrick had made it plain he wanted to keep Addie away from him. Or, she'd have to fight the woman to the death. Looking at the curvaceous but tough body on Jaycee, Addie didn't have much confidence in her chances.

"All right, who's hungry?" Addie asked, pretending she was neatly dressed and coiffed. "Charlie and I are making lots of pancakes today."

"Woo-hoo!" Brett yelled, jumping straight from Dimitri's arm to the porch floor. "Addie makes great pancakes. Can I have pie too?"

Without waiting for the answer, he raced inside, followed by Zane, who scrambled down from Dimitri, and then Robbie.

Jaycee put her hand on one hip. She wore a tight red tank top, equally tight black bicycle pants, and sneakers, as though she'd been jogging when called to meet up with Kendrick.

Jaycee looked Addie up and down but spoke to Kendrick. "Is she for real? What did you do, Kendrick, hire a Mary Sue human housekeeper? And why?"

Dimitri lost his infectious grin. "Hey now, she looks f-fine to me."

Addie decided she needed to stand her ground right away. "Watch who you're calling a Mary Sue, sweetie."

Kendrick's reaction was to rise slowly to his feet, face Jaycee, fix her with his green stare, and snarl. His nose wrinkled with the rumbling, his body stiff, eyes full of anger.

Jaycee's hand came off her hip, her face went pale, and she jerked back as though she'd been slapped. "Kendrick, I was just . . ."

Kendrick let out a full-throated roar, and Jaycee's tawny-brown eyes filled with tears. "I'm sorry."

"You sh-should be apologizing to *her*, not him," Dimitri said.

Jaycee flicked her gaze to Addie, the misery in it so great Addie's irritation turned to sympathy. "Sorry," Jaycee said, her voice sharp.

Addie waved her hand and spoke lightly. "Forget it. Come on in and have breakfast."

Jaycee drew a long breath, which pushed her ample bosom high. "Sure. You have meat?"

"Sausage and bacon. Plenty for carnivores." Addie turned away and went into the house, breathing a sigh of relief at the cool interior. The porch had heated up in more ways than one.

A touch on her arm stopped her, and Addie looked into Dimitri's handsome face. He had very nice eyes, dark gray and full of depth.

"D-don't mind Jaycee. She's just intense."

"I see that." Addie led the way to the big table in the front room. "Since you're first in, you get to pick where to sit."

Dimitri's grin returned. "Next to you, sweet babe."

No stammering at all that time. His look was warm, his interest apparent.

"I see what she means about a hose," Addie said. "Sit down over there." She pointed. "You can make sure the cubs don't spill anything."

Breakfast commenced without much problem. Kendrick disappeared into the bedroom, then reappeared in human form, dressed. He squeezed the shoulders of Jaycee and Dimitri as he passed them, and both Shifters visibly relaxed.

They need him, Addie realized. *The way they have to keep looking at him—it's like they've been incomplete without him.*

She wasn't sure how the two new Shifters would view her. Jaycee was already wary, angry that Kendrick had brought Addie into the fold. Dimitri, whose last name was Kashnikov, seemed friendly enough, but even he kept a cautious eye on Addison and Charlie.

The cubs were oblivious to any tension and ate heartily. Jaycee and Dimitri put away plenty of food, Jaycee making no secret of her vast appetite. As much as Addie knew she'd have problems with Jaycee, it was nice to share a table with a woman who didn't say, *No, I shouldn't eat that, it goes right to my hips*; or *Nothing for me, I'll be fine* while staring hungrily at the two bites of lettuce on her plate.

After breakfast, Addie as usual started to help Charlie clean up. She found the plates she'd picked up taken out of her hands by Dimitri.

"We'll d-do that, sweetie. It's our job."

Addie let him take the dishes, surprised. "You do the housework for Kendrick? What are you, his maid?"

Dimitri's chuckle vibrated in his throat. "Ain't you c-cute. A tracker's job is to help the leader, in any way p-possible."

Jaycee hadn't said a word but simply started carrying plates and bowls to the sink, moving Charlie out of the way to wash them.

"No offense, you two, but you're human," Jaycee said, mostly to Charlie. "*We* look after Kendrick. We do the stupid shit so he doesn't have to worry about it. He has more important things on his mind."

Addie watched them a moment, knowing she should not feel offended that someone else wanted to do the dishes. She should hand them the dirty plates and run. It was the *way* Jaycee took over that was offensive, she decided.

"I didn't notice Seamus rushing for kitchen duty," Addie pointed out.

Dimitri, who seemed to find everything funny, gave another chuckle. "Seamus is high on the d-dominance scale. Not much below Kendrick. He and Kendrick f-focus on large-scale plans. Jaycee and me t-take out the garbage."

"In more ways than one," Jaycee said, adding a snicker.

Charlie folded his arms and leaned against the counter. "Fine, but you be careful with them dishes. My wife spent a long time putting together that set."

"No one's more adept than a Shifter, old-timer," Jaycee said. "Don't you worry."

Charlie did not like being called *old-timer*, that was apparent. He shot a glance at Addie but jerked his chin in a gesture that told her to go.

Kendrick had disappeared again and so hadn't been around for the conversation. The cubs had moved to the wide front porch, the morning nice, playing with the toys Addie had bought for them at the discount store.

She sank down on a chair to watch them. "Where's your dad?"

Robbie shrugged. "Around. It's okay. Dimitri and Jaycee are here to watch us."

"Do they watch you a lot?"

"They take care of Dad," Robbie said. "So does Seamus, but in a different way. The three of them are—what does Dad call it? His inner circle."

"I see."

Addie sank into silence. Robbie, after giving her a puzzled look, went back to playing with the cubs.

Kendrick seemed to be surrounded by people who'd do anything for him. Even Robbie readily looked after the two younger boys so Kendrick wouldn't have to worry so much. Seamus had come charging out here as soon as Kendrick called to him, and so had Dimitri and Jaycee.

Addie thought about the embraces each of the trackers had exchanged with Kendrick, the nuzzling, the blatant demonstrations of affection. She wondered whether Jaycee leapt into Kendrick's bed every time he needed to work off some tension. She'd certainly intimated that she was willing.

All three Shifters had given Addie assessing stares, wondering how she fit into Kendrick's world. *Temporary aberration? Lover? Babysitter?* Seamus had been kinder, but Seamus was now in love with a human woman and likely understood better. Not that Addie herself knew what she was to Kendrick.

Dimitri bounded out onto the porch, evidently done with kitchen work. The cubs greeted him with glee.

"Uncle Dimitri—will you play big bad wolf for us?" Robbie asked him.

Dimitri growled. "I'm already a b-big . . ." He struggled with the next word, and gave up. "Wolf. Mean." He curled his fingers like claws.

The cubs laughed. "Do it, Uncle Dimitri."

Dimitri glanced at Addie and actually blushed. "C-can't be s-stripping down in front of Addie."

"Addie can turn around," Brett said. "Come on, Uncle Dimitri."

Addie rose. "I'll go inside. Just be careful."

All three boys cheered. They started chanting *Big Bad Wolf, Big Bad Wolf.*

Addie closed the front door, shutting herself into the dim interior. A few moments later, she heard vicious snarls, and quickly opened the door again.

A huge wolf stood on the porch. Its coat was not the gray or black she expected but a deep shade of red-brown. Dimitri had lowered himself to his belly, and was stalking the cubs, his ears flat, growls coming from his mouth. The boys were pretending to be afraid—Brett and Zane had become tiger cubs, but Robbie remained a boy, scrambling out of the way to come around behind Dimitri and pull his tail.

Dimitri howled in feigned outrage, saw Addie watching, and winked at her.

Addie bit back a laugh and decided to leave them to it.

She left the living room for the back, to make sure the cubs' room had been put to rights this morning. As she entered the hall, she saw Jaycee just going into the bedroom Addie was more or less sharing with Kendrick.

Addie hurried in behind her. Jaycee had halted in the

middle of the room and was looking around with her quick eyes.

"Hey," Addie said before the other woman could speak. "I've heard Shifters have a thing about territory. Well, this is mine."

Jaycee turned around and gave her a big, false smile. "And that's fine. I'm just getting the lay of the land. But Kendrick can't stay in here with you. Not safe."

"I think that's Kendrick's choice," Addie said stiffly.

"You're wrong about that." Jaycee looked her over. "We're Kendrick's seconds, his trackers, his bodyguards. He doesn't need human scent all over him. If he wants a quick release with you, that's okay, but unless he's crazy enough to mate-claim a human—and we'd do our best to talk him out of it—he can't cozy up to you. Too dangerous. Trust me, I've been keeping our guy out of danger for years."

"I see. How about when your compound was destroyed?" Addie said, angry.

Jaycee's condescending but tolerant look vanished. She zipped across the room before Addie could blink, grabbed Addie by the throat, and pinned her against the nearest wall.

"How do you know about that?"

"Kendrick told me," Addie said, or tried to say. Hard to talk with a hand squeezing her windpipe.

"He didn't tell you the whole of it—he never will. We were taken by surprise, we fought like hell, and then we followed protocol. We laid low until he summoned us. Well, now he's called us, and *we* take care of him, honey. Get that through your pretty head."

Jaycee shook Addie, not enough to hurt, but enough to tap her head against the wall. Jaycee released her, strode back to the dresser, and resumed pulling Kendrick's clothes out of the drawer.

Addie rubbed her throat. "You don't have to bother with that. I'll take mine out, instead."

Jaycee, her hands full of Kendrick's T-shirts, stopped, nodded, and put the shirts back into the drawer—neatly.

"That's a better solution. Find a small bedroom away from the rest of us. Don't worry, sweetie, I don't sleep with

Kendrick without his permission. If he wants *you*, he'll come to you."

Addie fetched the small tote bag she'd bought in San Antonio, stepped past Jaycee, and started putting her new clothes into it. She didn't say a word, because she knew she'd only start a knock-down, drag-out girl fight, and she was realistic enough to know she couldn't win. The strength in Jaycee's hand around Addie's throat, even with the woman holding back, had told Addie that.

Jaycee moved to the high bed and began to strip off its sheets. "No offense, honey, but I have to wash these. Too much human scent."

"Oh, you go right ahead," Addie said brightly. "I understand."

Jaycee nodded. "Good. I know it's hard for humans when they first come to us, but you'll catch on."

I'd bitch-slap her if I thought I could land it before she broke my arm. Addie swallowed her rage, picked up her tote bag with a jerk, and stalked out of the room.

She found Charlie in the kitchen doing a final cleanup. The dishwasher was running, humming and filling the room with the scent of soap.

"Charlie, will you give me a ride?" Addie asked.

Charlie tossed a last towel into the washing machine in the laundry alcove and returned to her. "Sure thing. Where do you want to go?"

"Home. It's in Loneview."

Charlie's face fell. "Aw, honey, you aren't going to leave me out here with all these Shifters are you?"

Why, when Charlie said *honey* did Addie feel warmed, but when Jaycee said it, Addie bristled and wanted to smack her?

"It's time for me to go. Dimitri is looking after the kids, Jaycee wants to clean every trace of me out of the house, and I shouldn't leave my sister to cope on her own. I think it will be safe enough now for me to go back." She'd find a real lawyer and ask Bo to vouch for her if the police went back to accusing her of abetting the shooting. She'd make them realize she had nothing to do with it.

Charlie shook his head. "I don't think you should run just because that woman is giving you a hard time. Stand your ground."

"It's not that." Addie drew a breath, surprised how much her chest hurt. "If I stay, I *will* stand my ground, and she'll break every bone in my body. I need to get away and think."

Charlie studied her, then gave a conceding nod. "I get it. You'd fight for him but you don't want to have to."

"I don't know *what* I'm feeling. That's why I need to just . . . go."

"Maybe you should talk to Kendrick first."

Addie hesitated. She'd been geared up to run, but Charlie was right. She should at least tell Kendrick to his face what she wanted to do instead of simply disappearing.

Plus, she could watch his reaction and see whether he really wanted her to stay or go. Men went on about not understanding women when *they* were harder to figure out than differential calculus.

"Where is Kendrick?"

Charlie shook his head. "That, I do not know. I saw him go up toward the barn, but that was right after breakfast."

"Thanks, Charlie." Addie slung the tote's long strap onto her shoulder and went out the back door.

Kendrick wasn't in the barn. The mare had been turned out into the large open corral behind it and was enjoying herself running around, but Kendrick was nowhere in sight.

Grinding her teeth, Addie headed back down the slope toward where Charlie kept his truck at the end of the long drive. She'd sit in the pickup and wait for Kendrick to return from wherever he'd gone, but she wasn't going back into the house. Not with Jaycee busy trying to eradicate Addie's scent from every inch of it.

As she went around the truck to the passenger door, a gigantic Bengal tiger shot out from the shadows of the tall cottonwoods and came right for her.

CHAPTER EIGHTEEN

Addie was too stunned to even scream. The tiger was orange and black, had intense, golden eyes, was larger than any animal she'd ever seen, and had her cornered against the truck in a heartbeat. Sunlight glinted from a silver and black Collar around its neck.

"Good tiger," Addie said. "Nice kitty."

The tiger's eyes narrowed but it didn't move. Addie reached for the door handle of the truck.

Instantly the tiger's heavy paw was on her hand. No claws, but Addie wasn't going to touch the truck anytime soon.

. . . There aren't any other tigers, Kendrick had said. Just the one she'd seen in the parking lot in San Antonio.

"How the *hell* did you find me?" she asked him.

The tiger growled again, but before it could finish, a black and white streak flashed around the pickup, and a white tiger bowled into the orange one. Both tigers went down in an explosion of dust.

Addie flung her tote bag through the open window of the truck and turned to face the snarling ball of teeth, claws, and striped fur. What she thought she could do, she didn't know, but just standing there wasn't going to cut it.

She turned around, cupped her hands over her mouth, and shouted, "Dimitri!"

Addie didn't need to bother yelling for him, she realized a moment later, because the red wolf was already charging down the hill, followed by the smaller, faster missile of a leopard. Both Dimitri and Jaycee hit the hindquarters of the orange tiger, whose roar rattled the truck's windows.

Kendrick was fighting hard, giant paws batting, huge mouth opening, ears back, snarls unceasing. The red wolf bit down on one of the Bengal's back legs, and the Bengal shook him off so hard Dimitri went tumbling. The leopard—Jaycee—darted in, her moves quick and precise.

But the Bengal was fast. He whipped around, swatted Jaycee aside, and returned instantly to battle Kendrick, giving him no time to take advantage of the distraction.

Dimitri gathered himself and tried again, this time aiming to land on the Bengal's back. Again, the orange tiger whipped around in a lightning-swift move, smacked Dimitri out of the way, and swung back to Kendrick. Dimitri fell to the dirt, landing hard. He tried to get to his feet, but collapsed with a whimper. Jaycee, who'd leapt at the tiger while he'd batted Dimitri, was hit with a giant paw, and went down.

Just as Addie started to go to her and Dimitri, the Bengal managed to throw off Kendrick and get around him to lope toward the house.

The cubs were up there. Addie started running for the porch, Kendrick ahead of her. Behind her, she heard Dimitri yelp again, nothing at all from Jaycee.

Kendrick was one stride behind the Bengal but couldn't catch him. The only reason Addie reached the porch first was that the Bengal stopped suddenly at the bottom of the steps, and Addie let her momentum carry her around both tigers.

"No!" she yelled. She stretched out her arms shielding the boys—who had all shifted—from the threat of the Bengal.

Addie knew she was completely useless. The tiger could fling her aside as easily as he had Dimitri and Jaycee—even more so.

The cubs and the wolf pup had crowded onto the porch

swing, watching with wide eyes. Kendrick used the Bengal's sudden stillness to land on top of him.

But the orange tiger, instead of spinning to fight, dropped to his belly. He extended his front paws, lowered his head, and huffed through his mouth.

Addie came down one step. "Kendrick, stop!"

Kendrick held himself back from bringing his open jaws down on the tiger's neck, but he kept his chest on the Bengal's back, pinning him.

The Bengal huffed again. Brett and Zane peeked down at him, then to Addie's astonishment, they half jumped, half fell from the swing and padded down to the orange tiger. Robbie as wolf followed more cautiously.

The Bengal did nothing. Brett, the bolder of the boys, touched one tiny white paw to the Bengal's giant one.

The Bengal let out another breath. Brett touched his nose, his green eyes full of interest.

"He's not going to hurt them," Addie said softly.

She didn't know how she sensed that. A part of her knew that the Bengal could be playing possum in order to snap his mouth over the vulnerable cubs, but Addie for some reason didn't believe that. The tiger had stopped his charge, had ceased fighting altogether, because he'd seen the cubs.

Kendrick very slowly eased himself from the Bengal's back. The Bengal remained still, doing nothing even when Brett bit his ear. Zane, encouraged by his brother's daring, tapped the Bengal's front paw.

Kendrick shifted into his human form, standing up slowly. "Tiger," he said, his voice gravelly rough. "What the fuck are you doing here?"

Jaycee, Kendrick saw when his trackers staggered to the porch, had only been winded—heavily so—but Dimitri had a broken wrist.

Kendrick remained standing over Tiger, his arms folded, while his cubs, growing evermore courageous, started crawling on him. Tiger raised his head and Kendrick tensed, but Tiger only met Kendrick's gaze without hostility.

Won't hurt them, Tiger was saying, in tiger. *Protect the cubs.*

"Get the hell away from them!" Jaycee came panting up, clutching her bare stomach. "Damn it, Kendrick, what are you doing?"

"Leave it alone," Kendrick snapped.

Kendrick was an alpha Shifter, a massive tiger, for the Goddess's sake, and neither he nor his crack team had been able to stop Tiger rushing for his cubs. Only Addison had managed to put herself in front of them, to try to keep the giant Bengal from the little ones.

A stupid move. Kendrick glared at Addison. Tiger could have killed her—easily.

Addison scowled right back at him. "This is the Shifter I saw, right? In San Antonio?"

Kendrick gave her a nod. Jaycee said angrily, "You mean she led him to us? He's Collared, Kendrick. We're screwed, because of her. What were you thinking? No humans are supposed to enter our territory until they're thoroughly vetted. Who made that rule? Oh, yeah. *You.*"

While this was true, Kendrick's temper frayed. "Addison is under my protection, and when the hell did you start questioning my judgment?"

"When you started thinking with your gonads," Jaycee snapped. "This is another thing trackers are supposed to do—point out when you're being an idiot."

Kendrick snarled at her. If she'd kept her leopard form, he'd have swatted her across the weed-choked lawn. As it was, he kept his admonishment a very loud growl.

Addison let out an exasperated breath. "Screw this. Charlie, can I get that ride now? You come with us, Dimitri. You need a hospital."

Dimitri hobbled toward them, cradling his arm, muttering in Russian. He never spoke Russian unless he was furiously angry or in serious pain. The man who conversed in fluent English without an accent couldn't remember a word of English in extreme circumstances. He didn't stammer when he spoke Russian either.

Charlie had come around the house to watch from a safe

distance. Now he averted his eyes from Jaycee's very full breasts and kept them on Dimitri's broken arm.

"I'll get you some pants," he said to Dimitri.

"He's not going anywhere," Kendrick broke in. "I'll treat him, and he'll be fine. Shifters heal fast." In fact, if Kendrick didn't set the arm very quickly, it would heal wrong and have to be re-broken by the end of the day. "Dimitri, come here."

Dimitri moved to him obediently, still cursing in Russian. Jaycee put her hands on her thighs, breathing hard.

Dimitri shouldn't have shifted—bones were different in each shape, and he might have caused more damage. Kendrick felt the arm, finding the pieces that moved. A clean break at least. He'd be fine by tomorrow.

"Charlie, do you have any bandages?" Kendrick asked. "A splint would be even better, but I'll take what you have."

"Lemme see." Charlie went, in his limping trot, around to the back of the house—not past the tiger lounging on the steps.

Kendrick caressed Dimitri's arm. "I'll do it quickly."

Dimitri nodded. He knew what was coming, but he gave Kendrick a stoic look.

Kendrick kneaded Dimitri's shoulder and then neck, trying to loosen him, send reassurance. But it would hurt, and any painkiller Charlie might have, short of a hefty dose of tranquilizer, wouldn't help.

Addison watched anxiously, dividing her attention between them and Tiger. Kendrick dimly wondered where she was asking Charlie to take her, but first things first.

He put firm hands on Dimitri's arm, waited until Dimitri steeled himself, and then snapped the bones back into place.

Dimitri yelled once, then let the yell cut off to be replaced with snarls. No words this time, just noise.

Charlie came hurrying with bandages and a sling. Kendrick had Charlie hold them while he quickly and competently wrapped Dimitri's arm. He'd done this kind of thing before—setting breaks, sewing up shallow wounds, removing bullets and pellets from Shifters who ran into hunters. Trackers had their jobs; Kendrick had his.

Dimitri's face was chalk white, moisture in his eyes, but he bore up, letting Kendrick settle his arm in the sling.

"You keep it still all day, even when it feels better," Kendrick admonished. "*Perfectly* still, you got that?"

"Sir, yes, sir," Dimitri said, his voice barely above a whisper. Apparently, he remembered English again. "H-hey, Addie, wanna play n-nurse?"

"He's all right," Jaycee said, her usual robustness dimmed.

"Good," Addison said. "Now what are you going to do about the tiger on the porch steps?"

She had a point. Kendrick approached, lifted a protesting Brett from Tiger's back, and nudged the Bengal with his foot. "You need to talk to me."

Tiger glanced up at him, worry in his tawny eyes. *She was trying to leave. She must stay.*

Kendrick didn't need to ask who he meant. His gaze shot to Addison. "Where were you thinking to go?"

She gave him a stubborn look. "Home. Only I didn't want to make a big production of it. Obviously, that ship has sailed."

"Why?" Kendrick asked, but he was drowned out by his sons who swarmed off Tiger and made for Addison. They clung to her legs, the little tigers' mewling shrill. Robbie sat down and howled.

"You can't leave the cubs," Kendrick said firmly. At the same time, he wanted to howl too. The thought of her going, and him discovering her absence too late, made a hole open up inside him. "You volunteered to help with them, remember?"

"You have plenty of people to take care of them now," Addison said. "I came along to make sure they were all right, and they are."

"Dimitri's down for a bit," Kendrick continued. Dimitri gestured at his sling, agreeing. "I need you here." Kendrick turned his head and scowled at Jaycee. "Jaycee, why didn't you tell me she was trying to leave? You were supposed to be watching out for her."

Jaycee flicked a hard glance at Addison. Addison returned the look neutrally.

Jaycee swallowed. "It's my fault," she said in a quiet voice. "I told—"

"No, it isn't," Addison broke in quickly. "I'm feeling bad about leaving my sister alone, that's all. I knew I couldn't stay here forever."

"Why?" Kendrick demanded. "Why can't you stay?" Robbie's wolf howls increased, an eardrum-piercing pitch.

Addison shouted over them. "Why? Because I have a life."

"The life where you work low-paying waitress jobs, go home, get up, and start all over again?" Kendrick snarled. "That's what you told me."

"Don't throw that back at me." Addison pointed her forefinger at him. "It's a better life than many people get. Plus I love my sister and kids, and they need me."

"*I* need you." Kendrick moved swiftly to her. "Get that through your head, Addison. Grab your things out of Charlie's truck and put them back in our room."

Addison didn't move, except to lower her hand. "And if I choose not to?" she asked.

"You. Can't. Choose. Not to." The words jerked out of Kendrick, his desperation growing. He couldn't let her out of his sight, and he couldn't safely be around her either. This was going to kill him.

"Way to woo a girl, Kendrick," Addison said, sparks in her eyes. "Who can resist commands and an implication that she's slow on the uptake?"

"What?" Kendrick had no idea what she was talking about. Addison belonged with him, the cubs loved her, he needed her, end of discussion. Why Dimitri looked like he wanted to burst out laughing, Kendrick didn't know. A second ago Dimitri had been tight with pain.

Jaycee, on the other hand, looked ashamed. Kendrick didn't know the why of that either. In fact, the only being in this group who didn't look tense was Tiger.

"Fine," Kendrick said, his voice hardening. "I'll woo you. Addison Price, under the light of the Father God and in front of witnesses, I claim you as mate."

CHAPTER NINETEEN

"*What?*" Jaycee's shriek jangled Addie's nerves worse than Robbie's howls—which had cut off abruptly as soon as his foster father had said the words, *I claim you as mate*. "Kendrick, you can't!" Jaycee cried.

Zane started yowling again, and Brett morphed to human and threw his fists in the air. "*Yesss!* I told you she was going to be our new mom!"

Addie waved her hands. "Hold on a sec, hold on a sec. I have no idea what that all means."

Dimitri boomed a laugh. "He mate-claimed you, sw-sweetie. This is awesome."

Addie felt herself losing control of her life, of everything, very fast. "What the hell is a mate-claim?"

"It means that I desire you to be my mate," Kendrick said. "I put my claim on you so all others will know you're no longer fair game. In time, we will go through ceremonies, one under the sun, one under the full moon, and join as one."

"We will, will we?" Addie's stomach had squeezed into a tight ball. "Says who?"

"Tell her she can refuse it," Jaycee said quickly. "Don't leave that part out."

"Suck it up, Jaycee," Dimitri cut in, sounding happy. "It's Kendrick's choice, not yours."

"I'm just saying, he can't force her. She should know that."

Kendrick remained silent, watching Addie with eyes that gave nothing away. The look eased the tightness in Addie's stomach, but her thoughts spun in confusion. She and Kendrick needed to have a very, very long talk.

The look on Jaycee's face was unmistakable—Kendrick's declaration had been a blow to her. Addie hadn't imagined her flash of despair. That despair made Addie speak gently instead of shouting as she wanted to.

"Tell you what, y'all—I'll think about it. Don't worry, little guys, I won't run away yet. Your father and I will talk about this first." Addie gave Kendrick a meaningful look, which he returned, his eyes sparkling.

Robbie ran around Addie's feet, tail waving. Brett yelled, "Yay! Yay! Yay!" until Zane jumped on top of him with his little tiger body.

Tiger—not ignored; no one could ignore Tiger—rose slowly to his feet. He gave Addie another golden-eyed stare, this one approving, then turned around and walked away, his striped back swaying.

"Where's he going?" Dimitri asked nervously.

"Probably to get his clothes," Kendrick said. "Addison, go unpack. Dimitri, get inside and lie down. Jaycee . . ."

Kendrick turned to her. He didn't lose his sternness, but his voice softened as though he knew Jaycee's feelings for him, had always known. "Jaycee, walk the bounds. Check out anything odd and report. I'm going to talk to our tiger friend."

He turned away before anyone could say a word and walked off after Tiger. The sun was fully up and shining hard, falling on his bronzed body and tight backside.

"I guess that's why he's the leader," Addie remarked. "He leaves before you can argue with him."

Dimitri nodded. "You hit the n-nail on the h-head."

"He's right about you, though," Addie said, frowning at him. "Inside with you and into bed. I'll ask Charlie to check on you later."

"Aw," Dimitri said, giving her a mock sigh, but he moved up the steps and into the house, a little unsteady on his feet.

Jaycee had already disappeared to obey Kendrick. Addie knew she needed to think very hard about what Kendrick had done, but she was numb as she walked to the pickup to fetch her bag.

Kendrick found Tiger a little way down the drive. He'd turned human—a giant of a man with orange and black hair—and was rummaging in a duffel bag he'd pulled from his motorcycle. Shifters liked duffels—easy to throw all kinds of clothes into them in case they had to shift away from home.

Tiger had already put on jeans and now eased on a blue T-shirt with *"SoCo Novelties"* on the front, silently unfolding it down his torso. He gave Kendrick a critical once-over, turned back to the duffel, then pulled out and tossed him a T-shirt and sweatpants.

Kendrick got into the clothes, more to keep the sun off his skin than any worry about modesty. He and Tiger were nearly the same size, Tiger a little larger, Tiger's eyes a golden version of Kendrick's green ones.

"What does Dylan want?" Kendrick asked him.

Tiger gave him a slow blink, looking slightly puzzled. "Dylan didn't send me."

Kendrick beckoned him under the shadows of a mesquite. Shade could take ten degrees off the three-digit temps that happened even in May. "Then why are you here, and how did you find me. Seamus told you where I was?"

"I haven't talked to Seamus," Tiger said. "I saw your mate in San Antonio. Knew she was yours. I looked for her to make sure she was all right. And your cubs."

Kendrick followed the disjointed speech with growing uneasiness. "How did you find us? How many others know? I can't have the entire Shiftertown coming out here." Not to mention the Shifters who wanted to kill him. If too many knew about this place, his plans would have to change again.

Tiger waited until he finished. "I can find people. It's what

I do. She broadcast scent—yours—in a big way. It took me two days to track her down. I told no one, and they did not notice what I did." He huffed in some irritation. "*Now* you tell me I could have hitched a ride with Seamus."

Kendrick folded his arms. "Now that you know where we are, what are you going to do? Report to Dylan? To Liam?"

Tiger shook his head. "I report to no one. Except to my mate." His hard face softened in a hurry. "Carly worries about me."

Kendrick couldn't blame her. Tiger had been created in a human laboratory, how, Kendrick didn't really want to know, and maybe even Tiger didn't know fully. Tiger had abilities that other Shifters did not—every sense heightened plus an uncanny way of knowing when things were going to happen. Kendrick had only met him once before but he'd been struck with how the quiet Tiger knew more about the world around him than any Shifter he'd ever met. He also didn't quite fit into that world, only looking comfortable when he talked about his mate, a human woman called Carly.

"Again, I ask—what are you going to do?" Kendrick said. "I don't want my Shifters, my cubs, my mate to be compromised. I have things to do, actions to plan."

"Is she all right?" Tiger asked, looking concerned. "Your mate? When I saw her in San Antonio, I knew she was with you, and I knew something was wrong."

Kendrick's alarm grew. "Something wrong? With Addison? What?"

"I don't know." Tiger said the words slowly. "That's why I came."

Kendrick looked up the drive toward the house. The door was closed now, everyone inside, Jaycee presumably walking the borders of the property, obeying orders no matter what her feelings.

He was going to have to have a talk with Jaycee about Addison. It would hurt Jaycee, which hurt him, but he needed her to understand.

"I haven't done anything to Addison," Kendrick said. "She's been caught up in my life. I could have shut her out, but I didn't. I want her to be with me. I know I should have let her go today."

Tiger studied him, his golden eyes shrewd. "It wouldn't matter. If you'd sent her away, you'd have found her again, or she'd have found you. If you are meant to be together, you will be together."

"The Goddess has planned it, you mean?" Kendrick asked skeptically. As Guardian, he had a measure of Goddess magic inside him, but he knew that the Goddess didn't interfere in Shifter business more than she could help it.

Tiger shrugged. "I was not made by the Goddess, but I know mates find each other. Why else would I have been running in the exact spot that Carly's car broke down? Why else would you have been with Addison when your life went wrong?"

"Went wrong-*er*," Kendrick corrected him. "We can argue about fate or destiny or the Goddess all day, but meanwhile I have shit to take care of." He met Tiger's gaze, neither of them looking away.

Kendrick knew that in the Austin Shiftertown, Tiger wasn't a clan leader or a leader of any kind—he wasn't regarded the same way other alphas were. But his dominance existed without question.

Tiger answered to no one and didn't care who answered to him. Within seconds of meeting him the first time, Kendrick had known that.

"I could use your help," Kendrick said. "If you're so good at tracking . . ."

Tiger cut him off. "I know all about you Kendrick Shaughnessy. Walker Danielson—the human who invaded your compound with smoke bombs and flash grenades—is my friend. He told me everything. Seamus is also my friend. You seek the rest of your Shifters, the ones you lost. You seek to build a new place for them. You are afraid that some of those Shifters have turned on you, will destroy you and all you have worked for. You aren't wrong. These are the same who are working to destroy all Shifters, hurting my friends." He stopped, tamping down growing anger, and gave Kendrick a quiet nod. "I will help you."

Kendrick exhaled in relief. Tiger would make a formidable ally—or an unstoppable enemy. He'd take ally any day.

"Thank you," he said to Tiger. "Here's what I need you to do . . ."

The ancient being known as Ben did his best research in bars and dives. He told himself this as he sat in the run-down bar in a hole-in-the wall town on the outskirts of Houston.

The giant city had grown out to swallow the countryside, but in this little town, the seedy dive was about all there was for entertainment. The roadhouse drew people from up and down the highway, or from out of the metropolis, giving them an alternative to chain restaurants or slick new gastro-pubs serving ultra-organic food no one had ever heard of.

This place was real enough. Gang bikers stopped off here, as did disreputable-looking men with nothing to do but down beer and stare at the small television above the bar.

Shifters came here too, ones hiding their Collars under hoodies and others with no Collars at all.

They didn't pay much attention to Ben, but then, Ben wasn't Shifter. Occasionally one of the Shifters would send Ben a puzzled look, but that was because Ben didn't smell human either.

He also wasn't Fae, but was technically a product of Faerie. More things lived in Faerie than the *hoch alfar*, or High Fae—those over-the-top arrogant but very powerful and cruel bastards who ruled the place. There were beings far more ancient in the Fae realms—the *dokk alfar*—Dark Fae—and the things like Ben, who were considered monsters by all but their own kind.

Ben had been living in the human world for a thousand years. He'd learned to look human, quickly growing tired of humans screaming and fleeing at the sight of him, or worse, trying to hunt and kill him. Humans in Ben's first days out of Faerie had called him demon and wanted to do unspeakable things to him, when all Ben had wanted was a beer.

Now he looked human, like one of the guys in this bar. The tatts helped him with his disguise and also kept more aggressive people away from him. No one wanted to tangle with a dude who looked like he broke necks for a living.

Ben had used this guise up in Las Vegas when he'd helped out Misty Granger—sweet girl—and her not-so-sweet mate, Graham. Well, those two kids were happy now and cubs would be coming to them soon.

In North Carolina, he'd taken the guise of Gil, part Native American cop and all-around nice guy. There, he'd helped another sweet woman, Kenzie, when she and her mate had been beset with problems. He'd worn out his welcome, though, at least with Kenzie's take-no-shit mate, Bowman, and decided to hit the road.

Why did the nice ones always end up with the hard-asses? Ben shook his head regretfully. He'd have to find him a woman who wasn't immune to the charms of Ben, the magical and all-wise.

Addison, now. She was pretty, and another sweetheart. He sighed. She'd gazed at Kendrick with obvious longing in her eyes, and Kendrick's look back at her told Ben that the man had already lost his heart but just didn't want to admit it.

It had to be the height, Ben decided. Shifter males were all about a foot taller than Ben, who clocked in at five eight on a good day. He'd learned how to change his appearance to blend in with humans, but so far, Ben had never been able to change his height. So unfair.

He hadn't come here, however, to think wistful thoughts about beautiful women, Shifter or otherwise. He'd come to eavesdrop on Shifters.

He could easily hear the ones who met at a table in the far corner—not because of any magical spell, but because he'd put a bug under the table where they habitually gathered. A small spell kept them from accidentally finding the little microphone, that was true, but technology definitely helped.

"Twenty more in place," a Feline's gravelly voice came in through the receiver in Ben's ear. "What about the stash?"

"Hard to get to," a Lupine answered him. "Dylan keeps

it pretty protected, and it's not easy to get past Dylan. I don't want him retaliating on me, or mine."

"We'll have to think of another way then," the Feline said.

"No shit. How did they get it in the first place?"

"The Austin Guardian's mate," the Feline said. "She's their 'in' with the Fae. But there are ways around that. But Collars are not our first priority, not yet. We'll work on it. Top priority is—have we found a place?"

"Maybe." The guy who answered was a bear, not one from the Austin Shiftertown. "If we do the deal right, no records will show that Shifters have anything to do with it. We'll need a human."

"I have an idea about that too," the Feline said. "My biggest worry, besides that interfering bastard, Dylan, is Kendrick. Kendrick's working for Dylan."

"Okay, I know you think that," the Lupine said, his voice heating. "But Kendrick would never work for someone like Dylan. He might be pretending to, but Kendrick always plays his own game. I say we should make Kendrick a friend, not an enemy."

The Feline reached across the table, his hand turning to claws. "Contact him, and I kill you."

The Lupine growled, not cowed. "Chill, kitty-kitty. It's only a suggestion. I haven't seen Kendrick or talked to him since the compound was destroyed, and I don't follow him anymore. I'm bringing it to the table for us *all* to decide. You're not leader yet."

The Feline snarled softly, but withdrew. "Fine. I vote no. No contacting Kendrick. Not until we know whose side he's on."

"He's on *Kendrick's* side," the Lupine said. "Trust me, I've known him forever."

The Feline went on in a hard voice. "Part of the reason we're doing this is the old leaders have screwed us standing. They're why we're practically slaves, wearing shackles to keep us tame. No more arbitrarily chosen leaders. We form the hierarchy the old-fashioned way, with challenges that are truly won and lost—not the shit rules of the fight clubs."

The bear spoke, his rumble holding caution. "In the old days, Shifters died when they lost a hierarchy struggle."

"Oh, well," the Feline said, with exaggerated indifference. "That was nature taking its course. We looked after our families and clans fine in the wild, everyone knowing their place."

"That's true," the Lupine said. "We can work it out so there's not so much bloodshed, though. Dominance can be established in the fight clubs, even with their stupid rule that a won or lost fight doesn't make a difference in the hierarchy. Such bullshit. Everyone knows it *does* make a difference."

The Feline thought about this, then nodded. "Good idea, Darien. We can use the fight clubs to figure it out as we go. Turn the Shifter leaders' rules to our purposes."

The bear and Lupine, Darien, liked that. They murmured assent and toasted their agreement with beer.

The talk slowed after that, and the Shifters drifted apart from each other, then departed at different times. A wise tactic—not coming and going in an obvious clump.

Ben waited until they were all gone, then walked casually past their table, as though heading for the bathroom, and removed the bug.

He left by the back door, becoming an inky shadow among other shadows.

The head Shifter, the Feline, was still in the parking lot. Ben watched him walk to his motorcycle and prepare to mount it. Before the Feline could climb aboard, another man approached him. Like Ben, this guy stayed within the shadows, obscuring his face. Ben could see the guy was male and wore a hoodie, and that was about it.

The Feline stiffened, coming up from bending over his bike, snarling softly. He seemed to know the man, however, because he stopped and listened as the man began to speak.

Ben had no idea what hoodie-guy said or what the Feline replied. They were a long way across the parking lot, traffic was roaring by on the highway, and Ben didn't have Shifter hearing.

Should have dropped a bug into the Feline's pocket. Oh, well. Live and learn.

Ben couldn't tell if the man were Shifter, human, Fae, or a whatever. While Shifters could scent the distinction, Ben couldn't—not that even a Shifter could smell much over the stench of Dumpsters and loose trash, oil, and exhaust.

The conversation ended. The Feline, not looking happy, climbed onto his bike, started it, and flowed away out of the parking lot. The man watched him go.

Ben couldn't see the guy very well, or hear his voice or smell him, but he recognized a stance of pure arrogance when he saw it. He didn't think the guy was Fae, though. They had a certain body shape that had been imprinted on Ben's mind from all the persecution his family had suffered from the *hoch alfar* shits.

That left human or Shifter, one who had something going on with the Feline but had waited to catch him alone. *Hmm*.

The man turned to fade back into the shadows, but for a moment, Ben felt a gaze resting on him. A pause, a stare, then a shake of head, and the man was gone.

Ben turned away to leave and found another Shifter directly in front of him. It was a Lupine but not the one who'd been in the bar. He wore a Collar and needed a bath.

"Dylan's pet," the Lupine said.

Ben decided to play stupid. "What are you talking about, man?"

"Shit," the Lupine said, his lip curling. "What are you? You stink."

The Lupine smelled like alcohol, whatever he'd been eating, and the strong odor of unwashed Shifter.

"Could say the same," Ben said.

"Dylan's a hypocrite, and you're a fucking Fae."

Ben scowled, fists clenching. This Lupine was spoiling for a fight. Ah, well, Ben would have to teach him a lesson.

"Never call me a *Fae*." His words hard, Ben swung his fist and contacted the Lupine's drunken face.

In the next moment, a sharp pain burned him in the abdomen. Ben glanced down in surprise to see a knife hilt sticking out of his stomach.

"A *knife*?" Ben asked incredulously. "Shifters don't fight with weapons. Have some self-respect."

As he spoke, fuzzy blackness took over his vision and he collapsed to the trash-strewn asphalt. At the last minute, Ben cast a spell that wiped the encounter from the Lupine's brain.

The Lupine blinked, looked around in bewilderment, and stumbled away.

Ben clapped his hand to his abdomen, pain washing through him. He managed to pry his cell phone from his pocket and press the name at the top of his speed dial, before he proceeded to pass out.

CHAPTER TWENTY

"What happened?" Addie demanded as she hurried out onto the porch, clad in the T-shirt and shorts she'd bought to sleep in.

Seamus and Tiger were carrying the recumbent form of Ben from the truck they'd taken him out of and up to the house. Kendrick, fully dressed, met them halfway, and helped them get Ben onto the porch. They laid him on blankets Kendrick must have already fetched.

"Ben," Kendrick said, touching the man's face. "Who did this to you?"

"He's pretty out of it," Seamus answered. "I got a call from him, but he couldn't speak more than a word or two. I tracked the phone—with a little help—to a bar outside Houston. There he was, stabbed half to death, left in a pile of trash."

Addie hurried to Ben's side, feeling Kendrick's warmth next to her. "Why did you bring him here?" she asked. "He needs a hospital."

"He's not human," Seamus said. "A hospital might mess him up."

Seamus didn't look very good himself. His face was wan,

and he kept pressing his hand to his side, as though he too had been stabbed, though Addie saw no blood on him.

Addie studied Ben's flat face, now-pale skin, and dark hair. "He isn't a Shifter, though, is he?"

"We're not sure what he is," Seamus answered. "Calls himself a goblin or a gnome, but I'm not sure if he says it as a joke."

"Well, he needs a doctor," Addie said decidedly. "If you pull that knife out of him, and it's pierced an internal organ, *you* could mess him up."

Kendrick nodded, face grim. "She's right. We need a healer."

"Finally," Addie muttered.

She was aware of Jaycee in the darkness of the porch beyond Kendrick, looking but not getting too close. Dimitri stood in the front doorway, in nothing but a pair of *very* brief briefs and the sling. He held his arm negligently, as though it had already healed a long way.

Seamus kept his hand against his side, but no longer pressing as hard. "Think you can trust him?" he asked Kendrick.

Kendrick didn't answer. Seamus seemed to know who Kendrick was talking about, but Jaycee and Dimitri looked nonplussed—they didn't. Tiger, stoic as ever, only stood in place, watching.

"Trust who?" Addie burst out. This cryptic Shifter glance-exchange thing was driving her crazy.

"A healer I've met," Kendrick said. "He doesn't answer to me."

"He doesn't answer to anyone," Seamus said. "He doesn't even answer his phone most of the time."

"I will find him," Tiger said. He didn't say it boastfully, but as a statement of fact.

Kendrick shot him a look. "You know where to start?"

"Yes," Tiger said. Without another word, he walked off the porch and into the darkness. A few moments later, they heard his motorcycle starting up, then he was gone.

Dimitri shivered. "He is *spooky*."

"You get used to him," Seamus said. "He's a good guy."

"Sure," Dimitri said. "And s-spooky."

Charlie had emerged onto the porch with a lantern flash-light. The cubs, of course, had woken up and come to see what the matter was, but they stayed in the doorway, shelter-ing behind Dimitri's bare legs. For once, they curbed their exuberance and watched with quiet eyes.

"He don't look good," Charlie said. "Want me to fetch a doctor?"

"We've sent for one." Kendrick unfolded to his feet. "We should make him comfortable and try not to move him too much."

Ben groaned and fluttered his eyes open. "Have a lot to tell you," he whispered.

"Later, my friend." Kendrick leaned down and put his hand on Ben's shoulder, his touch gentle. "I plan for you to live, so you can tell me when you're better."

Ben raised a bloody hand and clapped it around Ken-drick's wrist. "If I die, I want you to take that big sword of yours and run me through. It might not work, but I'd rather take a chance at getting to Shifter heaven than having my soul zipping back to Faerie. Wouldn't the Fae love to torment me then?"

Kendrick gave him a solemn nod. "You have my word."

"Thank you," Ben said fervently. "Now, any chance for some morphine?"

Addie remained on the porch with Kendrick as the others dispersed. Jaycee went out to patrol as her wildcat, as did Seamus. Dimitri disappeared into the house then reemerged, dressed but without the sling. He too walked away into the night.

Charlie had taken the cubs back to bed. They'd been somber, seeming to understand just how hurt Ben was.

They had seen death before, Addie realized as she gave them a second kiss good-night. The tigers' mother had died, and Robbie had lost both mother and father. They barely knew Ben, but they understood what his injury might mean.

Addie sat down on the porch swing next to Kendrick. Ben lay on blankets at their feet, where he slept fitfully. Kendrick had pulled a sheet over Ben's legs, but with the night still in the 90s, Ben had shoved it off almost immediately.

Addie felt Kendrick's arm against hers, then his thigh. In spite of the night's oppressiveness, his warmth wasn't overwhelming—it was comforting.

Addie gave up on trying to fight her feelings for him and leaned into him. "Who is this healer you're looking for?" she asked. "Why is Seamus worried?"

"He's kind of eccentric," Kendrick said. "You'll see." He let out a faint *mmph* noise. "I hate that Ben's hurt because of me."

"How do you know it's because of you?"

A reasonable question, Addie thought, but Kendrick growled. "He was poking around in things I'd been investigating. They must have caught him at it. They must know more about me and my friends than I realized."

"It could have been random violence," Addie suggested. "He might simply have been mugged."

Kendrick shook his head. "I doubt it." He stared off into the night, his entire body pressed the length of hers. She was aware of every twitch, every stillness, every beat of his pulse.

She laid her head on his strong shoulder. "Why do you want me to stay?" she asked softly.

Kendrick's shrug moved his body. "I need you."

The simple declaration warmed Addie's heart. "I've heard you say that to many people since I've met you. Dimitri, Jaycee, Seamus, Tiger. Even when you didn't say it out loud, that's what you meant. You seem to need a lot of people."

Another shrug. "I had a crappy upbringing," he said, forcing a light tone. "I have issues."

"An upbringing so crappy it made other Shifters rush to follow you to live in an underground compound in the middle of Texas?"

"Yep."

Silence descended, broken only by a chorus of crickets, the occasional crackle of brush as a lizard or snake slid by, and Ben's uneven breathing.

"Are you going to tell me about it?" Addie asked after a time.

Kendrick glanced at her. "You want to know?" He sounded surprised.

"I want to know everything about you." Addie rested her fingertips on his blue-jeaned thigh. "Have, ever since you walked into my diner."

He continued to study her in a puzzled way, as though he couldn't understand why she was interested. "When I was ten, my father died," he began. "He was a white tiger, an old Shifter, much older than my mother, and he came to the end of his natural life. My mother was still young, very beautiful. She was a tiger, but an orange one like Tiger. I'm an aberration."

"Is that what you call yourself?" Addie asked. "I'm sorry about your dad."

"I grieved. The Guardian of our clan sent him to dust, and my mother and I tried to get on with our lives. But that was back in a time when Shifter males far outnumbered females, and an unmated female like my mom was considered fair game. The strongest male around mate-claimed her, took her as mate under sun and moon, and then tried to kill me."

Addie's gasp was sharp. "Holy shit. Why?"

"Because a male doesn't want the offspring of another male to challenge him when that offspring grows up. He wants his own cubs to take over. My mother fought him tooth and nail—literally—to protect me. The male was a wolf, and though my mother wasn't as dominant, she was a tiger, the last of her line. I helped fight him off, already pretty strong. We couldn't get rid of him completely, though. It wasn't as acceptable for a female to deny a mate-claim then as it is now, and he was dominant to her." Kendrick let out a resigned breath. "I know now that if *he* hadn't forced the mate-claim, another Shifter would have. The Lupine got a few cubs on my mother, but they all turned wolf, not tiger. The offspring of two different Shifter species can go either way. My mom had no other tigers. Just me."

Addie pictured him, a small cub like Brett or Zane, scared and bewildered after his beloved father died. He'd have hated and feared his mother's new mate but stayed with his mom to make sure she was all right.

Kendrick went on. "I learned then that I couldn't do everything all by myself. I tried to fight my stepfather, tried to kill him, but I was one-third his size, so did little damage." His lips twitched as though he were amused at his foolish, younger self. "He did plenty of damage to me, though. My mother couldn't stop him anymore—she was usually pregnant, and each time she carried a cub it made her weaker. So I learned to form groups around me—we could pool our strengths to make things happen." He paused. "I finally did kill him."

Addie's eyes widened. "Oh."

"With some help. Dimitri's father had come from Russia and his mother was a red wolf from the North American wilderness. Dimitri was pretty formidable, even before his Transition. He helped me, as did a few others, who are gone now. We cornered my stepfather, fought him, killed him. My clan leader didn't punish me for it, because it was a legitimate kill—a son challenging his father's place in the hierarchy. In those days, fights for dominance were to the death. I was sixteen."

His look was empty, not defiant, not triumphant. He should not have had to face something like that so young. Addie squeezed his thigh. "I'm sorry," she said.

"It was necessary." Kendrick's rumble was low, and he rested his hand on hers, firm strength. "My mother, worn out, passed bringing in my youngest half brother. I took care of him, as I did the others."

Addie tried to imagine Kendrick with brothers and sisters and couldn't. He seemed so alone. "Where are they now?" she said.

"Two were killed by hunters," Kendrick said, staring into the darkness beyond the porch. "The other three were rounded up and Collared years ago. They live in a Shiftertown in Oregon. Trying to contact them would be dangerous—for them more than for me—so I let them go. They weren't too fond of me anyway. Apparently, I can be a hard-ass."

"No," Addie said with a straight face. "Never."

Kendrick glanced at her, his lips relaxing into a half smile. "Tigers are supposed to be loners. But I found out early on that I never could be."

And so he'd formed his own version of Shiftertown, outside the law, where he could gather everyone he cared about and protect them. Addie recognized that he wasn't simply a man reaching out to friends—he had a fanatic *need* to protect them, to keep the world from harming them.

Addie touched his face with light fingertips, as his eyes burned dark in the shadows. "You are an amazing man," she whispered, then rose against him and kissed his lips.

Kendrick went still as Addison's warm touch and kiss woke every yearning he'd been trying to suppress. He wrapped his arm around Addison's warm body and pulled her against him.

She moved in his embrace, her breasts flattening against his chest, the softness of her cutting through the horrific memories and the constant pain in his heart.

You are an amazing man. After everything Kendrick had just told her, about his stepfather and the brutal way he'd had to rid himself of his abuse, she called him *amazing*.

Kendrick couldn't think of anything romantic or poetic to say back to her. Words flitted through his head and out of his grasp. He could only groan softly and keep kissing her.

He turned the kiss deep, drawing her up into him, eyes closing as he tightened his arm around her. She was all that was warmth and goodness fighting against the harshness in him. His cock pushed against his jeans, his entire being aching for her.

A cough sounded somewhere at his feet.

"Hey," Ben rumbled faintly from the floor. "I'm not dead yet."

Addison broke from Kendrick. He couldn't see her face in the darkness, but her eyes were shining, and she wiped her cheeks.

"Ben?" she asked in concern. "You okay?"

"No." Ben's voice was weak. "I meant—I'm not dead yet, so keep going. Might be the last action I ever get."

"Stop talking," Kendrick said sternly. "You might move the knife."

"That's not how it's supposed to go," Ben croaked. "You unbutton her shirt from the top—one, two . . ."

"You're a shit," Addison said. "Just be quiet."

Ben rumbled a chuckle, which ended in a cough.

Kendrick got off the swing to check Ben's pulse and feel his forehead. The man hadn't developed a fever, which was good. Even in these days of antibiotics and other medicines, infection happened and could swiftly kill, and germs themselves were developing resistance to antibiotics.

Ben's eyes drifted closed, his lips parting. Kendrick pulled the sheet over his legs again—the wind that had sprung up was cooling off the hot night. This time, Ben didn't throw it off. He'd sunk into a stupor and responded to nothing.

Addison joined Kendrick on the porch floor. She smoothed the sheet then rested her head on Kendrick's chest. "I barely know him, but I don't want to see him die."

"I won't let him," Kendrick said. He put his arms around Addison and kissed her hair. "He did me a good turn, and I won't let him pay for it."

Addison shivered and Kendrick drew her closer. They returned to the swing and sat together as the night cooled, and they waited.

The horizon grayed around five, the night coldest just before dawn. Addison slept against his shoulder, her breathing even. Dimitri and Seamus checked in from time to time during the night, to report all was quiet. Jaycee kept her distance.

Kendrick sensed the motorcycle's approach before he heard the rumble and then saw it coming up the hill from the highway. He was on his feet, Addison rising and blinking sleepily beside him. Tiger brought his Harley up the drive, a big man clinging on behind him.

Tiger expertly turned and stopped the bike within feet of the porch steps, then looked up at Kendrick with an expression of vast irritation as he killed the motor. Well, the personage of Zander Moncrieff would piss anyone off very soon after meeting him.

The large man climbed off the back of the motorcycle, moving with inhuman grace. A duster coat floated around him, as did two long white dreadlocks that framed his face. The rest of his hair was in a buzz cut against his head, and unlike many Shifters, he wore a goatee beard around his mouth.

The hair on his head and in the thin braids was pure white, but he was not an old man. His facial hair was jet black, which matched his very black eyes.

Zander was a polar bear Shifter, a creature as rare as a white tiger. Still more rare, he was a healer, the gift of the Goddess running strong in him.

He was also batshit crazy.

"Greetings, Kendrick," Zander said, as he strode for the porch, his coat flaring behind him. "Who's the stiff?"

CHAPTER TWENTY-ONE

Addie stared in amazement at the man who bounded up the porch stairs with energy. He threw off his duster and thumped a canvas bag to the porch floor, his gaze on Ben. He'd braided blue beads into his dreadlocks, which caught the early light.

"Kendrick," the man said in a deep baritone as he pointed his forefingers at Ben. "I'm a *Shifter* healer. He's not a Shifter."

"I know," Kendrick said. "But you're his best shot."

The man sank to his heels and moved the sheet from Ben's legs, taking in the knife hilt sticking out of the bloody wound. "Poor bastard. My diagnosis—he's been stabbed."

Ben's eyes slowly opened. "Great. I'm dying, and I get a doctor who thinks he's hilarious."

"You're not dying." The man touched Ben's face with a surprisingly gentle hand. Then he let out a whistle. "Whatever you are, my friend, you're old. *Very* old. Old as the hills old. You've held on this long—maybe you will a little longer. If we're lucky. You." He looked up, his braids swinging around his face, and fixed his midnight gaze on Addie. "I need you to stand right there." He pointed to a spot next to him.

Addie left Kendrick's side to go to him. "Why? What can I do to help?"

The man raised his brows. "Nothing. You've got great legs—I just want to see them next to me."

"Oh, Goddess," Ben groaned. He grinned weakly at Addie. "But hey, he's not wrong."

Tiger growled from behind the man. "Heal him. *Now.*"

The man lost his smile as he glanced at Tiger. "Kendrick, where did you find this guy? I was minding my own business, meditating in my happy place, when he breaks down the door and demands I come with him. I'm Zander, by the way." The man held out a hand, now streaked with Ben's blood to Addie. "Alexander Johansson Moncrieff, but you can call me Zander. My ancestors were Norse, but I grew up in Alaska."

"Addie," she said, not reaching for his hand. "Short for Addison."

"Very pretty. Now, who can get me water, bandages, and a stiff shot of whiskey?"

"Whiskey for sterilizing?" Addie asked. "Charlie has rubbing alcohol."

"No, sweet thing, for me. It was a long ride down dusty roads. I figure as long as I'm stuck in Texas, I might as well be drunk."

Charlie had disappeared into the house, presumably to fetch the supplies. The cubs were at the living room window, eyes wide, as fascinated as Addie.

"Why are you stuck in Texas?" she ventured.

"Ask laughing boy there." Zander gestured to Kendrick and turned back to Ben. Even while he'd talked, he'd kept one hand on the man, and Ben, Addie thought, was breathing better. "Kendrick found himself a Shifter healer and decided he could reach out and grab him whenever he wanted."

"Zander says he loves the cold," Kendrick said mildly, "but he jumped at the chance to come to warmer parts of the world."

"Plus, I kinda wore out my welcome up north," Zander said, his fingers moving on Ben's side. "Figured I might as well hang out in Texas for a while."

Zander's neck, no longer hidden by the duster, was bare.

No Collar. "Do they know you were Shifter?" Addie asked him. "Your neighbors in Alaska?"

Zander shrugged. "A lot know, sure, but they say nothing. Those from the north like being left alone. Which is why they weren't happy with the polar bear rampage. But hey, it wasn't all my fault."

Charlie emerged at this point with a first-aid box and rolls of bandages. He hadn't brought any whiskey, but Zander didn't comment.

"He needs to be held very still," Zander said. "Big guy, you'd be good." He beckoned to Tiger. "This tiger threw me around like a rag doll when I . . . protested him interrupting my solitude."

"Turned bear and attacked me," Tiger clarified.

Tiger came up on the porch, his movements lithe despite his size. He sank down and held Ben's shoulders. Kendrick positioned himself to hold Ben's legs and feet.

"Kicked my ass is what he did," Zander said as he laid towels around the wound. "Embarrassing. Polar bear Shifters are the biggest predators alive, and I let a *tiger* kick my butt."

Addie knelt on Ben's right side, while Zander busied himself on his left. "Tiger's a special case," she said. "That's why we like him."

"I see how it is," Zander said, sending her a grin. "You have a thing for tigers. Maybe I'll get you to appreciate the greatness of bears. Now, let me do this."

Zander placed both hands around the knife, bowed his head, and closed his eyes. His body stilled, his braids ceased swinging and hung silently beside his face. He seemed to stop breathing altogether.

Then he made a long inhalation, air grating through his throat. The next sound that came out of his mouth was a long, low note, so low it was mere vibration.

The sound hummed for a very long time, longer than Addie would think any person could let out breath. Then Zander began to chant words in the same low, pulsing note. Addie didn't understand the language he spoke, but she saw

Kendrick bow his head, his lips moving in time with Zander's words.

Zander continued to chant, the sounds coming out in even syllables, the rumble of them vibrating the porch. Tiger didn't follow along as Kendrick did, he only stared at Zander as though he'd never heard the language before either.

Zander kept chanting, his body immobile, for a very long time. As he half spoke, half sang, the sky brightened, as though his words were pulling up the sun.

Addie wasn't certain, but Ben seemed to breathe more easily. He lay quietly, his eyes open and glittering, as Zander sat like a statue with sound pouring from his throat.

"He's c-calling the Goddess." A whispered voice in Addie's ear made her jump. When she came back to earth, she recognized Dimitri standing behind her in the near-light. "The h-healer of all things."

Zander didn't cease or even note the interruption. He slowly brought his hands together, until they met on the hilt of the knife.

Even more slowly he began to draw the knife out, a millimeter at a time. It took so long for the blade to rise from the wound that it seemed not to move at all. But at last, the tip appeared, dripping with blood.

Instantly, Zander dropped the knife, grabbed one of the towels, and pressed it to the wound. "Hold it there," he said to Addie. "Hard."

The change from Zander motionless to abrupt action made Addie react in the same way. She darted forward and pressed down on the square of towel. Ben grunted in pain but lay still.

Zander went back to chanting, but this time louder, the syllables more erratic. Kendrick stopped following along, as though these were words he didn't know. All the while Zander ran his hands over Ben's chest and the towel Addie held.

After a few moments of this, Addie understood why he'd had Kendrick and Tiger hold Ben down. As Zander's words rose and became a rapid ululation, Ben began to writhe. Spasms wracked his body, his spine twisting and arching.

Tiger and Kendrick held him firmly in place, but blood oozed from the wound, soaking the towel.

Without breaking his chant, Zander snatched up another towel and replaced the soiled one. Addie again pressed it firmly to the wound.

This happened again and again, until Addie feared Ben wouldn't be able to take the strain of it. He couldn't lose so much blood, fight to twist his body like this, and live.

Just as Addie's thoughts voiced this worry, Ben gave one final heave and dropped back to the porch. Addie leaned to him, fearing him dead, but Ben dragged in a long breath.

The breath was clean, no raggedness, no clog of blood or phlegm. Ben's eyes closed, his body relaxing. His hands dropped open at his sides, and he slid into the breathing of natural sleep.

Zander's chanting grew softer, his head bowed, braids swinging gently. He lifted his large hands from Ben and pressed his palms together, blood coating his fingers. His words became a whisper, then finally ceased altogether.

Zander raised his head, and Tiger and Kendrick climbed stiffly to their feet. The sun was well up now, bathing the porch in warmth and light.

At Zander's nod, Addie lifted the towel from Ben's abdomen. She found the skin beneath his shirt whole and closed, only a red, scabbing streak to show where the knife had been.

She turned to Zander in amazement. "How did you do that?"

Then she gasped. Zander looked terrible. His face was blotchy, his hands shaking. He met Addie's gaze for a brief moment before he doubled over, his hands pressed to his abdomen, and he collapsed.

Kendrick caught him. He laid Zander out across the porch floor, as he'd done Ben, easing him to lie full-length.

"He'll be all right," Kendrick said. "As I understand it, part of Zander's healing gift is that he takes the pain of his patient into himself. Not the actual wound or disease, but the sensations of it. It will disperse, in time."

"That's horrible." Addie smoothed back a braid that had caught on Zander's face. His hair was sleek, clean, pure white. "Why?"

Kendrick shrugged, weary. "The price the Goddess extracts? I don't know. It's hard to be Goddess-touched, trust me."

Dimitri laid a broad hand on Kendrick's shoulder. "Not all s-sunshine and roses, poor Guardian."

Kendrick climbed to his feet, Dimitri's touch remaining as though it gave Kendrick strength. "I didn't have to use the sword this morning," Kendrick said, relieved. "Thank you, Zander."

Zander groaned, his eyes closing tightly. "Don't mention it," he said, voice barely working. "Now, how about that whiskey?"

B en sat at the kitchen table, shoveling in everything Addie put in front of him, while Kendrick waited impatiently for the man to tell him all he knew.

Zander, recovering, was snoring on the sofa. Dimitri had vanished, likely to join Jaycee and Seamus in patrolling. It was nice, Kendrick reflected, to have Shifters he could rely on back with him. He had no need for a minute-to-minute report of their activities—he could trust that they knew what they were doing.

Tiger, not so trusting, remained in the house. He ate as much as Ben did, but kept a watchful eye on both Ben and Zander.

The cubs were clumped at the other end of the table, enjoying their breakfast. Kendrick never kept them away when he discussed Shifter business—one of them might become leader someday. Best they fully understood everything that was going on.

Around bites, Ben described what he'd done at the Shifter bar in Houston, and what he'd overheard.

Kendrick turned the information over in his head. They were looking for Dylan's stash of—what? Ben also said they were looking for a "place" and needed a human to do the deal. For what? Buying a building? A piece of property? Probably.

Dylan suspected they wanted to set up their own compound, so it must be related to that. They would need a human to purchase property, or at least make it look like the human was buying the property.

They wanted to use the fight club, at least at first, to determine hierarchy. *Hmm*. Kendrick could work with that.

"What did this Lupine look like?" he asked. "The one in the bar who told the others he knew me?"

Ben shrugged. He poured an entire glassful of orange juice into his mouth, swallowed it, and refilled his glass from the pitcher. "He looked like a Lupine. Shaggy black hair, gray eyes. Attitude."

Kendrick held on to his patience. "Anything else?"

"Scar on his forehead." Ben traced below his hairline. "The others called him Darien."

"Ah," Kendrick said, his heart sinking. Darien was a Lupine somewhat down the hierarchy, who'd given him no trouble before. Unnerving. "And the guy in the parking lot talking to the Feline? You couldn't tell what he was?"

"Shifter, human, one of those, probably. Not Fae—I'd have recognized that right off. I couldn't see very well though, and was too far away to hear him."

Kendrick fell silent. Ben had gathered a lot of information in one night, things he and Dylan hadn't been able to find out in months, so he couldn't fault Ben for not having the final piece of intel.

"What about the Shifter who stabbed you? Who was he?"

Ben looked sheepish. "He snuck up on me. I don't know if he clocked me planting the listening device but he sure saw me watching the lead Feline. Don't worry, I wiped his memory."

Addie, who'd been helping Charlie serve, sat down and looked at Ben in astonishment. "You can do that?"

Ben wriggled his fingers. "It's a talent I have."

"So, why don't you sit down with these Shifters and pretend to join them?" Addie asked. "Then when they've told you everything, wipe their memories for that time?"

"A thought," Ben said. Another glass of juice disappeared. Even Shifters couldn't eat like this guy.

"Drawbacks," Kendrick said. "They'd forget what they'd planned and plan it all over again, maybe changing that plan in subtle ways. We might be waiting for them to set up in one corner of the state and they'd have picked another without us knowing."

"Mm," Ben said as he swallowed. "Good point. I do have other talents, don't worry." He winked at Addie, and she gave him a warm smile.

"So, what do we do now, boss?" Ben asked.

Stuff all the crazy Shifters in a room and sedate them so Kendrick could explore the mate-claim with Addie.

"If they're using the fight club," Kendrick said, tamping down on his impatience, "we go to the fight club."

"What's a fight club?" Addie asked.

Ben answered before Kendrick could. "Shifters meeting to fight each other for fun. And profit—betting is heavy. They've been doing this for a few years now. Helps them work off steam, apparently. There are a few fight clubs around these parts. Secret, or supposed to be. A lot of humans go though, to cheer on their favorites and win money."

"Fight clubs are illegal," Kendrick said. "Both by human law and Shifter. Shifter leaders look the other way but humans shut them down."

"Who's this *we* who will go to the fight club?" Ben asked him. "*You*, my friend Kendrick, are distinctive. You might have been able to skulk in the corner at bars for a while, but among all those Shifters, someone's going to spot you. You've also become known as Dylan's man." He looked thoughtful. "So have I, for that matter."

"My trackers," Kendrick said. "They won't know who is loyal to whom anymore—Seamus has taken a fake Collar and is living with a former Shifter groupie. Dimitri and Jaycee have always been a little bit wild. Others *might* buy that the two of them have turned on me."

"Or you could send me," Addison said.

CHAPTER TWENTY-TWO

Both Kendrick and Ben glared at Addie and said, "No!" at the same time. Tiger was silent, his yellow gaze on her.

Addie raised her hands, her heart beating faster under their stares. "I'm not volunteering because I'm stupidly brave or anything. I'm saying I should go because none of Kendrick's Shifters have ever seen me before. At most, the ones who survived the diner caught sight of me diving for the floor in a waitress uniform. I can watch who you tell me to watch and report." Addie lowered her hands, meeting their eyes, though it wasn't easy. The thought of coming across one of the Shifters who'd shot up the diner was not pleasant, but the truth was, she was an unknown entity in this situation.

Kendrick rose, fists balled. "If they catch you, they will kill you, Addison. No."

Addie looked up at him, holding her ground. "You can make sure some of the Shifters you trust are also there, just not obviously with me. You keep talking about this Dylan. Apparently he's pretty mean stuff? You could ask him to keep the bad Shifters away from me."

Kendrick still scowled, although Ben looked as though he was starting to see her point. "You'd have to get close enough to hear what they say," Ben said. "And remember it. I might be able to fix you up with a listening device, but that's dangerous. If you're caught with a bug, even the law-abiding Shifters might try to take you out—they'd think you were spying for the humans."

Addie flushed, but sent Ben and Kendrick a triumphant grin. "Well, you're in luck. I have a terrific memory."

Both men looked dubious, and Tiger fixed his full attention on her, frowning.

"Go on," Addie said. "Ask me what meals I served the last day at the diner."

Kendrick said nothing, but Ben put his elbows on the table and said, "Tell me, what meals did you serve the last day at the diner?"

"I went in just before lunch," Addie answered, the images coming to her. "Right side, booth one—woman with bouffant hairdo had a Monte Cristo with a salad instead of fries; her friend with short blond hair had the soup of the day, which was chicken with rice. Left a tip of five dollars. Booth two, burger and fries, no lettuce, onion or pickle—he was one of the sheriffs' deputies—not one who arrested me. Booth three . . ." She went on, describing meals and what they'd tipped, while Ben listened with interest, and Kendrick retained his frown.

"Last customer had a grilled cheese with tomato," Addie concluded. "The cook was pissed off because he'd wanted to shut the grill down early, which he did right after he made the sandwich, and disappeared home. Then Kendrick and the cubs came in. Kendrick wanted apple pie with streusel and the cubs went for banana cream. But that wasn't hard to remember—they asked for the same thing every night."

"And it was good!" Brett said loudly.

"Impressive." Ben lifted his coffee and took a noisy sip. "Can you do that with anything?"

"No." Addie shrugged, a bit breathless from the recitation. "Not with math or science or anything that might get me a high-paying job. But I learned to notice things about people and couple it with what they say and do. I can't remember every meal I ever served, but definitely the last few days."

"I take back my original objection," Ben said. "I say, send her."

"My *mate*," Kendrick said, a growl in his voice. "Send my mate into the fight club, which is dangerous at the best of times, to get close to Shifters who are into shooting and stabbing other Shifters? It's a bad, bad, bad idea."

"She could go with Seamus's mate," Tiger said.

Kendrick's gaze snapped to him. Tiger had been so silent that his abrupt statement was jarring. "What?"

"Seamus's mate," Tiger repeated. "She used to be a Shifter groupie. She would know how to make Addie look the same."

Kendrick curled his fist on the table. "A Shifter groupie. Women who will do anything to have sex with a Shifter—you want Addie to go in looking like a groupie to a place full of Shifters who are happy to oblige?"

Tiger shrugged. "Seamus's mate has a brother. A soldier. He could protect them."

"Shit," Kendrick said. "No, Addison. It's a stupid idea."

"I know that," Addie said. "But I want to help you, Kendrick. I'm not happy that I was in the line of fire when these people came after you. They need to be stopped. I'm protecting myself as much as you. And the cubs. If I can do this, then why not?"

"I would protect her too," Tiger said. "I am always at the fight club. And Spike, Ellison, Ronan, Broderick . . . all the trackers."

"And me." A voice rose from the couch. Zander lowered his arm from his eyes, looking wide-awake. "I always like a good fight club. A tip—bet everything on me. I always win."

In the end, Kendrick decided to concede—sort of. He would send his trackers to covertly watch over her. Addison and Seamus's mate would go in separately and make no indication that they knew Kendrick's Shifters. Ben assured Kendrick that he had a spell that could remove Kendrick's scent from Addison so she wouldn't be announcing she was Kendrick's as soon as she walked into the arena.

The idea that a spell could do that unnerved Kendrick. Scent was important to Shifters—he didn't like to think someone could arbitrarily confuse the hell of out them by removing Shifter scent. He didn't like the idea of Addison not being protected by his scent either, but he couldn't have it both ways.

Kendrick would go as well. He didn't mention this, but he laid his plans. No way was he going to let Addison walk into a space full of adrenaline-hyped Shifters who'd be in animal form or naked as humans, willing to relieve their pent-up emotions with sex instead of fighting if the opportunity presented itself. Casual encounters were not forbidden to Shifters as long as they didn't poach someone else's mate. And with his scent off her, they would consider Addison fair game.

Addison would go with Seamus's mate, Bree, and her brother, with Seamus watching from the sidelines. Zander would go with Tiger—he'd been seen by the Austin Shifters before. Dimitri and Jaycee could slide in on their own. Shifters came from all over the state to the fight clubs, so it wouldn't be odd if they weren't well-known by the locals.

Once the plans were made, Kendrick removed himself from the house.

A run as tiger didn't help his pent-up impatience, anger, and need. He was sending Addison into danger. He'd mate-claimed her. Kendrick's first instinct was to carry Addison straight to the bedroom and bury himself inside her. But that would scent-mark her, and he couldn't risk that Ben's spell wouldn't erase the distinctive odor of a Shifter who'd gone mate-frenzied with her.

Kendrick's instincts to take her right away might get her killed. Addison's only hope at remaining unnoticed was for him to keep away from her until afterward.

Part of him whispered that if he did the scent-marking and let his mating frenzy go, he could keep her home and out of danger.

Probably not the best way to start a mating, he told himself dryly. And as much as Kendrick did not want to admit it, the others were right—Addison as an unknown had the best chance to get close to the Shifters Ben had overheard and see what the hell they were up to.

A leopard sprang out of a wash and loped along beside him, sending him a challenging look. Kendrick quickened his pace, then broke into a run, letting the impromptu race drag him from his thoughts.

Jaycee was fast, and she could outrun even Kendrick. She sprinted past him, then spun around in the dirt and met him face-to-face.

Kendrick stopped, dust flying up from under his paws. He growled at her, and Jaycee snarled back. Then Jaycee dropped down and rolled onto her back, showing submission. Kendrick brushed his breath over her, acknowledging, and gave the top of her head a nuzzle.

Jaycee stretched up and started licking his face. Kendrick backed a step but she kept it up. The tiger in him liked it—she was being affectionate as well as indicating her loyalty to him.

Kendrick shifted to human. Usually Jaycee would stop her licking when he did that, but today, she kept on, her tongue like sandpaper on his skin.

"Cease," Kendrick growled. She'd take off a layer if she didn't stop.

Jaycee shifted to her human form, coming to her feet with her arms around Kendrick, the licking turning to kissing.

She prodded at his mouth with hers, darting her tongue between his lips. She gave one swipe into his mouth before Kendrick could push her away.

"No," he said.

The hurt in Jaycee's eyes pained him, but Kendrick had never felt for her what she wanted him to.

Jaycee hung on to him. "If your scent is all over me and mine all over you, no one will pay attention to Addie. You know this."

Kendrick took Jaycee by the shoulders and pressed her gently aside. "Not the point."

"Kendrick, I love you."

"No." Kendrick shook his head. He brushed her cheek, his task as leader to reassure her even as he pushed her away. "I'm your leader. It's natural. I love you in return. But not as mate."

"I know." Jaycee's mouth firmed. "It's painfully obvious you don't want me that way. I've been true to you for *years*, was there for you when Eileen died, loved you through everything. Now, you see a cute human woman, and all that's for nothing. I don't understand. You *hate* humans."

"I can't explain it." Kendrick thought of Addison's ready smile, her sassy mouth, the softness of her when she held him.

Addison expected nothing from him, Kendrick realized. Demanded nothing. She looked at Kendrick as an equal, as a partner. But she stood on her own.

Jaycee would always demand. She was that kind of person. Everything given was payment for something she wanted in return. Addison gave without hope of reward.

Kendrick had watched Jaycee since she'd passed her Transition. She was courageous, dedicated, and loyal, fiercely so. He'd hoped she'd find happiness with Dimitri, who'd been friends with her since cubhood, but the two had never paired up. He suspected they'd had sex together, though he wasn't certain, but their relationship had never cemented.

Kendrick felt sorry for Jaycee, but at the same time his impatience returned. She'd expected him to devote himself to her after Eileen's death, when he'd been barely able to breathe. Jaycee had not hidden her anger when he hadn't reciprocated her desire.

Kendrick caressed Jaycee's cheek again. "Addison is my mate. When I first saw her, something inside me *knew*."

Jaycee jerked away. "Don't rub it in. But don't worry I'll make sure nothing happens to her at the fight club. I'm not that much of a bitch."

"I trust you."

Jaycee heaved a sigh, the anguish in her eyes receding the smallest amount. "I guess I'll have to be fine with that."

She swung away, started to run, shifted to her leopard, and sprinted for the horizon.

Fight clubs didn't meet every night, according to Kendrick, but most nights there was a fight club somewhere. Shifters couldn't stay penned up for long, even voluntarily.

Addie knew Kendrick was furious about her involvement, but she was going nonetheless.

She would go with Seamus to the house where his mate and her brother lived with their mother, and they'd leave from there for the fight club. Seamus and Bree were well-known at the fight clubs already, and there wouldn't be much surprise to see them there tonight. Addie's presence would be explained as being a friend of Bree's.

The others had already dispersed before Addie departed Charlie's, except for Ben, who'd go with her and perform the spell after she'd changed her clothes. Ben lingered as though in no hurry, lounging on the sofa while the cubs played at his feet.

Kendrick barred Addie's exit as she tried to follow Seamus out. His eyes held fire.

"Goddess go with you, Addison," he said in his deep voice. "Come back to me safe."

Addie's words got lost in her throat. She lunged at him, wound her arms around his neck, and kissed him.

Kendrick caught her against him, the strength of his embrace telling her how much he didn't want to let her go. It told her also that if he decided to insist she stayed, she couldn't fight him.

The force with which he kissed her back left her breathless. But Kendrick slowly released her, standing her away from him, holding her only with his gaze.

"Goddess go with you," Addie said softly.

Kendrick cupped her cheek with one hand, his eyes flaring heat, then he gave her a nod, stepped back, and let her go to where Seamus and Ben waited at the bottom of the steps.

Seamus drove Addie and Ben away from Charlie's ranch in a pickup that hummed smoothly beneath them. Ben rode in the bed, saying he wanted to enjoy being out in the air and alive.

"You have nothing to worry about," Seamus said as Addie watched the flat Texas landscape be swallowed up by late twilight. "I won't let one hair on your head be touched tonight. I love my mate, and I don't want to die."

"Kendrick won't kill you," Addie said with conviction. "I won't let him."

"Hunh." Seamus said skeptically, his eyes on the road. "You never know what Kendrick will do. When his mate died bringing in Zane, he went a little crazy. We were sure he'd die too, and he's the Guardian. Only a Guardian can send another Guardian to dust, and that was going to be a problem. And anyway, I love the guy. I hurt for him."

"All of you are devoted to him," Addie said, curious. "Why? I mean, I like him—he's compelling, and . . ." *Hot as a box of rocks on a summer afternoon.*

What do you mean, you "like" him? Addie told herself. *You've been jonesing for him from the minute he walked into the diner.*

Seamus glanced at her, amusement in his tawny eyes. "Kendrick's amazing. He held us together, protecting us, when we might have exploded from within. Shifters living together in close quarters—all different species—could have ended in a bloodbath or most of us going feral. He wouldn't let us. He's got an iron will, Kendrick does. I've never seen him as easygoing as I've seen him with you."

"Easygoing?" Addie asked in astonishment. "*That's* easygoing?"

"Believe it or not." Seamus nodded. "Even with his old mate, he wasn't tender. She was as hard-ass as he was, not a gentle woman. But they loved each other pretty intensely. With you, he's . . . different."

"He's lonely," Addie said. "I am too, and he recognized that in me. I saw his face when he found you and Jaycee and Dimitri. He missed you like crazy. I'm guessing the whole mate-claim thing will dry up once he's back to leading you."

Addie did *not* like the empty feeling she got when she said the words. Easy to pretend that once Kendrick had resettled himself, she could walk away and return to her old life without a problem.

Not true. Kendrick had changed her, and not simply

because she'd learned about Shifters. She'd seen him as worried father, caring friend, helpful to the weak, raw with emotion and need and fearing that state.

"I'm not so sure," Seamus said. "When I met Bree, I had this idea we'd never stick together once I figured out what was going on with me or found Kendrick. It doesn't work that way—I'm not leaving Bree, no matter what."

Seamus, though, wasn't a father, leader of Shifters, and a Guardian, with all the hang-ups that went with it. Kendrick, as he'd said himself, had issues.

Addie had supposed they'd go to a Shiftertown, but Seamus took her to a house that lay about forty miles south of Austin, in an area between housing developments. The house was old, had been there long before the walled communities in the distance had sprung up, with tall trees, a white picket fence, the whole works.

Floodlights blasted on when Seamus stopped the truck in the front drive, and a woman in a muumuu came out onto the porch.

"'Bout time you got here," the woman called down to them. "Bree's getting worried, and Lord, can that girl fuss when she's worried."

CHAPTER TWENTY-THREE

"This is going to be so much fun," Bree Fayette said as she put makeup on Addie in the downstairs bathroom. "I haven't costumed in a long time. I gave it up for a *man*."

Bree, with her short honey-colored hair and blue eyes, her Feline makeup already in place, laughed out loud as Seamus looked across the living room through the bathroom's open door. With his Shifter hearing, he'd follow every word, and Bree would know that.

"Hold still, sweetie." Bree's brow furrowed as she drew whiskers around Addie's nose.

Addie had never known there were such things as Shifter groupies. Apparently women put on fake ears and sometimes tails, made up their faces to look like cats or wolves, slid on provocative clothing, and chased after Shifters.

"Why?" she asked Bree.

"Is that a serious question?" Bree gave her an incredulous look. "Because they're *hawt*, that's why. I wanted to know everything about Shifters—wanted to sit next to them, watch them, *be* with them. It's not necessarily only about sex. It's about the experience. Remy, my brother, used to make himself up sometimes and go with me so he could ogle the lady Shifters."

A hard-bodied man with buzzed blond hair who was in the living room with Seamus called to them. "We can hear you." Remy's accent was soft Southern with a touch of Cajun. The Fayettes had come here from southern Louisiana barely a year ago.

Bree winked at Addie. "But now that I caught me a Shifter of my own, I don't have to dress up and go out. Well, not *go out* anyway."

"Goddess," came Seamus's voice, sounding embarrassed.

Bree gave Addie a last mark with her pencil. "You look great. Shifters will eat you up."

"That's what *I'm* supposed to prevent." Seamus moved to the bathroom door with his lithe ease. "No Shifters eating you. Not even touching. Kendrick will take my head off if they do."

"I won't let them anywhere near her," Remy said. He looked Addie up and down as she moved around Seamus and out of the bathroom. His blue eyes, mirrors of his sister's, warmed with appreciation. "Nice."

Bree had dressed Addie in a brief, tight skirt, a tank top with spaghetti straps and a lacy bra beneath, and gold, glittery sneakers with red hearts on them. Addie had expected mile-high heels but Bree said that since they were going to a fight club, Addie didn't want heels, trust her.

Addie had been given Feline makeup—the tip of her nose was black, her cheeks had drawn-on whiskers, her eyes were made up to look tip-tilted, and she wore a headband with fake ears on it. Bree also wore Feline makeup, and she'd complemented her costume with a short, lion-tufted tail.

Bree's mother, Nadine, came out of the kitchen, muumuu floating, cigarette in hand, and gave them a once-over. "You look like a trashy pair of tramps. Good work, Bree."

"Thanks, Mom," Bree said dryly.

"No sex with anyone but Seamus," Nadine said, turning away, cigarette smoke drifting behind her. "And even then, not where I can hear you."

"Mom," Bree growled under her breath.

"I like her," Ben said from where he waited in the living room.

Remy grinned at Addie. "She's winding you up. I'm proud to escort my trampy sister and her girlfriend. I have friends who'd shit themselves with envy." He frowned. "Then I'd have to punch them for looking at my sister and her friend like that."

"I'd be right there with you," Ben said. "Let's do this on the porch, Addie."

Ben led her outside, where he'd already laid out bowls and measuring cups he'd borrowed from Bree's mother. He lit a sage stick that he happened to have with him, and spent a lot of time wafting the smoke over Addie's body.

The scent-removing spell consisted of lots of chanting and Ben throwing different powders—some were kitchen spices—over Addie and her clothes. She wondered if there was truly magic in this or simply a matter of confusing animal noses with peppers, cinnamon, cardamom, and nutmeg, not to mention the sage smoke.

When Ben was finished, he returned to the living room, already deep into a discussion of cooking with Bree's mom.

Remy held out his arms to Bree and Addie, grinning hugely. "Let's go."

B ree drove Remy and Addie in the purring pickup to the fight club, which was in a grove fifty miles away, near the Colorado River that flowed through Austin on its way to the Gulf. At the end of back roads Addie never knew existed, they found a Shifter fight club.

This one was controlled by the East Texas Shifters, Bree explained. This was not technically Morrissey territory, though Dylan came here to fight as did his son Sean and many other Shifters from Austin.

Remy eyed his sister. "It's uncanny how you know all this, Bree."

Bree shrugged. "When I first moved here, I checked out everything Shifter, hoping to get lucky. I got so lucky, I found Seamus. I've come here a few times with him. He's a good fighter, and did I mention *hot*?"

"Just don't mention it to me," Remy growled.

Bree ignored him. "When we go in, stick close to me, Addie. I'll tell you which Shifters are all right to talk to—who will actually *talk* to you and not go all mating frenzy when you simply say hello to them."

"And I really don't want to know how you know *that*," Remy said. He exited the truck and helped Addie descend.

Remy had a quiet strength, fine blue eyes, and a body that a woman wouldn't forget in a hurry. Not only that, he had a sexy accent, and he was a gentleman. Addie should fall for *him*, not a huge white tiger with three cubs and abandonment issues.

But Addie knew it was too late. While she could admire Remy, like him, and knew she'd probably have fun with him, as soon as she thought about Kendrick—his green eyes, his white and black hair, his quiet watchfulness—all others faded before him.

Addison had been caught in Kendrick's gravity, like a wandering star pulled into the glory of a supernova. Potentially lethal, but her end would be spectacular.

Remy seemed to understand this. His look was resigned as he went arm-in-arm with her and Bree toward the arena.

Shifter fight clubs favored abandoned barns or hay shelters, Bree said—they liked places with roofs to keep the light from being obvious to passing aircraft. They liked places hard to get to, to keep the police away or nosy neighbors from reporting them.

This fight club was in an old riding arena with a giant metal awning covering it. The place had been part of a ranch that had raised show horses, gone broke, and been abandoned years before.

One-on-one battles were already in full swing when they arrived, the arena lighted by braziers in metal barrels and every kind of battery-powered lamp a person could carry.

Plenty of humans were here, Addie saw. Mostly men, but a good scattering of women, dressed similarly to Addie and Bree.

Addie looked around with interest that wasn't feigned. Many of the Shifters were unclothed, men walking upright and arrogant, wearing nothing but the Collars around their necks. No one seemed to think this weird, so Addie pretended not to be embarrassed by it. She'd take their bareness in her stride, as everyone else did.

Female Shifters didn't fight in the fight clubs, so Bree had told her. At least, not in the Collared Shifter fight clubs. Seamus had expressed surprised at this, saying Kendrick's Shifter females fought just as hard as the males, for fun or otherwise. Having met Jaycee, Addie believed it.

Speaking of Jaycee, she was there. She'd let her hair hang long and wore a shirt with a mandarin collar to hide the fact that she didn't have a Shifter Collar. She paid absolutely no attention to Addie, nor to Dimitri on the other side of the arena, or Tiger, who'd walked in alone.

Addie saw that all Shifters, and humans too for that matter, gave Tiger a wide berth. They didn't always do it consciously—whenever he walked by, humans and Shifters alike drew back and did not engage his attention.

Tiger didn't seem to notice this, or care. His golden eyes in his hard face took in everything, including Addie, as though he memorized all in his path.

Shifters were crowded around a fight going on at the far end of the arena, and Bree led them there. In a ring marked out by a single layer of concrete blocks was a giant of a man with very short black hair and brown eyes. He fought, in human form, against a man who was part wolf, part human.

The beast had a wolf's face, glaring gray eyes, a human-shaped body, and clawed hands. He and the man struck out, fought, punched, and wrestled, seemingly without rules. Five Shifter men hovered around the inside of the ring, watching the fight. The refs, Addie concluded.

The man-wolf furiously attacked his opponent—at the same time the larger man shifted to an enormous bear.

A Kodiak, Addie saw in stunned amazement. Holy shit, he was *big*.

The Kodiak roared. The wolf-man changed into a full wolf and leapt at the bear's throat. The wolf was much smaller than the bear in this form, but very fast. The bear swatted at the wolf, the Collar around the bear's neck emitting a shower of sparks.

The wolf's Collar sparked too, but neither seemed to be bothered. The bear shook off the wolf, who landed hard on his back, but he was up again almost immediately. Dust exploded upward as the two came together again and hit the ground, grappling, rolling, grappling again.

They both gained their feet once more, the wolf snarling, the bear shaking himself.

Then the bear let out a roar and went for the wolf. The wolf sprang at him, jaws opening, going for the kill.

The bear swatted one great paw into the wolf, catching him square in the chest and sending him flying. The wolf tumbled through the air and landed with a sickening crunch on the cement blocks.

The refs ran to him quickly, making sure he was still alive. The wolf breathed, but heavily, his limbs askew, his Collar arcing. The look in his eyes, however, was not pain, but pure savage rage.

The bear flowed back down into the huge man, breathing just as hard. Everything about him was big—*everything.*

The bear wiped his sweating face with a towel a scrap of a woman tossed to him, and strode to the wolf, ignoring the cheers of victory around him.

"You all right, Broderick?" the bear asked, peering down at the wolf.

The wolf shifted, slowly, groaning with it, until he was a dark-haired man, his gray eyes holding the same fury.

"I'll get you next time, Ronan. You fight like a girl."

A large woman at the edge of the arena laughed. She bent at the hips to look down at Broderick. "If you mean he fights like *me,* you're right."

"One day, Becks," Broderick said pointing at her. "You and me. One-on-one."

"For *fighting,*" the woman called Becks said. "Or my soldier boy mate will shoot you."

Broderick tried to climb painfully to his feet, groaned, and slid back down. "Of course for fighting. I have a beautiful mate. What would I want with you? Damn it, Ronan, I think you broke something."

"*I* broke something?" Ronan rumbled. "You did, Brod. It wasn't my punch, it was your landing."

"Ha, ha, the bear is funny." Broderick groaned and closed his hands around a brawny ankle. "I need a medic."

"No, you need a healer." Zander's booming voice broke through, preceding Zander himself, braids and duster swinging. "Move your damn hands. You'll make it worse."

Broderick looked up at Zander, recognizing him. "Oh, great. Just what I need to make my night perfect—an insane polar bear with delusions of grandeur. What are you doing here?"

Zander, ignoring the refs who were trying to clear the ring, sank down on his heels and put his broad fingers on Broderick's ankle.

"What am *I* doing here?" Zander asked, dark eyes wide. "Do you know what there is to do in the Arctic Circle on a Saturday night? Not a fucking thing."

As he spoke, Zander skimmed his fingers along Broderick's ankle, his mouth moving as he whispered words drowned out by the crowd.

Broderick clenched his fists, uttering one heartfelt groan. "Careful—that hurts."

"I told you to hold still," Zander said. He lifted his hand. "There you go."

Broderick blinked and flexed his foot. "Shit. That was fast."

"What can I say? I'm that good." Zander took one step away, then he yelped and collapsed to the ground, grimacing. "Be with you in a minute."

Addie couldn't go to Zander as she'd have liked to, not wanting to let on she knew him. She knew, though, that now his own ankle bore the pain and weakness of the break. She hated to leave him hurting but she forced herself not to make eye contact. Zander, for his part, pretended not to notice her at all.

Broderick, on the other hand, came right for them. "Bree!" he bellowed. "And my favorite ass-kicker, Remy." Broderick stopped in front of them. Addie sensed he wanted to embrace them, Shifter-style, then realized he was naked and sweaty. Shifters wouldn't mind but humans might. He pinned his gray stare on Addie. "Who's this?"

"Her name's Addie," Bree said quickly. "She's a friend of mine. She's new."

"Great. You bring her in just in time to see me get my ass handed to me." For a defeated Shifter, he was full of energy and fire. "Did you see that crazy polar bear heal me? Gives me the creeps, but hell, I can walk five minutes after I break my ankle. Hey, we should pit him against Tiger, see what happens."

"Tiger doesn't fight in the fight clubs," Bree said. "Everyone knows that."

"Yeah, well, maybe he could make an exception. I could win a pile of cash knowing Tiger could wipe the floor with him."

Zander got to his feet and limped away, at the moment not looking as though he could wipe the floor with anyone.

Broderick let him go. "Where's Seamus?"

Bree shrugged. "Around. I wanted to show my friend some fun. My brother decided to tag along and keep us safe."

Broderick gave Remy a sympathetic look. "Good luck with that. Shifters here are wild tonight. Some vibe in the air I can't place. But that's East Texas Shifters for you."

Broderick didn't stay to exchange more pleasantries. He clapped Remy on the shoulder, then walked away, calling a challenge to another Shifter. His body was tight, and most female heads turned as he went by.

"Who exactly are we looking for?" Bree whispered to Addie. "And how are we supposed to find them?"

Addie wasn't certain. Ben had described the Shifters he'd spied on, but the description could apply to any number here. Shifters fit a certain body type, and tatts and buzz-cut hair seemed to be popular.

Addie had never tried spying before, but being a waitress had been good training. People didn't pay attention to a server—they'd natter on about family secrets, real estate deals, bank deposits, their own extramarital affairs, their struggles to get a brother out of prison, without ever noticing that Addie heard every word as she refilled their glasses. The listeners of the world, she'd realized, could amass an amazing amount of knowledge.

Bree and Addie, with Remy, moved through the crowd, Addie trying not to obviously watch anyone specific. Another match started between the tatt-covered Shifter Addie had seen in the San Antonio parking lot and another, more rangy Shifter.

The crowd loved it, their frenzied screams heightening every time one of the Shifters landed a blow.

"Spike," Bree said into Addie's ear over the noise. "The one with the tatts. He's a favorite—a champion."

Addie couldn't see much of the fight through the mass of bodies around the ring, but the surge and ebb of the crowd's roar told her when Spike got in a good hit and when he took one.

She also knew when Kendrick arrived.

Addie didn't see him, not even a glimpse, but she knew with her whole being that Kendrick was there. Her body flushed, her need to turn around and search for him strong.

She knew that if she looked, she'd betray herself and him, but not looking was tough. She had no idea what the hell Kendrick was doing there when they were supposed to be practicing stealth, but she suddenly felt much better.

With the focus of the crowds on the fight, any covert activity would happen around the edges, where no one was looking, Addie reasoned. She slipped through the mass of Shifters and humans, walking nonchalantly toward the end of the arena as though doing nothing more covert than looking for the bathroom.

So it was that she saw a shadow detach itself from the scrub just outside the arena, move to Kendrick, and Kendrick turn and walk away with the man the shadow belonged to.

CHAPTER TWENTY-FOUR

Kendrick could barely breathe, could barely think as he followed the man in the hoodie away from the noise of the fights. When Ben had described seeing this person talking to the Feline Shifter he'd eavesdropped on in the bar, Kendrick hadn't had any idea who it could be.

He did now.

Kendrick followed him through the brush until they came to more open ground. Stars sprawled, thick and white, above them, across the moonless sky.

"Kendrick Shaughnessy," the man said. "You're still alive."

"And I thought you dead long ago," Kendrick said, making his tone not betray the rage that filled him. "I remember killing you."

"I survived." The man shrugged. "Barely."

He pushed back the hood of his jacket. The entire left side of his face was a scarred mess, left over from when Kendrick had raked it with his giant tiger claws.

"And now you hunt me?" Kendrick asked him, keeping his voice mild.

"Not necessarily," the man said. "I came here at the

behest of Shifters who needed me. Shifters who were tired of *you*."

Only Lachlan McGregor, a half-human, half-Lupine Shifter would use a word like *behest*. He'd always been full of himself. And seriously evil.

What he was doing alive, Kendrick had no idea. The man had died—Kendrick had sworn that. Nearly twenty years ago, Kendrick and his group had killed Lachlan and breathed a sigh of relief to be rid of him.

Kendrick would simply have to kill him again.

"You ordered Shifters to fire bullets at me," Kendrick said, maintaining the conversational tone. "Me and my *cubs*."

"No, I didn't. You know me better than that," Lachlan answered, derisive. "The shooting was Ivan's choice." He scowled, his gray eyes filled with hatred. "Why did you kill Ivan? He was one of yours."

"Because he was bent on hurting my cubs." Kendrick moved carefully to a fighting stance, readying himself to shift if he had to.

Half Shifters weren't necessarily weaker than full-blood ones. A half Shifter basically was a person who could shape-shift and had formidable Shifter strength, but who could easily blend in with humans. Half Shifters could pass for human and live among them without humans knowing any better. But Shifters knew. The scent was unmistakable.

"You're saying *my* Shifters sent for you?" Kendrick asked. Lachlan had come at their *behest*. "Which of them?"

"Ivan for one." Lachlan's mouth was partly scarred over—he couldn't move it well, and his words slurred a bit. Both his eyes were intact—bright, intense gray—though his left was surrounded by a shapeless mass of skin. "And others. They're tired of you always promising them paradise and never delivering."

Kendrick didn't rise to the bait. It was an old, old argument between the two—which style of leadership would keep the Shifters safe?

"If you haven't been dead, where have you been for twenty years?" Kendrick asked.

"Living." Lachlan shrugged. "Staying with humans who took care of me. I owed them my life. That is, until they tried to turn me in to Shifter Bureau. Then I killed them, and left."

Kendrick paused while more rage seeped through him. Lachlan could have made up the story to rile Kendrick, but he didn't think so. Lachlan had approved of the old-style Shifter existence, where threats were dealt with only by violence.

Kendrick gave him a wintry smile. "And you decided coming here was your best idea? Now I can kill you again."

"You couldn't do it the first time, Guardian." Lachlan moved his gaze to Kendrick's left shoulder. "Where's your sword? Don't tell me you left home without it."

"A friend is holding it for me," Kendrick said. He'd passed it to Zander on the way in. "He knows where to find me."

Lachlan grinned, his face pulling. "Rules of the fight club say no deaths."

"We're not at the fight club," Kendrick pointed out. "We're in a field outside it."

"True. So, what, you're going to kill an unarmed, injured man?"

"Yes," Kendrick said, and struck.

His pummeling fists found purchase in Lachlan's face and chest, but Lachlan brought his hands around to chop into Kendrick's middle, the man as strong as ever.

Kendrick punched him again, feeling his body start to shift before he told it to, his clothes stretching, tearing. He'd tossed Lachlan off the leadership throne for a reason, and there was nothing to say twenty years had changed the man.

Kendrick heard a rustling in the brush and grasses, and suddenly the field held twenty more Shifters, rising from the shadows.

They were Kendrick's Shifters—at least, they had been. Now they regarded Kendrick with anger in their eyes, their stances shouting that Lachlan had their loyalty now.

Kendrick noted the Feline, moving closest to Lachlan, who must be the Shifter Ben had overheard making plans in the bar. Figured. The Feline had been one of Lachlan's favorites.

They were all against Kendrick at this moment, ready to kill him.

Kendrick suppressed his shift, rose to his full height, and swept his gaze over the Shifters. A few wouldn't meet his eyes. Others did. They'd be the ones he'd have to take down first.

"You won't settle this one-on-one?" Kendrick asked Lachlan, disgust filling his voice. "Oh, yeah, the last time we did that, I kicked your ass."

"This time, you'll just be dead," Lachlan said. "Take him."

The Shifters surged forward, but none of them, Kendrick saw, wanted to risk being first to encounter him. In a few seconds, though, the group would decide to jump him at once, and that would be the end of him.

Kendrick didn't like the hollow feeling in his stomach this betrayal gave him. At the same time, strength ran through his limbs, fury begetting energy. He snarled.

His snarl was echoed by another throaty tiger snarl that came from behind Kendrick. Kendrick held his ground, and the line of Shifters edged back, the scent of sudden fear clogging the air.

Tiger, in his tiger form, stalked forward and halted next to Kendrick. His body was stiff, still, his golden eyes on Lachlan.

Behind him came an enormous black-maned lion, whose eyes were just as golden and just as hard. The Shifters edged back again, except Lachlan, who only looked on in contempt.

Kendrick knew Dimitri was behind him as well, though he didn't turn his head to look. And Seamus. No Jaycee, but that didn't mean she wasn't circling around to try to attack the Shifters from behind.

"So, the party's out here now?" Zander's voice rang across the field as he strode toward them. He flung off his duster and drew the Sword of the Guardian, the blade flashing. Starlight rushed up and down the runes on the silver. "Hey Kendrick, does this thing work? I mean for making Shifters bleed? I know—let's find out."

Zander swung the sword at a Lupine. The Lupine jumped out of the way. "Fucking crazy *bear*."

"That's right, dog breath," Zander said. "I'm completely off my nut. You can never be sure what I'll do."

Zander's voice sounded a little hollow, though. He was staring at Lachlan, his face fixed.

"Enough," Kendrick said with a low growl. "You can't win here, Lachlan. Take your children home. I'll meet you another day."

"That you will. Without your backup. I heard you had Dylan Morrissey in your pocket. Or maybe your pants." Lachlan's words ended in a sneering growl, but the Shifters who backed him were too nervous to laugh.

"Go," Kendrick said evenly, "before I let the polar bear rip off your head."

Lachlan had no fear of Zander or of Kendrick, or even Dylan, Kendrick noted. Lachlan reserved that fear for Tiger, who hadn't moved his gaze from him.

Lachlan growled low in his Lupine throat, and his Shifters changed stances from ready to fight to watchful. They surrounded Lachlan protectively, which was a bit sickening.

"I'll be seeing you," Lachlan said softly. "Maybe sooner than you think. Better look for your girl. I think she's in trouble."

Kendrick's gut clenched, and it was all he could do to keep from swinging around and searching for Addison. Lachlan, knowing this, laughed softly and walked away into the empty land, his Shifters fading with him.

As soon as they were gone, Kendrick moved from standstill to run, the others coming behind him.

He saw, as soon as he hit the arena, that when Lachlan had said *girl*, he hadn't meant Addison. He'd meant Jaycee, who was being dragged away by several Shifters, unnoticed by the rest of the locals, who were intent upon the fight by their champion, Spike.

Addie turned her head in time to see Jaycee in a sharp altercation with two Shifters who'd kept to the edge of the crowd. Jaycee leaned to them and snarled at them, the two males backing up a step.

That didn't stop a third Shifter coming up behind her and grabbing her.

Jaycee whirled, her Feline speed snaking her away from the Shifter who'd snagged her, but the other two stepped in, one slapped a hood over her head, and all three dragged her away.

Instead of fighting, Jaycee went limp. Addie couldn't tell why—either the bag contained an anesthetic, or maybe she was lying low for reasons of her own.

Addie scooted out of the arena and hurried after the Shifters and Jaycee. Kendrick and his crew were nowhere in sight. *Great*, just when she needed them.

Addie quickened her pace until she caught up to the Shifters. She pasted on a big, loopy grin, and stumbled against the Shifter who brought up the rear.

"Hey," she slurred, pretending to be a groupie long past drunk. "Where y'all going? Another party? Can I come?"

The Shifter, gray-eyed, snarled. "Out of the way, sweetheart."

"Aw, come on, tell me." Addie slid away from him and banged hard into Jaycee, loosening the others' hold on her. "Hey, what's wrong with her? Whatever she's on, can I have some?"

The lead Shifter swung around. "Shit, get rid of her."

One of the Shifters shoved the limp Jaycee onto his partner and swung a quick fist at Addie, a blow meant to knock her out.

Addie ducked swiftly but still was caught with a clip on her cheek. She staggered back and fell, then scrambled out of the way as a lion bounded past her and landed on two of the Shifters.

Addie rolled aside, narrowly missing getting kicked by fighting men. A hand reached down to help her up—Dimitri, looking grim.

Tiger and Seamus landed on the Shifter still standing. Kendrick pushed through the melee and lifted Jaycee. He held her as gently as he would a cub, carefully easing the bag from her head. He cradled Jaycee with unflagging strength but his gaze went straight to Addie.

"Thank you," he said.

Addie barely heard his words over the crowd's roar that went up over at Spike's match. The Shifters, on the ground, whimpered.

The lion shifted quickly, becoming a tall, dark-haired man Addie had never seen before. He had hard blue eyes and gray at his temples. "Kendrick," he said, and pointed.

From all sides of the arena, Shifters were converging on them, ones without Collars. They came from the darkness beyond the ring as well, surrounding them in a thick circle, homing in on Kendrick holding Jaycee.

Zander stepped in front of Kendrick, the big silver sword his hands. Dimitri, the bandage off his wrist now, flanked Kendrick's other side.

"Wait," Kendrick said, voice steely. He drew himself up, still holding Jaycee. When he spoke, his words carried. "Are you with Lachlan?"

The male Shifter in the front, one with golden brown eyes like Jaycee's, said, "Hell, no."

Kendrick acknowledged this with a nod. "Help me take her home, then."

Addie heard murmuring like a ripple of water. At the far side of the arena, Collared Shifters were celebrating their champion's latest victory. On this side, the un-Collared Shifters converged on Kendrick. Addie watched in amazement as they flowed toward him, hands reaching for him, expressions relaxing when they neared him.

Kendrick was mobbed, but no one pressed against him or hurt him, or Jaycee. They merely touched him, then moved aside so others could, keeping him the nucleus of their circle.

Dimitri took Jaycee from Kendrick, holding her gently against his chest, his face as he looked down at her telling Addie everything.

Kendrick stretched out his arms and welcomed his Shifters to him.

The Shifters followed Kendrick home. They came in trucks and old cars, on motorcycles, or stuffed ten and more into vehicles meant to hold four at most. They followed Kendrick and Addie and his trackers out into the empty lands of South Texas and to Charlie's old ranch.

Kendrick hadn't the heart to tell them to stay away for a little longer. He knew he'd been away from them too long, letting them fend for themselves. Not entirely his fault, but even so, it was time to become a family again. And so, Kendrick led his clan home.

Charlie waited on the front porch with Ben and the cubs. Charlie planted his hands on his hips.

"Now, this is a big ranch, but no way do I have enough bedrooms for all of them."

"Shifters are resourceful," Kendrick said as he left his motorcycle and came up the steps. "You have a barn, lots of fields, and a basement that's bigger than it first appears. They'll manage. I was thinking of buying the place from you anyway."

Charlie's graying brows shot up. "Buy it? But you're Shifter." He waved his hands. "No, never mind. We'll discuss it. Huh." He looked around the crowd climbing from vehicles, stretching, chattering. "Well, I'm gonna need some more groceries."

The Shifters surged around and into the house, through it, out into the back. Zane and Brett, who'd shifted to tiger, as they did when excited, ran among them. Robbie remained human but dashed about greeting the Shifters, being lifted for big hugs or kisses from the females, everyone babbling about a hundred miles an hour.

Kendrick knew full well that there could be enemies among them, spies Lachlan sent. Short of locking up every Shifter and interrogating them, though, he'd never find them. He'd have to trust his trackers to keep an eye out, and himself to spot a betrayal.

Addison moved among them without fear. She was wary, yes, but not afraid. She explained where everything was around the ranch, helped the younger ones, smiled at the older. Kendrick's Shifters seemed to understand without being told, without the scent mark, that she was with him, and there to stay.

Dimitri carried Jaycee into the bedroom she'd chosen for

herself and laid her gently on the bed. Zander followed and
checked her over. She'd been given a dose of some tranquilizer, Zander said, but she'd sleep it off.

"Good for you, Addie," Zander said when he came out.
"If you hadn't run after those guys, Jaycee could be who
knows where right now." He sent Kendrick a significant
look, as though Kendrick would never be able to figure out
that Addison had courageously saved the day.

Dimitri said nothing, but his glance at Addison showed
vast gratitude. Then he returned to Jaycee's room in silence.

Kendrick spent a long time walking among his Shifters,
settling them in for the night. They were used to living
rough, camping where they had to. The horse was a bit
nervous about all the animals moving in with her, but she
settled down when she started to grow interested and enjoy
the company. Horses were herd animals—they liked communities as much as Shifters did.

Some Shifters camped under the stars and the few bears in
Kendrick's group moved into the basement. As Kendrick had
found, a large door in the basement opened from a small space
behind the generator and icebox to cavernous rooms. Storm
shelters, he decided, or maybe built in the day when bomb shelters had been a popular thing. Whatever reason, Charlie had an
enormous basement under his house, and the bears liked it.

With Dimitri and Jaycee out of it, Kendrick had to rely
on Seamus, Ben, and Zander to move among the Shifters
with him and keep an eye out for any who might be Lachlan's. Seamus's mate had returned with him, along with her
brother, who started helping out without being asked.

In the small hours of the morning, Zander found Kendrick outside the barn with a crowd of his Shifters and put a
heavy hand on his shoulder. "Go to bed," Zander said in his
outsized voice. "You're all in, and your mate's already there.
Go snuggle up with her."

The Shifters of his band said, "Yeah go for it," and other
encouraging comments. Kendrick stretched his back, the
weight of the sword dragging at him. "You know what happens if I sleep with Addison," he said to Zander in a low
voice. "And what it will mean."

Zander's grin split his face. "Of course I do. We all do." His hand dug into Kendrick's shoulder, and he made an expansive gesture at the other Shifters. "It's natural—enjoy it. Take one for the team."

Kendrick shrugged off his hold. "She's human. Do *not* stand under the window cheering."

Amid disappointed groans, Zander said, "Aw, you know how to ruin all the fun. A leader in a mating frenzy is momentous, Kendrick. We'll cheer from the barn. And the basement. And the fields. It's catching, you know. Mating frenzy."

Kendrick knew that—especially a leader's mating. Other Shifters would catch the wave of need and find partners for the night.

Kendrick gave Zander a severe look. "If you get a cub on any of my Shifters, polar bear, you're taking care of it and its mother forever. No love 'em and leave 'em on my watch."

Zander raised his hands. "Don't worry. I wasn't planning on touching anyone. I like that you all love each other, but your way of life is . . . complicated. I like striding alone under the stars, on fields of endless ice."

"You lived in a house with satellite TV," Kendrick said. "And central heating."

"Hey, even polar bears get cold. And bored. You know, those programs about searching for ghosts are hilarious. Humans are good with comedy." Zander stepped back and let him go. "Need to talk to you about something after," he said.

Kendrick barely heard him. Afterward meant everything in his life would be different. He ended the conversation by turning his back and walking without a word to the house. Zander's laughter drifted after him.

Addison was in bed, as Zander had said. The room was warm, the windows shut, and Addison was sound asleep.

Kendrick locked the bedroom door, pulled off his clothes, and climbed into the high bed. He slid his hand under Addison's body, and when she fluttered her eyes open, Kendrick brought her up to him.

"Addison," he said, his voice low. "I can't stay away from you. I try and try, but you defeat me in the end."

CHAPTER TWENTY-FIVE

Addie came fully awake to find her arms around Kendrick's very naked, hot-skinned body. She flattened herself against him as his mouth came down on hers, and she kissed him back, tasting fire.

Something had changed in him, and not just the fact that he'd abandoned his vow to keep himself from her. Kendrick tonight was wilder, more vibrant, more *alive*.

She pressed her hands to his shoulders to break the kiss. "Wow. I'd say finding your friends really made you happy."

"*You* make me happy." Kendrick spoke in a growl. "Jaycee might have died, might never have come home—except for you."

"Yeah, throwing myself into three pissed-off, diabolical Shifters is nothing to me." Addie shivered. "Scared the shit out of me. Is she all right?"

Kendrick smoothed a lock of Addie's hair, fingers warm. "Zander says she'll be fine."

"He told me that too. But I mean, is she *really* all right?"

"Dimitri's with her. He'll take care of her."

Addie traced Kendrick's cheekbone. "Jaycee's in love with you."

"I know." Kendrick cupped Addison's face in his hands, his touch both hard and shaking. "I know she is."

"Dimitri loves her." Addie felt the need to add this.

"I know. All of us are fucked up."

Kendrick pushed her back into the mattress, hands dragging her T-shirt from her body. He dipped his head to lick one breast. Addie arched as her nipple went into his mouth, his tongue stirring fire. She stroked his hair, thick and sleek, his warm neck, smooth back.

Kendrick wasn't gentle—he tugged and pulled with his teeth, his hand coming up to cup her breast. He teased that nipple with thumb and forefingers at the same time he nipped and suckled the other.

Addie drew her foot up his leg, the covers dropping aside. It was too hot for blankets anyway. Addie pushed off the rest of the covers, nothing but the cool bottom sheet under them now.

High on this tall bed, it was as though they floated in an aerie, where nothing could reach them. Addie hugged Kendrick to her as he went on, his touch making magic. He knew how to pleasure with only hands and tongue, as he'd showed her in the barn, and Addie's body came alive in response.

When Kendrick released her breasts to take her mouth again, Addie let her hand move to the thick hardness between his legs.

Kendrick sucked in a breath and lifted his head, eyes glittering.

Addie gave him a hot smile. "You think only one of us can play that game?"

"I think you don't understand your danger." His voice was gravelly rough.

"I understand it just fine." Addie squeezed, and Kendrick let out a groan.

Bree had confided in Addie, confirming the rumor that Shifters were big. Very, very big. Addie had put this down to exaggeration, but she realized now that Bree was right.

It had been a while since Addie had been in bed with a man, but she'd never been shy about sex. She'd been curious and she'd discovered.

Exploring Kendrick opened up a whole new world to her. Addie wrapped her hand around his cock, marveling how sleek it could be. Kendrick growled, his eyes half closing then filling with something like pain.

Addie eased off. "Sorry—am I hurting you?"

Kendrick seized her wrist and pressed her hand over him again. "No. You're helping. I'm going to burn up."

"I know," Addie said. "It's hot tonight."

Kendrick squeezed his eyes shut and shook his head, kept on shaking it. "Not what I meant."

Addie had known exactly what he meant. Kendrick's body was fever-heated, his skin tight. Addie ran her hand up his cock, cupping the tip, and Kendrick arched into her palm.

"Like that." His jaw relaxed, his eyes drifting open again. "Like that, Addison. Goddess, you are so beautiful."

Addie touched his strong cheek, loving the rough of his whiskers. Kendrick looked straight into her eyes, the green of his bright in the starlight.

He kissed her as Addie stroked, his hips moving in time with what she did. Addie skimmed her hand all the way down to the tight balls at his base, the heat there the hottest. Wiry hair tickled her hand, and then Kendrick's strength came to her as he thrust up through her closed fingers.

Kendrick tore his mouth from hers and raised his hips away so she lost hold of him. "No. I need more. I need *you*."

"All right then," Addie said. "You'll have to help me out of my underwear."

Kendrick snarled. The fingers of one hand became tiger claws, which tore her bikini panties without touching the slightest bit of her skin. Kendrick's claws receded, and he pulled the shreds away.

"I knew I needed you as soon as I saw you," Kendrick said rapidly. "I put you in danger, but I couldn't stay away. I had to see you, be near you, every night."

"Aw, and I thought Bo's frozen pies were just that good."

"Stop." Kendrick brought his face to hers. "You are beautiful. Desirable. Perfect. Why the hell *wouldn't* I want you?"

Addie could think of many reasons, but his expression was furious, his gorgeous, heart-stopping body right on top of hers. This wasn't the time to tease, argue, play. This was the time to savor Kendrick and worry about the *whys* later.

"Have it your way," she said softly.

Kendrick snarled again. His strong hand moved her thighs apart, and he was speaking, but in such a low voice she barely caught the words.

"I can't go slow. I can't, can't. Damn it." He was at her opening, Addie so slick with heat there was nothing to keep him out.

She gasped out loud, her whole body opening as Kendrick closed his eyes and drove heavily inside.

Kendrick's words died as soon as he felt Addison around him. He opened his eyes again, finding her face softening with pleasure, her blue eyes warming.

He slid right in without barrier—she'd been with a man before. She wasn't hurting; her gasp had been surprise, but most human women weren't used to Shifters.

Shifters weren't used to human women either, as a rule, but Kendrick's body didn't care. Addison was warm, welcoming, hot, beautiful. The hunger he'd carried for her since he'd laid eyes on her rose up and consumed him.

She'd smiled at him when he'd first walked into the diner, she wearing that awful salmon pink polyester dress and holding a coffeepot. But her eyes had been kind, sparkling with good humor, her smile, genuine. Kendrick had pictured himself lifting her to the countertop, throwing aside the coffee, ripping open the ugly dress, and taking her.

The fantasy had sustained him every night, but every night he'd renewed it, going back to see her. He'd tried to stay away and couldn't.

He couldn't now. He was in grave danger, as was every Shifter out there who looked to him for protection. And Kendrick couldn't not be with Addison.

He stroked her hair back, lifting the weight of it. Kendrick kissed her as he pushed further inside, then raised his head as he eased back.

Addison's chest rose with her breath, her hips lifting with

his. Kendrick thrust, closing his eyes on the incredible sensation, opening them again to find her looking at him. She touched his face, pressed her fingers against his back, her body rising to him.

Kendrick eased out and thrust again, Addie making a faint noise in her throat. Kendrick balled his fist into the mattress, the next thrust coming faster.

Again he slid inside and out, speeding up, mating frenzy closing on him. *Addison.*

He didn't realize he'd said the word out loud until the guttural sound floated back to him. *Addison. Beautiful. Mate!*

Her cries joined his as Kendrick rocked faster, Addison winding her legs around him, drawing him deeper into her. Her face was flushed, her head turned on the pillow, eyes closing as she cried out.

Down into the bed, up only enough to make the next thrust deeper. Sensation became a swirl of color and light, like the stars against the night.

Growls escaped him, Addie's body tight against his while he buried himself deep inside her. The touch of her hands, legs, arms, propelled him on, any thought of gentleness gone.

They were bound together, rocking, he shouting, Addison laughing. Kendrick knew the noise they made floated to the Shifters inside and out—Shifter hearing being what it was. He didn't care. The frenzy caught him up and spun him around, and Addison clung to him, coming along with him.

Their bodies were slick together. Kendrick punched the bed beside him, need gathering deep behind his balls, telling him his coming would be powerful.

It was. Kendrick lost it too soon, but he was wrapped in Addison, his being dissolved in her. He cried her name as he gave up his seed, and she met him with her climax, the two of them clinging, holding, hungry.

After a long, long time they dropped back to the bed, Kendrick barely remembering how to breathe. He kept pushing into her, unable to stop, while she touched him and smiled.

A few Shifters in the distance *did* cheer, and Kendrick growled. He continued his thrusts as Addison laughed and kissed his chin, Kendrick moving until he could think and feel no more.

Waves of Kendrick's frenzy touched Dimitri, or maybe it was just all the noise they were making down the hall. He held Jaycee's hand more tightly, rejoicing she was home and well.

Jaycee opened her eyes. She took a startled look around, tried to sit up, then sank back with a groan.

"What the hell happened to me?" she demanded.

"Sh." Dimitri put a soothing hand on her shoulder. "You're at th-the ranch. You're all . . ." He couldn't make his mouth say *right* and gave up.

Jaycee put her hand to her head, brushing back her thick hair. Her golden brown eyes shone in the lamplight, so beautiful. "Are you going to tell me what happened?"

Dimitri gave her a truncated account of her near kidnapping, telling her how Addie had distracted Jaycee's abductors, giving Kendrick and the others time to come for her.

"Addie did that?" Jaycee asked in surprise. "I thought she'd have been glad to let them take me."

"She w-w-wou . . ." Again Dimitri gave up. His stupid stammer grew whenever he was agitated, and he got agitated a lot around Jaycee. "She's not like that," he said in a rush.

"Yeah, I know." Jaycee looked slightly disappointed that Addie wasn't as bad as she'd hoped, but also a bit more respectful. "So, what are you doing in here?"

"L-looking out for you."

"I'm all right." Jaycee's hand was still in Dimitri's. She closed her fingers around it, losing some of her bravado. "Thank you."

Dimitri squeezed her hand. "Any t-time."

They looked at each other. Whether Kendrick's mating frenzy was so strong it really did touch them, or they were simply alone in the night, lonely, relieved, safe for now—it didn't matter.

Jaycee lifted herself to Dimitri, cupped his face, and kissed his mouth.

Dimitri's heart hammered, and joy blossomed inside him. He slid his hand behind Jaycee's head, her hair trickling through his fingers, and pressed her up to him.

His return kiss parted her lips, wild fires building as his tongue swept over hers. Jaycee wrapped her strong self around him and pulled him down to the bed. Dimitri didn't even bother to fight his surrender.

"Lots of shagging going on tonight," Ben remarked.

Zander, flat on his back in the dirt and dried grass, arms outstretched as he gazed up into the stars, crossed his booted feet. "Yep."

Ben sat cross-legged next to him. Zander still wasn't sure what the guy was. Vampire? Fae? Creature from the Black Lagoon? But with so many Shifters getting busy in the house and barn—all rejoicing that their god on earth, Kendrick, was back in their lives—Zander had felt the need to walk away, seeking the isolation of the back fields.

Zander didn't belong here—he was not part of Kendrick's group—and neither was Ben. Therefore, the two outsiders left the others to their fun. Zander had also realized something tonight, an ugly truth that had smacked him in the face when he'd seen the scarred face of the half-human Shifter who'd confronted Kendrick.

"So," Zander said, studying the constellations that were slightly off from where they were way up in the northern latitudes. "Why aren't you with a lady? You have someone special waiting for you at home?"

Ben snorted a laugh. "Not me. I'm a thousand years old, the last of my kind. Any woman I took up with would live out her lifespan while I never changed. She'd get a little pissed off at me for that."

"A thousand?" Zander said in surprise. "Even Shifters will live out their lifespan before that. And we thought *we* had age hang-ups."

Ben shrugged. "I've gotten used to it."

No, he hadn't. Zander had a little bit of empathic ability in him, which was part of how he healed—as far as he knew. In all the years he'd been a healer, he hadn't figured out exactly how his Goddess magic worked. That empathy told him Ben was lonely and hated being alone, but didn't think there was anything he could do about it.

"What the hell are you, anyway?" Zander asked him. So much for being polite and giving him his privacy.

"Goblin," Ben answered readily. "That's as good enough term as any. I and my kind were kicked out of Faerie by the mofo bastards."

Interesting. "Out here is better," Zander said. "No Fae. More channels. Internet. No women who try to kill you after you have sex with them. Well, usually the women out here don't."

"Depends on your point of view," Ben said. "What about you? Special someone back in Alaska?"

"Nope." Zander folded his hands behind his head. "I'm a free spirit, not tied down, always on the move."

"You mean you struck out?" Ben asked, grin gleaming in the starlight.

"I mean I've never tried," Zander said, not offended. "I'm crazy, hadn't you heard? The Goddess reached out and gave me healing powers when I was ten years old and too young to fight her. Not that anyone can really fight the Goddess. But it made me half insane, and other people don't want to be near me for long, unless they're in serious pain or dying. *Then* they'll put up with me."

"I feel your pain."

Zander glanced over at Ben, who sat upright, head tilted back as he studied the heavens. "So, Ben, how about you and me blow this place, get roaring drunk, and find a few ladies for the night?"

Ben kept his gaze on the stars. He was silent a long moment, then said. "Nah."

"Yeah, you're right," Zander said. "Who needs uncontrolled, no-strings-attached, no-holds-barred sex?"

Ben chuckled. "You do. Tell you what—we'll sit this one out and next time we'll make a night of it."

Zander settled back down, staring up at the sky until he felt as though he were floating among the stars. "All right. It's a date."

Ben grunted another laugh and then they both fell silent, contemplating the night, lost in their own thoughts.

Addison woke to bright daylight and her nose against Kendrick's forehead.

For a moment, the previous day blurred, to coalesce into the memory of the fantastic lovemaking she'd had last night with Kendrick. He was here, lying with his chest against hers, his hand heavy on her side.

Addie lay motionless, soaking in his warmth, the scent of him. Sunlight touched his mottled hair, the white luminescent against the black.

The light traced his cheek, the dark lashes against sunbronzed skin, his mouth, which had so thoroughly kissed hers. Addie slid her gaze down his tight shoulder, arm folded against his body, his hand relaxed, fingers splayed just above her breast. The sunlight touched his bare hip and backside, down his leg to the curve of his calf.

Addie couldn't see the front of him, because it was pressed against her. But she could feel him. The hard planes of his chest cradled her breasts, and his cock, no longer rigid, rested heavily against her thigh.

Addie raised her gaze to his face again and found his green eyes open and looking straight at her.

"Hey," she said, suddenly shy.

Kendrick touched her cheek with a gentle fingertip. "Hey." His deep voice vibrated the mattress. "You okay?"

CHAPTER TWENTY-SIX

Addie considered. "The morning after great sex? Yeah, I think so."

Kendrick let out a small breath. "Good."

"Why good?" Addie frowned. "Why do you sound so relieved?"

He brushed back a lock of her hair. "Because I could have hurt you. I can be . . . focused."

"Focused on taking me to the best orgasm of my life?" Addie brushed a brief kiss to his lips. "I didn't mind."

A small smile touched his mouth. "The best?"

"Don't get a swelled head. But yes. Although the thing in the barn—that was pretty good too."

His smile turned wicked. "You bring out the playful in me."

"Oh, yeah?" Addie kissed him again. She liked how Kendrick tasted in the morning, and the fact that he kept his eyes open to watch her kiss him. "Do you feel playful now?"

"A little."

The growl in his throat made her shiver. "The others will expect you to get up soon, go out and see them," Addie said. "Maybe make a speech."

The growl escalated. "They can wait."

The warmth that squeezed Addie's chest grew. "Really? What for?"

Kendrick pushed her down into the bed, his fine weight on top of her. "The more you tease me, the less gentle you make me want to be."

"Mmm," Addie said, stretching under him. "Intriguing."

Kendrick's ongoing growl became a snarl. He backed away swiftly, seized her by the hips, and flipped her over. Addie squealed and struggled, but not very hard.

She went rigid in surprise, though, when his hand landed on her backside, the hot tingle of the swat spreading. Addie looked back at him. Kendrick knelt behind her, his cock straight out, his eyes sparkling like water under the sun. His palm smacked her backside again.

Addie squirmed. "What in the world are you—"

Her words cut off as Kendrick swatted her one last time, then raised her to her hands and knees and slid smoothly inside her.

Addie's eyes rounded, and she said, "Oh."

Kendrick slid out and back in, making Addie emit a louder, *Oh*. Then again, and again. In a short space of time, Addie was clutching the sheet, dragging it half off the bed, invocations to every deity coming out of her mouth.

"Goddess," Kendrick said harshly behind her. "Addison. Mate. *Mine!*"

Addie's words turned to screams, Kendrick's to mere sounds. The sun rose to heat the room, but nothing could be hotter than Kendrick, taking Addie to pleasure she'd never experienced.

Addie balled her fists into the bed to keep herself from falling, and let him.

Kendrick walked out of the bedroom an hour later—stiffly—to find Dimitri exiting Jaycee's room, buckling his jeans, a T-shirt resting on his shoulders but not pulled down.

Dimitri saw Kendrick and froze. They stared at each

other for a few heartbeats. "K-Kendrick. This is . . ." Dimitri's mouth worked, his agitation stealing his words.

"Not what it looks like?" Kendrick finished for him.

"No." Dimitri shook his head. "It's exactly what it l-looks like."

Kendrick waited while Dimitri settled the shirt on his torso and followed him down the hall toward the kitchen.

"How is she?" Kendrick asked in a low voice.

"Jaycee?" Dimitri paused a moment, then a beatific smile bloomed on his face. "She's fantastic."

Kendrick made himself not laugh. "Not what I meant, shithead."

"In all ways," Dimitri said. "Though she might try to k-kill me when she w-wakes up."

Kendrick and Dimitri made it through the living room and into the big kitchen. Seamus and several other dominant Shifters were grouped around the table, along with Zander and Ben. They looked up from eating when Kendrick came in, and burst into applause and hooting. Robbie and Kendrick's boys were there, and they cheered just as hard.

Dimitri went bright red, then he caught on and started clapping. "That's for you."

"Stop." Kendrick lifted his hands and swept them all with a severe look. "Don't embarrass Addison."

"I think *you* were the one embarrassing her," Zander said, drowning his waffles in syrup. "I'm surprised you can still talk. And that the windows stayed in one piece."

The only one not smiling was Charlie. Kendrick sat down in the empty chair at the head of the table, pushed there by Dimitri, who wouldn't let him serve himself. Charlie clumped over with a plate of eggs and sausage and clattered it in front of Kendrick.

"You do right by that little girl," Charlie said. "Or you'll hear it from me."

"Don't worry," Seamus said smoothly. "If he doesn't mate with her under sun and moon, we'll kick his ass."

"She has the right to say no," Kendrick reminded him.

"She won't," Dimitri said with confidence.

Seamus shrugged. "If she refuses, then we'll let her go with our blessing. If she accepts you, we'll make sure you make her happy for the rest of her life."

"Or," Zander said. "You know, the ass kicking."

Interesting that Zander thought he'd be looking in on Kendrick's Shifters. Well, they could use a healer these days.

Robbie, who'd finished his breakfast and slipped outside, now came running back in. "Dad. He's here."

"Who?" Kendrick was on his feet, expecting the twisted face of Lachlan to appear at the door, but the man who came in was Dylan Morrissey.

The Shifters around the table tensed until the air crackled with it. Seamus rose, both to confront Dylan and to keep the other Shifters from charging the man.

Kendrick got himself up and around Seamus. He needed to make it clear this was a leader-to-leader meeting, not an attack. There was no way Dylan had come out here without backup, and the situation could escalate into a pitched battle if Kendrick didn't keep things calm.

Kendrick spoke before Dylan could. "Welcome. Thank you for your help at the fight club."

His Shifters relaxed a fraction, though only a fraction. Kendrick was indicating to all present that this was his territory, Dylan was a guest, and so far, he would be tolerated.

The alpha in Kendrick couldn't help a touch of triumph. He'd been under Dylan's thumb for a while. Knowing he could throw Dylan off his turf anytime made him want to do a victory dance, like Brett did when he won a tussle.

Kendrick restrained himself. "What's up?"

Dylan gave him a conceding nod. The man was three hundred years old, venerable even for a Shifter, but he was strong, with the energy of his sons. His blue eyes were clear, his hair bearing only a touch of gray, and the lion in him could still win every fight in the fight club.

With the nod, he acknowledged that this was indeed Kendrick's territory, and Kendrick was master here.

"Tell me about this Shifter," Dylan said. "The one who tried to kill you last night." He shot a blue gaze past Seamus and around the table, knowing these were Kendrick's top men, who would defend their leader to the death. "And I wouldn't mind a cup of coffee, if you have it to spare."

Kendrick launched into his tale.

Twenty years before, Kendrick had joined forces with a half-human Shifter called Lachlan. They'd agreed, after the Shifters had been outed, that letting themselves be rounded up into Shiftertowns was a bad idea.

Though Lachlan was Lupine and only a half-blood Shifter and Kendrick was Feline, they had a common cause, and they became good friends. They wanted their families to remain free and without Collars.

They'd escaped from the humans rounding up Shifters and hidden out together in the wilds of the Yukon, staying far away from any human settlements. They'd realized that if they could find a place remote enough, they could live without detection.

If they didn't allow themselves to be Collared, with a record at Shifter Bureau and all that crap, most humans wouldn't even know they were Shifters. Lachlan, especially, could blend in, proving Shifters could live alongside humans—holding jobs, buying property, opening bank accounts—with no one being the wiser.

Since Kendrick was a Guardian, and Guardians by tradition weren't leaders, they agreed that Lachlan would be Shifter leader, with Kendrick as his second and the group's Guardian.

All went well at first. Kendrick found like-minded Shifters, helped them get away from the humans rounding them up and saving all the family members they could. It was tough—the humans ruthlessly herded Shifters into holding areas where they'd be processed. Cubs were separated from parents. Shifters young and old were taken away for experiments. By the time humans who were horrified at the treatment of Shifters had enough influence to stop the abuse, too much damage had been done.

In the meantime, Lachlan and Kendrick set up their hidden Shiftertown, chose trackers, established a hierarchy, made sure cubs were kept with parents, and that orphaned cubs were matched with adults who would care for them.

Different species who hated each other in the wild came together, willing to work to keep their families safe.

It was a heady feeling in the early days, Shifters joining together to be stronger, without having to surrender themselves and their entire lives. They made plans to grow the community, and in time, rescue every single Shifter from captivity.

And then Lachlan turned out to be insane.

It started with small things. Lachlan would make decisions—about whether a mate-claim would stand or a cub would or wouldn't accompany his parents into town—without consulting Kendrick. The decisions were arbitrary, and Kendrick received complaints.

Then Lachlan began to change his stance in the matter of Shifters breaking rules.

It had been agreed that a Shifter who broke one of the small laws of the community, such as taking a step into another's territory or getting into a fight, would be brought before Lachlan, who'd mete out justice.

At first Lachlan was reasonable—a territory violation meant an apology and the offending Shifter owing the offended a favor, to be called in at any time. An unwarranted fight had the two parties agreeing to let Lachlan or Kendrick listen to grievances and settle the question. Or, set up a controlled fight if the two Shifters simply had to battle it out.

Worse transgressions—hurting a cub, trying to force a female, robbery, assault—rarely happened, but when they did, the Shifter in question was banished on threat of death if he or she returned.

The simple justice worked. Then Lachlan decided to punish a Shifter who had borrowed another Shifter's motorcycle and then wrecked it, with a flogging. Kendrick had been away and had only learned about the flogging when he returned the next day. The punished man's family had cornered Kendrick about it, and Kendrick had confronted Lachlan.

Lachlan argued that making the transgressing Shifter buy the other another motorcycle was too tame. They needed to learn to take care of each other's things or there would be chaos.

Kendrick argued with him, until Lachlan became angry and said that Kendrick should be judge and jury by himself for a while, see how he liked it.

Things settled down, until a wolf cub got lost in the dead of winter. A search was made, the cub finally found deep in the frozen woods, and restored home alive and well. Lachlan decided that the father of the cub should be put to death for not watching him better.

Lachlan backed down quickly when Kendrick countermanded his decision, Lachlan explaining that he'd been very angry and worried about the cub. Now all was well, but in Lachlan's opinion, another Shifter should move in with the family to watch the cub.

As the winter wore on, Lachlan kept inventing transgressions that the cub's father had done, and finally claimed that he himself was the cub's sire. This was why he'd been so angry when the cub had gotten lost.

The cub's mother wasn't there—she'd been taken, Collared, and they'd been unable to rescue her. Therefore, she wasn't able to say whether Lachlan had fathered him. A DNA test was out of the question, because when a human lab saw Shifter DNA, they'd be betrayed.

Lachlan wanted to settle it with a fight—winner took the cub. The father protested that he was the true father but agreed to the fight. Kendrick forbade it but when Lachlan and the other Lupine met in secret and the Lupine was killed, Lachlan claimed the cub for his own.

When Kendrick confronted Lachlan, Lachlan said that the fight was just a battle for hierarchy. From now on, he said, claims on cubs and females should be settled by this method, which had worked for centuries. What bothered Kendrick was that other Shifters agreed with him.

Then had begun the split. Lachlan wanted to go back to the old ways—why should they follow human rules if they lived far from cities and towns? Shifters should be Shifters.

Kendrick had calmed things down and for a while there was no violence, but it simmered under the surface.

Then came the mate Challenges. Females were scarce and males who were lucky enough to make a mate-claim had to face Challenges from other males. Lachlan did not like the new rule that females could refuse the claim—their group didn't have enough cubs for females to be choosy, he said. Males claimed, and other males Challenged, whoever won the Challenge kept the mate, and that was the way it was.

Lachlan, of course, Challenged the first mate-claim that came after that. Being dominant, he won the fight, killing the other male, and Kendrick had to send the defeated Shifter to dust. The female, a feisty Feline, had refused Lachlan's claim, vowing to kill him instead. So, Lachlan abducted and imprisoned her, along with the cub he'd previously taken.

Kendrick and the Shifters he trusted most, including Seamus and Dimitri, went after him.

They cornered Lachlan in the mountains as a storm was beginning. Lachlan attacked before they could reach him, shooting one of the trackers with an automatic pistol. They'd been shocked—Shifters didn't use human weapons—which had allowed him time to shoot another.

Kendrick had gone tiger and attacked him, so swiftly that Lachlan had been forced to drop the gun and meet Kendrick as wolf. Seamus and Dimitri had joined in, and Jaycee had circled around them to find the female Shifter and cub.

But both were dead. From all evidence, they'd tried to get away from Lachlan, probably when they saw help coming, and Lachlan had killed them. The female had been holding the cub, trying to protect him, the child of another.

When Jaycee had shouted this information to him, Kendrick had thrown off any control and gone for the kill. Lachlan understood that and prepared to fight to the death. Seamus and Dimitri had let Kendrick lead, standing back to interfere only if necessary.

In the driving snow, Kendrick had slashed Lachlan to bloody shreds. Lachlan had fought to the last, finally falling in a bleeding, dead mess, staining the white ground around him.

Kendrick had been so furious that he'd violated his vow as Guardian, and instead of dusting Lachlan after he killed him, left the man for the animals to feed on. If Lachlan wanted to return to wild ways, let him return to nature as they'd originally done. If his soul was stolen by a Fae, he'd pay for the torment he'd given to the Shifters he'd killed.

Kendrick had sent the female and cub to dust, blown their ashes to the wind with a prayer to the Goddess, and gone home.

Later, Kendrick had second thoughts about not sending Lachlan to dust—not for Lachlan's sake, but so the Fae wouldn't be able to claim a Shifter. Kendrick's job was to not allow Fae to take even the worst of the Shifters—though Kendrick wondered if he shouldn't feel more sorry for any Fae who got stuck with Lachlan's soul.

But when Kendrick went out into the night to complete his task, he couldn't find Lachlan. The blizzard had been a bad one, covering all traces of the fight. Kendrick had never been sure whether animals had dragged Lachlan away to feast on him or if the heavy snowfall and ice had simply buried him. Either way, no one had ever found trace of him.

Kendrick had moved the Shifters after that, relocating farther south, near the Canadian-US border, and taking over as leader. Even the Shifters who'd agreed with Lachlan welcomed him as leader, and everything calmed. Or so Kendrick thought.

Kendrick finished the tale and bowed his head in the silence of the room. Remembering the details of Lachlan's crimes had dredged up memories of death and fear he'd wanted to forget.

He became aware of Addison, leaning on the doorframe, listening. When Kendrick looked up at her, he read shock and sympathy in her eyes.

Dylan spoke into the quiet. "So you didn't dust him."

"No." Kendrick let out a breath. "I should have, but I didn't. I fucked up."

"He was *dead*." Seamus leaned forward to emphasize his words. "No one could survive being ripped up like that. He had no more flesh on his bones. I was there. I saw him."

"Dead as a d-doornail," Dimitri added.

"Apparently not," Dylan said dryly. "Though the odds of his survival were not good. Not unless he found himself a Shifter healer." His unnerving blue gaze went straight to Zander and stayed there.

CHAPTER TWENTY-SEVEN

Zander looked around with a start as everyone stared at him. He raised his hands. "Hey, there are more Shifter healers in the world besides me."

"There are." Kendrick agreed, but Addie saw him give Zander a thoughtful look.

"And what would I have been doing in Canada anyway?" Zander went on, his eyes snapping. "I was trekking the polar ice back then."

"You still could have done it," Dylan said.

"*Could* have," Zander returned. "Or a passing Shifter might have helped him out, not knowing who he was. Or a passing human—same thing. Or a mama bear dragged this Lachy to her den and nursed him back to health."

"Was he feral?" Dylan asked Kendrick. "Being confined, even voluntarily, can do that."

Kendrick shook his head. "No, this was different. Lachlan never lost himself to his animal. He remained clear-headed the whole time."

Zander nodded, his expression grim. "There are other ways to go insane."

"I plan to ask him," Kendrick said. "Right before I dust

him for certain this time. Any idea where he went last night?"

Seamus broke in. "I followed him, with some of Dylan's trackers, including Tiger. We lost him."

"*Tiger* lost him?" Kendrick asked, surprised. "I thought he was some kind of tracking genius."

"He is," Dylan said in a hard voice. "This Lachlan is apparently tricky. But we'll find him. Tiger won't give up. Lachlan has met his match in him." Dylan paused. "If I find Lachlan first, do you want me to save him for you?"

Addie watched Kendrick ponder Dylan's question, emotions flickering rapidly behind his eyes. "Make the kill," he said finally, his voice quiet. "We can't risk him hurting others. That's more important than me facing Lachlan personally to gloat. But *I'll* send him to dust. I'm his Guardian."

"And the others?" Dylan asked. "His followers?"

More emotions. These kinds of decisions were hurting Kendrick, Addie saw, but there was no one else who could make them. "Contain them. I'll speak to them. But be careful. Lachlan's followers have been using guns and knives."

"That's all we need," Seamus said. "Shifters with guns. I hate the things, meself."

"That's because you're s-sane," Dimitri said. "Don't know how humans can st-stand them."

"Don't be so hard on humans," Ben said quickly. "They can't turn into ferocious beasts to fight their enemies. They've had to invent ways to defend themselves."

Kendrick ended the discussion. "Whatever the philosophy on human weapons, *Shifters* shouldn't have them. It would be the end of us."

"Agreed," Zander said. "We'll rip the guns out of Lachlan's hands and stomp them into little pieces. But we need to find him, first."

"So glad you volunteered," Kendrick said, his tone dry. "A bear would be handy, as would a healer."

Zander made a face but didn't argue.

Addie noticed that Kendrick had told the tale and discussed Lachlan's demise with his cubs in the room, without sending them away. They listened even now, eyes on their father. Addie knew Kendrick hadn't forgotten they were there—he'd included them in his eye contact as he told his story. He must have decided that they deserved to know about their enemies and the danger.

The Shifters began discussing the technical details of the hunt—who would go with whom and where they would look. Addie slipped away and down the hall to check on Jaycee.

Jaycee was sitting up in her bed in a tank top over her T-shirt, her golden hair tangled. Any other woman might look haggard like that, but not Jaycee. She looked pleasantly mussed, like a pinup girl at an old-fashioned mechanic's shop.

"Kendrick giving you the spiel about Lachlan?" Jaycee asked when Addie entered. She tapped her ear at Addie's surprised look. "Shifter hearing."

"Yeah, he did. Lachlan sounds like a peach."

"There was always something wrong with him." Jaycee looked troubled. "Kendrick doesn't say, but he admired Lachlan, even wanted to be like him. Lachlan had a lot of courage and, at first, was very protective of his people. Then . . . something happened. Everyone says he snapped but I think he was finally showing his true colors."

"Well, whatever he is, he has everyone spooked," Addie said. "He wasn't dragging you off to do anything good, that's for sure."

Jaycee flushed dark red. "I heard how you stopped them. Thank you." The words came out awkwardly, and Jaycee flicked her gaze away from Addie's.

"I was scared to death," Addie said. "I had no clue what to do but getting in their way seemed the best thing."

"You didn't have to." Jaycee brushed her hair from her head with one plump hand. If she were human, she might worry she was "overweight" and frantically go on crash diets, each one weirder than the last, but Jaycee looked exactly right to Addie. Her form fit her perfectly—strong but with curves, soft rather than hard.

"Didn't have to do what?" Addie asked. "Save you from crazy Shifters? I didn't, in fact—I only delayed them until Kendrick could get there."

"I haven't exactly been nice to you." Jaycee's flush deepened. "Not real subtle of me, trying to keep you from Kendrick."

Addie waved it away. "Oh, please. If I gave up everyone who wasn't nice to me to kidnappers and murderers, the population of my hometown would dwindle real fast. It doesn't matter if we don't get along, Jaycee. You're Kendrick's family—or as good as. Families stick together, even if they fight. Just ask my sister. We used to go at it when we were kids—we still do if I think she's being ridiculous about something." She said the last with a pang in her heart. She looked forward to a nice cozy talk with Ivy when this was all over.

Jaycee watched Addie in surprise. "I didn't think a human would understand that."

Addie huffed a laugh. "You don't know much about humans do you? We're not that bad. Well, some are, some aren't. Probably a lot like Shifters."

"How do you tell?" Jaycee hugged her knees to her chest, the sheet tight against her legs. "How do you know the good humans from the bad? With Shifters, at least, we have scent, body language, warning signs."

"They're there with humans too. You just have to learn them." Addie lifted her shoulders in a shrug. "Truth to tell, it's mostly trial and error. If I was better at it, I wouldn't have let myself get engaged to a total jerk. I had a lucky escape but only because *he* dumped *me*. I would have gone through with it."

More surprise. "You were going to mate? I mean, get married?"

Addie nodded, the pain of those memories having lessened a long way in the last few days. "Yes, because I thought it was what I needed to do. But I see now that it would have been a mistake of colossal proportions."

Jaycee's gaze turned awestruck. "The Goddess was keeping you for Kendrick." She groaned and buried her face in her knees. "I was trying to thwart the will of the Goddess. Oh, I am so stupid, stupid."

She banged her forehead with each *stupid*. Addie, alarmed, sat down on the bed.

"What are you talking about? My engagement was a long time ago. It has nothing to do with this."

Jaycee lifted her head, eyes glittering with tears. "That's what you think. You were abandoned by this man because you weren't meant for him—you were meant for Kendrick. The Goddess knows what she's doing."

Addie started to laugh. "No, he broke it off because he was an asshole. I knew he was—I just tried to tell myself he was better than nothing. Guess what? He wasn't. It has nothing to do with Kendrick, or your Goddess, or you. Don't worry."

She patted Jaycee's knee, something she wouldn't have dreamed of doing when she'd first met the woman. Addie now felt a sort of protectiveness toward her—Jaycee had showed her vulnerable side and Addie had new sympathy for her.

Jaycee's gaze rested on Addie, misery in her eyes. "You have it. The mark of the leader's mate. You have the compassion, the ability to surrender yourself to it. I never did. I don't know why I thought . . ."

Jaycee bowed her head again and began to shake with sobs.

"Oh, honey." Addie moved closer and daringly stroked Jaycee's back. "I'm so sorry."

Jaycee continued to cry, rocking a little, but she didn't shake off Addie's hand. When she raised her head, her face wet and nose running, Addie grabbed a box of tissues from the nightstand and shoved it into her hands.

"See?" Jaycee plucked out five tissues and mopped her face. "You know how to take care of people."

"I was a waitress for a long time," Addie said. "I guess I'm used to it."

Jaycee gave a watery laugh. "It's more than that, and you know it. I should have seen . . ."

"That's enough of that," Addie said briskly. When strong people fell apart, in Addie's experience, they could really go to pieces. "Kendrick needs you to help him, not blubber in the bedroom. Dimitri . . . he needs you too."

Jaycee groaned and clapped more tissues to her face. "Dimitri. Oh, Goddess. I was hoping last night was delirium."

"Why?" Addie set the tissue box down again. "Dimitri's *hot*. I love red-haired guys."

Jaycee wiped her nose with the tissues. "I've known Dimitri forever. We're trackers. We fight together, we train, we spar . . . He's always known how I felt about Kendrick."

"*And* he's hot," Addie said. "I think that's important to point out more than once. You could have pushed him away last night. You didn't."

"Crap on a crutch," Jaycee whispered. She looked at Addie in so much dismay that Addie laughed.

"You clean yourself up and come out and join everyone," Addie said, getting to her feet. "They need you. And don't be afraid of what happened with Dimitri. Own it."

Jaycee slanted her an ironic look. "I could say the same for you. You have a rabbit-in-the-headlights look, and I don't blame you. Kendrick is a powerful man. But some advice— Kendrick isn't good with close relationships. He shuts people out, you might have noticed."

Addie sat down again. "He hugs everyone," she said. "*You* were kissing all over his tiger face."

"That's him being leader," Jaycee said. "He comforts and reassures us. When Shifters are with someone as dominant as he is, we turn into kittens. Or puppies." She gave a dismissive wave to the Lupines. "It's part of the whole being Shifter thing. But Kendrick does shut people out, retreats into being leader so he doesn't have to deal with them one-on-one. Dimitri thinks it's because of what happened with his step-dad. Did he tell you about that?"

Addie nodded, remembering Kendrick's terrible story about his abusive stepfather and having to kill the man to save his mother. "He did."

"Kendrick was only sixteen, which for Shifters is still a

young cub, but he had to fight the man who should have been taking care of him. Then Kendrick had to watch his mother die. It broke him."

Addie sat quietly, trying not to imagine Kendrick as a cub, finding himself suddenly orphaned and alone. He'd have been crushingly lonely.

Jaycee laid her hand on Addie's, her touch surprisingly gentle. "Don't let him shut *you* out, Addison. He needs you."

Addie nodded. "I'll try."

"Do more than try. Don't be afraid of being with him. *Own* it."

Addie made a noise of exasperation and got off the bed. "*You* are a smartass, missy. Come on and get out of bed. Comb your hair, get back to your beautiful self, and don't let those guys out there have all the fun."

Jaycee gave her a startled look. "You think I'm beautiful?"

"Well, yeah." Addie said. "Look in the mirror. But don't take too long. They're going to go hunting for Lachlan soon and I want someone with them who will keep them out of trouble."

Jaycee was gazing at her in stunned amazement but Addie was finished playing counselor. She'd started the fence-mending with Jaycee. Now to see if it took.

Kendrick noted Jaycee slip into the crowd as the Shifters gathered outside, awaiting his orders. He knew damn well Addie had something to do with rousting her—Addie remained on the back porch but looked pleased when she glanced at Jaycee.

Addison astonished him more every day. Jaycee, when she experienced what she perceived as a failure, could be morose for days. Kendrick didn't have time to rally her and Addie had done it for him, as though she'd known exactly what both Jaycee and Kendrick had needed. His blood warmed.

Kendrick stepped back into leader mode and began to instruct the Shifters what to do. His role now fitted him like a glove—a change from the very first time he'd faced these men and women. He'd been shaking and sick and knowing he needed to take care of them all and not entirely certain how.

He quickly divided up the forces into teams, each led by one of his top trackers. The Shifters looked eager but confident as they broke off into groups they'd worked in all their lives.

Dimitri, Seamus, and two other trackers turned to their assigned Shifters to prepare them for going after Lachlan but Kendrick decided to hold Jaycee, Ben, and Zander in reserve. Jaycee gave Kendrick a look of fury as he approached the porch where she and Addie waited.

"What, I don't get a troop because I was tardy?" Jaycee growled. "You need me, Kendrick."

"I know." Kendrick studied his hot-tempered female tracker who gave him her usual belligerent look. Something had changed about her, something he'd figure out when he wasn't so distracted. "I need you for the most important mission of all, Jaycee. To take care of Addison."

Jaycee's eyes widened. "Seriously? You're launching a full-scale hunt, and you want me to play *babysitter*?"

"Jaycee's right," Addison said quickly to Kendrick. "You should send her out to kick Lachlan's ass. She deserves that after he tried to snatch her."

Kendrick knew right then he was in for an interesting time with his beautiful mate. She'd never roll over and do what Kendrick said just because he said it.

"No, she's wrong." Kendrick fixed Addison with his gaze, which she met. "Lachlan will know that the best way to get to me is to go after my mate and my cubs. I'm sure he's even now gathering intelligence on who is most important to me these days. I've got Ben and Zander on my cubs—I want Jaycee with you."

"Why *me*?" Jaycee argued. "Zander, as crazy as he is, could do as good a job. Better—he's bigger and stronger than I am."

"But he can't follow Addison into the bathroom," Kendrick pointed out. "Can't watch over her while she takes a shower. I'd have to kill him if he did that."

"Aw, come on," Zander said from the yard. "Let a bear have some fun."

Kendrick ignored him. "I need you on this, Jaycee. Sort it out."

"You mean *suck it up*." Jaycee slammed her arms over her chest. "Fine. I'll do it. But only because *she's* nicer to me than you are."

Kendrick simply gave her a nod. He felt the change in dynamic between Jaycee and Addison, and again, he knew Addison was behind it. He stepped to his mate, who stood above him on the porch steps, leaned into her, and kissed the curve of her neck.

Her scent flowed around him like a meadow of sweet flowers. Kendrick wanted to sink into her and stay there forever.

When he was finished with Lachlan, he would. He would take Addison someplace safe, and not come out for days.

Kendrick raised his head, uncaring that Ben, Zander, Jaycee, and Dylan surrounded them, not even pretending not to watch. Kendrick brushed a kiss to Addison's lips. "Goddess bless you."

The tender moment was broken by the ring of Dylan's cell phone. Dylan walked away to answer it, and Kendrick brushed his fingertips over Addison's cheek, touched her parted lips.

Dylan was back in less than a minute, his expression grim. "We don't have to worry about hunting Lachlan," he said. He hadn't spoken a word to whoever had called him, simply listened, grunted a syllable, and hung up. "That was Spike. He and Tiger found Lachlan." He met Kendrick's gaze, the bleak rage in his eyes enough to flatten a mountain. "He's taken over the San Antonio Shiftertown."

CHAPTER TWENTY-EIGHT

"How many live in that Shiftertown?" Kendrick asked as Dylan headed to his pickup.

"Sixty-five." Dylan turned back to answer, tension boiling off him. "Lots of females and cubs. I'm more or less its leader though there's another Shifter technically in charge. A strong alpha—but I can't find him anywhere."

"Lachlan's tricky," Kendrick said. "I wouldn't be surprised if your alpha is dead—I'm sorry."

Dylan sent him a severe look over the roof of his pickup's cab. "Don't take the blame for someone else's evil. You weaken yourself and allow him to win."

Kendrick shared a look with him for a long moment. "You're right," he said. "Let's go rip him apart."

Dylan gave him a nod and slid into his truck, starting it up.

Kendrick returned to the porch where Addison waited with his sons. His fury with Lachlan rose. He'd found hope, a chance, and Lachlan had arrived in time to take it away from him. Knowing Lachlan, he'd planned that.

Not this time.

"Addison." Kendrick felt the speech he was going to make to her slip away. He got himself up on the porch and pulled her into his arms, burying himself in her for a brief moment. He inhaled her scent and breathed out his mark on her. *Mine*.

"Don't you dare get hurt," Addison was saying, her whisper warm in his ear. "You hear me?"

Kendrick eased out of the hug and cupped her face in his hands. "I killed him before—I can do it again."

Jaycee, standing in the shadows, already taking her bodyguard duties seriously, looked worried. "Make sure you kill him all the way this time, Kendrick."

Kendrick shot her a look. "No worries there. Addison—you'll be well with Jaycee. Look after my sons."

"Of course." Addison touched his face, her hand cool. "Go get 'em, tiger."

At her feet, both Zane and Brett burst out laughing. "Go get 'em, tiger," they repeated in their shrill voices.

Kendrick crouched down to them. "You two take care of Addison, all right?"

"We will," Brett said. "If Lachy and his traitors come here, we'll wipe the floor with them."

"Yeah," his brother said. "We'll go all tiger on their asses."

Kendrick gathered his boys to him, his heart aching. If he didn't return . . .

No good thinking like that. Kendrick would take care of the problem and come on home.

He hugged both boys tightly and set them on their feet. "Tell you what—when I come back we'll have a big cookout, Texas style, and pie. Lots and lots of pie."

"Yay!" Both boys said. "We'll help Addie make pies," Brett said. "Even the apple one you like." He made a face.

Kendrick hugged them once more then let them go. They'd focus on the celebration, not the danger.

"Robbie."

Robbie, who'd hung back from Kendrick and his blood sons, now came forward. He was old enough to understand the kind of danger Kendrick faced and the consequences. He also understood that because he wasn't Kendrick's biological son, his position would be precarious if Kendrick died or was too hurt in the fight to resume leadership.

"Addison will take care of you," he said. "No matter what. She's my mate. So will Zander. Understand?"

Robbie listened, gray eyes round, and nodded. Robbie was so serious, having been forced to grow up too quickly. Kendrick vowed that he'd make a place where Robbie, the orphan he'd come to love, could be a cub, and play and run without worry.

Kendrick hugged Robbie and nuzzled his cheek. Robbie nuzzled him back, his body shaking, but he gave Kendrick a nod when they released each other, letting Kendrick know he'd be strong.

Kendrick unfolded to his feet again. Addison was watching him, understanding what it cost him to leave his cubs behind to go into battle. She also understood that the battle was necessary.

Kendrick slid his hand to the back of her neck and kissed her. "Goddess keep you," he said, his heart full.

Addison rose on tiptoes and put her lips to his ear. "I love you too, Kendrick."

The shock that jolted through Kendrick nearly knocked him off his feet. He blinked down at her, pulling away, and Addison slanted him a wicked smile.

"*That's* distracted you from your tearful good-byes," she said. "Go kick ass, Kendrick. I'll keep the coffeepot warm for you."

Kendrick growled, his heart pumping, triumph taking the place of rage. He crushed another kiss to her lips, turned, and leapt from the steps. His heart raced and was light at the same time.

He swung around and raised his arm at his Shifters, who were hurriedly getting into or onto vehicles, ready to depart.

"To me, my friends! Let's get him!"

His warriors whooped, men and women alike taking up the battle cry.

Kendrick climbed onto his motorcycle, settled the sword on his back, and waved his arm, signaling his Shifters to follow. He shot down the drive in the wake of Dylan's white pickup, and headed east, into the summer sun.

The San Antonio Shiftertown lay outside the city a little to the east and south. A few years ago, so Dylan had said, it had been run by a Shifter doing diabolical things—that Shifter had been killed by Dylan's son. The human government couldn't let a Shiftertown be leader-less, so they appointed a Shifter they thought they could control. That Shifter was loyal to Dylan first, however, and Dylan still wielded almost total power here.

The San Antonio Shiftertown was more or less in the middle of nowhere, among flat, dry land. A hand-painted sign said, "Welcome to Shiftertown," with the numbers after it crossed out, new ones put in over the crosses. "Population sixty-five Shifters, twenty-two horses, seven dogs, and twenty cats."

Everything was silent and deserted. The air was still, not even a breeze to stir the heat. Even in May, this far south in Texas afternoons could climb into the three-digit temperatures.

Kendrick had dispersed his Shifters to come at the town on all sides. They were to look for signs of resistance and capture those Shifters. No killing. The Shifters with Lachlan were still under Kendrick's protection.

Kendrick and Dylan had parked their vehicles at the entrance to the town and now walked in via the main road, not hiding their approach. A series of long, low houses surrounded the main streets, huddled together under the sun. Trees had been planted, mature now, the only things giving shade in this empty place.

Tiger and Spike, a Feline Shifter with body-covering tattoos, met them under one of these trees.

"He's holed up in the leader's house," Spike said without preliminary, his voice deep and strong. "I wanted to go in, but Tiger insisted we wait for you."

"He's strong," Tiger said in his slow way. "And cornered. If we break in, he will kill."

Kendrick knew the truth of that. Lachlan was certain to have hostages, possibly the entire population of this little town, with him. The leader's house wasn't very large at first glance, but looks were deceiving.

Tiger gave Kendrick his golden stare. "He wants you."

"No kidding." Kendrick studied the leader's house, which didn't look much different from those around it.

"He will do everything in his power to have you," Tiger went on.

"I know." Kendrick scanned the road, noting his own Shifters filling the shadows beside walls, under trees, ready, waiting. "I'd like to do this without too much bloodshed."

"That would be best," Dylan said calmly. "Humans won't mind their own business if a bunch of Shifters get killed."

Dylan wasn't only worried about the human police's reaction, Kendrick knew. Dylan shared Kendrick's need to take care of those in his realm. Though Dylan had conceded leadership of the Austin Shiftertown to his oldest son and "retired," he was still a leader at heart. The hierarchy of office was one thing; a Shifter's protective instinct was another.

Dylan was joined by a younger man who shared his looks—dark hair, blue eyes, Irish accent—and this man carried a sword. His son, Sean, the Guardian of the Austin Shifters.

Sean gave Kendrick a nod, an exchange among equals. "You know, Dad," Sean said, "We'll have to expose a lot of secrets to Shifters we don't know to pry this Lachy out."

Kendrick sent him a wry look. "Lachlan will have no trouble exposing them for you. Don't worry, I and my Shifters can keep our mouths shut."

Sean gave Kendrick a smile that was tight but genuine. "I thought you would. We all have secrets."

"Tell me about it," Kendrick said under his breath.

Sean's eyes warmed and Kendrick knew he and this Guardian could be friends.

"How do you want to do this?" Dylan asked Kendrick. "You know the man best."

"I once thought I did," Kendrick answered. "I'm not so certain now." He looked around, having thought about this a lot while he'd ridden out here, though he'd waited to make his final assessment until he saw the lay of the land.

"I go in," he went on. "Lachlan will have taken hostages, and he won't hesitate to kill if we do an all-out attack. I walk in and talk to him. If he wants me, he can let the others go to have me."

"And doesn't that sound like suicide?" Sean asked. "Are ye mad?"

Kendrick gave him a wintry smile. "I didn't say I would walk in alone." He turned to the Shifter at his side. "How about it, Tiger? Are you up for some cunning? Tigers together?"

Tiger's eyes flickered, moving the slightest bit from side to side as though he were running through scenarios and choosing the best one.

His eyes stilled, and he gave Kendrick a nod. "Tigers together."

"Besides, you'll know your way around," Kendrick said. "Dylan—here's what I want to do."

"**Y**ou know where white tigers come from, don't you?" Ben asked from where he lazed on the porch swing.

The laziness was feigned, Addie knew. Everyone on the porch—Ben, Zander, Jaycee, Robbie—was tense. The exceptions were Zane and Brett, who played as tiger cubs, content and unafraid.

"It's a genetics thing, isn't it?" Addie asked.

She'd had Charlie make up a big batch of iced tea, and she served it, pretending this was simply a fine summer morning to lounge outside. Never mind that her mouth was dry, no matter how much tea she poured into it, and her heartbeat wouldn't calm. Kendrick might die today, and Addie couldn't do a damned thing about it. She'd had to ask Charlie to make the tea or she'd have thrown the glass pitcher, ice, and tea across the room.

The tiger cubs did stop scampering and sat down to listen to Ben. Ben skimmed his hand, hanging down from the swing, across the porch's board floor.

"White tigers were bred especially for the Fae princes,"

he said. "Most Fae princes are arrogant s.o.b.s, and they competed with each other to own the most unique Shifters. Any unusual strain, like snow leopards and black panthers, were prized, but the white tigers were prized most of all. It was so rare that a white tiger bred true that any prince who had one could boast he owned something unmatched."

"That's awful," Addie said. "And I don't even know what a Fae prince is."

Zander answered. "Total bastards. Fae made the Shifters centuries ago, with breeding and magic. I don't want to know how—it was probably pretty disgusting. I have to say, they did a good job, because all these years later, we're still here, we can cross-breed, we can have cubs with humans. We're stronger than ever."

"The princes were the worst—*are* the worst," Ben said. "The warriors and generals at least understand the cost of what they achieve and can think with their brains. If they don't, they're dead. The princes are products of inbreeding and cushy living. They never leave their pristine palaces except to go on overly elaborate hunts. They *invented* glamping."

Addie thought about Kendrick, his strength, his surety. "How did the white tigers feel about being prizes for these princes?"

Ben snorted a laugh. "Let's just say that when the Shifters as a whole decided to fight back, the white tigers were in place, nicely close to the princes. A lot of princes lost their lives at that time. Of course, unfortunately, so did most of the white tigers. They sacrificed themselves to start the Shifter-Fae War. That's why there are so few white tigers now."

"Kendrick is unique," Addie said, thinking of his rare flashes of smile, his emotion-filled green eyes. So were his cubs, who were watching Ben with all seriousness.

"Unique," Zander said with a laugh. "That's one word for him."

The man had been lying flat on his back across the top step of the porch, and now he sat up. "I have to confess something. It's kinda burning a hole in my chest."

"What?" Addie's alarm returned.

Zander, his braids swinging on either side of his face, looked ashamed and chagrined. "Dylan was totally right," he said. "I was the Shifter healer who found Lachlan. I'd been traveling around, seeing the world, and I came across a mostly dead Shifter. I had no idea who he was, or why he was half dead, so I took him back to my hideout, and I healed him."

CHAPTER TWENTY-NINE

"What?" Addie was on her feet, her agitation surging into anger. "You said you had nothing to do with it!"

Zander rose, unfolding with grace. "No, I said there were other Shifter healers in the world and asked what I'd be doing in Canada. I never said it wasn't me."

"Splitting hairs." Jaycee had come up off her chair and was next to Addie. "Polar bears have a lot of hair. Why didn't you admit it?"

"With Kendrick and all his angry Shifters sitting there?" Zander asked in amazement. "No way. I wanted to live until dinner. I planned to take him aside this morning and tell him, but I didn't get a chance. Anyway, I had no idea who Lachlan was or what he'd done. All I saw was a Shifter clawed up and bloody, unconscious and unable to speak. I'm a healer. I couldn't walk away. I patched him up, and when he was well enough, I left him. Had places to go, things to do. I didn't know what had happened to him. I barely said two words to him and he didn't talk to me. I didn't even ask his name."

"Because of you, Kendrick might get himself killed," Jaycee flared. "You should have left Lachlan alone to die."

Zander lost his embarrassed look and became stern. "That's *not* what healers do. We don't decide who to save and who to let die. That's not our job—we save a *life*. Anyway, Kendrick should have dusted him. He didn't do *his* job."

"Don't you dare blame Kendrick for this," Jaycee said hotly. "You should have told him."

"Why? It's ancient history, and I didn't know the guy had anything to do with Kendrick until I saw him at the fight club last night."

"How do we know you aren't with Lachlan?" Jaycee demanded. "I should kill you, just in case—"

Addie stepped in front of her. "Stop it. He says he didn't know, and I believe him."

"I didn't," Zander said. "I promise you. I'd never seen the guy before. But I know he's tremendously strong. He'd never have survived otherwise, doesn't matter how good I am. And I'm good."

"Glad to hear it," Addie said, looking Zander up and down. "You can go out to the Shiftertown right now and make sure Kendrick doesn't die. If he gets a paper cut, you heal him. All right? So get going."

Zander didn't move. "You deserve to be pissed off at me, Addie, but I'm not running across Texas and leaving you unprotected. Kendrick told me to look after you. Those are my orders."

"You keep saying you're not one of Kendrick's Shifters," Addie pointed out. "So why are you obeying him all of a sudden?"

"Because you and his cubs are more precious to him than anything else in the world," Zander said. "If he lives and you die, he'll give up. I see that in him. He's been through so much and he wants this happiness that's dangling in front of him. He might harm himself—well, after he kills and dusts *me*."

"If Kendrick dies, *I'm* going to be upset," Addie said. "Not to mention his cubs and the rest of his Shifters. What do you figure your chances are against all of us?"

Zander's dark eyes were hard. "You're saying either way, I'm screwed."

"Pretty much."

Zander sat down again with a sweep of his duster, which he kept on despite the hundred degree temperature. "Then I'm staying."

Addie balled her fists. "No, you—"

The electronic jangle of a phone cut her off. Zander reached into his pocket, frowning, while Addie's heartbeat escalated to a sickening pace. A phone call meant news, probably bad.

Zander swiped his thumb across the screen. Addie noted absently that while the other Shifters had older model phones, Zander's was brand new.

"Whoa," Zander said.

He turned the phone around to show Addie the scarred and bent face of Lachlan.

"Addison," Lachlan said. He spoke calmly, without hurry. "It's you I wanted to reach, but your phone seems to have been disconnected. I want to show you something."

Lachlan turned the phone around. Its camera pointed to a window, through which Addie saw the slightly blurred images of her sister, Ivy, and Ivy's kids, Tori and Josh. They were in a kitchen, the familiar one of their own house.

Addie's mouth went dry, her fingers going numb. "You leave them alone!" she yelled, her voice cracking. "Ivy!"

Zander glared into the phone, looking more furious than Addie had ever seen him. "You just made a big mistake," he snarled at Lachlan and snapped off the phone.

Addie lunged for it. "No! He'll hurt them."

Ben was up, tight with anger. "No he won't. We won't let him."

"I'm with you," Zander said. He swung around, already walking away.

Jaycee leapt after him and grabbed at his coat. "Hello? Can you say *trap*?"

Zander shook her off. "I know it's a trap. But are you willing to sacrifice those kids to not spring it?"

"And how did he know to call *your* number?" Jaycee continued.

Zander scowled. "I don't know. Maybe he asked someone."

"Or maybe you're working with him, like I said," Jaycee went on. "You healed him, he showed up here, he calls you when he has a threat."

"I told you—I didn't know anything about him, and I never saw him again after he was awake and alive."

"Yeah?" Jaycee stepped to him. "How can you just walk away from patients you heal? You have to form some kind of bond with them—what you do is Goddess magic, like the Guardians have. Are you saying you get inside someone like that to heal them and you feel *nothing*?"

"Of course I feel something!" Zander shouted. The air shook as his bear growl burst out of him. "Why do you think I'm so crazy? If I hang around and take that person into my heart, I'd be more nuts than I already am. And when I *can't* save them? When they die no matter what I do—how do you think *that* makes me feel?"

He glared at Jaycee and she glared back at him but she began to falter. Ben strode off down the porch.

"While you're arguing, that bastard has Addie's family. Are you coming with me to crush him or not?"

Zander's anguish drained out of him from one heartbeat to the next and he swung around after Ben.

Addie ran after them, reaching Zander's motorcycle at the same time he did. "I'm going with you."

Zander opened his mouth to argue, his dark eyes still filled with anger and sorrow, then he closed it, understanding.

"All right."

Behind them Jaycee started to splutter. Addison ignored her. She knew that between Jaycee and Ben, they'd arrange for the cubs to be safe. The cubs were becoming her family, but Ivy and her kids were *Addie's* family, and she'd never abandon them to their fate.

Kendrick had never lived in a house in a Shiftertown. He knew of Shifter clans' propensity to hoard valuables through the years—though his Shifters had always kept their prized possessions in safe places around the world, while living simply and traveling light. Because they didn't wear Collars, Kendrick's Shifters could usually use banks or highly secure storage facilities without a problem.

Collared Shifters didn't have the luxury of anonymity or of traveling anytime they wanted to, so they'd built secret places in their homes to keep their valuables. Each clan had its own treasures, which they kept from humans' notice.

The San Antonio Shiftertown leader's house was small, at least aboveground. The single floor held a living room and a kitchen, plus a narrow hall that led to bedrooms.

A door in the hallway led to a closet that housed a false wall. Tiger depressed a catch that opened the wall to reveal stairs descending into a chill basement—the way to this Shiftertown's store of treasure.

Kendrick had to take off his sword to go through the low doorway and down the cramped stairs. At the bottom, another false wall gave way to reveal lit paneled corridors that led a long way underground. The walls bore faded rectangular patches, all regular and evenly spaced. Kendrick touched one.

"Dylan's stash," he murmured.

Tiger gave him a questioning look.

"Ben told me the Shifters he'd overheard said they wanted to find Dylan's 'stash'," Kendrick explained. "He must have meant the treasures of Dylan's clan—some Shifters collect artwork." Artwork, precious stones, and historic pieces kept their value through the centuries, while currency and investments might go up or down or vanish altogether. Regardless of how much paper money was worth, someone would always want a Rembrandt.

"Most of it is down there," Tiger said, pointing to the darkness at the end of the hall.

"Of course it is." Kendrick hadn't slung the sword over his back again, and now he loosened it in its sheath.

He and Tiger continued down the hall toward the gloom. Rooms opened out onto the corridor, but Kendrick heard nothing behind them, scented nothing. Apparently neither did Tiger. Tiger was scanning the walls, taking in scent, stopping to listen.

Nowhere did they see or sense any hostages, other Shifters—anyone. They were alone down here.

The ordinary-looking door at the end of the hall opened to reveal a steel door behind it with a coded lock. While the rest of the house appeared to have been built in the seventies, this door looked to be brand-new, the keypad lock state-of-the-art. Dylan must have installed it as soon as the old leader had died.

"Know the combination?" Kendrick asked.

"No." Tiger moved past Kendrick and let his finger hover over the keypad. "But . . ." He hesitated a few seconds, then touched numbers.

The lock clicked, and the door opened.

"Remind me to ask you how you did that," Kendrick said as they peered into the room.

It was dark. Kendrick's Shifter vision saw plenty of shapes but he couldn't make out anything clearly. Tiger, on the other hand, scanned the room as though he saw everything without a problem.

"Light switch there," he said, pointing a little way down the wall. "If you need it."

Tiger didn't sound superior; he was stating a fact. Kendrick moved toward the switch, which was a push button, and pressed it.

Lights flickered to life. By them, Kendrick saw that every cabinet door was either open or hanging broken from its hinges, and that glass cases that had decorated the middle of the room had been smashed. Any valuables that they'd housed were gone.

"Dylan needs to see this," Kendrick said, turning.

Tiger was just inside the doorway, looking around. As soon as Kendrick swung back to him, Tiger jerked his head up, peering sharply at the ceiling.

The big man shouted, *"No!"* then a sharp, grating sound cut off the word.

The main door was set back in an alcove. From the top of this alcove, a solid metal door screeched downward, cutting Kendrick from the entrance, and Tiger.

The door was a single, smooth sheet, no handles, keypads or anything on it. Tiger slammed into it from the other side, but the door stayed in place, not budging.

All the lights in the treasure room went out. The darkness was complete, even to Kendrick's Shifter vision.

He drew his sword, hearing it but not seeing the flash of the blade or flicker of runes. Tiger thumped the door from the other side again, and then there was nothing.

Kendrick was alone in the dark and the silence.

A ddie had never shot through the town of Loneview so fast in her life. Zander was riding far over the speed limit—if the local police wanted an easy ticket, they'd have it today.

Not that Zander would bother to stop for them. Addie clung to him as they zoomed past the town square, Zander following her bellowed directions to her house.

Ben came behind them on another motorcycle, riding with Jaycee. She was taking seriously her commitment to not leave Addie alone for a single moment. She'd made arrangements for the strongest of the Shifters left at the ranch, and Charlie, to take care of the cubs.

Ivy's house loomed up in the heat of the afternoon. Addie's heart thumped as Zander halted in front of the familiar Bermuda grass yard with the live oak tree, Josh's bike resting against the garage door.

Addie was scrambling off the motorcycle before Zander shut it down. She ran for the front door, but Jaycee caught her, spinning her back.

"Don't even go in there before we check it out," Jaycee said sharply. "Don't be a too-stupid-to-live heroine."

"My *sister* and her kids are in there!" Addie yelled. "With that *monster*."

Jaycee's grip on Addie's arms tightened. "Addie, he's just a Shifter. Zander and I are plenty tough enough to fight him, and I'm guessing Ben can do something to help, or Kendrick wouldn't have left him with us. Plus Zander's a polar bear, and they're just *big*. We'll take care of this."

"Lachlan is a Shifter with a love for firearms," Addie pointed out. "It won't matter how strong or fast you are if you have bullets in your body."

"We can also surround him and take him down, no matter what weapon he has." Jaycee's words were low and rapid. "But you don't go rushing in when you don't know what's waiting for you."

Addie forced herself to acknowledge the truth of this. Still, it was very difficult for her to remain hidden behind the thick bole of the tree while Zander disappeared around to the back of the house, Ben went to the side window, and Jaycee approached the front door.

Jaycee went into a crouch. As Addie watched, her limbs started to change, becoming larger and more muscular, the seams of her shirt tearing.

Jaycee didn't change to a leopard—she became a leopard-beast, with the height and dexterity of a human but the lithe strength of her wildcat.

She leaned to the door, listening. Jaycee was motionless, somehow blending into the shadows around the overhang of the entrance. The way the leopard-woman became almost invisible was uncanny.

One of the others must have signaled her, because Jaycee instantly became alert. The next moment, she dug immensely strong fingers through the crack in the doorframe, and yanked the door from the wall.

Addie heard screaming inside. Without being aware she moved, Addie dashed across the yard and barreled into the house in Jaycee's wake.

CHAPTER THIRTY

Addie followed close behind Jaycee as the woman raced into the kitchen. Tori, the dark-haired eleven-year-old girl standing next to the refrigerator, dropped the full glass of iced tea she was holding and screamed.

Her screams joined those of Ivy, who had picked up a chair to face Zander. Zander hadn't shifted or become a beast like Jaycee, but he was plenty scary with his snapping dark eyes, giant bulk of a body, and wild hair.

Only Josh wasn't yelling—he was heading for the cell phone that rested on the counter.

"Ivy!" Addie shouted into the cacophony.

Her sister jumped and swung around, her eyes going wider still. "Addie! Look out! What . . . ?"

Addie lifted her hands. "Could everyone please stop screaming!"

Tori closed her mouth and the sound cut off. Tea spread in a pool at Tori's feet amidst ice and broken glass.

Ivy's chest rapidly rose. "Addie . . . *What* is going on?"

"Where is he?" Addie demanded.

Ivy blinked. "Where is who?"

"Not here." Ben came in from the living room, holding something his hand. "I'm thinking he never was."

Addie stared. "What are you talking about? What is *that*?"

"Webcam." Ben held the small piece of white plastic with lens in his palm. "Positioned on the tree so it would look into this window." He indicated the wide kitchen window that gave onto the side yard and another live oak. "From the angle, it would seem like someone standing outside looking in. What he showed through his phone was probably feed through a computer monitor."

Addie could barely breathe. "What the hell?"

"Addie!" Ivy raised her big-sister voice. "Who are these people? *What* are they?"

"Jaycee, could you . . ." Addie waved her hand.

Jaycee looked annoyed but she gave a leopard snarl and sank down into her human form. Her torn shirt showed glimpses of her ample curves.

"These are my friends," Addie said. "Ivy, I thought you were in danger. Did anyone come here today?"

"Today? No."

Tori spoke up. "Yesterday some guys came to repair the electricity on the house next door." She pointed out the kitchen window.

"They set the camera," Zander said. "Probably Lachy's thugs."

"Why?" Jaycee demanded. "Why would they trick Addie like that?"

Zander gave her a hard look. "To get us all out here, of course. We'd charge to the rescue, while Lachlan slips back around to do his evil deeds."

Addie gasped. "The cubs!"

"Are protected," Zander said. "Some of Kendrick's and Dylan's best Shifters are at the ranch. No, what Lachy-kins really wants is—"

"Kendrick," Jaycee and Addie said at the same time.

Jaycee whirled, running out. Zander went after her. "Wait—Jaycee—" He stopped at the door to the living room. "Damn it."

"Addie." Ivy's fear was fading, anger rising. "You tell me what's going on right now. And where have you been? The police came here—they think you're on the run. I told them you were just trying to calm down and get over what happened at the diner—I had to lie to the police, Addie."

The kids were watching Addie in bewilderment. Josh at least hadn't gone for the phone.

"I'm sorry." Addie's heart squeezed. "Truly, I am, and soon I'll sit you down and tell you about my adventures. But right now, I have to go, and I have to ask you not to tell *anyone* you saw me. All right? I'll explain when I can. Please, Ivy—*trust me.*"

Addie looked at her in appeal. Ivy had supported Addie through all her woes—her failed engagement, her need for a place to live, her hope to start working her way through school. In it all, Ivy had kept her big-sister attitude—*Poor little Addie needs help again.*

Now Addie was asking Ivy to trust her as an equal. Ivy shook her forefinger in Addie's direction. "It had better be a good explanation."

"Oh, it will be entertaining, I guarantee. Ben, do you know where Kendrick went?"

Ben nodded. "I know the place."

"Good. Zander—follow Ben. And maybe could you be a *little* less speedy on the turns?"

Zander grinned as he herded her out after Ben. "Hey, this is tame. You should see me when I open up my bike on the ice floes. I can really get going then."

Addie would have shuddered, but her thoughts were all for Kendrick, far away and in danger.

The darkness was absolute. Shifters could see in the dark, but that was because there was usually more light in a space than human eyes could detect. In the absence of all light, Shifters were as sightless as any human.

Kendrick sheathed the sword and shifted to his between-beast, half man, half tiger. He bent all his strength to the door, trying to wrench the steel slab back up into its slot. He heard Tiger on the other side attempting the same thing.

The door didn't budge. It was a thick piece of metal, and the mechanism that dropped it had locked it in place. Kendrick considered tearing his way through the walls themselves, but this was a vault, built to withstand fire and natural disasters. The walls would be solid concrete reinforced, likely several feet thick.

Tiger would make his way out and bring help. Dylan and Kendrick's Shifters would get the door open sooner or later.

For now, Kendrick was the mouse in Lachlan's trap, waiting for it to spring.

"That won't work."

Lachlan's voice came from behind Kendrick, on the other side of the room. Kendrick couldn't see the man, but he could hear and smell him. He didn't need sight to attack a target.

He rushed Lachlan, not waiting to ask questions or issue a challenge. At the instant before he should have contacted him, Lachlan leapt aside, and Kendrick smashed into the far wall.

His reflexes had him cushioning the blow, pushing himself away and to his feet even as he hit.

Kendrick grabbed for Lachlan again, and again Lachlan moved at the last minute. The man shouldn't be able to see any better than Kendrick, and Kendrick didn't remember Lachlan having superior hearing or scent. If anything, Kendrick, the full-blood Shifter, should have the advantage.

"You're wearing night-vision goggles," Kendrick realized, trying to catch his breath. "You see my body heat."

"You're like a flame, my old friend," Lachlan said. "Fire in the darkness."

"Take them off or turn on a light. Fight me straight up."

"Why?" Lachlan said. "I want to win. Shifters fight dirty all the time, so don't give me any crap about honor."

"I won't," Kendrick said. "I just want to see your face when I rip off the other half of it."

"Fine." Kendrick heard a rustle and then lights flashed on. Kendrick quickly dropped his gaze to the floor, blinking to adjust to the sudden glare. Lachlan discarded his goggles on an empty table.

He straightened and faced Kendrick, neither his jeans nor T-shirt showing the telltale bulge of a gun. That didn't mean Lachlan didn't have one holstered somewhere else about his person, though Kendrick smelled no metal or gunpowder.

"It's going to take your new friends time to open the door," Lachlan said. "We might as well discuss a few things."

"No, I'm just going to kill you." Kendrick drew his sword. "I'm guessing there's another way out—you weren't in here when we came in."

"Of course there's another way out. The last leader of this Shiftertown must have been one paranoid son of a bitch. There are tunnels and shafts all over the place, some not rising to the surface for miles. Sounds like a place you'd love. You always liked multiple exits and contingency plans."

"For good reason," Kendrick said. The sword's hilt felt good in his hand. "It's not safe to be a Shifter these days."

"Not when you weigh yourself down with clingy Shifters who can't make a go of it on their own," Lachlan sneered. "You should have cut them loose, let humans round them up and slap Collars on them. Saved us a lot of bother."

Kendrick's heart burned with rekindled anger. "I believed you when you said you wanted to keep Shifters free. I didn't realize you meant only select Shifters *you* chose."

"The strongest, yes. Shifters will only prevail if we band together and attack our captors. Like the Shifters did the Fae—we need to become the Battle Beasts again, but for ourselves."

"Meanwhile, all those cubs and less dominant Shifters should be rounded up and shocked, experimented on, confined, barely allowed to live?"

"Some of them like it," Lachlan said, with a laugh of disbelief. "They think it makes them stronger. Trust me, when I was trying to build a group from the Shiftertowns around here, I ran into that screwed-up way of thinking time and again. *Shiftertowns made us a community, gave our cubs a safe place to grow up. We're getting stronger.* Goddess, they reminded me of *you.*"

Kendrick held his sword steadily but at the same time watched every twitch Lachlan made. The moment the timing was exactly right, Kendrick would be on him.

"We *are* getting stronger," Kendrick said. "Having more cubs. What I'm proving is that we don't need human controlled Shiftertowns and shock Collars to do it. What did you do with all the goods in this room? The treasure of this particular Shifter clan?"

"Stole it," Lachlan said. "We need it for bribes to get the Fae gold."

"Fae gold?" The statement caught Kendrick off guard.

Lachlan made a noise of disgust. "It's the secret to getting Shifters safely *out* of Collars. Didn't Dylan share that with you? My reward to Shifters who follow me is to rid them of their Collars. No waiting their turn or until the Shiftertown leaders think it's safe or any of that bullshit. Every Shifter who follows me will be out of his or her Collar, and I'll lead them to victory."

"But only the strong ones, right?" Kendrick finished. "All the others are SOL?"

"Doesn't matter. They'll be freed sooner or later, when we win."

"Meanwhile, every Shifter, whether they follow you or not, gets slaughtered trying to rise against the hundreds of millions of humans in this country. Well thought-out."

"It's that kind of attitude that will always keep you on the run. Join me, Kendrick. We made a hell of a team once. Dylan already trusts you—get him to join us too. Nothing will be able to stop us."

Kendrick was done. "You killed a cub and the woman you wanted as mate when they tried to get away from you. You killed the humans who helped you. We don't kill those we protect. That's the end of it."

"I killed my mate and cub to protect them from *you.* I knew what you'd do to them if you captured me."

"I would have released them to return to their families.

You killed them because you wanted to. I tried to avenge them then—I'm back to finish what I started."

Lachlan gave him a pitying look. "You poor, deluded bastard. You'll learn, though, with that cute little woman you want as mate. Do you think she obeyed you, sitting at home where you told her to stay? No, the minute your back was turned, she rushed home, convinced her sister was in trouble."

Kendrick's rage burst through him along with a cold wave of fear. He tried to tamp both emotions down—Lachlan was baiting him. "If you've touched her or her family . . ."

"You'll what? Kill me faster? Or slower? No, no, I just distracted her and your friends. I love the Internet. With a webcam and a tablet even the rankest amateur can create the illusion that he's somewhere he's not."

Kendrick's fears escalated but he wasn't going to scream them at Lachlan. "Shut up, and let's do this."

Another condescending look. "You didn't think I'd bring you down here so I could fight you one-on-one, did you, my friend? Live and learn."

He clicked something in his hand and the lights went off again.

Damn it. Kendrick had started moving as soon as he'd seen Lachlan press his thumb down, sword going for its target. Lachlan moved, but not fast enough. The blade caught Lachlan and he grunted.

Not a lethal blow. Kendrick heard the man rushing away through the total darkness.

The night-vision goggles—had Lachlan snatched them up, or left them? Kendrick groped his way to where he thought the table was. He bumped into it, painfully, and then his hand landed on plastic and soft straps.

In two seconds, Kendrick had the goggles oriented and on. He glanced around the room in time to see Lachlan duck out through another opening.

He followed, sword held out of his way. Lachlan was sprinting, unencumbered, down the cement reinforced tunnel.

The best thing about chasing Lachlan down tunnels under a Shiftertown was that Lachlan was *here*. Not at the ranch closing in on Addie and his cubs or lying in wait at Addie's sister's house. The man was where Kendrick could put his hands on him. He'd finish him off, go home, and celebrate.

Lachlan ducked down another corridor, and Kendrick ducked after him. Kendrick wasn't about to wait for Lachlan to spring his trap—he would kill the man *now*.

The corridor ended in a wide room. Lachlan didn't need to see to find it, he only needed to follow the narrow hall and to smell all the Shifters waiting inside. Kendrick's Shifters.

Kendrick let his body shift to his between-beast again, crouching down under the low ceiling, but retaining the sword. He leapt into the room after Lachlan.

Lights went on, rendering the goggles useless. Kendrick flung them off and turned to face his Shifters, old and trusted friends and followers, who were now grimly lined up behind Lachlan.

CHAPTER THIRTY-ONE

Zander got another call as they were heading down the back highway toward San Antonio. He abruptly pulled to a halt, making Addie's stomach roil, and answered it.

"*What?* Shit."

That was all. Zander shoved the phone back into his coat, lifted his feet, and guided the bike back to the road.

"What's wrong?" Addie shouted.

Zander turned his head and the motorcycle crossed into the far lane. "Kendrick's gone. Lachlan has him."

He swerved out of the lane, narrowly missed by a truck that had been coming straight for them, and sped to catch up with Jaycee and Ben.

Ben led them on highways around the city of San Antonio and out into countryside again. Growing up in Texas, Addie had been almost everywhere in it but she hadn't come to the empty area south and east of San Antonio, bypassed by most people on their way to Houston or down to vacation on South Padre Island.

She certainly hadn't been along the stretch of deserted road that ended in a cluster of houses, a corral with bored-looking horses in it, and a sign that read "Welcome to Shiftertown."

Shifters milled around a house under the westering sun, the afternoon heat intense. The hottest part of the day happened in the hours before sunset.

Jaycee came and helped Addie from the motorcycle, Zander swinging off behind her. None of the Shifters seemed to notice or comment on Jaycee's torn clothes, not even Dimitri. They understood that she'd had to shift while dressed, which meant she'd run into some kind of danger.

"Kendrick's in there?" Addie asked breathlessly as she reached Dylan.

Seamus pushed through the crowd to Addie, not looking happy. Tiger, his yellow eyes glowing with rage, turned to her. "The scarred Shifter trapped him down there," Tiger said.

"We can't get to him," Seamus added.

"So what are you doing?" Addie demanded. "Is there another way in?"

"There is, but it's highly r-risky," Dimitri said. His face was damp with perspiration, his red hair raked back from his forehead. "It's a f-fortress down there, meant to be d-defended. We can only go in one at a time, which means Lachlan's Shifters can c-cut us down one at a time. *If* we can find them."

Addie stared at him. "Are you saying you haven't gone inside yet? You don't know where Kendrick is?"

"We were waiting for you," Seamus said. Shifters fanned out behind him and Dimitri, none of them wearing Collars—Kendrick's fighters. "You're leader's mate, Addie," Seamus went on. "It's your call what we do."

"Mine?" Addie jabbed a finger at her chest. "How can it be *my* call? I barely know any of you."

Jaycee, next to her, said, "Doesn't matter. When the leader is down, everyone rallies to the leader's mate. The seconds and the trackers carry out the orders, but *you* give them, until it's certain he's . . . gone." Jaycee swallowed on the last word.

Addie's chest tightened. *Gone.* The word echoed hollowly in her head. Beyond hope.

"And until we know, *I'm* in charge?" she asked, her voice rasping.

"Yeah," Seamus said. He gave her the ghost of a grin. "Scary, isn't it?"

"Kendrick might have mentioned this when he started all the mate talk," Addie said. "I'm going to have to save his ass so I can kick it. But I don't have any idea how to go in there and get him out."

Zander answered. "That's why you take advice. But not from me. From Kendrick's trackers." Because he was an outsider, Zander was saying. She had to trust the people who'd been loyal to Kendrick for years.

"Right." Addie drew a sharp breath. "Seamus. Jaycee. Dimitri." She looked at each of them in turn. "What do you suggest?"

The Shifters attacked Kendrick with fury in their eyes. Kendrick's body grew cold as he defended himself—had they hated him all this time? Was that why Lachlan had so easily turned them?

Kendrick knew all these men by name, knew their families, their clans. Knew some from cubhood, through their Transitions. He'd seen them through illnesses, through grief of loss. And now, as one, they came at him, ready to kill him.

Kendrick did not want to kill in return. He was being pushed into this choice by Lachlan.

He dodged claws and teeth coming at him, slammed his fist into bodies—human, animal, half beast. He'd never prevail—they'd drag him down and slaughter him.

Kendrick backed hurriedly, giving himself room to heft the sword. The blade, runes glinting, made the Shifters hesitate. Killing a Guardian was unheard of, supposed to bring bad luck to the Shifter who did it, maybe even to his entire clan.

"Superstition," Lachlan growled. "He's only a Shifter, like you. Give him a pretty sword and everyone is afraid. Kill him and see if he bleeds."

Most of the Shifters surged forward with renewed determination. One leapt—a Lupine, in his between-beast state. Kendrick had to swing the sword. The Lupine howled, blood on his chest, and fell back.

The others made noises of rage. Twenty, Kendrick counted, all furious now that he'd drawn blood.

This was Lachlan's revenge, he realized. Not simply Kendrick's own Shifters turning on him, but Kendrick being forced to kill them to survive.

A leader didn't kill his own. Kendrick had fought Lachlan and driven him out to prove that point. Now Lachlan forced Kendrick into a terrible choice.

"No!" Kendrick stepped back, breathing hard, shifting down to be fully human-shaped. He rested the sword back on his shoulder like a baseball bat, keeping his blade well away from the others. "I won't kill my own Shifters. Rally to me and we'll sweep this mess out of here."

"Why?" A man in front, a big Feline, snarled. "You've led us nowhere, Kendrick. Lost us our homes, our families. We hide like cowards. When we had to leave the compound, we trusted you, we waited for you. And you never came."

"I know." Kendrick held his ground. "I was making a deal with a devil called Dylan Morrissey, so we'd all be left in peace—so the Collared Shifters would help us instead of betray us. I finally found a place where we can start again. I even found a new mate. Who is with me?"

A few paused. A leader with a mate promised more stability than one without. Grief over a broken mate bond could drive a Shifter insane, make him go feral, or at least dangerously depressed—dangerous for all the Shifters he led.

The Feline sneered. "Have you forgotten your mate bond so quickly? Eileen has been gone only four years."

"The mother of my cubs will be forever in my heart," Kendrick said. "But a new mate bond is forming—and that bond is strong."

It was. Kendrick could feel it twining around his heart, whispering to him. Addison was near, he knew it.

When she shouldn't be. He growled in anger—Lachlan must have tricked her here. Zander, Ben, and Jaycee should have tied her up and sat on her. Kendrick would have to explain what he'd meant by *keeping Addison safe*.

Yet another Shifter drew back, indecision on his face. Lachlan had worked these men into fighting frenzy, feeding on their insecurity, their fear that their leader had abandoned them.

Lachlan. A swift glance around the room told Kendrick he'd vanished.

"Damn it," he snarled. "He turns you against me and leaves you to your fate. Help me find him."

The lead Feline didn't budge. "You've shit on me for years, Kendrick. Now you get to know what it tastes like."

He attacked. A few of his friends joined him. Kendrick swung the sword in a perfect arc, which would have taken off the Feline's head if that had been Kendrick's intent.

Kendrick timed it so that the tip grazed the man's throat, leaving a tiny line of blood seeping out where a Collar would be.

"Is that what you want?" Kendrick demanded. "Certain death or captivity? You keep on like this, the humans will find you and lock you in a cage."

The Feline, not learning, attacked again. Kendrick shifted his weight and swung his body all the way around, bringing up his right leg in a roundhouse kick. The Feline danced back from the blow, but Kendrick kept spinning, coming up next to the Feline to bring the hilt of his sword down on his head.

The Feline crumpled into a ball with a grunt and went still.

"Where's Lachlan?" Kendrick called to the remaining Shifters. "I want him."

Half of them roared, raising fists in fealty and swarming to his side. Kendrick had to stop them trying to touch him for reassurance and led them out into the next corridor.

Which way Lachlan had gone was anyone's guess. Lachlan had been right that the place was a maze, with blind corners everywhere. Kendrick needed a tracker, an exceptional one, like Tiger.

He brought his party to a halt. They would look for a way to the surface, join with the rest of his Shifters and Dylan's, and scour the grounds for Lachlan. Kendrick started to give the orders for the Shifters to split and begin searching for a way out, when a rumble alerted him to danger.

Kendrick knew that noise. He hadn't lived in underground places most of his life to not understand what it meant.

"Run!" he shouted. "Find exits—meet at the leader's house!"

His words were drowned by a tearing roar as the ceiling of the tunnels started to come down, tumbling huge slabs of concrete and a half ton of dirt onto the Shifters below it.

The earth shook under Addie's feet. She and Kendrick's Shifters, plus a few of Dylan's, had moved around to the back of the house, where Tiger said tunnels emerged from the extensive cellars.

The roar of an explosion rumbled across the ground, and dust and debris shot out of the open back door of the leader's house.

"Shit!" Dimitri was running toward the house, Seamus and Ben behind him.

Jaycee stood her ground next to Addie, but the anguish in her eyes told Addie she wanted to sprint after them.

"Tiger!" Addie called. "Where is this other way down? The risky one Dimitri talked about?"

Tiger growled and pointed into the open fields beyond Shiftertown. "There."

Very specific. "Well, come on then," Addie said. "Show me."

"Hold on," Jaycee seized her by the arm. "Are you crazy?"

Another Shifter came to them, big and gruff—Addie wasn't familiar enough with Shifters yet to tell what kind he was. "What are your orders, ma'am?"

Addie's thoughts whirled. Her only desire was to find Kendrick any way possible, to drag him out and hold him to her.

"Find a way in," she said, her voice barely working. "Come at him from all sides you can and grab this Lachlan guy on the way. Do anything you have to. Ask Seamus to organize it."

"Yes, ma'am." The Shifter looked a bit doubtful, but he gave her a nod and an encouraging look.

"Jaycee," Addie said, turning to her, "if you're supposed to guard me, you stick with me. Tiger supposedly can find anyone. Zander, we might need you—if . . . *when* we find him . . ."

"If he needs a little healing?" Zander finished for her. "You got it, sweetheart."

"We should let Seamus and the others dig their way down first," Jaycee said. "And you should stay up here and wait. Sit in Dylan's truck."

Logically, Addie understood that Jaycee was right. She knew damn all about rescue missions, explosions, and underground tunnels.

But something propelled her to follow Tiger, to rush headlong toward Kendrick, wherever he was. A frantic heat gripped her heart, making her feet move out into the open land instead of back to the safety of the vehicles.

Tiger was quickly heading for the horizon. Addie sprinted after him, and Jaycee bounded along behind her, as fast and sleek as her leopard. Zander jogged after them. "Where's he going?" Zander asked.

Tiger disappeared over a fold of land, and they hurried to catch up. They found Tiger tearing squares of sod from what looked like boards lying on the ground. As Addie neared him, she realized they were doors, like the entrance to a storm shelter.

"In there?" she asked.

Tiger didn't answer. He finished digging the sod out of the way and yanked the doors up.

A waft of dust poured out, closing up Addie's throat. She coughed. Jaycee sneezed. Zander peered into the darkness of the hole, his arm over his nose.

"Of course," Zander said. "Kendrick is hiding in the deep, dark, smelly hole. And *you* want us to go down there." He pointed an accusing finger at Tiger.

Tiger gave him an unreadable look. He forestalled any questions by lying on the edge of the doorframe, feeling inside, then righting himself and starting down what appeared to be a ladder.

Addie made herself wait until Tiger had gone a long way down. Following him without knowing how sturdy the ladder was or where it led would be stupid, even though every instinct in her was urging her to scramble down after him.

"You all right?" she called.

Tiger took so long to answer that Addie's heart thumped in worry.

"Forty rungs," Tiger's rumble came to them. "Solid floor. The ladder will hold you."

Before the others could prevent her, Addie slipped over the side and climbed down in Tiger's wake.

CHAPTER THIRTY-TWO

Kendrick inched his way out from under a pile of rubble, struggling to breathe. He was trapped between the rock fall that had rushed into the corridor, creating a mound of debris, and the low ceiling, which remained intact. There was very little space for Kendrick's body between the rubble and the ceiling, and he slid through darkness on his belly.

Lachlan didn't bring firearms, because he went for explosives.

The air was thick with dust and Kendrick couldn't get a breath. He coughed and spat but had only sand and dirt to inhale.

He shook his head, trying to find clean air. Kendrick had only one thought beyond immediate survival—*Lachlan is out there, and Goddess knows what he'll do to Addison and my cubs*.

That thought galvanized him, made him harbor no idea of giving up and dying. He'd dig his way out of here, find Addison, and kill Lachlan. He'd finish Lachlan as fast as he could and send him to dust.

But first he had to get out. Though Kendrick had returned

to his between-beast state, strong enough to throw chunks of concrete from his path, his progress was slow.

Something hummed in the darkness. Kendrick knew exactly what it was, having heard that sound resonating deep in his body since the day he'd stood under a grove of trees during the Choosing and was touched by the Goddess.

Smacked by the Goddess was more like it. He'd been standing there, minding his own business, never dreaming he was a good candidate for Guardian. He'd attended the Choosing only because every male past their Transition in his mother's clan was required to.

A shaft of light had struck him, pulling him off his feet. While Kendrick's heart had pounded in terror the clan leader had announced, "The Goddess has Chosen."

Since that day, the damned sword had been singing to him, either so faintly as to blend into the background, or, like now, soaring into a resounding chorus.

Kendrick knew its music could save his life. He dragged himself forward, angling through the rock fall toward the humming sword.

Light flashed. Kendrick froze, expecting Lachlan to come climbing over the rubble and shoot him, but the light emanated from the ground and not from a flashlight.

The runes on the sword were flashing in the gloom, letters outlined with fire. Not all the Guardians bothered to learn what the inscriptions said—and Kendrick acknowledged that a lot of it was gibberish to him. He'd taught himself to read the ancient Fae he could decipher, so he could understand part of it.

One of the lines was in invocation of the Goddess, similar to the ones Shifters used to begin any ceremony of worship:

Goddess, mother of us all, lady of the moon, we beseech thee to be with us.

Another line was an incantation to her husband the God, asking for his blessing.

Then there was the curious sentence Kendrick had mulled over for a long time:

The power lies not in one.

Not in one *what*? Or not in one person but more than one? In that case, why was the Guardian the only person who could wield the sword? If another Shifter caught it up and stuck it through a dead Shifter's heart, the Shifter's body would remain intact, but with a sword sticking out of it.

A few months ago, a non-Guardian Shifter, Broderick, had performed a Guardian duty on a dead Guardian in Montana, but from what Kendrick had gleaned, Broderick had been temporarily Goddess-touched at the time.

Here Kendrick was, all alone, the sword singing away, telling him to get his butt over there and rescue it. Growling, Kendrick squirmed and wriggled over to the sword, pushing more debris out of his path as he went.

The sword lay on top of a pile of crushed stone, just out of reach. Of course. Kendrick clawed his way to a relatively open spot—not much space between the fallen stone and what was left of the ceiling.

He reached up, his between-beast claws changing back to a human hand so he could wrap his fingers around the hilt.

Instantly the sword went into paroxysms of joy. The sword jangled and sang, vibrating on the rocks.

"Shut up," Kendrick told it in irritation. "You'll bring the rest of the ceiling down."

The sword muted its song the slightest bit but the happy noise went on. Kendrick knew it couldn't be heard except by himself—maybe others couldn't see the glowing runes either. Kendrick was just one lucky sod, wasn't he?

The tunnel seemed to be filled fairly uniformly from the cave-in, the narrow crawl space near the ceiling sloping a little way down to the sides of the corridor. Kendrick knew that whichever direction he went, he was likely to find a total collapse in his way or he'd cause one.

But what the hell? He couldn't stay here debating about it. Kendrick picked a direction and started crawling.

He'd gone, he calculated, about twenty yards, the sword lighting his way, when he heard sounds. He snarled at the sword, which was humming in his ears, to *shut up* again and listened as hard as he could.

The noises were groans. Eventually, Kendrick distinguished them into separate ones, two of them, one louder than the other. They were male voices, of Shifters in great pain, unable to make any sounds but the moans that came from their throats.

Kendrick carefully scrambled down and over stones, making his way to them. The rock fall sloped downward farther on, flowing out of an open door. The doorframe had remained upright, the lintel supporting the walls, but the entire ceiling inside the room had collapsed.

Kendrick spied a hand poking from this debris. He dropped the sword near it and started pulling rocks away from the man buried beneath. The groans increased as Kendrick moved the concrete away to reveal a Shifter, one of the ones who'd joined Lachlan. Lachlan had trapped him in here to die.

The Shifter—a Lupine called Darien—opened his dark eyes, and his next moan became a sigh of relief. "Thank the Goddess. I won't die without a Guardian."

Kendrick felt Darien's chest, arms, legs, neck, and gently slid his hands across his abdomen. "You might not die at all. You're pretty tough."

Darien's dirty face split with a grin. "Yeah, so my mate tells me."

Kendrick knew Darien's mate, and his cubs. "You'll see them again. I promise you. There's another down here with you. Can you help me find him?" The other voice had grown fainter still.

Darien tried to raise his head, grunted, and gave up. "Five of us. Lachlan told us to wait for you here in case you came back this way."

"Bastard. Why the hell—?" Kendrick bit off his question. Rescue now, interrogate later.

Darien put his dirt encrusted hand on Kendrick's arm. "Because we needed a leader. We're *Shifters*, Kendrick. We like hierarchy and alphas. Life is hard to figure out—we need someone to lean on when it gets too tough."

"I was still there for you," Kendrick said in a hard voice. "Even if you didn't see me."

"I know, but like I said, we're Shifters. We need someone to hold our hands sometimes—literally."

And Lachlan had played on that need and dependency. A leader's Shifters weren't much different from his own cubs—his followers thrived on attention as much as the basics like food and a safe place to sleep.

"I'm sorry," Kendrick said. "Truly. You're right. I should have been there for you." He closed his hand around Darien's fingers where they rested on his arm. "Tell you what, when we get you and your friends out of here, you can smack me upside the head."

Darien grinned again. "I wouldn't have hurt you." His other hand came to rest on Kendrick's as though he took strength from the touch. "Much."

Kendrick grunted a laugh as he continued to unbury Darien and helped him to sit on the pile of rubble. He left Darien to catch his breath and crawled to where he heard movement. Kendrick began pulling away rocks and gravel, the Sword of the Guardian lighting the way.

Kendrick's heart dropped when he uncovered a Shifter, dead. The man had been crushed, no hope of survival.

Kendrick knew him, as he knew Darien, as he knew every Shifter under his command. Immense grief flowed through him as he lifted the sword and plunged it into the dead Shifter's heart. There was a faint whisper, and the Shifter disappeared into dust that dispersed and vanished.

But there was still someone alive under here. Another groan sounded, and rocks moved near where Kendrick crouched. Kendrick let the sword drop with a clatter and dug through the rubble with both hands. Darien joined him, and soon they uncovered another Shifter.

It was the Feline who'd been Lachlan's main supporter. The man opened his eyes, dark orbs shining among the white dust that coated his face.

"Guardian," he whispered.

The Feline's body was broken. Blood seeped from between his lips, and his bones had been shattered.

Kendrick laid his hand on the Feline's chest, feeling his heart beating erratically—struggling for life.

"I know a healer," Kendrick said quickly. "He can get here soon. Crazy asshole, but he's got the gift."

The Feline gave him a wan smile. "I'm not going to make it out in time, he's not going to make it in, and you know it." He closed a bloody hand around Kendrick's wrist. "Lachlan's a bastard. So are you, but *he* left me to die."

"I'll avenge you," Kendrick said. "Trust me."

"Yeah, I know you hate him. Just tell him before you kill him that I'll be waiting to kick his ass in the Summerland."

"I will," Kendrick promised. More sorrow swamped him. "I'm sorry I failed you, my friend."

The Feline snorted. "Get over yourself. Just do it. I want to see my mate and cub. I can feel them reaching for me." His mate had passed long ago, trying to bring in a cub that had also died.

Kendrick brushed his hand over the man's forehead. He hated this part of his job, but he also knew that he sent the Shifters off with some comfort.

"Goddess go with you," Kendrick said. He lifted the sword, which sang and glittered, and drove it into the Feline's heart.

"Thank you," the Feline whispered, and then he was dust.

Tears streamed down Darien's cheeks, plastering the dirt to them. "He was a good man." He sniffled and wiped his face with the back of his hand. "For a Feline."

Kendrick cleared his throat, trying to contain the pain in his heart. "Help me find the others."

The final two Shifters Darien said had been with him were farther down in the rubble, already dead. Kendrick dispatched them, then bowed his head for a time, resting his weight on the sword, unable to move.

Addie felt sick when she saw the rubble blocking the tunnel at the bottom of the shaft.

Kendrick was behind there. Zander's flashlight roved the seemingly solid wall of boulders. A slight indentation at the ceiling showed that the debris had filled in nearly to the top of the tunnel.

"Are you sure he's through there?" Addie asked Tiger. "Dylan said there were many ways out."

Tiger touched the rocks and bent his head. "Yes," he said after a moment. "This is the closest path to him."

Jaycee, who'd climbed down directly after Addie, clicked off the cell phone she'd used to contact Dimitri. "Dimitri says Kendrick hasn't come out. The main entrance has completely collapsed. Dylan and his trackers are checking all the side tunnels, but they're not optimistic."

"No," Tiger said. "He is behind here."

Zander slapped his hand to a boulder. "It's nothing but rock. We'll never tunnel in there. Going around has to be better."

Tiger had both hands on the fill now, his head bent, while Addie watched worriedly. She could barely breathe in this stuffy place, and her wildly pounding heart didn't help.

"I can see," Tiger said, his eyes closed. "Heat, moving . . . now it's gone."

"Gone?" Addie ran two steps to the rock and flattened her hands against it, as though she'd be able to feel something through it as Tiger did. "What's gone?"

"The heat. Someone was alive. Now dead."

"Kendrick?" Addie's word came out a whisper.

"No," Tiger said. "Another."

"Let's hope it was Lachlan," Jaycee said.

Tiger shook his head. "Another. A Feline." He remained frozen for a few more seconds, a giant of a man with his hands spread on the rock, as though listening to what the debris had to tell him.

He turned abruptly, eyes flashing gold, and started up the ladder.

Addie, instead of screaming at him to wait, climbed quickly out after him. She'd figured out that Tiger didn't answer direct questions or take orders or bother to explain what he was doing. He did what he did and everyone else had to figure it out. Jaycee followed Addie, Zander coming behind her.

Tiger stood at the top of the ladder, looked around for a few moments, then started off to the west, his strides even. Counting paces, Addie realized as she hurried after him, his strides never varying.

The sun touched the horizon. Red and gold rays streamed up into the soft blue sky, a Texas sunset in all its glory.

Tiger moved about a hundred paces from the entrance to the shaft, then turned and walked south. He stopped on a patch of ground that looked no different from any other to Addie—the grasses and dust were identical to all other grasses and dust around it.

"Here," Tiger said. "This is the best way in."

Zander scanned the ground, his white braids swinging. "You see a hidden door that I don't? Nothing here but solid earth." He stamped one booted foot on the grass.

"Here," Tiger said, and started taking off his clothes.

CHAPTER THIRTY-THREE

Addie stared as Tiger's body came into view, then she spun on her heel when he started to slide down his jeans. She saw the jeans land on the grass, a very small pair of underwear on top.

There was a rush of air, and Zander said in awe, "Holy shit."

Addie risked a glance behind her. The giant tiger that had confronted her at Charlie's ranch stood like a statue on the vast plain, the dying sun's light burning its orange fur golden. Tiger let out a tiger growl, then he planted his sharp claws in the grass and started to dig.

"Seriously?" Zander said to him. "You're going to dig forty feet down with your bare paws?"

Tiger paid no attention. In the space of a minute, he had soft earth moved aside and was going deeper.

"Thirty-nine feet now," Addie said, coming to the hole. "Don't stop him unless you have a better idea."

"A backhoe and a giant drill," Zander said. "But what the hell. I can't let a tiger best me."

He threw his duster to the ground, tugged off his boots,

and peeled his T-shirt from his torso. He was as tightly built as Tiger and almost as big.

Addie averted her gaze as Zander slid out of his jeans, and saw that Jaycee was undressing as well.

Zander growled and Addie looked at him in time to see him complete the shift to very large, snowy white polar bear. Addie had never seen a polar bear apart from ones in zoos, and then only from a distance. Now she stood an arm's length from Zander, who was larger than any wild polar bear would ever be. His black nose and claws stood out vividly from his pale fur, as did his very dark eyes.

Zander gazed at her soulfully for a moment, then he put his giant paws down next to Tiger's and began to dig.

Jaycee was much smaller than both of them but her leopard was a thing of grace. She darted in between the males and began to dig, her paws spewing up dirt faster than they could.

Addie, not to be outdone, found a piece of board and joined them. She couldn't dig as well as they did, but she could scrape the loosened earth out of the way.

They worked while the sun sank, bathing the sky in hazy purple twilight. By the time it was fully dark, a half-moon rising, they'd made it down about fifteen feet.

Zander decided they needed to shore up what they'd dug out, or the walls would collapse. He shifted back to human to ask Addie to help him drag over the doors from the hidden entrance, and used the timber to brace the shaft they were creating. Zander didn't bother dressing for this, but by this time Addie was used to Shifters thinking nothing of standing around naked. Zander was beautiful, though, the man with stark white hair and black eyes, touched by moonlight.

Kendrick was even more beautiful.

Zander sent Jaycee running back to the main house to bring help and more supplies. They'd need rope if they were going to climb down and fetch Kendrick.

Tiger said nothing at all, never returned to his human form. He simply dug.

The moon was high by the time Dylan had arranged for more diggers, equipment to move the earth and solidify the hole, and rappelling gear.

"You know I'm going down there," Addie said to Dylan.

Dylan looked at her a long time, then amusement entered his hard eyes. "I know."

"Don't be crazy," Zander said. He still hadn't bothered with clothes. "I'm a *Shifter* healer. There's nothing to say I can help *you* if you get hurt."

Addie faced him, hands on hips. "Well, one thing about working for Bo is he was good about making sure his employees had an insurance plan. If I'm hurt, just drive me to a hospital in Austin. I'm covered."

Zander stared at her, eyes unmoving. "Not my point."

"I know. But if I worry about shit like that, I'll break down and never get up. I *have* to go down and help Kendrick. That's all there is to it."

Zander watched her for another moment. "If you're hurt, you know he'll kill me."

Addie shrugged. "Suck it up."

Zander gave her another black-eyed stare, then he nodded. "You're his mate. What'cha gonna do?"

Jaycee wasn't so sanguine but she declared she'd go down right in front of Addie. She'd been assigned to be Addie's bodyguard, and that was that.

Finally they had the shaft clear to the depth Tiger wanted it, the ropes and pulleys ready.

"I go first," Tiger said.

No one argued with him. Addie was coming to understand, both from observation and comments by the others, that Tiger had unique abilities for search and rescue.

Tiger had resumed his jeans, shirt, and boots before he approached the hole and settled the rappelling gear around his chest and thighs. Now he leapt backwards into the hole, not bothering to wait to see if Dimitri, who was securing the ropes, had done it right. He simply trusted Dimitri had.

The nylon ropes whirred as Tiger went down, snapping

tight when he stopped. He made his way gradually down into the darkness—he had no light, saying he could see better without it.

The ropes went slack abruptly, then Tiger tugged at them, indicating Dimitri should haul them back up. "Wait," Tiger called, then went silent.

Addie heard a faint clinking of metal against rock. After an interminable time, Tiger's gravelly voice floated back to them.

"I'm through."

Addie breathed a sigh. Tiger had found a way into the tunnels after all.

"Me next," Zander said.

"No," Tiger called upward. "No room. Jaycee, then Addison."

"No," Dimitri said abruptly. "Z-zander, and that's it."

Jaycee glared at Dimitri. She'd restored her clothes, but they were too shredded to cover her much. Dimitri glared right back at her, his red hair shining in the moonlight.

"Addie's insisting," Jaycee said. "Which is her right, as mate. And I have to take care of her. That's my job."

Dimitri's wolf gaze landed on Addie. "Add-Addie . . ."

"I'm going down there, Dimitri," Addie said. "Jaycee doesn't have to come."

"Yes, I do." Jaycee heaved an exasperated sigh. "What am I supposed to do? Disobey an order from my alpha to keep his *mate* safe? Because *you* might be worried?" She pointed at Dimitri. "There's no connection between you and me. I don't care if we had a great night in the sack."

The other Shifters crowding around didn't pretend to mind their own business. They listened, interested.

"No c-connection?" Dimitri asked, rage in his eyes.

"Nope. So you have no call to tell me what to do."

Dimitri drew himself up. "Jaycee Bordeaux, under the light of the Goddess and in front of witnesses, I claim you as mate." His voice rang clear, his stammer gone.

"What?" Jaycee shrieked. "Are you out of your mind?"

"No." Dimitri said. "You going to refuse?"

Jaycee opened her mouth, very likely to hotly say *yes*. Then she subsided. "No. I don't know. I have to think."

Dimitri's eyes flared with triumph. "Mate-claimed. Stay out of the hole."

"Don't even start with me." Jaycee grabbed the harness and began buckling herself in. "You're not my mate yet, and you can't override the alpha's command until then."

Addie twined her fingers together to keep herself from grabbing the gear from Jaycee and plummeting downward herself. She asked Dimitri, "Does she mean you can tell a Shifter leader to stuff himself if you think his orders might hurt your mate?"

"Yep," Dimitri said. His smile beamed. "L-looking forward to it."

"What if your mate *is* the Shifter leader?" Addie went on.

Jaycee snapped the last strap into place and lifted the supplies she'd carry down with her. "Then you're screwed. Watch that rope real close, Dimitri."

Dimitri growled, the wolf in him responding, but Jaycee didn't wait for any more argument. She sat on the lip of the opening, swung her legs over, and disappeared inside.

Dimitri sweated while the ropes played out, holding the end even though it was secured by a big hook to an equally large metal loop driven into the ground.

He didn't relax until Jaycee called back up, "I'm down," and sent the gear to the surface again.

Addie shook as Dimitri helped strap her into the harness. She'd never done any rappelling before, or any even moderately dangerous sport for that matter. She took walks, went on occasional country hikes with the kids, and that was it.

"You sure this will hold me?" she asked Dimitri nervously as she slipped on the leather gloves he handed her.

"It held Tiger," Dimitri said. "And he's much bigger than you. You don't have to go down," he added.

"Yes, I do. Thanks, Dimitri." Addie impulsively gave the man a hug. Dimitri responded gladly, squeezing her in a tight embrace. "I'll tell Jaycee she'd be a fool to refuse you."

Jaycee yelled up, "I can hear you! Don't encourage him."

Addie patted Dimitri's shoulder, sat on the edge of the

hole as she'd seen Jaycee do, braced herself, and gingerly slid into the shaft.

The ropes zipped through the buckles faster than Addie thought they would, and she yelped. She applied the brake as Dimitri had showed her, and yelped again as she dangled in mid-air.

Jaycee had brought a flashlight with her, knowing Addie couldn't see in the dark like Shifters. Jaycee shone it around now, and Addie saw a wall with dirt brushed away from it, a hole in the wall, and empty space beyond.

She released the belaying device and let herself down a little more slowly, grateful for the gloves. When she reached the bottom, a tight space, Jaycee helped her unlock the ropes and step out of the harness.

Tiger waited for them at the opening. Without speaking, he turned and squeezed through. Addie went next, and Jaycee followed, holding the flashlight so it would light Addie's way but not blind Tiger.

They moved through an almost round tunnel shored up with solid stone pressed together and mortared. Someone had made this long, long ago.

"What is this?" Addie asked. "What's it for?"

"Escape tunnel," Tiger said. "Looks like it was abandoned. There's air coming through it."

Addie had noticed that. Instead of the stuffy, dusty air she'd expected, it was cool, with a flowing breeze.

Tiger led them unerringly down this tunnel, their feet crunching on gravel. It was very dry, no dankness announcing the presence of water.

After a long time of trudging, the opening left far behind them, Tiger stopped. Though the tunnel went on, beside him was another opening, half filled with rubble.

He started digging through this, the rocks rolling out behind him. Jaycee started pushing the debris he shifted ahead of them into the tunnel, so it wouldn't block their way back. Addie, after realizing what she was doing, helped.

Tiger stopped digging. "Addie," he said.

Addie went to him, her heart beating faster. He'd found something.

Before Addie could ask a question, Tiger boosted her up and over the pile of rocks he'd tunneled into. She slid down a slope on the other side, skittering and bumping in the dark, heading for a faint glow below.

As she neared the glow, a large form rose in front of it, and she ran headlong into it. Addie tried to stop herself, but was lifted and steadied by the strong arms of Kendrick.

"Addison—what the hell?" Kendrick's words were a croak, his voice gone after hours of being trapped beneath with no water.

Addison's cool hands were on him as she touched his chest, arms, face. "Kendrick—thank God you're alive."

She flung her arms around him, and Kendrick held her, the relief that she was safe and whole almost making his knees buckle. He lifted her against him, tension flowing away as he clung to his mate. Addison was all right.

Addison kissed his cracked lips. "Tiger found a way down." She called behind her. "Jaycee, get him some water." She turned to Kendrick again, then started as she saw Darien on the rubble a few feet away. "Hello . . ." Her breath brushed Kendrick's face. "I'm Addie. We're here to rescue you."

Darien stared, then he let out a breath. "She's your mate all right. Damn, Kendrick, you move fast."

"When it's important. Give Darien the water, Jaycee. He's been hurt."

Jaycee was already unstrapping a bottle of water she'd carried down. "Whose side is he on?"

Her voice held all kinds of suspicion, but she went to Darien and unscrewed the cap of the water bottle. Darien took it.

"The Guardian's side," Darien said. "He proved himself the better." Darien sipped water but didn't take much before he was passing the bottle to Kendrick.

"Kendrick shouldn't have to *prove* himself to you," Jaycee told Darien hotly. "You should have trusted him."

"Enough." Kendrick drank, wiped his mouth, and tried not to crumple in gratitude for the cool liquid in his throat. "Tiger, Jaycee, take him out of here, and call Zander to come out and look at him."

"Zander's here," Addison said. "Just outside. You go first, Kendrick. We'll take care of Darien."

"Doesn't work that way." Kendrick helped Darien to his feet. "Jaycee, get him out safely and stay with him. Don't let anyone kill him. I'm relieving you of your duty to look after Addie and assigning you Darien."

Jaycee sighed in exasperation. "Sometimes it sucks being a tracker. Especially a tracker with an unreasonable leader."

"You can yell at me later," Kendrick said. "Tiger—there are other Shifters down here. Some remained Lachlan's followers, but it doesn't matter. They're *all* my Shifters, and we need to find them."

Tiger nodded. "On it. You next, though."

Kendrick knew damn well he wouldn't leave this place until all his Shifters were accounted for and Addison was safely above. "What about Lachlan?" Kendrick asked. "Tell me someone found him and gutted him. Don't worry about saving him for me."

"Haven't seen him," Tiger said.

"He tricked me into thinking he'd taken my sister and her family hostage," Addison told him. "So he could get you. *I* want to gut him."

"I bet he's as trapped down here as you," Jaycee said. "Caught under all the rubble like he wanted you to be."

"We need to make sure," Kendrick said. "Tiger, send as much help down as you can."

Tiger gave another nod and assisted Darien up over the rubble. Tiger boosted Jaycee out then looked Kendrick and Addison over with his strange eyes.

"Touch of a mate," he said, then he scrambled up over the rocks and was gone.

Addison looked after him in bewilderment then turned to Kendrick. "What does that mean?"

Kendrick opened the bottle of water and took another

welcome drink. "Touch of a mate heals," he said. "When the mating is true."

"Did he mean you were hurt?" Addison's hands moved over his chest again. Kendrick was sore, cut, bruised, and aching but he'd live. Not that he'd stop Addie touching him for any reason.

"I'll be all right," he said.

"Did Lachlan do this?" she asked. "Cause the cave-in?"

"Yep. He came down here, robbed the Shifters that lived here of everything they had, lured me down, and collapsed the tunnels, trapping me *and* his own followers. That's the kind of fine Shifter he is."

"I thought he'd taken Ivy. I couldn't stay at the ranch and let that happen."

Addison spoke defiantly, as though she expected Kendrick to grow enraged, but he only kissed her soft hair.

"A leader has to make decisions like that," he said, enjoying her warmth. "You weigh your safety against that of others and make your choice. I don't blame you for going."

"Really?" Addison blinked at him in the glow of the flashlight Jaycee had left. "Jaycee was convinced you'd skin her alive."

"She kept you safe. That's all that matters." Kendrick made himself release Addison. "They should be out by now. Show me the way."

He boosted her to the top of the rubble then handed her the flashlight. Kendrick turned to retrieve his sword from where he'd stuck it point-first into the rocks and watched in momentary confusion as the boulders seemed to part and turn to dust.

A flash blinded him, then came a roaring in his ears. "Addison!" he shouted, but couldn't hear his own words. "Go!"

The rock in front of him parted and became dust, the rest of the room falling on him. He saw Addison roll back down toward him as a slab fell on the opening she'd been about to crawl through.

Rock and debris rained down on Kendrick's back. Addison slammed into him, and Kendrick swiftly put her under him, trying to block the worst of the fall from her. He was pinned, trapped, and the rock was crushing him, filling his mouth, his nose, his lungs.

A light shafted through the dust, and into it strode Lachlan. He kicked Kendrick's head where it protruded from the rock fall, and another blinding flash flared before Kendrick could see no more.

CHAPTER THIRTY-FOUR

Addie wriggled and squirmed, trying to fight free of the weight crushing her back. The flashlight had gone out, buried, but a pinprick of light pierced the blackness.

She heaved herself onto her hands and knees, and the weight slid away, along with a cascade of pebbles.

Coughing, Addie turned, groping in the darkness. "Kendrick," she sobbed. "Kendrick . . ."

The light brightened, something underneath a pile of stones making them glow. Addie shoved away rock and halted, stunned, when she saw that the light came from the Sword of the Guardian.

It lay lengthwise, unsheathed, the naked blade and hilt flashing silver fire. Addie turned her head from the sudden glare, her eyes screwing shut.

After a time, she pried her eyes open again, a crack at a time, letting herself adjust to the light. She saw that the chamber they were in was small and now crammed with even more rubble. The sword's light illuminated it better than the brightest flashlight. By that light, Addie saw Kendrick.

He lay facedown, half buried in rock, and she realized

he had been the weight she'd climbed out from under. His shirt had been torn open, revealing his spine and neck covered in blood. His white and black mottled hair, which Addie had admired since the first time she'd seen him, was now drenched with dirt and gore.

"Kendrick!" Addie shouted.

She scrambled back to him, the sword flaring with still more light. Its glow brushed the broken wreck of Kendrick's hand that reached out toward the sword. The hand was unmoving, as was Kendrick's entire body.

Addie quickly slid her hand to his neck, searching for a pulse. She found nothing—no beating to tell her he was still alive, no breath, nothing.

"Kendrick." The word turned to a sob. Addie collapsed onto Kendrick's back, choking with tears, her body watery with fear. "Kendrick, please, no. I love you so much."

"Aw, very sweet."

Addie jerked her head up to see Lachlan climb into the room from the direction the blast had come. The sword's light flooded his face, half of it ruined by old scars from Kendrick's claws.

Addie launched herself up, fury and grief giving her strength. She slipped, her leg throbbing, and fell to the rocks beside Kendrick.

"No, stay there with him," Lachlan said. "That way I can skewer you together. Won't that be nice?"

Lachlan reached down and snatched up the sword.

The next instant, he yelled and dropped it, wringing out his hand. Addie saw a black streak, like a brand, burned across his palm.

"Son of a fucking . . ." Lachlan snarled, and he shifted into his half-wolf, half-beast state, his T-shirt and jeans splitting as he did. His hands became wolf claws, his face fierce and terrible, half its fur gone, revealing scarred, bare skin.

Beneath Addie, Kendrick moved the slightest bit. Addie's relief, fear, and anger twisted together until she could barely see, barely think.

"Addison," Kendrick whispered. "Sword."

Lachlan struck. Addie tried desperately to deflect him, but he was too swift, too strong. Lachlan's blow landed on Kendrick's back, claws digging in. Kendrick grunted in pain, and blood flowed where Lachlan ripped.

Kendrick needed the sword. But it was white-hot—Addie had seen it burn Lachlan. She wouldn't be able to pick it up.

She grabbed for Lachlan, getting her fingers around the waistband of his torn jeans. She tried to pull him away from Kendrick, but she might as well have tried to pull over a well-rooted tree. Lachlan shrugged her off as though he barely felt her and went for Kendrick again.

Damn it. Addie wrapped her shirt around her hand and lunged for the sword.

As she seized the hilt, she realized it wasn't hot at all. In fact, no matter how much light the sword radiated, it was comfortably cool.

Surprised, Addie freed her hand from the shirt and grasped the hilt with her bare fingers. The sword flashed, but was easy to hold, not as heavy as she'd feared.

Behind her, Lachlan struck at Kendrick again. Kendrick managed to drag himself up enough to grasp Lachlan around the waist and pull him down to him.

The two men grappled on the rocks, slipping and sliding, Kendrick trying to get a lock on the man's throat. But he was hurt and Lachlan was whole, strong, unyielding.

Addie snarled at Lachlan and smacked him with the sword.

Lachlan scrambled up and spun around, his gray wolf eyes widening. "Hey, watch where you're swinging that."

Kendrick got to his hands and knees. Lachlan turned and kicked him in the stomach. Kendrick, blood dripping from his mouth, went down.

Addie shrieked. She held the sword in both hands and started beating Lachlan with it, not sure whether she hit him with the flat or the edge. Lachlan, a ferocious beast with a scarred wolf face, backed under her onslaught.

In a moment, he would turn on her, batter the sword away, and kill her. Addie knew that. But then he'd kill Kendrick, and Addie would prevent that for as long as she had breath.

"I'm a *waitress*," she yelled at Lachlan. "I'm supposed to make *coffee*, not fight mythical beasts with magic swords. Why don't you just go *away*?"

"Don't play with that, little girl," Lachlan said, his voice a guttural snarl. "Stroking Kendrick's sword won't get you anything from him. Why don't you stroke mine instead?"

Addie's rage escalated. She continued beating him, then behind her, she was aware of a long, low, growl.

The growl held the fury of ages, an old, old anger that reached back to its ancestors, who'd been forced to fight for the princes of the hated Fae. A white tiger, battered and bloody, rose from the debris, his ears flat, his body moving with the deliberate, slow, almost trembling stalk of a cat intent on its kill.

Lachlan howled, the primal cry of a wolf. He went for Kendrick, his massive arms spread, his claws primed to gouge his enemy.

Addie heaved the sword in her sore arms, brought it around, point-first, and drove it straight into Lachlan's side.

Lachlan's howl turned to a roar of anger. He grabbed the sword's blade that stuck out of his ribs, then cried out again as the sword burned him.

The sword was still cool to Addie's hands. She stared as Lachlan fought it but she didn't let go.

Blood gushed from Lachlan's side, but Shifters, it seemed, were tough to kill. Lachlan jerked himself around, the sword tearing from him, and lunged for Addie, his wolf mouth open and ready to rip into her.

Kendrick sprang. He was filthy with dirt, his front leg hung askew, and blood coated his mouth, but his spring was true and elegant.

He leapt directly at Lachlan, a cat moving in a precise arc to take down his prey.

Lachlan whirled from Addie to face Kendrick's attack, but he didn't have a chance. Kendrick landed on Lachlan without flinching, opened his tiger jaws, and tore out Lachlan's throat.

Blood, hot and red, gushed from the wolf as he howled and scrabbled, trying to get Kendrick off him. Kendrick yanked his head back and spat blood. Lachlan's hands slipped from Kendrick's white fur, the howl quickly becoming a drawn-out cry of agony.

Kendrick shifted back to human, his naked body shaking under the glow of the sword, his face stark, his broken left arm folded across his chest.

But his eyes were green and steady as he turned to Addie. "Addison. The sword."

Addie grabbed it, the blade coated with Lachlan's blood. Kendrick snatched it by the hilt, tried to get to his feet, and fell back to his knees. Addie was next to him, her hand under his shoulder, helping him up again.

Lachlan was still breathing, blood all over his throat, chest, and face as he slowly shifted back to human.

"Fuck you, Kendrick," he whispered. "I'll see you in the Summerland—and I'll best you there."

"You'll see me," Kendrick said. "Goddess go with you, Lachlan."

Kendrick touched Lachlan's face. Lachlan, who'd moved feebly to bite him, suddenly sank back, the enraged expression vanishing from his face. He gazed up at Kendrick with pain in his gray eyes, and sudden loneliness and need.

"Guardian," Lachlan said, his voice fading. "Don't leave me this time."

Kendrick brushed Lachlan's hair from his forehead. "I won't," he promised, his voice gentling. "See you on the other side, my old friend."

Lachlan gave one feeble, very brief nod.

Kendrick drew a long breath. He raised the Sword of the Guardian, which flared anew, lighting every facet in the rocks around them and making them glitter like jewels.

He thrust the sword unerringly into Lachlan's chest. Lachlan flinched, then breathed a sigh, and smiled. "Thank you, Kendrick," he whispered. Then his eyes closed, his body shimmered, and he slowly dissolved into dust.

Kendrick bowed his head, the sword point resting where Lachlan's body had lain. A moment later, Kendrick threw his head back and roared, a sound of grief and pain so heart-wrenching that tears sprang to Addie's eyes.

She wrapped her arms around him from behind, resting her head between his broad shoulders. Kendrick's roar died into a moan and tears wet his face.

"He was my friend, once," Kendrick said, then he drooped, falling against Addie, who fought to hold him.

Kendrick lost his grip on the sword, which fell full-length with a clatter, the brilliant light fading until it was only a faint glow. Kendrick's breath rattled in his throat, and he sagged down into the rubble, Addie clinging to him all the way.

"No, Kendrick," she sobbed. "Don't leave me."

"Love you," Kendrick whispered. He squeezed his eyes shut, taking shuddering breaths.

Addie held him, anguish gouging her. "We have to get out of here. *Kendrick.*"

"The sword," Kendrick managed. "Get the sword."

Addie groped for it, her heart pounding. Did he mean for her to use it on him? Or to take it out to the other Shifters?

"Keep it for me," Kendrick said, his voice ragged. "And hold me again, Addison. I need you to."

Addie lay down right beside him and wrapped him in her arms, clutching the glowing sword tightly in one hand.

"I love you," she whispered.

Kendrick lay very still for a moment. Then his body shuddered, *moved.*

He was shifting. For a few seconds, Addie lay half on Kendrick's human body, then she was lifted from the rock as he expanded into the form of his tiger.

Addie found herself on the white tiger's back, her fingers sinking into his warm fur. With a grunt and huff of breath, the tiger moved painfully forward, stumbling over the rocks to the opening Luchlan had made.

Though he limped, and one paw dragged, Kendrick slunk out into the tunnels so adeptly that Addie never brushed any of the low ceilings or fallen debris. She hung on to him, feeling every move of his body as he crept on elastic muscles.

The tunnel outside went on, up and up, the tiger flowing like water, his footfalls silent. Addie felt as though she moved under the deep night sky on the back of a magic beast. The Sword of the Guardian was still in her hand, the rocks above her reflecting its light like twinkling stars.

When the tunnel finally ended at a narrow opening, through which came night air and true starlight, Kendrick stopped, his sides heaving. He collapsed just inside the tunnel, Addie with him.

His body jerked, and Kendrick became a man again, naked and bruised, his skin dark with blood. He gazed up at her with green eyes that burned into her heart.

"Love you so much," Kendrick whispered. Then his eyes filmed over, and he went still.

Addie gave a cry of anguish. "No. Please, we're almost there. Kendrick, please, I can't lose you."

Her sobs were drowned by the sound of grating rock, and she raised her head with a gasp. But instead of the cave-in she expected, a tiger as large as Kendrick, but orange and black, snaked through the opening and stopped, studying her with yellow eyes.

Behind him came Zander, the healer, and Kendrick's trackers—Seamus, Dimitri, Jaycee. Ben too, with Dylan, all of them wading in to help.

The three trackers and Zander lifted Kendrick gently between them, carrying him out. Ben got Addie onto her feet, his touch tender with understanding.

They carried Kendrick out and laid him under the stars, where he lay still. The sword Addie held flashed once, then its light cut out and vanished, leaving them in darkness.

CHAPTER THIRTY-FIVE

Kendrick opened his eyes as pain roared through him. Sound burst out of his throat, a cry from the depths of his soul.

Every nerve was on fire, every blood vessel straining to burst. His head pounded, his throat was desert dry, and his lungs could grab no breath.

He peeled open his eyes—even his eyelids hurt.

On one side of him knelt Addison. Her face was covered with grime and scrapes, her dark hair matted with blood, perspiration, and dust. She clutched one hand around the hilt of the Sword of the Guardian, which no longer glowed, the other hand resting on his chest.

Kneeling behind Kendrick's head was Zander, his two white braids brushing Kendrick's face, the beads in the braids catching the moonlight. Zander was chanting in his deep voice in a strange language, both hands placed on Kendrick's shoulders. Pain burned where Zander's hands touched him and rippled down the rest of Kendrick's body.

"Son of a . . ." Kendrick writhed, trying to throw off Zander's hold, but the big man pushed him back down.

"Stay still," Addison said. "He's healing you."

Kendrick's head banged back down to dirt and prickly grass. He was naked, but alive, cool breeze touching his sweating skin. He was also outside, no more tunnels. The sky stretched far overhead, the constellation of the Shifter bear and her cub circling the polar star in their endless dance.

"Holy Goddess," Kendrick snarled, his voice strengthening. "That fucking *hurts*."

Zander opened his eyes, the blackness of them deeper voids in the darkness. "Hey, you were mostly dead," he said, sounding weary. "Of course it hurts. Think what I get to look forward to."

Kendrick tried to feel sympathy—Zander would experience Kendrick's pain exactly as Kendrick had. But no emotion touched him beyond agony.

Kendrick's muscles were fusing back together, his bones knitting. If he had spent a few months in a hospital bed, he'd have accomplished the same thing. Having all the healing happen at once was excruciating.

Addison moved her hand on Kendrick's heart. The warmth there cut through the hurt, relaxing Kendrick the slightest bit.

Zander bowed his head again and continued chanting. As Kendrick's body relaxed, he became more aware of what went on around him. He saw Shifters milling about, and beyond them, the bulks of houses in the dark, warm lights shining in their windows. He heard men talking, the higher-pitched, lighter tones of women, the smaller voices of cubs.

So normal. So absolutely, bloody normal.

"My Shifters." Kendrick tried to rise. There could be more trapped below, and who knew if the ones up here were still against Kendrick?

Zander landed all his weight on him. "Stay down. I'm not finished. You take a step on that front leg, you'll shatter it again."

Front leg? Kendrick realized Zander meant his left arm, which, as tiger, Kendrick had limped out of the tunnels on.

The sensible part of him said it would be wise to let

Zander finish. The alpha tiger in him made Kendrick want to run around making sure everyone was all right.

"Hold him, Addie," Zander said. "He won't throw *you* off."

True. Kendrick settled into the grass as Addison came down to him. She rested her head on his chest, and Kendrick brought up his good hand and stroked her hair.

"Addison," he said. "My mate. You should have seen her, Zander. She went after Lachlan with the sword like a warrior."

Addison hugged him tighter. "Like a scared woman afraid he'd hurt her mate."

Kendrick ran his hand through her hair again. It was tangled and dirty, but he'd wash it clean for her in the deep claw-foot bathtub at the ranch. After that, they'd do many more entertaining things.

"Does that mean you accept my mate-claim?" Kendrick asked.

He waited, his heart beating hard with hope. Addison raised her head, regarding him with her dark blue eyes.

"Is it like accepting a proposal of marriage?"

"I'm not sure," Kendrick had to admit. "I don't know much about the mating rituals of humans."

"Yes," Zander said, the words snapped. "It's exactly like that, but more binding than a human engagement. The mating ceremony is mostly a formality."

Addison wrapped her hands around Kendrick's. "So we'd be married. As in . . . I live with you and your cubs for the rest of my life. Wherever you go, whatever happens to you. Whether you live in a house or a bunker, with dozens of Shifters following you around."

Kendrick's hope started to fade. "Yes. I'm Shifter leader, and you'd be leader's mate. With all that entails."

"I hope they all don't expect me to make coffee for them and serve them meals," Addison said, her expression stern. "Because I'm hanging up my apron."

"Don't throw it away altogether," Zander said. "Kendrick might want you to play dress-up."

"Shut it," Kendrick growled. "It's your choice, Addison.

I can't force you to stay with me. I can't even promise that it will be easy. I can only promise to love you, no matter what."

"In that case." Addison leaned down and pressed a warm kiss to his lips. "I accept the mate-claim."

"Good thing you have a witness," Zander rumbled. "If you didn't, it wouldn't count, and you'd have to do it all over again in front of everybody."

Kendrick opened his mouth to tell Zander to shut it again, but he cut off the words. Zander was sitting upright now, his face gray, the pain of Kendrick's wounds starting to grip him.

"Take it easy," Kendrick said. "Addison, help me."

Kendrick sat up, feeling much better if not ready to run and fight. He and Addison laid Zander down on his back. His coat lay beside him, removed to work on Kendrick, and Addison rolled it into a pillow to slip under Zander's head.

"Will he be all right?" Addison asked. The big man groaned.

"To tell the truth, I don't know," Kendrick said. Zander was the first Shifter healer he'd ever met—healers were rare and enigmatic.

"Be fine," Zander mumbled. "Just in a shitload of pain for a while. Do me a favor." He beckoned them close. Kendrick leaned over him, hand on Zander's chest, wishing he could make the man feel better.

"What?" Addison asked him, anxious.

Zander lifted his head the slightest bit. *"Go away."* He dropped his head back, letting out another groan.

"Should we?" Addison said as Kendrick climbed to his feet and reached to help Addison to hers.

"Probably not."

Zander made a feeble gesture, as though brushing them aside. *"Please.* Go."

Kendrick understood. Zander wasn't physically hurt, not like Kendrick had been. This was part of the process he had to endure, the sacrifice for his gift. The Goddess wasn't always easy to work for.

Kendrick guided Addison away, though he limped

heavily, and it was she who held him up. He should probably find some clothes, but the thought of cloth rubbing his sensitive skin right now made him queasy.

Several Shifters broke away from the main knot and came to them—Jaycee and Dimitri, followed by Dylan.

"You all right?" Dimitri asked, reaching them first. "Zander made us stay away—we th-thought you were done for." He reached out and touched Kendrick's upper arm, both seeking reassurance and trying to reassure.

Kendrick covered Dimitri's hand with his. "I'll mend. Zander is a genius, and the touch of my mate kept me alive."

"Sh-she acc-accepted?" Dimitri asked, his gray eyes widening. "D-did you?" he said to Addison. Dimitri's stammer worsened in his agitation, but by the huge grin on his face, he didn't notice or care.

"Yep," Addison said, sounding shy.

"Yes!" Dimitri grabbed Kendrick, kissed him on the cheek, grabbed Addison, kissed her too, then hauled the protesting Jaycee into his arms and planted a kiss on her mouth.

"Hey!" Dimitri shouted into the crowd. "Kendrick has a *mate*!"

Jaycee, looking startled and flushed at Dimitri's kiss, went first to Addison and hugged her. "Awesome, Addie. Thank you." She turned to Kendrick, hesitating, as though unsure he'd welcome her.

Kendrick stepped to Jaycee and gently drew her into his arms. "Thank *you*, Jaycee, for everything."

Jaycee's tension eased, and she hugged him back. "You did good, Kendrick. You'll be happy." She released him and gave Addie a warm look, then another embrace. "The Goddess go with you both."

Kendrick didn't have time to comment on her generosity, because Dimitri's whoops had brought the rest of the Shifters over. Kendrick and Addison were surrounded by the Shifters he'd known and led for so many years—then came the hugs, congratulations, kisses, back thumps, Shifters losing their fear and anger in the joy of the moment.

As it should be, Kendrick thought. Addison had just

become the linchpin that would secure the Shifters together, uniting them once more.

A ddie followed Kendrick in a daze, though with more confidence than she thought she would have. Kendrick's Shifters greeted her with warmth and exuberance, smothering her in hugs as much as they did Kendrick. People she'd never met in her life were hauling her into their arms, crying and kissing her. There were some who held back, uncertain, but for the most part, they welcomed Addie as one of them.

The Shifters rejoiced without restraint that Kendrick was back among them. They'd been scared and worried without him, adrift, like kids suddenly finding themselves without parents. Now Kendrick was with them again, and his voice took on a softness and warmth Addie had only heard him use with her and his cubs.

The Shifters responded, happy and celebrating, though they didn't stint on the teasing and lewd suggestions. They weren't *tame* Shifters.

There were still problems to solve. Dylan joined Kendrick. "We've found them all," he said, his voice pitched low so the now-partying Shifters wouldn't overhear. "Three dead. The rest injured but all right."

Kendrick gave him a nod, his face drawn. "I'm sorry I brought him here," Kendrick said. "Truly."

"It's done," Dylan answered. The words were final. No recriminations to be made.

"You had treasure in the vault," Kendrick went on after a brief silence. "I saw the place, but it was empty. Lachlan cleaned you out."

Dylan nodded, his brows together. "I had taken some of it previously," he said. "But the rest, no. Either it's buried down there or Lachlan moved it somewhere." He sighed. "We'll find it. Another task in the ongoing task of taking care of Shifters."

"About that," Kendrick began. "I told you I was finished working for you. I don't take that back. I need to settle my

Shifters, and I've found a good place. But I'm happy to help you find the others who still might cause trouble. Not *all* my Shifters have come back to me."

Dylan didn't change expression, but Addie thought she saw relief in his eyes. "I will help you set up your new home—make sure the humans don't get word of it," Dylan said. "No matter what my rep, I'm not rushing to put more Shifters in Collars. You might want to wear fake ones, to keep out of trouble, but it's your choice."

"Done," Kendrick said.

They studied each other, two alphas telling themselves it was better to come together than fight.

Dylan stuck out a hand. Kendrick took it. The two locked grips, fingers tight, then they mutually pulled each other into an embrace. They held each other in acknowledgment, no competition. They'd be partners, equals.

Kendrick and Dylan released at the same time. "For now, let's get everyone the hell home," Kendrick said. "Before nosy humans find out something's going down out here. I'm glad this Shiftertown is so remote."

"Which is why Lachlan chose it," Dylan said. "At least we stopped him before he hurt too many."

Kendrick nodded again, his look going somber. He took the sword from Addie, who'd been carrying it for him as he struggled to walk, and silently turned away.

Addie knew what he was going to do, and she followed, not liking the bleak expression on his face. Kendrick's stride grew stronger as he approached the bodies laid out on the grass, watched over by Seamus and Spike.

He gazed at each dead Shifter in great sorrow. They were strangers to Addie, but Kendrick had known these men for years, had led them, loved them. Kendrick kept Addie by his side while he said a prayer to the Goddess and sent each of them to dust.

Kendrick lingered for a while as the dust faded on the wind, his head bowed. This task as Guardian was so difficult for him, Addie saw, and tonight he'd had to perform it too many times.

Addie touched his hand. Kendrick snapped his eyes open and gazed down at her, then he scooped her up to him for a long kiss.

His mouth was plenty strong, his arm holding her steady. He seemed to draw strength from her as well as comfort.

Addie rested her hands on his chest and rose into the kiss, her heart swelling with love. Kendrick pulled her up to him, groaning a little in his throat, his heart beating quick and hard. Whatever Zander had done to heal him had taken away his injuries, leaving him as stalwart as ever.

That strength let him kiss her hard, his mouth opening hers. Their tongues tangled, the kiss fierce, promising that when they were alone, wrapped around each other, he'd be fiercer still. Addie remembered his words, spoken in his harsh voice: *I want you every way I can have you, and I don't want it gentle.*

She shivered, holding him, letting him know she wanted him as much as he wanted her.

Kendrick at last eased from the kiss, cupping Addie's face in his hands. "The power lies not in one," he said softly.

Addie frowned at him. "What are you talking about?"

Kendrick's grin warmed his eyes. "Something the sword was trying to tell me. We did it together, you and me. It's why you could touch the sword and Lachlan couldn't. It means I can't prevail alone. I need *you*."

Addie still wasn't sure what he meant, but they'd have time to discuss it when they were snuggled up together in bed. Well, *maybe* they'd have time to talk in bed. "If you mean we kicked ass, yeah, we did." She felt a moment of triumph, then she shivered. "I was really, really scared."

Kendrick touched his forehead to hers. "So was I. You have much courage, Addison. My mate."

Heat flared in his eyes when he said *mate*. Addie was coming to know that the declaration, in all its intensity, meant the same as *I love you*.

"My mate," she said softly in response.

Kendrick's heat flared. He leaned into her, his body the length of hers, hands hard on her back.

Addie struck his chest gently with her fist. "What were

you thinking running straight into Lachlan's trap? He could have killed you! I might have lost you . . ."

Her bravado drained in an instant, and Addie was crying, leaning on Kendrick's chest. Kendrick gathered her to him, tumbling her hair, kissing away her tears.

"Addison," he whispered, breath warm in her ear. "My love. I know."

This was what he did, she understood. Rushed headlong into danger so others didn't have to. He'd gone after Lachlan to protect his cubs, his friends, *her*. Kendrick would do so again and again. It was who he was.

Addie lifted her head. His eyes held anguish, and she touched his cheek. "I'll be okay." She scrubbed her hand across her face. "Just every now and again, I'm going to go to pieces worrying about you. I think that's my privilege, as leader's mate. But don't worry. I'm made of pretty strong stuff. You have your butt grabbed all day by repellant guys who stiff you on the tip and see how tough it makes you. Facing down homicidal maniac Shifters is nothing." She waved it away.

Kendrick only watched her, his eyes filling with rage. "Give me their names," he said. "I'll go have a chat with these repellant men."

Addie enjoyed picturing it, the more repulsive clientele of the diner facing Kendrick, his eyes hot with anger, pinning them with his terrifying stare. He wouldn't even have to turn into a tiger to scare them shitless.

"No," she said. "Let them live. If I hadn't put up with them, working at the diner, I wouldn't have met you."

Kendrick pulled her to him again, warm arms around her. "I'd have met *you*," he said. "I'm certain of it. I was meant to."

"It was fated?" Addie asked, feeling herself smile. "Not sure I believe in that, but what the hell? We met—that's all that matters."

Kendrick's heart beat strongly beneath hers. He started to speak, then his words left him, and he tugged her into him for another long kiss.

No more talking. This bliss was so much better. Fear and

worry dissolved as Addie melted into Kendrick, and his mouth warmed her with every beat of her heart.

The gruff voice of Tiger, who'd been helping the injured Shifters near them, suddenly cut into their joy.

"Time to go," he said.

Kendrick reluctantly broke the kiss to look at him. Tiger stood next near them, gazing at both Addie and Kendrick with unblinking golden eyes. Addie sensed his agitation, however, a new fear that boiled off him in waves.

"Tiger, what's wrong?" Addie asked, her own worry returning. "Has something happened at the ranch?"

Tiger shook his head. "My mate is having our cub. *Right now.*"

"She is?" Addie slid out from Kendrick's embrace. "Then what are you doing here? Why did you even come out here? You need to go."

"She has just begun," Tiger said. He hesitated, casting his gaze around the darkness. "Tell Zander to come."

"You think she'll need a healer?" Addie asked, eyes widening. "She isn't Shifter, is she?"

"The cub is," Tiger said. "And I'm not . . . right."

Addie had no idea what this meant, but Tiger's distress was palpable. Kendrick put a strong hand on Tiger's shoulder. "Don't worry, big guy. We'll get him there."

"And you," Tiger said. "You're tiger. Please come. And Addie. Carly will like you."

Kendrick did not want to leave his Shifters, that was obvious. But he seemed to see past Tiger's stoicism to his deep fears, and gave him a reassuring nod. "We'll be there."

"Go," Addie said, giving Tiger a push. "Sometimes babies come faster than expected, and it's a ways to Austin. You don't want to miss it."

"I do not." A mix of joy and worry flared in his eyes. Without further word, Tiger turned and headed for his motorcycle, its engine roaring to life, blaring through the noise of the celebrating Shifters.

CHAPTER THIRTY-SIX

Tiger's mate, Carly Randal, had been taken to a clinic not far from the Austin Shiftertown, one of the few medical facilities that treated Shifters.

Kendrick did not *want* to walk in there in front of all the humans who ran the place, and neither did Zander, he sensed, but they did it. Tiger had a way of compelling people.

Dylan had given them fake Collars to wear. Though Kendrick had worn a fake before, he hated how it felt on his neck. Zander spent the first ten minutes trying to scratch under his.

Zander was still hurting from healing Kendrick, he knew, but the man had climbed to his feet and allowed Kendrick and Addison to tow him to Dylan's pickup. Kendrick had driven, with Zander stretched out in the bed, complaining about every bump from there to Austin.

Addison was far more excited about attending the birth than Kendrick. She'd gone through it with her sister—twice, she said. Nothing to worry about.

But Addison's sister was human and had given birth to human children. Carly was bringing in the cub of a Shifter who was an unknown quantity.

Kendrick had been present when his mate, Eileen, had brought in Zane, and he'd had to watch Eileen die of it. She'd had no healer, no help. Only Kendrick to ease her final breaths.

His mouth was dry as he entered the room where Carly lay. As was Shifter custom, the men of her family—which were represented by Dylan's sons and nephew, formed a circle around the bed, facing outward. By custom, they were there to protect the Shifter woman from being hurt or killed by rival clans. Lachlan's attack had proved that such dangers weren't necessarily things of the past.

"Hey, Tiger," a tired but light voice came from the bed, Carly's Texas accent warm. "'Bout time you got here. Oh, and look, you brought friends."

There were other humans here as well. Three young women and an older one, all looking enough like Carly to be her family. They gazed with interest at Zander and Kendrick, undismayed by the presence of more Shifters. Another woman looked in the door, older than the others, but very lovely. She said in an accent that Kendrick thought was French, "You will do beautifully, Carly. Then we will celebrate."

The whole thing seemed to be a celebration instead of an intense worry. The human doctors had ways to ease some of the pain of the birth—maybe there were a few good things about trying to integrate with humans.

When the time came, the doctors wanted everyone out except the father. Tiger insisted that Zander stay, and Kendrick and Addie. He was adamant about them witnessing the birth.

Kendrick thought he knew why. Tiger was alone in the world, one of the few tiger Shifters in existence. He had no family, no clan, coming from nothing.

Tiger and Kendrick shared genetic material from somewhere in the distant past, which made Kendrick the closest thing to Tiger's clan. Kendrick was also Guardian, who could send the cub to dust if necessary. Kendrick prayed and prayed to the Goddess that wouldn't happen.

Why Tiger wanted Addison as well, he wasn't as clear. Except, Tiger just liked her.

Carly liked her too. She said, "Sorry I can't get up and say hey more politely, but I'm a little busy."

Addison gave Carly her warm laugh. "We'll get to know each other later. You're going to have to tell me what to expect living with a tiger."

"You bet," Carly said, then her contractions came, and she had other things on her mind.

The cub was born as the sun rose. A heavily tinted window gave out into the dawn sky, the sun's rays flooding the room as the cub came forth.

Addison's hand in Kendrick's squeezed hard. Kendrick held his breath while the doctors cleared the cub's lungs and cut the cord, and he opened his mouth and screamed his displeasure at being yanked into the cold world.

Carly laughed wearily, exhausted but with a smile on her face.

Tiger stood as one stunned. He looked down at the baby laid on Carly's chest, her hand coming up to cradle it as it took its first meal.

"Do you want to hold him?" Carly asked Tiger after a time.

Tiger stood still for another few seconds, then he made himself take the last step to the bed and lay his hand on the child's back.

The three of them shared a moment of completeness, Tiger's huge hand on the tiny cub, Carly looking up at him in absolute trust.

Tiger then took a breath and lifted the cub into his hands. The little guy had streaks of orange in his very black hair, and he stared at Tiger with belligerent golden eyes.

Tiger's hands dwarfed the cub's body. When he turned to face the others, Kendrick saw tears in the big man's eyes.

Tiger's voice was perfectly strong as he lifted the cub to Kendrick, Addie, and Zander. "Behold, my *cub*!"

The word roared through the room and down the hall. The triumph on Tiger's face competed with joy. The Shifters outside cheered, as did Carly's family and friends. Addie said, "He's beautiful, Tiger."

Tiger's son, in human form for now—he'd start shifting

when he was about three—gazed down upon his new friends and family, then screwed up his face, opened his mouth, and roared.

The sun was well up by the time Kendrick and Addison wandered into the parking lot, heading for the white pickup that waited at the end of the row. Addison leaned into Kendrick and wiped her eyes.

"I'm so tired. But that was worth it."

"Then why are you crying?" Kendrick asked, his voice gentle. He'd probably never understand human women but he intended to try for a long time.

"Because it's so beautiful," Addison said. "I always cry when babies are born."

Kendrick laughed. He needed to laugh, needed the cleansing of his soul. He drew Addison into his arms and hung on.

"I love you so much Addison Price."

"I love you too, Kendrick. Thanks for coming to my diner."

"Hey." Kendrick leaned down and kissed her lips. "You serve a mean piece of pie."

Addison wrapped her arms around him, no inhibitions, no hesitation. Just love and joy. Her kiss tasted of the champagne the Frenchwoman and her husband had brought— apparently they did this sort of thing all the time.

She also tasted of Addison, of the goodness of her, and the sass, and the strength. Kendrick had been empty for a while, and Addison had come to fill those aching spaces. His heart held fire as he felt the true mate bond strengthening between them.

Zander strode by them, his duster floating out behind him. "Guess I wasn't needed. Thank the Goddess. Now, I've got to go. Things to do." He whirled around and pointed both forefingers at them. "Later, kids."

"What things?" Addison called after him. "How will you get wherever you're going?"

Zander only swung away and kept striding, waving a hand as he went. He disappeared into the city streets and the morning light.

"He's totally crazy," Kendrick said. "Always will be."

"He saved your life," Addison said, watching Zander's fluttering coat in the distance. "So I think he's the most wonderful Shifter alive."

Kendrick feigned a frown. "Wait—have I already slipped in your hierarchy?"

Addison gave him an innocent look. "Of course not. You're my mate—and you need to teach me whatever the hell that's going to mean exactly. And I love you." She touched his lips. "I really do, Kendrick."

"Good." The word rang strong into the morning. "Then let's go the hell *home*."

Zander made it to the Austin Shiftertown after hitching a ride with two young women who were very cute and astonishingly friendly. They waved him good-bye outside Shiftertown, expressing interest in meeting up with him again.

Zander ignored the stares of the Austin Shifters, many of whom were blearily wandering off to bed in the light of day.

He knew the way to the large bungalow in the middle of the Shiftertown. Before he approached the front door, it flew open, and a small boy with white hair ran out.

"Zander!" the cub, Olaf, shouted.

Zander grinned at him, his heart lightening. He reached the cub and they bumped fists, first Olaf on top, then Zander. "My man," Zander said. He grinned at the watching she-bear and her soldier mate who had come out onto the porch, then returned his attention to Olaf. "We polar bears gotta stick together, right?"

Olaf, a lad of few words, alone in the world like Zander was, threw his arms around Zander and held on tight.

Addie was right that Kendrick would love her savagely when they made it home. He ensured the cubs were fine, that Charlie and the Shifters left behind had taken care of them well. Brett and Zane were excited and demanded to know the full story, so it was a while before Robbie suggested they run off with Charlie and let their father rest.

Kendrick more or less shoved Addison into the bedroom, and his hard fingers all but tore off her clothing. His sweat-pants and T-shirt he'd borrowed from one of the bear Shifters slid off quickly.

Addie found herself on her back, her mate on top of her. Kendrick pinned her with rough hands, fingers clamped around her wrists. He didn't prepare her this time, only slid inside her, thrusting as though he couldn't stop himself. Groans came from his throat, blending with Addie's.

They loved in frantic silence, need tearing at them. Fear and pain, death and darkness, had gone, and they'd survived. They took each other, holding hard, until their throats were hoarse with their cries, bodies exhausted. Then Kendrick gathered Addie into his arms, bowed his head into her shoulder, and held on to her until he stopped shaking.

The mating ceremony was held a few days later, under the light of the full moon, the sun ceremony having been done earlier that day.

Addie didn't know what to expect, but what she got was Shifters everywhere, partying with abandon. They did the ceremony at the ranch, where Kendrick was settling in his Shifters. They were making plans to alter the place where the Shifters could live in comfort and privacy. Charlie was happy to accommodate—he was selling the place outright to Kendrick and would stay on to run it. He enjoyed having the Shifters there, Addie could see, his ranch coming alive again.

Dylan arrived to do the blessing, Kendrick having asked him to perform the ceremony. Dylan and Kendrick were still working together, but as equals, making all kinds of pacts that Addie didn't want to know about. Likewise, Zander had confessed to Kendrick that he'd healed Lachlan all those years ago, not knowing what a monster he'd saved. Kendrick understood—Zander was a healer whose instinct was to help those in pain, and he'd had no idea what kind of trouble Lachlan would cause all these years later. Also, Zander's healing had no doubt saved Kendrick's life. Still, Kendrick said with a humorous glint in his eyes, if Zander felt bad about Lachlan, he could keep his cell phone on in case Kendrick needed him again. Zander growled, but Addie saw the guilt in his eyes ease.

Addie's sister, Ivy, arrived with the kids for the ceremony. Ivy was bewildered at first, but understood that Addie staying with Kendrick made her happy. Tori and Josh acclimatized faster, and were soon running and playing with Robbie, Zane, and Brett, and other Shifter children.

Under the silver moonlight, Dylan called down the blessing of the Goddess and united Kendrick and Addie. Moonlight gleamed on Kendrick's sword, its shimmer cool and white rather than the hot silver flashes it had blazed in the tunnels.

"By the light of the moon, the Mother Goddess, I proclaim you as mates!" Dylan said in his firm voice. The Shifters around them howled and roared, a mating completed being cause for crazed celebration.

The loudest roar had to come from Tiger, who'd arrived with Carly and the new little cub, whom they'd named Seth, nestled happily in his mother's arms.

Even louder were the shouts of Zane, Brett, and Robbie. "I told you!" Brett said at the top of his voice. "She's our new mom!"

As the celebration escalated—every Shifter wanting to embrace Addie, the cubs wanting to be lifted into her arms—Kendrick managed to break them away, especially as the beer started flowing.

He towed Addie out into the fields beyond the house, down the far side of the rise.

"Where are we going?" Addie asked in curiosity. She didn't much care, as long as she could be with Kendrick.

"Somewhere away from the light."

Kendrick led her a long way, but before Addie could grow tired, he stopped. "Here."

He unstrapped the sheathed sword and laid it down, then pulled from the shadow of a bush a couple of blankets he must have stashed earlier. Kendrick shook them out and spread them on the ground.

He dropped down onto his back and patted the blanketed space beside him. "Remember?" he asked. "I promised to tell you about the stars."

Addie's heart beat faster as she slid off her shoes, stepped onto the blanket, and settled in next to him.

They lay back, the heavens, cloudless, flowing around them. The moon had become a small disk high above, and stars thickly blanketed the sky.

Kendrick pointed straight upward at a very bright star. "The humans call this one Vega. Shifters see it as a mother, a Lupine, who beams her light, looking for her cubs." Kendrick shifted his arm to the right and Addie snuggled into the curve of it. "The wolf cubs have run away on the back of a dragon. See them there? Their mother chases them across the heavens all night, and they laugh and fly away. Robbie really likes that story."

Addie ran her fingers across Kendrick's chest, catching on his soft button-down shirt. "I'm not surprised. What else?"

"That, we call the Tiger." Kendrick moved his arm to point between two other bright stars. "You call those Deneb and Altair and divide all the stars between into a couple different constellations, but Shifters grouped them together as a tiger, his head turning as he stalks his prey." Kendrick looked at her. "Then there are the Lovers."

Addie pretended that heat hadn't flooded her body. She scanned the sky. "Where are they?"

"Not up there," Kendrick rumbled. "Can't see them until winter."

"Then why bring them up?"

She dissolved into laughter when Kendrick rolled onto her, the weight of him a fine thing. "We'll just have to make do with the lovers down here," he said, his breath warming her skin.

"Mmm." Addie laced her arms around his neck. "Maybe they'll name constellations after us."

"Not right now." The hunger Addie had glimpsed that

last night at the diner returned to his eyes full force. "I'm busy. Gonna be busy for a while."

"Good," Addie whispered, and sank into Kendrick's kiss.

A few moments later, she was humming in pleasure as Kendrick stripped from her the light summer dress she'd donned for the ceremony. Addie returned the favor by ripping open Kendrick's shirt, sending the buttons flying. She kissed his chest, which was whole now, only a few faint scars showing where he'd been hurt.

Kendrick growled, rolling Addie down into the blankets, his bare body on hers. He brushed her cheek with a tender touch, then parted her legs and slid inside her.

"Addison." His voice shook, rough with need. "I love you. My *mate*."

Addie wrapped herself around him, her body hot, full. Her heart tingled with what Kendrick had told her was the mate bond, the true twining of souls. She ached where they joined, an ache that dissolved to pure, ecstatic pleasure as he began to thrust.

"I love you," she said in a clear voice. "Mate of my heart."

Kendrick groaned and sped his thrusts.

Addie held him, her hard-bodied Shifter with white-black hair and beautiful eyes. He gazed down at her as he loved her faster and harder, his green eyes outshining the sparkling river of the night sky.

Turn the page for a sneak peek at the
next book in the Shifters Unbound series,

GUARDIAN'S MATE,

coming from Berkley in September 2016

Rae's job on the day of the Choosing was to stand behind her foster father and hold the absent Guardian's sword. Absent, because the Guardian was dead, had been for months.

The woods were quiet, dark, cold. Any sane Shifter would still be in bed, snuggled under a few blankets, looking forward to a warm shower and a hot cup of coffee.

But no, the Shifters of the Western Montana Shiftertown had crept out just before dawn, following Eoin, Rae's adoptive father and leader of this Shiftertown, to see whether the Goddess was in a good mood.

Four times in the last six months they'd trudged out here in the gloom and cold, waiting for the Goddess to pick a new Guardian. They'd come at a full moon, a new moon, a waxing moon, a blue moon. They'd turn toward wherever the moon happened to be—above or below the horizon— and wait.

All the young men of the Montana Shiftertown who were past their Transition were required attend. They formed the now-familiar circle around Rae and Eoin. Some were excited, some fearful, some simply wanted to go back to bed.

Eoin, a Feline Shifter who was mostly mountain lion,

sent Rae an encouraging smile. Rae was a Lupine, black wolf, but she conceded her foster dad was handsome—for a Feline. He was currently mateless, which made him a target for every female Shifter near and far. What some of them would do to try to sneak into his bed was beyond ridiculous. Rae sometimes felt like his bodyguard rather than his daughter.

"Not long now," Eoin said softly to her. Even speaking low, his voice was a full rumble.

"Then we can go out for breakfast?" Rae asked. "I could use a stack of waffles. With bacon."

"Sure."

He turned to the circle. Beyond the young males, the rest of the Shifters waited, anxious and impatient.

Months ago, their Guardian, Daragh, had been killed by humans, his sword stolen. Rae still fumed over that. The humans had been found, punished, the sword returned by an unlikely messenger, but no new Guardian had been chosen. The Goddess had not answered their call.

The faintest light came through the stand of trees. The mist that had gathered became ghostly white.

The Shifters dropped into silence, and Eoin raised his arms.

"Goddess, mother of us all, lady of the moon," Eoin began, "we beseech thee. Send us your light to touch the Guardian, the most holy of men, so that he may do thy work."

Rae loved hearing her father chant in his deep baritone. Her earliest memories were of him reading her books, soothing her to sleep, wrapping her in comfort, knowing she was protected when he was near. The sword, which she held point downward, vibrated with his voice.

The sword gave her the creeps, but no one else would touch it. Even Eoin's trackers, the bravest of the brave, refused to hold it, so Rae'd had to step up. She didn't mind so much when it was sheathed, but for the ritual, it had to be naked, the runes etched in the silver catching the dawn light.

She'd done this four times. Rae prayed to the Goddess that the fifth time was the charm, so she could hand it to the new Guardian and never hold it again.

Eoin went on chanting. He repeated his lines over and over, his arms raised.

In the old days, Shifters probably had worn robes and crowns of leaves and crap like that. Today, Eoin wore jeans, sweatshirt, and thick-soled boots, sensible attire in the Rocky Mountain woods. Rae, and every Shifter here, wore something similar.

Maybe they should have donned robes and painted themselves with moon goddess symbols. Or danced naked at midnight. It would make the same difference. The Goddess wasn't coming. She never did.

"We beseech thee!" Eoin shouted.

His words echoed through the woods as the sun climbed higher, brushing the treetops high above. The mists thickened, the ground becoming colder. Autumn should involve the last of the summer cookouts and playing football, not standing around in the woods in the cold.

The sun kept climbing. The mist turned to fog. The Shifters shivered and rubbed their arms, wanting to shift, cuddle up to something furry, or at least go the hell home.

Eoin finally lowered his arms, letting out a sigh, defeated. A whisper of breeze echoed his sigh, then died.

The Shifters didn't look happy. Eoin, as Shiftertown leader, was supposed to solve problems like this. Ask the human government to bring in a Guardian from another Shiftertown, figure out a way to use the sword himself, *something*.

If they got too restless, the more dominant ones would start challenging, and then things could really hit the fan. The human government didn't allow Shifters to change leaders without their approval, but that wouldn't matter if Eoin were dead.

Rae picked up the sword's sheath from the grass, her braid of black hair falling over her shoulder.

A thin finger of light made it through the fog to dance on the blade as she lifted it to slide it into the sheath. The runes glittered and moved.

They did that sometimes. It was one creep-toid piece of metal.

The tip of the blade jerked out of the leather sheath. Rae stared at the sword in surprise, then let out a cry as the sword shot upward, dragging her arm with it.

Rae tried to drop the sword but her hand was fixed to the hilt, her fingers not obeying the command to open. The sword jerked again, nearly pulling her arm out of its socket.

Rae grabbed the hilt with her other hand, holding on while her heels came off the ground.

"Dad!" she yelled. "Help!"

Eoin, who'd moved off to speak to his trackers, swung around. At the same time the sword yanked itself upward and Rae's feet came all the way off the ground.

She yelped in terror. She couldn't let go. What if the thing shot up into the trees, dumping her off when it got twenty feet up? She had no idea what the damn thing was trying to do— return to the Goddess? Fly to the next real Guardian?

Eoin ran for her, his trackers behind him, but before he could reach her, a brilliant shaft of light shot down from the treetops and enclosed Rae, the sword, and the sheath on the ground.

Pain burned through her, as though every cell in her skin, every bit of iron in her blood suddenly began to boil. Her Collar, the metal embedded into her neck, went off, arcs of electricity ringing her throat.

Rae screamed. The sound echoed up through the trees, crescendoed into a piercing shriek, and swooped back down again. The Shifters clapped hands over ears, some falling to their knees.

Rae was lifted a few more feet in the air, then her body crumpled and she slammed hard into the ground. She'd lost hold of the sword, and the blade plummeted toward her.

Eoin dove for it but too late. The sword landed, blade down, straight into the earth between Rae's outstretched arms. It stilled, the light died, and the pain faded.

"What the hell?" one of the trackers growled.

Eoin halted a few feet from Rae. Rae slowly climbed to her feet, groaning all the way, having to use the hilt of the stupid sword to brace herself.

Eoin's face was gray, his eyes wet. "The Goddess has Chosen," he said in a hushed voice.

"What?" Rae tore her hands from the sword, which slowly toppled to the ground. "What are you talking about? There's no way. It was a lightning strike, or something . . ."

Eoin seized Rae's hands and turned them palm upward. Burned into her skin was the symbol of the Celtic knot, the sign of the Goddess. Though Rae's hands were branded, she felt no pain, not even itching.

Her heart hammered. "No way. Dad—*no!*"

Eoin was openly weeping. "The Goddess has Chosen," he repeated, his voice breaking. "We have our new Guardian."

The rest of the Shifters stared at Rae in absolute shock.

An elderly Shifter man gave voice to the thought in the head of every Shifter present.

"But she's a *woman!*"

Z ander's cell phone rang. "Aw, son of a . . ."
Zander vented to every deity, familiar and obscure, as he hoisted himself from the chair at the stern of his boat. His fishing pole, secured to the deck, went on enjoying itself dangling bait in the water, while Zander trudged down the gently rocking boat to where he'd left the damn phone this time.

He should just throw the cell phone overboard. The point of being in a fishing boat all alone off the coast of Alaska was being *alone*.

He knew why he didn't toss it even as the thought formed. If someone had dire need, and they couldn't reach him, he'd never forgive himself.

Zander's two braids with blue beads woven through them swung against his cheeks as he reached for the phone he'd left on top of the cooler. He figured he might as well grab another beer at the same time, and came up with a phone in one hand, a can in the other.

He thumbed the phone on and put it to his ear. "Go for Zander."

He stilled as a voice from far away rumbled in his ear. If it had been anyone other than Kendrick, white tiger Guardian, he'd have snarled something and hung up, but Zander glued the phone to his ear and listened. His reflection in the window of the wheelhouse showed his dark eyes growing wider and wider. At the end of the boat, the fishing pole started to buzz, the bait taken, but Zander ignored it.

He yelled, "You want me to *what*? Seriously, Kendrick, what the fuck? How am I supposed to teach her to be a Guardian. Hello? *I'm not a Guardian.*"

"I know," Kendrick said. "But she needs—"

"I'm *busy.* I don't have time to babysit a woman who thinks she's been chosen by the Goddess to be a Guardian, for crap's sake. There are no female Guardians! *I'm* supposed to be the crazy one, Kendrick. When you regain your sanity, call me back."

Zander moved the phone, but Kendrick's stern voice had him listening again. "Oh, you've got to be kidding me."

Over the whirring of the fishing pole came the drone of a motor, a boat rushing at him across the deep waters.

"Seriously?" Zander shouted into the phone. "Do you know how much shit you're in right now?"

Kendrick rumbled something else, not keeping the amused bite out of his voice. The man and his cute little mate must be laughing their asses off.

Zander clicked off the phone and threw it to the deck. The boat came closer. Three figures stood on its deck—the man piloting it, a tall, stern-looking Feline Shifter, and a smaller woman, a Lupine, with a Sword of the Guardian strapped to her back. The sword's hilt gleamed in the strong sunshine.

"Perfect," Zander said. "Just effing perfect."

He squeezed the can of beer until the pop-top burst open, then he poured the cold liquid down his throat, wiped his mouth, and strode to meet the intruders.

From *New York Times* bestselling author

JENNIFER ASHLEY

MATE BOND

A Shifters Unbound Novel

To cement the leadership of his North Carolina Shiftertown, Bowman O'Donnell agreed to a "mating of convenience." Two powerful wolf Shifters, he and Kenzie keep the pack in order and are adored by all. But as strong as their attachment is, they still haven't formed the elusive mate bond—the almost magical joining of true mates.

Now with a monster threatening the Shiftertown community, Bowman and Kenzie will have to rely on their instinctive trust in each other to save their Shifters—and the ensuing battle will either destroy them or give them the chance to seize the love they've always craved.

"Danger, desire, and sizzling-hot action!"
—Alyssa Day, *New York Times* bestselling author

jennifersromances.com
facebook.com/ProjectParanormalBooks
penguin.com

FROM *NEW YORK TIMES* BESTSELLING AUTHOR

JENNIFER ASHLEY

"Sexually charged and imaginative . . . Smart, skilled writing."
—*Publishers Weekly*

jenniferashley.com
facebook.com/ProjectParanormalBooks
penguin.com